The Silent Governess

Books by
Julie Klassen

Lady of Milkweed Manor

The Apothecary's Daughter

The Silent Governess

The Girl in the Gatehouse

The Maid of Fairbourne Hall

The Silent Governess

JULIE KLASSEN

BETHANY HOUSE PUBLISHERS
Minneapolis, Minnesota

Published by Bethany House Publishers
11400 Hampshire Avenue South
Bloomington, Minnesota 55438

Bethany House Publishers is a division of
Baker Publishing Group, Grand Rapids, Michigan.

Printed in the United States of America

Library of Congress Cataloging-in-Publication Data

Klassen, Julie.
   The silent governess / Julie Klassen.
      p. cm.
   ISBN 978-0-7642-0707-5 (pbk.)
   1. Governesses—England—Fiction. I. Title.
PS3611.L37S55   2009
813'.6—dc22

                                      2009035948

To Carlisa,
treasured friend & first reader

The virtue of silence is highly commendable,
and will contribute greatly to your ease and prosperity.
The best proof of wisdom is to talk little, but to hear much. . . .

—SAMUEL & SARAH ADAMS, *THE COMPLETE SERVANT*, 1825

❧

Remember Who it is that has placed you in your present position;
perhaps you have no home,
perhaps you have experienced a reverse of fortune; no matter what!
It is God who has willed it so,
therefore look to Him for guidance and protection.

—HINTS TO GOVERNESSES, BY ONE OF THEMSELVES, 1856

Prologue

For years, I could not recall the day without a smoldering coal of remorse burning within me. I tried to bury the memory deep in the dark places of my mind, but now and again something would evoke it—a public house placard, a column of figures, a finely dressed gentleman—and I would wince as the memory appeared and then scuttled away, like a silverfish under the door. . . .

The day began wonderfully well. My mother, father, and I, then twelve, rode into Chedworth together and spent a rare afternoon as a harmonious family. We viewed many fine prospects and toured the Roman ruins, where my mother met by chance an old friend. I thought it a lovely outing and remember feeling as happy as I had ever been—for my mother and father seemed happy together as well.

The mood during the journey home was strained, but I chalked it up to fatigue and soon fell asleep in the gig, my head lolling against my mother's shoulder.

When we arrived home, I remained in such buoyant spirits that when my father dully proclaimed himself off to the Crown and Crow, I offered to go along, although I had not done so in many months.

He muttered, "Suit yourself," and turned without another word. I could not account for his sudden change of mood, but then, when had I ever?

I had been going with him to the Crown and Crow since I was a child of three or four. He would set me upon its high counter, and there I would count to a thousand or more. When one has mastered one hundred, are not two, five, and nine so much child's play? By the age of six, I was ciphering sums to the amusement and amazement of other patrons. Papa would present two or three figures and there before me, as if on a glass slate, I would see the totals of their columns.

"What is forty-seven and fifty-five, Olivia?"

Instantly the numbers and their sum would appear. "One zero two, Papa."

"One hundred two. That is right. That's my clever girl."

As I grew older, the equations grew more difficult, and I began to wonder if the weary travelers and foxed old men would even know if I had ciphered correctly. But my father did, I was certain, for he was nearly as quick with numbers as I.

He also took me with him to the race clubs—even once to the Bibury Racecourse—where he placed wagers entrusted to him by men from Lower Coberly all the way to Foxcote. Beside him, with his black book in my small hands, I noted the odds, the wins and losses, mentally subtracting my father's share before inscribing the payouts. I found myself caught up in the excitement of the race, the smells of meat pasties and spiced cider, the crowds, the shouts of triumph or defeat, and the longed-for father-daughter bond.

Mother had always disliked my going with Papa to the races and public house, yet I was loath to refuse him altogether, for I was hungry for his approval. When I began attending Miss Cresswell's School for Girls, however, I went less often.

In the Crown and Crow that day, being twelve years of age, I was too old to perch upon the high counter. Instead I sat beside my father in the inglenook before the great hearth and drank my ginger beer while he downed ale after ale. The regulars seemed to sense his foul temper and did not disturb us.

Then *they* came in—a well-dressed gentleman and his son, wearing the blue coat and banded straw hat of a schoolboy. The man was obviously a gentleman of quality, perhaps even a nobleman, and we all sat up the straighter in defense of our humble establishment.

The boy, within a year or two of my own age, glanced at me. Of course we would notice one another, being the only young people in the room. His look communicated disinterest and contempt, or at least that was how I ciphered his expression.

The gentleman greeted the patrons in gregarious tones and announced that they had just visited a lord somebody or other, and were now traveling back toward London to return his son to Harrow's hallowed halls.

My father, cheeks flushed and eyes suddenly bright, turned to regard the boastful gentleman. "A Harrow lad, ey?"

"Just so," the gentleman answered. "Like his old man before him."

"A fine, clever lad, is he?" Papa asked.

A flicker of hesitation crossed the gentleman's face. "Of course he is."

"Not one to be outwitted by a village girl like this, then?" Papa dipped his head toward me, and my heart began to pound. A sickening dread filled my stomach.

The gentleman flicked a look at me. "I should say not."

Father grinned. "Care to place a friendly wager on it?"

This was nothing new. Over the years, many of the regulars had made small wagers on my ability to solve difficult equations. And even fellows who lost would applaud and buy Papa ale and me ginger beer.

The gentleman's mouth twisted. "A wager on what?"

"That the girl can best your boy in arithmetic? They do teach arithmetic at Harrow, I trust?"

"Of course they do, man. It is the best school in the country. In the world."

"No doubt you are right. Still, the girl here is clever. Is she not, folks?" Papa turned to the regulars around the room for support. "Attends Miss Cresswell's School for Girls."

"Miss Cresswell's?" The gentleman's sarcasm sent shivers down my spine. "My, my, Herbert, we had better declare defeat before we begin."

My father somehow retained control of his temper. Even feigned a shrug of nonchalance. "Might make for a diverting contest."

The gentleman eyed him, glass midway to his lips. "What do you propose?"

"Nothing out of the ordinary. Sums, divisions, multiplications. First correct answer wins. Best of three?"

That was when I saw it—the boy's look of studied indifference, of confidence, fell utterly away. In its place pulsed pale, sickly fear.

The gentleman glanced at his son, then finished his drink. "I don't find such sport amusing, my good man. Besides, we must be on our way. Long journey ahead." He placed his glass and a gold guinea on the counter.

"I don't blame you," Papa rose and placed his own guinea on the bar. "A bitter pill, bein' bested by a girl."

"*Pu-ppa* . . ." I whispered. "Don't."

"Well, Herbert, we cannot have that, can we." The gentleman

poked his son's shoulder with his walking stick. "What do you say, for the honour of Harrow and the family name?"

And in the stunned dread with which son regarded father, I saw the rest. I recognized the fear of disappointing a critical parent, the boy's eagerness for any morsel of approbation, and his absolute terror of the proposed contest. Clearly he was no scholar in mathematics, a fact he had perhaps tried desperately to conceal— and which was now about to be exposed in a very public and very mortifying manner.

"Excellent," my father said. "Ten guineas to the winner?"

"Per equation? Excellent," the gentleman parroted shrewdly. "Thirty guineas total. Even I am skilled in ciphering, you see."

I swallowed. My father had not meant thirty guineas. Did not *have* thirty guineas, as the gentleman must have known.

My father did not so much as blink. "Very well. We shall start out easy, shall we? First with the correct answer wins."

He enunciated two three-digit numbers, and the sum was instantly before me and out of my lips before conscious thought could curtail it.

I glanced at Herbert. A trickle of sweat rolled languidly from his hairline to his cheek.

"Come, Herbert, there is no need to act the gentleman in this instance. You may dispense with 'ladies first' this time, ey?"

Herbert nodded, his eyes focused on my father's mouth as though willing the next numbers to be simple ones, as though to control them with his stare.

Papa gave a division problem, not too difficult, and again the answer painted the air before me.

And again the young man did not speak.

Go on, I silently urged. *Answer.*

"Come, Herbert," his father prodded, features pinched. "We haven't all night."

"Would you mind repeating the numbers, sir?" Herbert asked weakly, and my heart ached for him.

I felt my father's pointed look and heard his low prompting, "Out with it, girl."

"Six hundred forty-four," I said apologetically, avoiding the gazes of all.

Murmurs of approval filled the room.

The gentleman stood, eyes flashing. "There is no way the girl could figure that in her head. I see what this is. A trick, is it not? No doubt we are not the first travelers to be taken in by your trained monkey who has memorized your every equation."

I cringed, waiting for my father to rise, fists first, and strike the man. Cheaters infuriated him, and many was the time I'd seen him fly into a rage over a thrown game or race. Yes, he'd take his share of other men's winnings, but not a farthing more.

"Let us see how she fares if *I* propose the question," the gentleman demanded. "And the first correct answer wins the *entire* wager."

Would my father abide such an insulting insinuation?

The proprietor laid a hand on his arm, no doubt fearing for the preservation of his property. "Why not, man?" he quietly urged. "Let Olivia prove herself the clever girl we all know she is."

My father hesitated.

"Unless you are afraid?" the gentleman taunted.

"I am not afraid."

My father's eyes bore into the face of the proud traveler, while I could not tear mine from the son's. Such humiliation and shame were written there. It was one thing for a girl to be clever—it was unexpected. A parlor trick, however honestly come by. But for a son, his father's pride, and no doubt heir, to be proven slow, to be made a fool by a girl? I shuddered at the thought of the piercing reprimands or cold rejection that would accompany him on the long journey ahead. And perhaps for the rest of his life.

The gentleman eyed the hop-boughed beams as he thought, then announced his equation. No doubt one he knew the answer to, likely his acreage multiplied by last year's average yield. Something like it, at any rate. Against the background of the boy's pale face and bleak green eyes, the numbers appeared before me, but lacked their usual clarity. Instead they swayed and slithered like that old silverfish and slid beneath the door.

The young man's eyes lit up. He had likely hit upon the number by memory rather than calculation, but as soon as he proclaimed the answer, I knew he was correct. The relief and near-jubilation on his face buoyed me up for one second. The answering smile and shoulder-clap from his father, one second more. Then the disapproval emanating from my own father's eyes pulled me around, and I saw the terrible truth of what I had done. Too late, I saw. Never again would he take me with him. Never again would he call me his clever girl, nor even Olivia.

The gentleman picked up my father's guinea from the bar. "I will take only one guinea, and let that be a lesson to you. I shall leave the rest to cover your debts to the others you have no doubt tricked over the years." Turning with a flourish, the gentleman placed a gloved hand on his boy's shoulder and propelled him from the room.

I watched them go, too sickened to be relieved that all I had cost my father was one guinea. For I knew I had cost him far more—the respect of every person in that room.

Slowly I became aware of their hooded looks, their unconscious shrinking back from us. Now they would believe the traveler's accusation that my ability had been a trick all along. All their applause and ale and wagers accepted dishonestly. In his eyes—in theirs—they had all been made fools by us. By me.

By my silence.

It is nought good a slepyng hound to wake.

—GEOFFREY CHAUCER

Chapter 1

Twelve years later
November 1, 1815

*H*eart pounding with fear and regret, Olivia Keene ran as
though hellhounds were on her heels. As though her very life
depended upon her escape.

Fleeing the village, she ran across a meadow, bolted over the
sheep gate, caught her skirt, and went sprawling in the mire. The
bundle in her cape pocket jabbed against her hip bone. Ignoring
it, she picked herself up and ran on, looking behind to make sure
no one followed. Ahead lay Chedworth Wood.

The warnings of years echoed through her mind. *"Don't stray
into the wood at night."* Wild dogs stalked that wood, and thieves
and poachers camped there, with sharp knives and sharper eyes,
looking for easy game. A woman of Olivia's four-and-twenty years
knew better than to venture into the wood alone. But her mother's

cries still pulsed in her ears, drowning out the old voice of caution. The danger behind her was more real than any imagined danger ahead.

Shivers of fear prickling over her skin, she hurled herself into the outstretched arms of the wood, already dim and shadowy on the chill autumn evening. Beneath her thin soles, dry leaves crackled. Branches grabbed at her like gnarled hands. She stumbled over fallen limbs and underbrush, every snapping twig reminding her that a pursuer might be just behind, just out of sight.

Olivia ran until her side ached. Breathing hard, she slowed her pace. She walked for what seemed like an hour or more and still hadn't reached the other side of the wood. Was she traveling in a circle? The thought of spending the night in the quickly darkening wood made her pick up her pace once more.

She tripped on a tangle of roots and again went sprawling. She heard the crisp rip of fabric. A burning scratch seared her cheek. For a moment she lay as she was, trying to catch her breath.

The pain of the fall broke through the dam of shock, and the hot tears she had been holding back poured forth. She struggled up and sat against a tree, sobbing.

Almighty God, what have I done?

A branch snapped and an owl screeched a warning to his mate. Fear instantly stifled her sobs. Hairs prickling at the back of her neck, Olivia searched the moonlit dimness with wide eyes.

Eyes stared back.

A dog, wiry and dark, stood not twenty feet away, teeth bared. In silent panic, Olivia scratched the ground around her, searching for something to use as a weapon. The undergrowth shook and the ground pulsed with a galloping tread. Two more dogs ran past, one clenching something round and white in its jaws. The head of a sheep?

The first dog turned and bounded after the other two, just as Olivia's fingers found a stout stick. She gripped it tightly, wishing for a moment that she still held the fire iron. Shivering in revulsion,

Olivia thrust aside the memory of its cold, hard weight. She listened for several tense seconds. Hearing nothing more, she rose, stick firmly in hand, and hurried through the wood, hoping the dogs wouldn't follow her trail.

The moon was high above the treetops when she saw it. The light of a fire ahead. *Relief.* Wild animals were afraid of fire, were they not? She tentatively moved nearer. She had no intention of joining whoever had camped there—perhaps a family of gypsies or a gentlemen's hunting party. Even if the rumors of thieves and poachers were stuff and nonsense, she would not risk making her presence known. But she longed for the safety the fire represented. She longed, too, for its warmth, for the November night air stole mercilessly through her cape and gown. Perhaps if another woman were present, Olivia might ask to warm herself. She dared move a little closer, stood behind a tree and peered around it. She saw a firelit clearing and four figures huddled around the flames in various postures of repose. The sound of men talking and jesting reached her.

"Squirrel again tonight, Garbie?" a gravelly voice demanded.

"Unless Croome comes back with more game."

"This time o' night? Not dashed likely."

"More likely he's lyin' foxed in the Brown Dog, restin' his head on Molly's soft pillows."

"Not Croome," another said. "Never knew such a monkish man."

Laughter followed.

Every instinct told Olivia to flee even as she froze where she stood. This was no family, nor any party of gentlemen. Fear slithering up her spine, she turned and stepped away from the tree.

"Wha's that?"

A young man's loud whisper stopped Olivia's retreat. She stood still, afraid to make another sound.

"What's what? I don't hear nofin'."

"Maybe it is Croome."

Olivia took a tentative tiptoe step. Then another. A sticky web coated her face, startling her, and she stumbled over a log onto the ground.

Before she could right herself, the sound of footsteps surrounded her and harsh lamplight blinded her.

"Well, kiss my bonnie luck star," a young man breathed.

Olivia struggled to her feet and pushed down her skirts. She brushed her fallen hair from her face and tried to remain calm.

"Croome's got a mite prettier since we saw 'im last," said a second young man.

Beside him, a bearded hulk glowered down at her. In the harsh, gravelly voice she had first heard, he demanded, "What are ya doin' here?"

Panic shot through her veins. "Na—nothing! I saw your fire and I—"

"Looking for some company, were ya?" The big man's leer chilled her to the marrow. "Well, ya come to the right place—hasn't she, lads?"

"Aye," another agreed.

The big man reached for her, but Olivia recoiled. "No, you misunderstand me," she said. "I simply lost my way. I don't want—"

"Oh, but we do want." His gleaming eyes were very like those of the wild dog.

The stout stick she had been carrying was on the ground, where it had landed when she fell. She lunged for it, but the man grabbed her from behind. "Where d'ya think yer going? Nowhere soon, I'd wager."

Olivia cried out, but did manage to get her hand around the stick as he hauled her up.

"Let go of me!"

The burly man laughed. Olivia spun in his arms and swung

the stick like a club. With a *thwack*, it caught the side of his head. He yelled and covered the wound with his hands.

Olivia scrambled away, but two other men grabbed her arms and legs, wrestled the stick from her, and bore her back to the fire.

"You all right, Borcher?" the youngest man asked, voice high.

"I will be. Which is more'n I can say for her."

"Please!" Olivia implored the men who held her. "Release me, I beg of you. I am a decent girl from Withington."

"My brother lives near there," the youngest man offered.

"Shut up, Garbie," Borcher ordered.

"Perhaps I have met your brother," she said desperately. "What is his na—?"

"Shut yer trap!" Borcher charged forward, hand raised.

"Borcher, don't," young Garbie urged. "Let her go."

"After the hoyden hit me? Not likely." Borcher grabbed her roughly, pinning both arms to her sides with one long, heavy arm and pressing her back against a tree.

She tried in vain to stomp on his foot, but her kid slippers were futile against his boots. "No!" she shouted. "Someone help me. Please!"

His free hand flashed up and clasped her jaw, steely fingers clamping her cheeks in a vise that stilled her shouts. She wrenched her head to the side and bit down on his thumb as hard as she could.

Borcher yelled, yanked his hand away, and raised it in a menacing fist.

Olivia winced her eyes shut, bracing herself for the inevitable blow.

Fwwt. Smack. Something whizzed by her captor's ear and shuddered into the tree above her. She opened her eyes as Borcher whirled his head around. Across the clearing, at the edge of the firelight, a man stood atop a tree stump, bow and arrow poised.

"Let her go, Phineas," the man drawled in an irritated voice.

"Mind yer own affairs, Croome." Borcher raised his fist again.

Another arrow whooshed by, slicing into the tree bark with a crack.

"Croome!" Borcher swore.

"Next time, I shall aim," the man called Croome said dryly. Though he appeared a slight, older man, cool authority steeled his words.

Borcher released Olivia with a hard shove. The back of her head hit the tree, where long arrows still quivered above her. Even the jarring pain in her skull did not diminish the relief washing over her. In the flickering firelight, she looked again at her rescuer, still perched on the stump. He was a gaunt man of some sixty years in a worn hat and hunting coat. Ash grey hair hung down to his shoulders. A game bag was slung over one of them. The bow he held seemed a natural extension of his arm.

"Thank you, sir," she said.

He nodded.

Glimpsing the stout stick by the light of the forgotten lamp, Olivia bent to retrieve it. Then turned to make her escape.

"Wait." Croome's voice was rough but not threatening. He stepped down from the stump, and she waited as he approached. His height—tall for a man of his years—and limping gait surprised her. "Take the provisions I brought for these undeserving curs."

She accepted a quarter loaf of bread and a sack of apples. Her stomach rumbled on cue. But when he extended a limp hare from his game bag, she shook her head.

"Thank you, no. This is more than enough."

One wiry eyebrow rose. "To make up for what they did to you—and would have done?"

Olivia stiffened. She shook her head and said with quiet dignity, "No, sir. I am afraid not." She handed back the bread and apples, turned, and strode smartly from the clearing.

His raspy chuckle followed her. "Fool . . ."

And she was not certain if he spoke of her or of himself.

Olivia walked quickly away by the moonlight filtering through the autumn-bare branches, the stick outstretched before her like a blindman's cane. She stayed alert for any hint of being followed but heard nothing save the occasional *to-wooo* of a tawny owl or the feathery scurrying of small nocturnal creatures. Eventually her fear faded into exhaustion and hunger. *Perhaps I should not have been so proud,* she thought, her stomach chastising her with a persistent ache.

Finally, unable to trudge along any further, she curled into a ball beside a tree. She searched her cape pockets for her gloves, but only one remained—the other lost in the wood, no doubt. She again felt the firm bundle in her pocket but did not bother to examine it in the dark. Shivering, she drew her hooded cape close around herself and covered her thin slippers with handfuls of leaves and pine needles for warmth. Images of her mother's terrified eyes and of a man's body lying facedown on the dark floor tried to reassert themselves, but she pushed them away, escaping into the sweet forgetfulness of sleep.

Send her to a boarding-school,
in order to learn a little ingenuity and artifice.
Then, Sir, she should have a supercilious knowledge in accounts . . .

—R. B. SHERIDAN, *THE RIVALS*, 1775

Chapter 2

*O*livia awoke to birdsong and mist, her hand still grasping the heavy stick. It reminded her once more of the fire iron, and she was tempted to hurl it away. But was it not her only protection from wild dogs if not wicked men?

The sunrise glimmered through the canopy of branches, beribboned with sparse, tenacious leaves. Her limbs were stiff, her toes numb from sleeping on cold, rooted ground. She rubbed warmth into her hands, then her feet, before replacing her shoes. If she had known what would happen yesterday, she would have taken time to lace on half boots instead of wearing her flimsy kid slippers.

The dreadful scene replayed in her mind.

She'd come home late from her post at Miss Cresswell's

school. Found her father's coat on an overturned chair. Her slippers crunched on broken glass. What had he thrown this time? A drinking glass? A bottle? A shrill cry pulled her into the bedchamber, dark, but light enough to see a chilling sight—the back of a man with his hands around her mother's throat. Her mother's eyes wide, gasping for air . . .

Olivia had not thought, only reacted, and suddenly the fire iron was in her hand. She raised it high and slammed it down with a sickening clang, and he fell facedown on the floor. The force of the blow reverberated up her arm and into her shoulder. Numbing shock followed like an icy wave. She stared, unmoving, as her mother sucked in haggard draws of air.

Then her mother was beside her, pulling the fire iron from her stiff fingers, and drawing her from the room, through the kitchen to the front door, both of them trembling.

"Did I kill him?" Olivia had whispered, glancing back at the darkened bedchamber door. "I did not mean to do it. I only—"

"Hush. He breathes still, and may revive any moment. You must leave before he sees you. Before he learns who struck him."

By the light of the kitchen fire, Olivia glimpsed the welts already rising on her mother's neck. "Then you must come with me. He might have killed you!"

Dorothea Keene nodded, pressing shaky fingers to her temples, trying to concentrate. "But first I will go to Muriel's. She will know what to do. But he must never know you were here. You . . . you have left the village . . . for a post. Yes."

"But where? I don't know of any—"

"Far from here." Her mother squeezed her eyes shut, thinking. "Go to my . . . go to St. Aldwyns. East of Barnsley. I know one of the sisters who manage the school there. They may have a post, or at least take you in."

Her mother turned and hurried across the kitchen. Reaching up, she winced as she pulled a small bundle from behind a portrait frame.

"I cannot leave you, Mamma—you are hurt!"

Returning, her mother gripped her arm. "If he should die, it will be the noose for you. And that would kill me more surely than he ever could."

She shoved the bundle into Olivia's cape pocket. "Take this and go. And promise me you will not return. I will come to you when I can. When it is safe."

A low moan rumbled from the other room, and panic seized them both. "Go now. Run!"

And Olivia ran.

The scene faded from her mind, and Olivia shuddered. She drew forth the small bundle, studying it by morning's light. At first glance, it looked like an old, folded handkerchief, but on closer inspection, she saw that it had seams and a small beaded clasp.

Why had her mother made this? Had she foreseen last night's events and Olivia's need to flee? Or had she been prepared to make her own escape, from a husband whose violent temper had been escalating for months?

Olivia opened the concealed purse and examined its contents. Four guinea coins were tacked in with thread, to keep them from jingling and giving away their hiding place, she supposed. There was also a letter. She picked it up, but saw it was firmly sealed with wax. She turned it over and read the tiny script in her mother's fine hand: *To be opened only upon my death.* Olivia's heart started. *What in the world?* She thought once more of her father's jealous rages—the overturned chairs, the broken glass, the holes punched in the wall. Still, Olivia had never believed he would actually harm his own wife. Had her mother feared that very thing? Curiosity gnawed at her, but she quickly returned the letter to its place.

As she did, she felt a thin disk within the folds of fabric, apparently a fifth, smaller, coin. A small tear in the lining revealed its would-be escape route. Curious, she worked the coin with stiff fingers back to the hole. As she extracted the shilling, a scrap of paper came with it. It was an inch-by-three-inch rectangle, torn from a newspaper, yellowed with age. It appeared to be a brief portion of a marriage announcement.

> . . . the Earl of Brightwell of his son,
> Lord Bradley to Miss Marian Estcourt
> of Cirencester, daughter of . . .

Brightwell . . . Estcourt . . . the names echoed dully in Olivia's mind. She could not recall her mother mentioning either name before. Why had she kept the clipping?

Her stomach growled and Olivia tucked away the paper—and her questions—for another time. Gingerly she rose and began pulling leaves and needles from her hair. Brushing off her cape and dress, she grimaced at a long tear in her bodice. Her shift and one strap of her stays showed. Thinking of her peril of the previous night, she shuddered, realizing the damage could have been far worse. She pulled up the hanging flap of bodice and tied it crudely to the strip of torn cloth at her shoulder. She hoped she didn't look as dreadful as she felt.

She tried to run her fingers through her hair and discovered it was a knotted mess, her neat coil long-since fallen. She longed for a bath and a comb. *No use in fretting about it now*, she told herself. *If I don't get moving, no one but the trees shall see me anyway.*

Olivia once more wove her way through the trees and underbrush, wondering if the schoolmistress her mother knew would really take in a stranger, and what Olivia would do if not. She bit the inside of her cheek to hold back self-pity and tears. She breathed a quick prayer for her mother and kept walking, her breath rising on the cold morning air.

The trees thinned as the sun rose higher in the sky, lifting her spirits with it. She saw a ribbon of road ahead and decided to follow it, knowing she could return to the shelter of the wood if necessary.

She walked along the road for several minutes, then accepted a ride in the back of a farmer's wagon. His wife looked askance at the stick in her hand but did not comment.

After many jostling, jerking miles, the farmer called a welcome "whoa" to his old nag and smiled back at Olivia. "That's our farm up the lane there, so this is as far as we can take you."

Thanking the couple, Olivia climbed stiffly from the wagon and asked the way to St. Aldwyns.

"Follow the river there," the farmer said, pointing. "It'll be quicker than the road, though you'll not meet another wagon."

Olivia followed the river as it passed through a rolling vale, skirted a tiny hamlet, then another. Soon after that, the river disappeared within a copse of trees. *Not another wood . . .* Olivia lamented. She did not wish to lose her way, so she took a deep breath and entered the copse.

The trees were not dense, and through them she saw an open field beyond. Having had her fill of trees the previous night, she walked faster.

A sound startled Olivia, and she stopped abruptly. Listening over her pounding heart, she heard it once more. Barking. Her stomach lurched. More wild dogs? Coming fast! She was running before she consciously chose to, stick banging against her leg. With her free hand, she hiked up her skirts and darted onto the field. Ignoring the cinder burning in her side, she ran on, not daring to pause to look behind her. Another sound joined the first—a low rumble, growing louder. Thunder? A search party?

The dogs drew closer—she could hear the barking distinctly now—they were nearly upon her. Panic gripped her. Something nipped at her skirts, and she spun around, swinging the stick and yelling at the top of her voice.

"Be gone! Go!" The barking dogs skidded and jumped. She grazed one on its rump, and it yelped and ran away.

Slowly the blur of mottled fur came into focus and she realized these were not wild dogs at all. Horse hooves thundered around her. She looked up in a daze as a small army of scarlet coats and black hats—men in hunting attire—charged up on all sides.

"Stand clear!" one of the riders shouted, his roan galloping dangerously close.

She leapt out of his way. Then she screamed and lifted her arms over her head—for she had jumped right into the path of an oncoming horse. Its rider pulled up sharply and the black horse skittered and reared up. Dirt flew, splattering Olivia's face. The horse's hooves flashed inches from her chin and then exploded onto the ground before her.

"What on earth do you think you are doing?" The rider of the black yelled down. "Are you mad?"

Other riders—whippers-in and gentlemen on field hunters of white, grey, and chestnut—circled around her, their voices raised and angry.

"You have spoilt an excellent hunt!" This from the elderly master of the hunt, silver side-whiskers showing beneath his telltale velvet hat. His lined, aristocratic face was nearly as red as his coat.

"She tried to kill the hounds!" another accused. "The lead dog is limping."

"I thought they were wild dogs!" Olivia sputtered in lame defense.

"Wild dogs!" the huntsman echoed, copper horn hanging from his neck. "I don't believe it. Are you daft?"

She wiped her sleeve across her eyes to clear the mud and her mind. "No. I . . . I—"

"I believe her, gentlemen." The rider of the black horse dismounted and grabbed the stick from her hand. "She is obviously armed to ward off wild dogs."

"From the looks of the chit," the stout rider of the roan called down, "I'd say she battled a mud puddle—and lost."

The other men laughed. Ignoring the jeers, Olivia kept her

eyes on the tall young man before her. Though not the master of the hunt, and by all appearances no older than she was, he was clearly a leader of men and cut an imposing figure in his hunting kit and Hessian boots.

Forcing her voice into cool civility, she said, "I am sorry about the dog. Now kindly return my stick, sir."

His eyes were glittering blue glass in a face that would have been handsome were it not imperious and angry. "I believe not. You are far too dangerous."

Olivia could feel her anger mounting as the men continued their laughter and taunts. But it was the disdainful smirk of the young man before her that threatened her self-control, already worn thin by recent stress and lack of sound sleep. She thrust out her hand. "Return it to me at once."

The elderly master of the hunt called derisively, "Have you any idea whom you are addressing, *ghel*?"

Keeping her eyes on the haughty young man before her, she answered levelly, "Someone with very poor manners."

The others reacted with barely concealed snorts of laughter. *Good*, she thought. *See how he likes being laughed at.*

Some new emotion flickered across the man's face, but the expression was quickly overlaid with contempt. Broad shoulders strained against his close-fitting coat as he carelessly flung the stick into the brush some thirty yards away.

Olivia opened her mouth to protest, but the old master called down a steely warning. "Careful, ghel. Bradley there is magistrate as well as lord. You don't want to risk his wrath."

She looked once more at the young man called Bradley. Golden side-whiskers indicated fair hair beneath his hat. Under its brim, blue eyes rested on a bit of dirt on his coat sleeve. With the merest glance at her, he flicked it away with a finger, and in that one gesture Olivia knew she had been dismissed as thoughtlessly.

"Ross!" he called, and a younger man, by appearance his groom, jogged over. "How is Mr. Linton's hound?"

"He is well, my lord, merely bruised."

"Still, bear him on your horse. Linton's kennel-man will want to have a look at him."

"Yes, my lord."

"Thank you, Bradley," the master said. "I think we must call off the hunt for today."

The huntsman nodded and pocketed his horn. "That fox is in Wiltshire by now at any rate."

"Perhaps *she* could be our fox." The stout roan rider jeered, gesturing toward Olivia with his riding crop.

"Excellent plan," another said. "Quite sorry, constable. We thought the sorry creature a fox."

"No—a mad dog!" A second man poked Olivia on the shoulder with his crop, and soon three of them were circling her on their horses, laughing all the while.

"Gentlemen!" came a loud command.

The three men reined in and looked at Bradley.

"That is quite enough," he said. "Peasants are not for prodding."

"Just so," another snorted. "They are for paying rents."

Lord Bradley scowled, clearly not amused.

"Take heart, gentlemen," the master consoled. "The season has barely begun. We shall have many more hunts come winter."

Lord Bradley prepared to remount his tall black horse. He paused, his icy glare resting briefly on Olivia. "Are you still here?"

She expelled a dry puff of air. "No, sir. I have disappeared utterly."

His eyes narrowed. "Have you not somewhere to go?" It wasn't a question.

"I—"

"Go!" he commanded, jerking his crop to the south.

Olivia strode blindly across the field, humiliated and indignant. She was angry at herself for obeying, for fleeing in the exact direction he pointed. Was she a dog herself? He surely had not meant for her to go in any specific direction. Only away. *I was traveling in this direction at any rate,* she thought hotly, and trudged toward the river once more.

Always remember to hold the secrets of the family sacred,
as none may be divulged with impunity.

—SAMUEL & SARAH ADAMS, *THE COMPLETE SERVANT*

Chapter 3

*T*he sun was high in the sky when Olivia knelt beside the river to wash her face and hands. She scrubbed at the stubborn dirt encrusted in the lines of her palms and beneath her nails. She hoped the dirt on her face did not cling as tenaciously. Nor the guilt she felt. Had there been no other recourse? Surely she might have thought of another way to stop her father. She might have called the constable or a neighbor. But it was too late now. Olivia splashed cold water on her face, wishing she could wash away the memory—the regret—as easily.

She found but two hairpins still tangled within her fallen curls and, in the end, tore a strip of ribbon edging from her shift and tied back her hair with it. She did not wish to enter the next village looking like a beggar. Or worse.

The water, while too frigid for comfortable washing, seemed inviting to her dry throat and she bent low to drink, using her now-clean hand as a cup. Cold and delicious. She bent low over the water once again.

"I say! Hello there! Don't— Are you all right?"

Still on her knees, Olivia turned at the call. A man in a black suit of clothes and tabbed white neckcloth briskly approached. Behind him followed a spotted dog and four young boys, a sight which put Olivia more at ease than she would otherwise have been.

"I am well. Only thirsty."

"Oh!" He stepped nearer. "I feared you might be about to do yourself harm. Though I suppose the river is too shallow and gentle here to pose much danger."

"No, sir. I was not."

"Of course not. Forgive me. A young lady such as yourself could have no reason to be so desperate, I trust."

She hesitated, her lips stiffening. "No reason . . ."

"I am Mr. Tugwell," he said, doffing his round, wide-brimmed hat of black felt. "Vicar of St. Mary's."

"How do you do." She guessed him to be in his midthirties, with light brown hair and soft, mobile face.

He extended his hand. "May I offer you a hand up?"

"I fear mine are wet and cold, sir," she apologized as she placed her hand in his.

He pulled her to her feet. "You were in earnest! A cold fish comes to mind." He grinned. "Never fear, I have handled far worse."

She found herself grinning in spite of her recent ordeal. "And my face. I suppose it is a fright?"

He cocked his head to the side and appraised her. "Your face is charming." He nodded toward his boys. "You fit right in with my lot here. These are my sons—Jeremiah, Ezekiel, Isaiah, and Tom. Amos, my eldest, is at school."

"Hello. I am Miss Keene." The name was out of her mouth

before she could think the better of it. But how could she lie to four such angelic, albeit dirty, boys?

Mr. Tugwell handed her his handkerchief, then tapped a broad finger to a spot along his jaw.

Blushing, she wiped the same place on her own jaw. "I am afraid I have fallen and made a mess of myself."

"Have we not all done so, Miss Keene?" he asked, a twinkle in his kindly hazel eyes. "Have we not all?"

Not knowing how to respond, she returned the handkerchief and asked, "And who is this?" of the spaniel sniffing at her skirts.

"That is Harley," little Tom supplied.

"Harley likes these wanders as much as we do," Mr. Tugwell explained. "The lady of the house believes a great deal of exercise keeps male animals from tearing about the place." He grinned. "The dog as well."

She smiled. "Might you direct me to St. Aldwyns, sir?"

"With pleasure." Tucking the handkerchief back into his pocket, the vicar said, "We are for Arlington, which is on your way. May we escort you that far at least?"

"Thank you." She thought a moment. "I suppose my first task will be to repair my appearance. Is there someplace in Arlington where I might purchase a needle and thread and perhaps a pair of gloves?"

"Indeed there is. Eliza Ludlow's shop. Miss Ludlow is a friend of ours. Might we have the pleasure of introducing you?"

"Yes, that would be most kind. Thank you."

In company with Mr. Tugwell and his boys, Olivia crossed a stone bridge near the village mill and turned up the high street, passing the Swan Hotel and a row of weavers' cottages—evidenced by stone troughs for washing and dying cloth, and the narrow mill leat flowing past. They crossed the cobbled street and approached a cluster of shops—a chandler's, a wool agent's, and the promised ladies' shop with a display of hats and bonnets in its many-paned bow window.

"Please await me here, boys," Mr. Tugwell said. "And do keep Harley from the chandler's wares this time, hmm?"

The vicar opened the shop door for her. Quickly smoothing back the wisps of hair at her temples, Olivia stepped inside while the bell still jingled.

The shop was small, neat, and sweet-smelling. Shelves displayed gloves, scarves, stockings, fans, and tippets. A dress form wore a flounced walking dress of white cambric muslin. The front counter held fashion magazines and an assortment of cosmetics and perfumes.

A woman in her thirties, dressed in an attractive, vested gown of striped twill, stood at a tidy counter. She smiled brightly at the vicar. "Mr. Tugwell, what a lovely surprise."

Her ready smile dimmed only fractionally as Olivia stepped near.

"Good afternoon, Miss Eliza." He made a slight bow. "May I present Miss Keene, of . . . ?"

Olivia faltered. "Near Cheltenham."

"Who is in need of your services."

"Of course." Miss Ludlow turned warm brown eyes in Olivia's direction.

Mr. Tugwell straightened. "I shall leave you ladies to it. I know little of such falderals, and confess I prefer my ignorance." He smiled at Olivia. "But you may trust Miss Ludlow implicitly, I assure you."

The woman blushed at his praise.

Mr. Tugwell rubbed his lip in thought. "I don't wish to be presumptuous, Miss Keene, but it does grow late, and St. Aldwyns is still a few miles off. You would be most welcome to stay the night in the vicarage guest room. Miss Tugwell will make you quite welcome, I assure you."

"You are very kind. I . . . Perhaps I shall, indeed. If you are certain it is not too much of an imposition?"

"Not at all. And the boys and I promise to be on our best behavior. Though I cannot speak for Harley." He grinned, then turned once more to Miss Ludlow. "If you would be so good as to point out the way, Miss Eliza, once your business is concluded?"

"Of course."

"Then I shall bid you adieu for now." He bowed to both ladies and made his exit.

When the jingle of the shop bell faded, Eliza Ludlow asked kindly, "And how may I help you, Miss Keene?"

"I hope to find a situation, you see . . . " Olivia began.

The woman's dark eyebrows furrowed. "I am afraid this little shop barely provides for me."

"Oh no. Forgive me, I did not mean here. I understand there is a girls' school in St. Aldwyns."

"Yes, I have heard of it. Managed by a pair of elderly sisters, I believe. I cannot say whether they need anyone, but you might try."

"I plan to. But I should not go looking like this." Olivia pulled back one shoulder of her cape, exposing the crudely tied fabric of her frock. "I am afraid I suffered a mishap—a few of them, actually—on my way here."

Miss Ludlow tutted sympathetically. "You poor dear."

"Have you needle and thread I might purchase to put this to rights?"

"Indeed I have. Blue thread?"

Olivia nodded. "And, perhaps, a hairbrush and pins?" Her stomach rumbled a rude complaint, and Olivia ducked her head to hide a blush.

"Of course, my dear." Eliza Ludlow smiled sweetly. "And you must come up to my rooms and repair yourself properly. Perhaps you would join me for tea and cake?"

Tears pricked Olivia's eyes at this unexpected generosity. "You are very kind. I thank you."

An hour later, Olivia's hair was combed and securely pinned, and her gown repaired and brushed reasonably clean. She wore a new chip bonnet, two gloves, and a small reticule dangling from her wrist. She'd had money enough to purchase the bonnet, but Eliza had insisted on giving her a lone glove, saying she'd lost its mate and wasn't it nearly a perfect match? Not wanting to deplete her funds, Olivia had gratefully agreed and accepted. Now her mother's small purse, a new comb, and a handkerchief were encased within the reticule, which Miss Ludlow had sold her for a suspiciously low price.

Prepared to take her leave, Olivia listened as Eliza described the way to the vicarage. "Continue up the high street as it angles to the north. The vicarage is just past an old white house with a dovecote."

"Is it proper, do you think, for me to accept the vicar's invitation?" Olivia asked. "Mrs. Tugwell won't mind?"

"You mean *Miss* Tugwell, his sister."

"Oh. I thought—"

"Mrs. Tugwell died several years ago, poor soul."

"How tragic. Those poor motherless boys . . ."

"Yes." Miss Ludlow's brown eyes glowed sympathetically. "Still, I think it appropriate. Unless you would feel more comfortable in the Swan, though the inn might be more expense than you wish to bear."

"I am afraid it would be."

"Then we shall hope and pray the school has need of you directly."

Olivia pressed the shopkeeper's hand. "Thank you. You have been prodigiously kind, and I shall never forget it."

"You are more than welcome." Miss Eliza was suddenly distracted by a bandbox on the counter, her dark brows knit in perplexity or irritation. "Oh, fiddle . . ."

"Are you all right?"

The woman sighed. "I would be better had Mrs. Howe paid for this feathered cap she ordered. Said she wanted it for a party at Brightwell Court, but the party is this very evening, and still she has not sent anyone round to collect it. And *bon chance* trying to sell this piece of London frippery to anyone else in the village."

"I am sorry," Olivia murmured, but her mind had caught on something else Miss Ludlow had said. "Brightwell Court?" Olivia asked. She remembered the name *Brightwell* from her mother's newspaper clipping.

"Yes. Do you know it? The largest estate in the borough, save the Lintons'. There is a party there this very evening." She winked at Olivia. "But I seem to have misplaced my invitation."

Olivia grinned at her joke. "As have I."

Promising to call on her new friend when she was able, Olivia thanked her once again and let herself from the shop.

The evening was already growing dark, the hours of daylight quite abbreviated in the final months of the year. The wind pulled at her cape and she shivered. It was indeed too dark and cold to continue further. At least by foot.

She walked up the high street where it curved to the north, and passed the village square. She saw a stately church beyond it, which she supposed to be St. Mary's. Several fine carriages passed, and one coachman stopped to ask if she would like a ride.

"Are you for St. Aldwyns?" she asked hopefully.

He shook his head. "Not bound for Brightwell Court like every other fine lady in the borough? Big doings there tonight."

Brightwell . . . There it was again.

Olivia shook her head. "Thank you anyway."

She waited while the carriage passed, then watched as it turned through a gate and up a long, torchlit lane. Had her mother some connection to the place? Olivia felt compelled to lay eyes on this Brightwell Court. Then she would make her way directly to the vicarage.

Olivia walked through the gate, up the graveled lane, past several small outbuildings, and then, there it was. A tall, grey Tudor manor in an E-shape, with a many-peaked roof.

Had her mother friends here? Had she once visited or had a post here? Olivia certainly was not going to knock on the door and ask, especially while the owners were entertaining.

She started to turn back when the lively, happy music caught her attention. It swirled in her ears and swelled in her chest. She stepped carefully across the lawn, drawn by the light spilling from large mullioned windows. As she drew near she received her first good look into one of the grand rooms. Lovely women in fine gowns and distinguished gentlemen in black evening attire stood in groups, talking, laughing, bowing, eating, and drinking. A sigh escaped her.

Mesmerized, she slowly walked past the first wing, glimpsing a buffet graced by a life-size ice swan, towering jelly molds, a stuffed boar, and a huge golden bowl overflowing with fruits. She walked past the recessed courtyard of the shorter leg of the E, and then around the final wing, staring in each window, as if watching vivid tableaux lit by a hundred candles. As she rounded the manor, she walked by another window, open, she guessed, to release cigar smoke or the heat of the crowd. Her steps faltered. Inside what appeared to be a library, a dapper middle-aged gentleman embraced his middle-aged wife. They were alone. The man kissed the top of her head and stroked her back, murmuring some reassurance or encouragement near her ear. The gentle tenderness stung Olivia's heart. She knew she should turn away, respect their privacy. But she could not. Then the man put his hands on either side of her face and said something. The woman nodded, her pale cheeks wet with tears. The man brushed them away with his thumbs and kissed the woman full on the mouth.

Embarrassed, Olivia lowered her head and walked away. She leaned against a shadowed tree to catch her breath. If only her mother and father might have shown such affection to one other instead of brooding silences and heated arguments. If only she herself might one day know such tender love.

A side door opened. Olivia froze beside the tree. Footsteps sounded on the flagstones of the veranda, followed by another set.

"Edward, wait."

"This is not something I wish to discuss before the assembled company, nor the servants."

"Must we discuss it at all?"

Olivia peered from behind the tree, looking for a way of escape. The veranda was mottled shadow and moonlight. Upon it, she glimpsed the same older gentleman from the library standing before a taller man, whose back was to her.

The taller man sputtered, incredulous. "Am I to simply forget what I read?"

"No, I don't suppose you could. But it need not be a disaster, my boy."

"How can you say that?"

"I have known all along and it has not altered my feelings."

"But how did you . . . ? Where did I come from? Who was my mother, my—?"

"Edward, lower your voice. I will tell you one day if you really must know. But not today. Not on the eve of our departure."

Olivia was chagrined to overhear such a personal conversation. What should she do? If she moved at all, even to lift her hands to her ears, they would see her.

The elder man put his arm around the younger man's shoulder. "I am sorry you had to learn of it at all, and especially now, but nothing has changed. Nothing. Do you understand?"

The younger man slapped his chest, his voice hoarse. "Everything has changed. Everything. Or will. If . . ." His voice broke, and Olivia missed the rest of his sentence.

"There is nothing we can do about that now. Promise me you will not attempt to ferret out anything more until we return. Let it lie for now, Edward. Please. You have been given enough to adapt to already."

"That is an understatement indeed, sir."

The father turned his son back toward the manor. "Come inside, my boy. How cold it is. Your mother will wonder what became of us."

The young man muttered something inaudible as they stepped to the door and Olivia released a breath she had not realized she was holding.

"May we *not* burden your mother with this right now?" the older man asked. "I want nothing to spoil this journey for her."

His son sighed. "Of course. Her health must come first." He held the door for his father. "After you."

The older man pulled a sad smile and disappeared inside.

Olivia stepped from behind the tree, ready to make her escape at last. But the young man stopped suddenly, hand on the open door. He stood, staring blindly in her direction. Had he seen her? Heard her?

Her heart pounded. She took a step backward, hoping to further conceal herself in the shadows, and instead collided with something solid and warm. She cried out as a foul sack descended over her head and wiry arms grasped her by the shoulders and hauled her away.

A poacher becomes an infirm old man if he be
fortunate enough to escape transportation or the gallows. . . .

—THE GAMEKEEPER'S DIRECTORY

Chapter 4

When the sack was pulled from her head, Olivia found herself in a small parlor, staring at a bald man and a round, aproned woman. The man introduced himself. "I am John Hackam, village constable. Again."

"Again," the woman echoed. "No one else will take 'is term."

The constable nodded to the woman. "My good wife."

"What did the earl's man catch 'er at," Mrs. Hackam inquired. "Thievin'?"

"Mayhap," Hackam replied.

An earl? "No," Olivia protested. "I took noth—"

"No time to hear your tale o' woe now, girl. I've an inn to run, and we are full up tonight."

"Full up." His wife nodded.

Mr. Hackam took Olivia's elbow. "It's the lockup for you tonight, and we'll sort it in the morning."

The constable led her from the inn's parlor and out a side door to a windowless octagonal building some twenty yards distant.

"Court is held here at my humble inn regular-like, but the JPs are all at Brightwell Court tonight and can't hear your case at present."

He unlocked the heavy door and firmly, though not roughly, compelled her inside. The door shut behind her, enveloping her in darkness. She heard the key scrape in the lock and footsteps retreating. Weariness and fear competed for precedence within her.

Was this God's judgment for what she had done? She berated herself yet again for not going directly to the vicarage.

Olivia blinked, trying to adjust her eyes to the darkness. Not complete darkness after all—a small red glow shone several yards away. A rat's eye? No. A lit cigar. Suddenly a flame sputtered and sparked to life, illuminating a big man holding a candle stub in one hand and the cigar in the other.

Her heart lurched and stomach seized. Borcher!

The big man held up the candle and peered at her. She prayed he would not recognize her from Chedworth Wood.

"Well, well. What have we here?" He stepped closer and held the candle near her face. In the wobbling light, his fat lips curled into a feline smile. "The hoyden from the wood."

"No. I—"

Tossing aside the candle, he slammed her hard against the door. Pain shot up her spine. She turned and banged on the door. "Help! Please help me!" A scream caught in her throat as Borcher slapped one hand over her mouth and with the other gripped her arm, pulling her back against him. He laughed a ghoulish giggle in her ear, his foul breath making her gag.

"I told ya I'd get ya, girlie. And now I have done."

She struggled and tried to call out, but only a muffled murmur escaped his thick hand. Her mind reeled, *No, no, no!* She opened her mouth and tried to bite his hand.

"Not this time, pet." He released her mouth only to grasp her neck with both hands. He squeezed until Olivia thought his thumbs would crush her windpipe. Something popped within her throat.

Olivia choked and struggled against the pain and suffocation, panic soaring as she struggled to suck in the thinnest stream of air. Was this what her mother had experienced? At least Olivia had been able to save her. *Oh, God,* she prayed. *Please forgive me. I only meant to stop him. . . .* She hoped he would not try again. *Please watch over her,* Olivia silently pleaded as her mind clouded over, the shutters of her brain closing tight.

Blackness.

Vaguely she heard something. A key in the lock? The door banged open, though Olivia could see none of the lamplight that surely was flooding in. Borcher growled and pushed her roughly away as he released her. She would have fallen, but strong arms caught her. She tried to breathe through a throat that felt sealed off. Crushed. She gasped painfully and smelled a man's sweat and pipe smoke. Sputtering and sucking in panting breaths, her vision returned. The constable righted her, then scowled—first at her, then Borcher.

"You there." He glared at her attacker. "An extra fortnight for you. And you, come with me. There is someone to see you."

A fortnight? Olivia thought dumbly. *That is all my life is worth?*

Relieved to be leaving the lockup, she asked no questions. With a trembling hand, she tentatively reached up to survey her burning throat. She thought it a miracle her neck was not broken. As it was, her legs shook from the shock and violence of the ordeal. When she stumbled, the constable took her arm and pulled her along. She would not have remained upright otherwise.

"Lord Bradley wants to question you." The constable sighed in a long-suffering manner. "Wants to see the trespasser properly punished, no doubt." He whistled low. "Looks dreadful fierce, he does."

He led her back into the Swan, pushed open the door to the same parlor, and propelled her within.

She shrank at the sight of the tall man in full evening dress, his blue eyes intense with scrutiny and suspicion, but not, she thought, recognition. She, however, recognized him at once. The haughty young man from the hunt. Lord Bradley. His father was an earl? *Theirs* was the conversation she had overheard?

She looked down, hoping he would not remember her. She imagined she appeared quite altered with a clean face, her hair neatly pinned back—at least it had been—and a proper bonnet over all.

Olivia could feel his glare on her bowed profile. She registered his finely shod feet, then slowly raised her head. *I am not a dog to cower in the corner,* she encouraged herself, forcing her gaze to meet the man's icy blue eyes. He scowled, his countenance darkening. Had he just recognized her from the spoilt hunt?

Staring at the slight figure before him, Edward Stanton Bradley bade his heart rate to slow and his anger to calm. His mind still reeled, not only with the stunning sledgehammer of news he had barely had time to assimilate himself, but with the terrifying prospect that someone had overheard the tidings he hoped with all his being to bury forever. He fisted his hands, ineffectively trying to quench the irrational desire to squash this unknown foe, to silence her before she might open her mouth and devastate them all.

When she looked up at him, Edward felt the barest hint of recognition, but it quickly flitted away. He knew not this sorry creature. *Good heavens, what had befallen her?* She seemed barely able to walk, let alone stand. Had Hackam not held her arm, she seemed certain to fall. Her face was ashen, her neck . . . *What the plague?*

"Hackam, what have you done to the chit?"

"Nothing, my lord."

"Did my man do this to you?" he asked her directly, knowing Hackam would not hesitate to lay blame at the gamekeeper's feet.

Eyes glazed, the girl shook her head.

"Dash it, Hackam. Punishment before a hearing?"

"No, my lord. It was another prisoner. Gordon didn't tell me he'd put a poacher in the lockup. I thought it empty."

Biting back an oath, Edward grimly shook his head. Still, he believed Hackam. He was not a cruel man, but he was busy with his inn and held little patience for his secondary role as constable. The quarter sessions and more frequent petty sessions brought business to his establishment, so he begrudgingly took up the unpopular duty year after year when no one else stepped forward.

"Do you not wish to hear about the poacher, my lord?" Hackam asked. "Likely to be one of the lot what evaded us all summer. Is that not good news, my lord?"

Edward ignored the man's attempt at diversion. "The next session is not for a fortnight, and there is no question of calling an early hearing. My father is leaving the country on the morrow, and Farnsworth is already on the continent. If this is what happens in half an hour, what would become of her in a week?"

"I plan to send her up to Northleach. Let the justices up there deal with her."

Hackam referred to the new house of corrections—a fortresslike prison only about as old as Edward himself. An improvement over the gaols of old, where men and women were held together, but a prison just the same. "That will not be necessary."

" 'Course it is. Your man said she were trespassing, maybe even a thief."

The young woman swayed, and Hackam tightened his grip.

"Have you any evidence she meant to steal anything?" Edward asked. He knew trespassing was a petty offense, unless accompanied by theft, nuisance to the land, or injury to a person. But could not great personal injury come of her eavesdropping? Not to mention the repercussions his father would face should his deception be made known?

"Well, she weren't an invited guest, now, were she? What else would she be doin' there?"

"That is what I should like to know." Edward turned to the pale-faced woman. "What is your name?"

She opened her mouth to speak, her small lips forming a silent O. Wincing in surprise, tears swamping her bright blue eyes, she raised thin fingers to her rapidly discoloring throat.

Could she really not speak, or was she a consummate actress?

"Could have her flogged on the pillory," the constable jovially suggested. "That would loosen her tongue."

The girl's pale skin blanched nearly white.

"Or hung in the stocks on the village green. An example to other would-be thieves." The constable rocked on his heels as he considered. "Or ducked on the ducking chair. Haven't used that contraption since my first term."

The woman's eyes flared, then drooped, her posture rigid. She was falling forward before he realized it, her eyes open but unseeing. Hackam's grip was insufficient to stop her fall, and she crumpled to the ground.

Returning to her senses sometime later, Olivia peered through her lashes to find a bespectacled middle-aged man leaning over her. She shrank back instinctively, only to realize she was lying flat while he sat peering down at her, touching her throat in the gentlest of palpations. An apothecary, she guessed. Or a surgeon. She closed her eyes once more and listened to the conversation above her.

"Such an injury could indeed render a person speechless for a time. Have you reason to think her pretending to muteness?"

"She was caught trespassing on our estate." Lord Bradley's voice.

"A great many people were at Brightwell Court this evening. Why do you think her intentions nefarious?"

Lord Bradley did not respond. Instead he asked, "Can she be moved?"

"I think so. Doesn't seem to have any broken bones. Even so, I have given her laudanum. That neck injury must be dreadfully painful."

"Moved, my lord?" The incredulous voice of the constable. "Moved where?"

"Clearly I cannot leave her here, Hackam. Nor do I wish her taken to Northleach for mere trespassing. Release her to my custody for now."

Hackam's voice rose. "Are you certain that is wise, my lord?"

"She doesn't look dangerous to me," the medical man offered.

"Is that your professional diagnosis?" Bradley's tone was acerbic. "I shall hold you to it."

"But—" Hackam tried once more. "She might turn out to be a thief, after all."

"Then you shall have your chance to flog her yet."

Olivia sank into darkness once more, from a hefty dose of laudanum. And fear.

Edward and the constable helped Dr. Sutton settle the young woman into the back of Sutton's cart.

"Speaking of moving," the doctor said. "I dearly hope the trip to Italy does your mother good."

"Thank you, Sutton. As do I."

"Many in my profession attest to the benefits of a warm Mediterranean winter for their patients."

"Do you concur?"

"What I *can* attest to are the benefits of avoiding a damp English winter. That I heartily recommend. When do they depart?"

"Tomorrow."

The doctor nodded. "Then I wish them Godspeed."

The constable had just bid them good-night and returned to the Swan, when the Reverend Mr. Charles Tugwell crossed the cobbles toward them. "Bradley. Sutton." His gaze flicked from the men to the prone girl, concern drooping his hound-dog eyes. "I say, what is happening here?"

"Mr. Tugwell," Edward said quickly. "I am afraid you have come upon me at an inopportune time. Might I come round the vicarage next week?"

"Of course. But that young woman. I know her."

Edward was stunned. "Do you?"

"That is to say, I met her today near the river. What has befallen her?"

"She was caught trespassing at Brightwell Court and, I am afraid, was injured in the lockup by a male prisoner."

"Good heavens!"

"Sutton here believes she will shortly recover."

"Thank God." The clergyman shook his head. "A young lady such as she, locked in with a criminal!"

"We do not know that *she* is not a criminal as well."

The clergyman shook his head. "She seemed a genteel, well-spoken young lady to me."

"Lady?" Edward sneered. "What sort of *lady* lurks behind trees, unchaperoned at night, eavesdropping on private conversations?"

"A desperate one, to be sure, but let us not be too quick to judge. I myself escorted her to Miss Ludlow's to replace the gloves she had lost in some mishap. I believe she said she was on her way to St. Aldwyns, seeking some post or other."

"And of course *you* believed her."

The clergyman eyed him speculatively. "Have you some reason to suspect her of more than curiosity? My own boys were tempted to sneak over and have a look-in at Brightwell Court tonight. All the fine carriages and horses, footmen and musicians, and I know not what. I had to send Zeke to bed without his supper and forbid Tom to leave his window open in hopes of hearing the music.

Everyone in the village knew of the party. Why, I imagine Miss Ludlow mentioned it to her. The young lady was to come to the vicarage tonight and sleep in our guest room."

"Was she indeed?"

"I wondered what became of her and dropped by Miss Ludlow's just now to see if she had changed her plans. I imagine she took a brief detour to see the goings-on at the manor and that is all. Pray do not besmirch her reputation by calling her a criminal until she recovers and you learn her true intentions."

"Regardless of her *intentions*, she has likely—" Edward broke off, glancing at Sutton, and waited while the doctor climbed onto the bench of his cart.

"Likely what?" Tugwell urged.

Edward lowered his voice. "I cannot say. But it is imperative that I learn who she is, and whether she plans to use whatever she may have overheard for mercenary ends."

"Good heavens, Edward. What is it?"

"Forgive me, Charles. I am not at liberty to say."

His friend's eyebrows rose. "Even to me?"

Edward grimaced. "Even to you."

People leave their native country, and go abroad
for one of these general causes—
Infirmity of body, Imbecility of the mind, or Inevitable necessity.

—Stearne, *A Sentimental Journey through France and Italy*

Chapter 5

*I*t was nearly midnight when Edward faced his prim house-keeper. Fortunately she was still dressed, the party having only recently broken up. He held the young woman in his arms, still limp from laudanum. He found it ironic that a figure so light could weigh so heavily on his mind. His future.

"This girl was injured in the village," he began. "Attacked by a suspected poacher."

"In the village?" Mrs. Hinkley repeated, wide-eyed.

He hesitated, remembering Tugwell's request, and did not mention the arrest.

"Yes. I don't know all the details, because her injury—there you see her bruised throat?—seems to have rendered her unable to speak."

"Merciful heavens." She opened the door to her small parlor and gestured for him to lay the girl upon the settee.

"Her attacker is in the lockup, Mrs. Hinkley. There is no call for alarm."

"Shall I send Ross for Dr. Sutton?"

"Sutton has already seen her. In the Swan. In fact, we bore her here in his cart."

He could see her brain working, trying to add up his disjointed sentences and make them equal a reasonable explanation for bringing the young woman to Brightwell Court.

"And you thought I . . . could . . . ?"

"I want to see her recover. I feel some responsibility, as she was injured in our village. Being the new magistrate and all."

Again he could see the wheels of her mind turning. Could guess her thoughts. Would not the vicarage be better suited? Or Dr. Sutton's offices. Or even the almshouse? But the woman had not risen to her position by questioning her masters.

"Shall I see to her here in my parlor, my lord? The nurserymaid recovered here after she wricked her ankle."

"Excellent. Dr. Sutton will call tomorrow, but he does not believe her injury severe. In the meantime, I would rather not inform Lord or Lady Brightwell. I do not wish anything to spoil their departure in the morning."

"I see, my lord. As you wish."

❧

After a fitful sleep, Edward bid a stilted farewell to his father, and warmly embraced his mother as they prepared to depart. Once the coach disappeared up the lane, Edward went directly to the housekeeper's parlor. He was determined to discover how much the girl had heard and if she had understood its import. He'd had insufficient time to grasp the potential consequences himself. He had barely slept for thinking of what might happen were she to sell such news to the highest bidder, or even to let it slip in company, where it would spread like barley fire through the county, through the London ballrooms and clubs, to the Harringtons, and the Bradley relatives. He would lose all—his reputation, inheritance, title, his very home.

Could one slip of a girl ruin his life as he knew it?

Mrs. Hinkley met him at the door with a curt nod and let him in, closing the door discreetly behind him. The young woman half reclined on the settee, some foul-smelling poultice wrapped around her neck. Whether the work of Dr. Sutton or Mrs. Hinkley he did not know or care. She wore the same light blue gown, neither that of a hussy nor a lady. A scratch marred one cheek. Her complexion was still pale, but not ashen as it had been the previous night. Her dark hair was neatly coiled at the back of her head. Her intense blue eyes regarded him levelly from between black lashes. She clasped and unclasped her hands, then stretched one out, indicating he should sit as though receiving guests in her very own drawing room.

He remained standing. "If you will excuse us, Mrs. Hinkley?"

The matronly housekeeper hesitated, pressing her thin lips into a disapproving line, but let herself from the room.

When she had gone, he said briskly, "Now that you are somewhat recovered, I must put several questions to you."

She hesitated slightly, then nodded her acquiescence.

"Have you regained the power of speech?"

Again she hesitated, then parted her small lips. A broken rasp came from her throat, and her eyes immediately filled with tears. She gingerly touched her wrapped neck and shook her head, her expression apologetic.

How convenient, he thought, far less than charitably. "Very well, then I shall pose questions and you will nod or shake your head as appropriate."

She nodded.

He took a deep breath. "Was it your intention to spy on us last night?"

She shook her head no.

Well, what would she say? "You overheard my father and I speaking to one another on the veranda?"

Shame flushed her pale cheeks, and she looked down at her clasped hands before nodding.

His heart hammered. "You heard . . . everything?"

Not meeting his eyes, she nodded once more.

Dread twisted his stomach. *Burn it, I am ruined.* "Were you here on anyone's behest?" He began pacing before her. "Did someone send you?"

The girl shook her head.

"Sebastian's solicitor? Admiral Harrington?" He leaned near and stared into her eyes, daring her to lie. Seeing her shrink from him, he pulled back quickly, trying to rein in his emotions. Never before had he dealt so harshly with anyone.

"Where do you . . . ? That is, do you live nearby or . . . ?" He ran agitated fingers through his hair. "Dash it, this is maddening."

She imitated the act of scribbling.

"You can write?"

She nodded and had the cheek to roll her eyes at his skepticism.

He helped himself to the small desk in the housekeeper's parlor and produced a piece of paper, quill, and pot of ink. He placed them on the low table before the settee and waited while she opened the ink and took up the quill. She looked up at him, expectant as a schoolgirl awaiting her tutor's instructions.

He asked, "What is your name?"

She dipped the quill but hesitated. She bit her lip, then wrote, *Miss Olivia Keene.*

Suspicion filled him. "Is that your real name?"

Avoiding his eyes, she merely nodded.

"And where do you come from, Miss Olivia Keene?"

Again, that slight hesitation. *Near Cheltenham.*

She was being purposely vague. But why? He was familiar with Cheltenham; a school chum had recently relocated to the area, but he had no enemies there. Did it signify?

"How old are you?" he asked.

She wrote, *24.*

His age. That surprised him. She looked younger.

"What brought you to our borough?"

I came seeking a post.

"So our good vicar said. Godly man. Always believes the best in people. Sometimes to his cost. Why did you come to Brightwell Court?"

Again that maddening hesitation as she apparently calculated her answer to best effect. She wrote, *Miss Ludlow mentioned the party. I only meant to glimpse the place.*

"And to eavesdrop?"

She shook her head. *That was a mistake. I regret it.*

"As well you might," he muttered. "Did you know of Brightwell before the helpful Miss Ludlow mentioned it?"

She nodded—sheepishly, he thought.

"Where had you heard of it?"

She reached for a folded handkerchief on the settee beside her and, from it, withdrew a yellowed newspaper clipping. She handed it to him.

Skeptically, he read the old type, taking several seconds to recognize the announcement for what it was. *What the devil?* "Where did you get this?"

She wrote, *I found it in Mamma's purse.*

"Did you indeed? How extraordinary. And why would *Mamma* have this in her purse?"

I don't know.

"Do not lie to me."

She shook her head, shrugged once more.

"And you wish me to believe you came here with no other

motives? When you had the names Brightwell and Bradley in your possession?"

No other motives, my lord.

It was his turn to hesitate. He was surprised she addressed him thus. He was also surprised she wrote with such a fine hand, but of course did not verbalize the compliment.

Even if she were innocent of all but eavesdropping, what was he to do with her? Let her go? Extract a promise of silence from her? Bribe her?

She bent over the paper and wrote again. As she did, twin coils of hair came loose and fell forward. When she looked up once more, with dark curls framing her pale face, he recognized her with a start as the girl from the hunt. He had been ready to believe her—that she had stumbled upon his estate with no ulterior motives. But this . . . To have her interrupt the hunt and then appear outside his very door? The names Brightwell and Bradley on her person? It was too much of a coincidence. He looked from her face to the final words she had written. Words that pricked his pride.

You have nothing to fear from me.

"I, fear you? You will find, Miss Keene, that *you* had better fear me. As acting magistrate, I hold the power to see you imprisoned, or worse. Do I make myself clear?"

She nodded, but did not look as frightened as he might have wished.

When the housekeeper knocked and tentatively stepped back into her own parlor, Edward straightened and announced, "Mrs. Hinkley, good. It seems Miss Keene would like nothing more than a *trial* post at Brightwell Court. Three months. Is that not so, Miss Keene?"

Again, that irksome hesitation. Did the chit think he was giving her any choice? He glared at her as a myriad of thoughts passed wordlessly behind those bright blue eyes. What he would give for a transcript.

Finally, she nodded. Almost meekly, he thought.

"What is she fit for?" the housekeeper asked, clearly dubious about the notion.

"Emptying chamber pots?" Edward offered helpfully. "Or scrubbing laundry, perhaps?" He liked the idea of assigning Miss Keene to the laundry. She would spend her time in the washhouse and have little contact with the other servants, and none at all with the family.

Miss Keene narrowed her eyes at him.

"Look at them hands, my lord. She has never seen the inside of a laundry, and that's a fact."

"Well, it is never too late to learn a new skill, is it?"

Mrs. Hinkley tapped her chin in thought. "With Miss Dowdle gone and Becky still hobbling about on that ankle, the nursery is shorthanded. We could use an under nurse. One of the housemaids has been lending a hand, but none too happily."

"And what does an under nurse do, Mrs. Hinkley?" Though he addressed the housekeeper, his eyes held Miss Keene's.

"Why, she bathes and dresses the children. Carries up the breakfast and dinner trays, and attends the older children. Nurse Peale, of course, is chiefly engaged with the infant."

The idea of consigning Miss Keene to the nursery also appealed to him. High on the top floor, eating and sleeping separately from all the servants save a nurserymaid and old Nurse Peale, who had been his own nurse and was loyal to him to the last. And what of Judith? She went more rarely to the nursery than he privately thought she ought, but when she did, she was certainly not one to encourage the confidences of a servant.

Could he trust Miss Keene with the children? He believed so. He would have a word with Nurse Peale and ask her to keep a sharp eye on the new girl.

And when she did happen upon another servant or family member in the course of her duties, she was not likely to ask for a paper and quill, was she? Yes, the nursery seemed an excellent plan.

"Under nurse, it is, Mrs. Hinkley." He turned to the girl. "You shall not leave the premises until I give you leave to do so. Nor post any letters without my consent. I trust I make myself clear?"

She opened her mouth as if to reply—or protest—but closed it again and nodded.

So until her voice returned, he should be safe enough. At least until he could figure out if he could trust this secretive, silent newcomer.

A Young English Person wishes to obtain a SITUATION as NURSE, Lady's-maid, or Teacher in a school.
No objection to travel.

—ADVERTISEMENT IN THE *TIMES*, 1853

Chapter 6

*W*hen Lord Bradley had skewered her with his shrewd, icy-blue glare and pronounced that she would like a trial post at Brightwell Court—*"Is that not so, Miss Keene?"*—Olivia had known it was a command, not a question. Still, she had hesitated.

A part of her panicked at the thought of staying there. She had not gotten far enough away from Withington. Nor had she made it to St. Aldwyns as planned; her mother would not find her at Brightwell Court. But in truth, she needed a post and bore only the faintest hope of finding one at an unfamiliar girls' school. With only a few coins left in her purse, and no character reference, she could ill afford to refuse a situation and a place to live. And really, had he given her any choice?

As soon as she was able, she would send word to the school,

asking the proprietress to let her mother know where she was. What had she said? *"I will come to you when I can. When it is safe."*

But would Olivia be any safer here? For she had overheard a good deal of the conversation between Lord Bradley and his father and could piece together the rest. Could not such knowledge put her in more danger than ever?

Mrs. Hinkley had allowed Olivia a few more hours' rest, then removed the poultice. She gave Olivia a long white apron to wear over her gown—the sole dress in her possession. Only the footman and the coachman had livery, she explained. The female servants wore modest frocks and plain aprons.

Without ceremony, the housekeeper lifted Olivia's frayed hem, took one look at the thin, stained slippers, and said, "It'll have to be new half boots for you when you get your first wages. Eight guineas per annum, paid quarterly."

Eight guineas? A trifling sum indeed.

"You'll have your own small room off the nursery, once Doris moves her things out."

Olivia nodded, taking it all in. The fact that the young lord had children surprised her. *Was he the Lord Bradley mentioned in the marriage announcement Mother saved?*

"Come along. I shall help you get your bearings and introduce you to Miss Peale."

Olivia followed Mrs. Hinkley out of her parlor, where the woman paused. "To the left are the butler's pantry and serving room, which supply the dining and breakfast rooms there ahead of us. Below us are the menservants' quarters, kitchen, and servants' hall. You shall see those another time."

Mrs. Hinkley turned right, striding into the lofty central entry hall with its double front door, tall windows, and white-and-black marble floor. "On the other side of this hall are the library, billiards room, and drawing room. You'll not need to see those."

Olivia followed the housekeeper up the hall's stone, canti-levered staircase, gripping the carved banister to steady herself.

When they reached the first floor up, Mrs. Hinkley did not pause. "The family bedchambers and Lord Bradley's study are on this floor."

Olivia was huffing by the time she reached the top floor, but Mrs. Hinkley marched up the stairs and along the corridor with a soldier's unaffected vigor. "And up here are the nursery, children's sleeping chamber, and schoolroom. The nurse and housemaids have rooms up here as well." She knocked on a pair of double doors and pushed both open without awaiting a reply from within. She gestured Olivia in beside her.

In the bright, cheery nursery, Olivia glimpsed a thin adolescent girl blackening the fireplace grate, and an elderly woman rocking a child. The woman rose gingerly at their entrance, the rocking chair still swaying behind her. The chubby baby in her arms sat upright of his own strength but was less than a year old. He wore a long white gown and had a halo of white-blond wisps about his head. The child did resemble his papa.

"Miss Peale. This is Olivia Keene, your new under nurse. She has not been in service before, so you will need to instruct her in her duties."

The old nurse frowned. "Never been in service? At her age? What has she been about all this time?"

The housekeeper pursed her lips. "I am afraid I do not know. My Lord Bradley offered her the post."

The grey eyebrows rose. "Did he indeed? Who recommended her?"

"No one that I am aware of. She presented no letter of character."

Both women looked at her as though she were a freak of nature. Even the adolescent maid paused in her work to stare.

Olivia attempted an apologetic smile.

Nurse Peale narrowed her eyes. "And what have you to say for yourself, my girl?"

Mrs. Hinkley cleared her throat. "Nor has she the ability to speak, I am afraid."

The old woman stared, incredulous. "What? A mute?"

"Only temporarily, or so Dr. Sutton says. She suffered an injury but should recover her voice in time."

"And *Master Edward* offered her a post?"

"Yes, as I believe I said. So. I will leave the two of you to become acquainted. Olivia does read and write, should you want to communicate that way."

The woman's eyes clouded briefly, then sparked. "I shall make myself understood, Mrs. Hinkley. Never fear. But the care of Master Andrew and Miss Audrey . . . without sayin' a word? What good she'll be, I shudder to think. It's children what is to be seen and not heard, not their nurses."

Mrs. Hinkley smiled stiffly. "Yes, well. I trust the two of you will come to a suitable arrangement."

Once Mrs. Hinkley left them, the old woman resumed rocking herself and the child, studying Olivia shrewdly. "I was Master Edward's own nurse. Did he tell you?"

Olivia shook her head, trying not to stare at the wiry, inch-long grey hairs poking this way and that from the vague arc of Miss Peale's eyebrows.

"Such a fine lad he was. And always so kind to me. It was me who looked after him and tended to all his wants. It was me he poured out his troubles to."

Uncertain how to respond, Olivia was relieved not to be expected to reply.

Nurse Peale tipped her head to the side, resting her silver hair against the baby's blond curls. "This is Master Alexander. Ten months old, he is. So like Master Edward at that age. Isn't it a wonder?"

Though she saw nothing to wonder at, Olivia smiled politely.

Nurse Peale lifted a hand toward the young maid. "And that's Becky, the nurserymaid what does the cleanin' and such."

Becky smiled across the room at her, still scrubbing away, and Olivia nodded in return. Olivia thought a girl so young should be in a schoolroom, not in service, but knew many girls were put out to work even younger.

With a bang and a shout, two brown-haired children burst into the room wearing coats, hats, and gloves. Their attire, as well as their red cheeks, proclaimed them just returned from out of doors. A young woman puffed in after them. She wore a grey cape over a plain green frock and an apron identical to Olivia's. A simple muslin cap and ginger hair framed a wide, freckled face, punctuated by bright green eyes and a squat nose.

Upon seeing Olivia, she halted and clapped her hands. "The new under nurse?"

When Olivia nodded, the maid rushed forward and took one of Olivia's hands in both of her own, squeezing it warmly. "Oh! I cannot tell you how relieved I am you've come! Now *you* may have charge of these wild animals and I shall enjoy the peace of cleaning perfectly quiet rooms."

"We are *not* wild animals, Dory," the girl said. "You oughtn't to say so."

"Are you not wild? I'll say you are. Lions and tigers the both of you."

At this, the little boy raised his "claws" in the air and let out a great roar. Olivia flinched.

"What did I tell you? Well, they're yours now, love. You've a friend in me forever. That scamp is Master Andrew and this is Miss Audrey."

The little boy was six or seven years of age and the girl eleven or twelve. Surely too old to be Lord Bradley's children. Unless he was older than he appeared. And besides, they looked nothing like him. They must favour his wife.

"And I'm Doris." The ginger-haired maid looked at Olivia expectantly. "What's your name, then?"

"This is . . . uhh, Olivia," Nurse Peale said. "Rather a fine name for an under nurse. We shall call her Livie."

Olivia parted her lips to object, but just as quickly pressed them closed. Even if she could speak, she had little grounds to insist on *Miss Keene.*

Doris was staring at her, her head tilted to one side. "You always this quiet?"

"She cannot speak at present," Nurse Peale explained. "She suffered an injury to her neck—so Mrs. Hinkley tells me."

Dory's eyes widened. "Are you the girl what got strangled in the lockup? I heard tell of it last night. A poacher, was it?"

Had the tale gotten round already? Lord Bradley would not be pleased. Nor was Olivia eager to spread word of her imprisonment.

"Or did it happen in the Swan?" Doris asked. "That's what Johnny said, but I heard the lockup."

Olivia lifted a faint shrug, and Doris's eyes narrowed.

She turned to the nurse. "Is she daft as well as dumb?"

"I shouldn't think so. Master Edward himself engaged her—with good reason, I don't doubt. Now, what are you standing there for? Do I not see muddy boots on the young ones' feet and coats what need airing out?"

In the tiny chamber that would be hers, Olivia placed her list of duties, which Nurse Peale had told Doris to write down for her, on top of the dressing chest. Olivia had been impressed the maid could read and write—until she had looked at the list. The scrawled hand—the spelling!

Opening the top drawer, she placed her reticule and her gloves inside. Then she hung her cape and new bonnet on a hook behind the door. She had ridiculously little to put away, to make the room her own.

The chamber was narrow, and the ceiling, which was high above the single bed, pitched steeply down to the outside wall, effectively reducing the walking space to half for anyone above three feet tall. The room was paneled in white, the cast-iron bed covered in white tufted cotton. One small dormer window offered the faint glow of afternoon sunlight. From it, she looked down onto a fallow field and the distant wood beyond. Which direction? From the angle of the light, she guessed her room faced northwest. The direction from which she'd come. The direction of home, though home no longer.

What was happening there now? Had her father regained consciousness? Had Muriel Atkins treated his injury and her mother's as well? Or had he . . . died? Was the constable even now mounting a search for her?

Why, oh why, had she given her real name? The shock and weariness had left her mind sluggish. She had not thought quickly enough. And once she had told the vicar her name, she dared not give another to anyone else. Could she hope to remain hidden here—a menial servant on the top floor of this great manor?

Pushing self-centered thoughts away, she contemplated once more what she had overheard and what it might mean for Lord Bradley and his wife and children. Was his wife very disappointed, assuming he had told her? And what of poor Andrew, the eldest son?

The sound of hooves and a shout brought Olivia to her small window once more. Through its wavy glass, she looked down upon the long lane below. A liveried footman hopped down and opened the carriage door, and Olivia watched as a woman appeared in the open frame, a small hat angled upon a head of blond curls. A dark cape flowed around her feet as she stepped gracefully down. The children's mother, Olivia guessed. *His* wife.

As if on cue, Lord Bradley entered the scene and greeted the woman a short distance from the carriage. The woman leaned close to his ear, perhaps to confide something or kiss his cheek; Olivia could not tell from this distance. Arm in arm, the two walked majestically toward the manor and out of view.

Olivia had not heard the nurse refer to a Mrs. or Lady Bradley. Only to Lady Brightwell—"gone to Italy, poor soul." But if this was the children's mother, Olivia knew she would meet her soon enough.

That very lady swept into the nursery a quarter of an hour later. She now wore a lace cap over the golden blond curls curtaining her brow. Her pale blue eyes were round and her cheeks rosy, giving her the look of an angelic little girl. That comparison ceased, however, when one's gaze lowered from her face to the generous curves evident beneath her close-fitting gown of dove grey.

Olivia felt far too shabby to stand in the same room with her.

The woman's large eyes fastened on the infant in Nurse Peale's arms. "There he is. How is my little man today?"

"He is well, madam," Nurse Peale said.

Audrey approached the woman almost shyly. "Alexander smiled at me," she said. "Look, I shall make him smile again."

"Never mind, Audrey. He is smiling at his mamma now."

Andrew left his toy soldiers and tugged on the blond woman's skirts, smiling up at her.

"Oh, Andrew, do wipe your nose," she said.

Before Olivia could move, the little boy obediently swiped his sleeve beneath his dripping nose.

The boy's mother winced, and looked heavenward as if for patience.

Olivia rushed forward with a handkerchief, helping the little boy tidy his sleeve and smeared cheek.

Nurse Peale lifted a spotted hand in Olivia's direction. "This is our new under nurse, Livie Keene."

Olivia curtsied and smiled politely at the woman.

The woman regarded her closely, and if Olivia wasn't mistaken, approval lit in her eyes. "Welcome. I trust I may depend upon you to tend well to Audrey's and Andrew's needs?"

Olivia nodded and curtsied once more.

The woman turned back to her youngest, hands extended. "Come, Alexander, come to mamma. Lord Bradley wishes to see how big you've grown."

Watching her, Olivia thought, *His wife is lovely indeed.* At closer inspection, she appeared to be in her late twenties, perhaps a few years older than Lord Bradley.

The woman took the child in her arms and strode from the room, babbling and cooing to her youngest as she went. Olivia closed the door after her, remembering Nurse Peale's admonition to keep the rattles and cries of the nursery well contained.

"That was Mrs. Howe," Nurse Peale said.

Mrs. Howe? Olivia tilted her head to the side in question.

"The earl's niece. A widow, I am afraid."

Ah. That explained the dull grey dress.

"Her husband died. . . . I forget exactly when, but more than a year ago, before Alexander was even born. Audrey and Andrew are her stepchildren, from his first marriage. That wife died in childbirth, I understand."

That explained why Audrey and Andrew looked nothing like either Lord Bradley or Mrs. Howe. Olivia nodded her understanding, readjusting her thoughts. Not Lord Bradley's wife, then, but his cousin. Living there out of necessity after the death of her husband. Or were there other reasons as well?

Olivia was relieved Lord Bradley was not married. This meant he had no wife and no future heir to disappoint. She found herself remembering what Nurse Peale had said about little Alexander looking like Lord Bradley and "wasn't it a wonder." Did it signify?

Doris stayed in the nursery the rest of that afternoon to explain Olivia's various duties, saying she was fortunate that Becky did most of the nasty work, the cleaning and the hauling of heavy bathwater. Still, how Olivia would miss her post at Miss Cresswell's.

Later, Doris brought up the dinner tray and they sat down

together like an odd family—Nurse Peale, the venerable grandmother at the head of the table. Alexander had already been fed
and sat on a quilt on the floor, shaking a well-chewed rattle.

After the meal of pea soup, cold beef, mashed potatoes, and
carrot pudding, Becky rose and began stacking the dishes.

"Let's give these wild animals a good clean, hmm?" Doris said.
"It's grotty, they are."

While Becky took the tray belowstairs and hauled up the water,
Doris and Olivia got the children ready for their baths. As Becky
filled the copper tub, Andrew ran across the room naked as God
made him and splashed water about with a great *whoop*. Again
Olivia flinched at the loud sound, so foreign in the sedate corridors
of Miss Cresswell's. Boys would take some getting used to.

Doris managed Andrew with a good-natured firmness—that
came from having a younger brother, she explained—and Olivia
followed her lead as they bathed the children and helped them into
their nightclothes.

From the corner of her eye, Olivia saw Doris yawn. Olivia
pointed to herself, and gave Doris a gentle push toward the door.
The maid squinted, somewhat bleary-eyed and not comprehending.
Olivia pointed to Doris and then tilted her cheek against clasped
hands, closing her eyes to mime sleep.

"Really? You'll put them to bed on your own?"

Olivia nodded.

"Thank you, love. I knew you were an angel the moment I laid
eyes on you. Bless me, I am near off my feet. Be good for Livie,
you lions and tigers. No eating your new under nurse on her first
night, all right?"

Audrey nodded. Andrew roared.

After Doris left, Olivia pulled a chair before the fire, and
there combed Audrey's damp brown hair until it hung straight
and smooth. Andrew had settled down and now sat in his bed,
looking through a picture book Olivia had found in the nursery.

She wished she might read to them, as her mother had always read to her. A psalm, poem, or short tale, though nothing frightening before bedtime. There were no books on the stand between the two beds, which Olivia found odd. Did not Nurse Peale or Mrs. Howe read to the children?

Looking at Audrey and Andrew, Olivia put a finger to her lips, then lifted that same finger in the sign for "wait."

Taking a candle lamp with her, Olivia let herself from the sleeping chamber and back into the nursery. Holding the lamp high and looking about the room, it seemed Andrew's picture book was the only book to be found. She saw a child's table and chairs, a rocking horse in the corner, a chest of toys, and a line of pretty dolls sitting on the window seat, but no books.

She looked at the closed door at the other end of the nursery, which Nurse Peale had pointed to with a dismissive wave as "the schoolroom."

The schoolroom . . . Olivia had always adored its confines and endless horizons. The melodious purr of the teacher's voice rising up and down her lessons like a musical score. And the sight of book spines—black, blue, green—lined up side by side like London townhouses. Each leather rectangle a gift waiting to be opened and explored and savored.

Cautiously, Olivia tried the knob and opened the door with a creak. Though Nurse Peale had indicated the former governess had not been gone long, already the room held the cloying mustiness of disuse. But over this arose the fragrances Olivia loved. Chalk dust, old leather books, wilted wild flowers, paint and paste. Olivia closed her eyes and breathed deeply, transported back to her recent idyllic days as Miss Cresswell's assistant.

Raising the candle lamp, she swept the room with its light— the governess's desk, the chairs around a table set with slates, the world globe in one corner, the bookshelf in the opposite. She would have loved to take it all in, study the books and the prints on the walls, but the children were waiting. She lowered herself before the bookshelf and skimmed the spines. Aesop, Mangnall, Hannah More, Fordyce's *Sermons to Young Women*, Sarah Trimmer's *Fabulous Histories*, more commonly known as *The History of Robins*. And an elegant volume of the New Testament and Psalms.

She selected the latter two and bore them with her from the schoolroom, carefully closing the door behind her.

Back in the sleeping chamber, she listened to Audrey's and Andrew's prayers, surprised their stepmother did not come up to do so. Then she sat on Audrey's bed beside the girl and waved Andrew over to join them. The children seemed surprised by this, but did not object. The young maid, Becky, already lay on her pallet on the floor. She was supposed to be the first to hear if one of the children wanted for anything. But from the look of her, the poor thing would be sound asleep before a single sentence was read.

Olivia opened the book to Psalm 46 and followed along with her finger as Audrey read aloud. She encouraged Andrew to follow along as well, though she doubted the boy could read many of the words.

Then she opened *The History of Robins* and encouraged Audrey to read aloud once more.

"... the Robins ate their meal with all possible expe ... expe-dition, for the hen was anxious to return to her little ones, and the cock to procure them a breakfast; and having given his young friends a serenade, he did not think it necessary to stay to sing anymore. ..."

By the time Olivia closed the book, she realized Audrey was resting her head against her shoulder and Andrew was curled beneath her other arm. A small bittersweet pang struck her soul. *Thank you for delivering me to such a place, Almighty God.*

Mrs. Goddard was the mistress of a . . .
real, honest, old-fashioned boarding school,
where a reasonable quantity of accomplishments
were sold at a reasonable price.

—JANE AUSTEN, *EMMA*

Chapter 7

The following morning, Nurse Peale sent Olivia down to the kitchen for the breakfast tray. Olivia hoped she would not get lost. She jogged lightly down the many pairs of stairs until she reached the basement. There, she passed two closed doors, the open door of a larder, and a white-paneled stillroom with shelves of china and jarred preserves. The clank of pans and smells of savory sausage and warm bread led her to the kitchen, its small high windows proudly declaring it only mostly underground. A massive stove fitted with spit and pot hooks filled most of one wall, while the others held floor-to-ceiling cupboards and shelves of tins and utensils. A long worktable dominated the center of the room. From its head, a wide, well-padded woman in her fifties directed two thin young kitchen maids in a firm but kindly voice.

Mrs. Hinkley swept in from a second door, her face set in stern lines, her bearing one of clear authority. A tall footman followed in her wake.

"More coffee is needed abovestairs, Mrs. Moore. And why, may I ask, is breakfast not yet laid in the servants' hall?"

"Never fear, Mrs. Hinkley," the plump woman assured. "We are but one thin minute behind schedule. Here you are, Osborn." She handed the footman a silver coffee urn. "Take this upstairs. And, Edith, take this tray into the servants' hall before Mr. Hodges has an apoplexy."

Seeing Olivia hovering at the threshold, Mrs. Hinkley's stern countenance darkened further.

"Mrs. Moore," she said. "This is Olivia Keene, the new under nurse."

Mrs. Moore paused in her frantic preparations to give Olivia a friendly smile. "Aren't you a lovely one. Welcome, my dear. The nursery tray is right there all ready for you. Do let me know if you want something more than bread and milk. That is all the children want, but if you'd like porridge or eggs, you need only ask."

Olivia warmed to Mrs. Moore instantly, but Mrs. Hinkley soon dashed her spirits.

"This is not a hotel, Mrs. Moore," the housekeeper said. "She shall eat what you have provided and be grateful. Come, girl, let us introduce you to the others and have done." She lifted her hand and waited none too patiently as Olivia came forward.

As she stepped into the long narrow servants' hall ahead of Mrs. Hinkley, Olivia's nerves jingled and her ears heated, self-conscious at so many pairs of eyes turning to regard her.

Mrs. Hinkley stood at her place at the foot of the table. "If I may have your attention, please. This is Olivia Keene, the new under nurse."

"Nurse Peale said we are to call her Livie," Doris interjected.

Frowning at being interrupted, Mrs. Hinkley continued, "She

is here on trial—new in service as of yesterday. Due to an injury she received before coming to us, she is unable to speak at present."

Doris leaned close to another maid and whispered loudly, "Did I not tell you?"

A young auburn-haired man grinned across the table. "Some of us might wish you were so afflicted, Dory."

Mrs. Hinkley silenced the two with an icy glare. "You are not to speak to her unless necessary to your duties. If she has a question, she will come to me with it."

"How will she ask, if she cannot speak?" the stodgy butler asked from the head of the table.

"She can read and write, Mr. Hodges, or so I understand." The housekeeper's skepticism was apparent, and Olivia felt her ears burn anew.

Mrs. Hinkley gestured with a snap of her wrist toward each in turn, rattling off a quick inventory of the gathered servants. On Mrs. Hinkley's left was a pretty lady's maid, Miss Dubois. Mrs. Moore, the rotund cook, set a platter of sausages on the table, then took her seat to the right of Mrs. Hinkley. Next to her were Doris and Martha, the two housemaids, and kitchen maids Edith and Sukey. At the other end of the table, Mr. Hodges nodded curtly to her. The male servants sat clustered at his end of the table—the coachman and hall boy, whose names she did not catch; Osborn, the snooty footman in livery, just returning from abovestairs; and the auburn-haired groom, who smiled shyly at her.

She doubted she would remember all the names, but as Nurse Peale had warned her, she "need not get chummy with the staff." Except for holidays, or when the children ate with the family, Olivia would take her meals in the nursery with only Nurse Peale, the nurserymaid, Becky, and the children.

Olivia attempted to direct a smile toward the table in general, but her face felt stiff and she was fairly certain her lips did not manage more than a quiver. Mrs. Hinkley sat and everyone bowed their heads while Mr. Hodges began the prayer. Olivia had been dismissed.

❧

"I met the new under nurse last evening," his cousin Judith announced as she stepped into the library. "Have you seen her?"

Edward was instantly wary. "Yes." He slid the life-changing note beneath the cigar box on his father's desk.

"Most unusual, do you not think? That Mrs. Hinkley should engage such a girl, I mean." Judith bit her full lower lip. "Something isn't right there."

He stilled, pulse accelerating. He wondered what Judith had heard or guessed, but asked only, "What are you implying?"

"Only that there must be more going on than meets the eye." She seemed delighted at the prospect.

"I don't follow." He felt himself frowning. "Do you mean, because she cannot speak?"

"Of course. What did you think I meant?"

He did not respond to that. "Are you concerned about leaving the children in her care?"

"Not at all." She gazed above him, musing. "But it is interesting, is it not? Never been in service before. Doesn't speak a word." She returned her gaze to him. "Who wrote her character, do you know?"

"I do not." He hesitated. "I am surprised at you, Judith. You have never taken an interest in the servants before."

"You have never engaged a mute before, have you?" Her round blue eyes suddenly lit up. "Perhaps she is not mute at all but only pretends to be."

This snagged his interest, though he tried not to show it.

"What if she only pretends to be mute or dumb, or whatever the word is, so she need not reveal her secrets? She might be the daughter of some powerful lord who is bent on forcing her into an arranged marriage."

"Such marriages are no longer legal, Judith. As you well know."

"La! Fathers still wield a great deal of pressure—that I do know."

"All right. If she is nobility, why have we never seen her in London?"

Judith pursed her lips. "Locked in the tower, perhaps? Or . . . I know! She doesn't speak English!"

He leaned back in his chair. "I have seen her write perfectly good English, and she understands everything said to her."

Judith ran her finger along the table globe on his father's desk. "Then perhaps she speaks with an accent, and is afraid that if she spoke she would give herself away. She is a" —Judith twirled her slender hand with dramatic flair— "Prussian princess, escaping a cruel husband."

His interest lagged. "What nonsense, Judith. You read too many novels. I have always said so."

She sighed. "Ah, well. You are no doubt right." She poked through the dish of candies on the desk and changed the subject. "Did your parents depart without incident?"

"Yes, right on schedule."

"I was so sorry to miss their party. I intended to return in time but was delayed at Mamma's." Judith helped herself to a ginger drop. "Ah, Italy . . . Dominick and I took our wedding trip there, you know."

"Did you? Yes, I believe I do remember that."

"You were at Oxford at the time. Left us right after the wedding breakfast."

Dominick Howe had died only two years later, Edward recalled, from injuries received during the Peninsula War.

Judith sighed once more. "How I should love to visit Italy again. I do envy your parents."

"Don't. This trip is more about convalescence than pleasure. Though Father hopes that, should the climate improve Mother's health, they might take in some of the sights."

"It is their first time in Italy?"

"Yes."

"Did they not take a wedding trip?"

He inhaled, pursing his lips. "I do not know. A bit before my time."

She raised one perfect blond brow. "You have never asked?"

"No."

She studied him through narrowed eyes. "You certainly haven't much curiosity, cousin."

"Whereas, you, dear cousin, have enough for the both of us." He rose and the two left the library together.

"Would you be a dear and bring Alexander down to me?" she asked, pausing before the drawing room door. "I cannot face all those stairs at present."

"Of course. I thought to see how the children were getting on at all events. Shall I bring all three? Perhaps I might give the older two a riding lesson, if you do not mind."

"If you like."

He bowed and stepped into the hall.

She called after him, "And do observe the new under nurse while you are there."

He turned back, brows raised. "And what shall I look for? A royal brooch she has forgotten to hide away? An indentation on her ring finger?"

She gave him a sidelong glance. "Mock me if you will, Edward. But in time, I shall discover her secret."

❧

Olivia had just finished plaiting and securing a ribbon in Audrey's hair when the door to the nursery creaked open. Young

Becky was out dumping the children's bathwater and Nurse Peale was still dressing little Alexander.

"Cousin Edward!" Andrew tossed his ball aside and ran across the room. Lord Bradley dropped to one knee as the boy launched himself into his arms.

He chuckled. "Good morning, Andrew. I take it you slept well."

"I dreamt I was a kite!"

Lord Bradley smiled good-naturedly. "You certainly fly about like one."

Audrey walked toward him as he rose but stopped several feet away, eyes both shy and admiring at once, tugging at the end of her plait and biting her chapped lip.

Lord Bradley smiled at Audrey, bestowing the attention she so obviously sought. "Good morning, Miss Audrey. Don't you look lovely today. I like your hair."

"Our new nurse did it."

He hesitated. "Did she indeed."

His eyes roved the room and met Olivia's where she stood in the doorway to the sleeping chamber. She dipped a curtsy. His eyes lingered on her a moment longer before returning to Audrey.

"Well, I've only come to see how you all were getting on." He laid a hand on each child's head.

"We are ever so happy, now Miss Dowdle has gone," Andrew said. "No schoolroom for us! No lessons for us!"

Olivia bit her lip.

"But Miss Livie did have us read our prayers before breakfast," Audrey said. "And one of *Aesop's Fables*."

"Oh, which?"

" 'The Wolf in Sheep's Clothing.' "

One fair brow rose. "What an interesting choice. Do you recall its moral?"

"Frauds and liars are always discovered eventually," Audrey answered. "And pay accordingly for their deeds."

"Something I do hope each of you will remember." Again his gaze flickered to Olivia, and she felt herself flush self-consciously.

Andrew grinned. "Livie made Audrey start over when she tried to skip a whole line. Audrey thought she mightn't know, but she did!"

Audrey ducked her head.

"Well, do not become accustomed to life without lessons," Lord Bradley said. "For your mamma will no doubt engage another governess soon."

Andrew groaned.

"Now." Lord Bradley clapped his hands. "Who wants to ride today?"

Both children chimed in with great enthusiasm.

"Very well." He looked up, his smile disappearing, his eyes focusing somewhere over Olivia's head. "Please dress them in their habits and bring them to the stables at ten."

Olivia nodded, but inwardly, she sighed. As Lord Bradley took little Alexander down to his mamma, Olivia began the process of undoing all the bows and fasteners she had just done up.

❦

At ten minutes before the appointed hour, Olivia ushered her young charges down the stairs and out the rear garden door. Or rather, her young charges ushered her. Audrey took Olivia's hand, as though directing a blind person instead of a mute. Meanwhile, Andrew bounded across the damp lawn, his little legs full of energy. He turned around, running backward to gauge their progress. She would have liked to urge him to be careful but, of course, could not.

He tripped over a tree root and would have toppled to the ground had not the auburn-haired man she'd seen at breakfast leapt forward and caught him. Olivia pressed a hand to her chest in relief and smiled at the groom.

His smile widened in return. He was nice looking—not too tall, but broad-shouldered, with fair freckled skin and brown eyes. The groom she had seen at the hunt, she now recalled.

"I'm Johnny Ross," he said. "And you're the girl who can't speak. Miss Livie, was it?"

She nodded.

"You can hear, though?"

She nodded again, trying not to grin. Of course she could hear—did he think she could read minds?

"Lots of fellows might like a girl who can't talk." He added hastily, "Not me, I mean, not that I mind if a girl can't, but I don't mind if she can do either." Flustered, his face reddened to match his freckles.

She bit her lip but could not hold back the smile this time. She dipped her head, then stepped around him to catch up with Audrey and Andrew. They had continued on to greet Lord Bradley, who stood in the stable yard, awaiting their arrival. It would not do for him to see her chatting, or rather not chatting, with the groom.

"I shall hope to see you later, miss," Ross called after her.

As she approached, Lord Bradley consulted his pocket watch. "Right on time. Excellent. I shall return them to the nursery when we are finished."

Olivia would have liked to stay and watch the children ride but understood a clear dismissal when she heard one.

With time on her hands, Olivia went to the kitchen, hoping for one of Mrs. Moore's smiles and an almond biscuit. She found the cook hunched over her worktable.

"Oh, fiddle," the woman murmured, clearly distressed. She squinted at the recipe in her fleshy hand, and Olivia wondered if the woman needed spectacles.

Mrs. Moore glanced up and met Olivia's quizzical look. "Hello, love. Don't mind me." She nodded toward the biscuit tin. "Help yourself."

Olivia removed her cape, then selected a biscuit and seated herself on a stool.

Mrs. Moore waved the recipe in the air. "You see, Lady Brightwell sometimes 'borrowed' the Lintons' French man-cook for parties and such," she explained, clearly offended by the practice. "All the best houses prefer a man-cook—a Frenchman most of all," she huffed. "Now Miss Judith wants me to make his *coq au vin* again, but bless me if I can read his French scrawl."

Olivia set down her biscuit and held out her hand.

The older woman hesitated, then handed over the grease-spotted paper. Olivia scanned the lines and nodded, gesturing for a quill. The cook quickly procured one, along with ink from her small escritoire and handed both to her.

Taking a moment to study the handwriting, Olivia dipped the quill and began rewriting the ingredients and mode in English.

"You've a lovely hand, Livie," Mrs. Moore said over Olivia's shoulder.

Olivia smiled up at her, then bent once more over the quill. Within a matter of minutes, she completed the translation and handed it to Mrs. Moore with an impish little bow.

Shaking her head and clucking her tongue, Mrs. Moore said, "Thank you, my dear. You've certainly earned that biscuit."

After her visit to the kitchen, Olivia went upstairs to the schoolroom, wanting to see it in the full light of day.

Stepping inside, she took a deep breath of chalk dust and memories.

Her mother had arranged their own schoolroom, in the attic of their cottage, and there had been her sole teacher until she had begun attending Miss Cresswell's School for Girls. What a row her parents had fought over it too. In the end, her mother had appealed to her husband's pride. Did he want his neighbors to think he could not afford to educate his own child? Did he not want the pleasure of hearing his daughter touted as the top of her class? She had even vowed to pay for the school herself, out of her own wages from the needlework she took in each week and the occasional pupil.

She had won.

How Olivia had loved those hours at Miss Cresswell's, where adults spoke firmly but gently, even in reproof. Where students smiled in wonder as Miss Cresswell read to them from her favorite poems or novels or histories, bringing each character to life in her rich, musical voice. Yes, there were difficult hours too, of struggling to translate French and Italian or declining Latin verbs. The girls had performed plays together and went on nature walks and quizzed each other on spelling and vocabulary. They beamed at Miss Cresswell's praise and strived all the harder under her admonitions.

How Olivia longed to be a teacher like that. To inspire children to learn, to introduce the world of literature, the beauty of music and the music of mathematics, the wonder of creation in geography and the sciences, and so much more.

She had gotten a taste of it as Miss Cresswell's assistant, but now those dreams seemed further from her grasp than ever.

Sighing, she closed the door and returned to her duties as Brightwell Court's new under nurse.

A POACHER generally exhibits characteristics of his profession; the suspicious leer of his hollow and sunken eyes, his pallid cheek, his wide, copious and well-pocketed jacket.

—THE GAMEKEEPER'S DIRECTORY

Chapter 8

That night, Olivia had just stripped down to her shift when a knock sounded on her door. Forgetting herself, she opened her mouth to call out, "Yes?" but only a croak emerged. Warily, she opened her door a crack and was relieved to see the friendly maid Doris standing there.

"Look slippy, love, and let me in," she whispered.

Olivia opened the door and then closed it softly behind the ginger-haired girl.

"Don't want me to get the push, do you? If Mrs. H. caught me in here talking to you . . . 'Course she can't do that, can she—you can't talk! I can barely imagine. Well, at least you don't rabbit on like Edith." She pressed a wadded bundle of cloth into Olivia's hand. "Here's an old nightdress a'mine. You can have what's left of it. Isn't much."

Thank you, Olivia mouthed, accepting it gratefully. She had not looked forward to sleeping in the same underclothes she'd worn for days. Now she could wash out her shift and let it dry overnight.

"Do you mind if I tell you something?" Doris asked. "I have to tell someone or I'll burst my stays. And you're a safe one, are you not?"

Olivia nodded, sure she would not get a word in even if she were able to speak.

Still fully dressed, Doris plopped down on the bed and crossed one leg under the other, patting the mattress. Olivia sat beside her.

"It's Martha, poor love. Got herself in a real muddle." Doris leaned closer. "She's going to have a babe, and her not married, nor even a sweetheart, far as I know. She won't say who the father is. Mrs. H. found out, and that means the master will hear soon enough. Do you know what happened the last time a maid got herself into trouble?"

Olivia shook her head.

"I heard the old master, the fourth earl—or was it the third?—put her out on her ear. Without a bean to her name. So, if you're a prayin' type, say one for Martha. If she's not past prayin' for."

Olivia's stomach dropped at the mere thought of finding herself in such a predicament. Poor Martha!

Doris cocked her head to the side and regarded her earnestly. "I been wonderin' about you, love. How you come to be here. No character. No valise. I suppose you run from home—is that it?"

Too stunned to deny it, Olivia nodded.

"Thought so from the first. A man, no doubt. A cruel husband, was it?"

Olivia shook her head.

"Your father, then. A mean crust? A scapegrace?"

Olivia nodded again, tears filling her eyes at this unexpected empathy. What a relief to talk with someone, even though she could not say a word.

Doris squeezed her hand. "Mine too. Ran out on my mum when my brother and sister was only babes. I've had to work since I was ten. Scoundrel." She cheered instantly. "There, there, ducky. That's the way of it. No use feelin' low. You and me get on well enough, don't we? A pigeon pair."

Olivia blinked back tears and grinned at the girl.

"Well, I had better dash to my room before Martha wonders where I've got to. Now not a word about what I told you. But you can't, can you?"

Doris threw her arms around Olivia in a stinging embrace before launching herself toward the door. Opening it a sliver, she paused to peer down the corridor, then smiled over her shoulder.

"Night, love." And she was gone.

Olivia did not pray as often as she should, but now, confronted with a young woman in worse straits than her own, she did just that.

❧

The following afternoon was fine, so Olivia took the children out of doors for exercise. She and Audrey walked about the lawns while Andrew kicked a ball this way and that. After much cajoling on his part, she and Audrey gave in to a halfhearted game of football.

Olivia had little experience with such sport, and within a matter of moments, the ball flew right past her. Olivia turned to gauge its destination. The ball rolled to the edge of the wood, coming to a halt beneath a rowan sapling still bearing several fronds of bright red leaves. Olivia ran after it and bent low. She reached her hand beneath the sapling, where the ball lay amid a nest of fallen red leaves. She picked up the ball and rose, but then stopped, staring in dismay. The orb bore a red smear as if stained by the leaves themselves. Or was it . . . blood?

She looked up, over the sapling, and sucked in a silent shriek. A tall old man stood there, stone-still among the swaying tree limbs. His gaunt face was a stiff mask—a beak of a nose bracketed by deep scowl lines leading to a thin mouth. Long ash grey hair hung to his shoulders.

It was him. The old man from Chedworth Wood. Had he followed her? Had he saved her from Borcher only to track her down and harm her himself?

She felt rooted to the spot, afraid to turn her back on him. Beneath wiry, untamed brows, his narrow, silvery eyes stared at her, then down at the ball in her hand. He lifted a brace of dead birds by way of explanation. A reedy relief threaded through her. Only the blood of birds . . .

"Here," he rasped, holding out his hand for the ball.

Olivia was confused. Had he come to poach game and now wanted a child's ball as well? Numbly, she extended her gloved hand. He snatched the ball with stained, gnarled fingers.

She watched, still rooted, as he wiped the ball on his coat sleeve, inspected it again, then handed it back.

She accepted it and looked down at the ball, now unmarred. Andrew ran over to see what the matter was, but when she looked up once more, the man had utterly disappeared, only the merest swaying of a tree branch to testify that he had ever been there at all.

❦

While the children played quietly in the nursery, Olivia paced. Should she tell Lord Bradley she had seen a poacher? Could she do so without admitting where she had seen him before? She had overheard something about the poacher problem in the area. As magistrate, he would want to know. Had the old man come to free

Borcher from the lockup? Just thinking of those two men wandering the estate made her perspire. She had to tell someone.

Olivia penned a brief note.

> When I was taking exercise with the children, I saw a strange old man in the wood, bearing a brace of dead birds. Possibly a poacher?
> I thought you would wish to know.

Leaving the children with Becky and Nurse Peale, Olivia carried the note to Lord Bradley's study, one floor down. She had seen him there from the landing when she had brought the children upstairs. Knocking on the open door, she stepped inside and handed him the note before he said a word. While he read it, she surveyed the room. It was like a small library, with fitted bookcases and a desk littered with ledgers, papers, and writing implements—quills and a wax jack for melting sealing wax. Statues of rearing horses stood atop the fireplace mantel.

He frowned as he read, but then his countenance cleared. "Man about sixty, very thin, long grey hair?"

She nodded.

"I daresay that was Croome."

Croome! Yes, that was his name, Olivia remembered. But how did Lord Bradley know? Was this Croome a wanted man? A known criminal?

Her stunned expression seemed to amuse him. "I do not blame you for being startled by old Croome. I grew up in fear and trembling of the man myself."

She stared at him, perplexed by his levity.

He sat forward, elbows on his desk. "Croome is our gamekeeper. Been with us for years."

Brightwell's gamekeeper?

He clearly misunderstood her uncomprehending look, for he explained, "As gamekeeper, he is responsible for the estate's preserved land. Stocking game, controlling vermin, predators, poachers . . . In fact, he is the man who caught you on the grounds and bundled you off to the constable."

Her mind was whirling so quickly she nearly missed the implication that she was of a kind with predators and poachers. *A gamekeeper in league with poachers?* It made no sense. Had he recognized her before he whipped that sack over her head? She had wondered why the "Brightwell man" had deposited her with the constable and departed before she had even laid eyes on her captor. Was he worried she would have recognized him? Reported him to the constable in turn?

Yet the man had saved her once and had done her no harm when he'd had the chance. She decided she would not reveal anything more about him for now. Lord Bradley had enough to worry about at present.

One further thought followed her back upstairs to the nursery. If she had overheard a conversation no one was meant to hear . . . had Croome heard it as well?

Chapter 9

*M*rs. Hinkley, looking rather put out, asked Olivia to come down to her parlor. It seemed the vicar wished to see her, and the housekeeper could not very well allow one of the servants to receive callers in the family's drawing room. But nor could she ask the good parson to descend belowstairs to the kitchen, where most servants received the occasional caller. Mrs. Hinkley sighed, and Olivia had the impression that the housekeeper thought the new girl more than a bit of bother.

"What does the parson want with you?" Mrs. Hinkley whispered.

Olivia shrugged.

"Said he met you when you first arrived in the village and

wanted to see how you were getting on." She said it as though such a thing must be suspect indeed.

For her part, Olivia was pleased to know the man remembered her. She certainly recalled his kindness in introducing her to Miss Ludlow. She regretted that she had not gone to the vicarage that night as she'd intended. She hoped he and his sister had not laid a place for her at their table nor stayed up late expecting her. How sorry she would be if they felt their hospitality had been rejected.

Mr. Tugwell rose when she entered. "Miss Keene. How well you look! Much more fit than when I saw you last, I daresay! Are you well?"

She nodded, mildly taken aback. Had she looked so poorly at the river that day?

"Excellent. You do remember me, I hope? Charles Tugwell, vicar of St. Mary's?"

Again she nodded.

"When you did not come to us that night, I—"

She put her hand out in entreaty, eyes wide.

"Never mind, my dear. I understand completely. I learnt what befell you and was grieved indeed to hear it. In fact I saw you that very night, though you were not aware of my presence. The laudanum, you know. How I prayed for you."

Now she understood. He had indeed seen her at her worst. She felt tears misting her eyes at his kindness and managed a wavering smile.

"There, there, my dear. All is well now, yes? I had hoped to see you in church, but as I did not, here I am to see how you fare." He tilted his head to one side. "Your throat is bruised, I see. Am I to understand from your silence that your voice has yet to return? Or have I not allowed you to get a word in edgewise?"

She shook her head, biting back a grin.

"Your ability to walk seems unhindered, and it is a fine day. Might I interest you in a stroll?"

She looked at him, mouth ajar.

"Forgive me. You have a position here now, I understand. I confess I forget how blessed I am to be able to walk about whenever I desire, barring a christening or marriage to perform. I even compose my sermons whilst walking, did you know? Of course not—how could you? Yes, I find a brisk stroll just the thing to spur the mind and lift the spirits." He paused for a breath, then grimaced. "Forgive me. I do prattle on, I know. I warn you that when you do attend services you shall find my sermons much the same. I cannot seem to say anything succinctly. As several parishioners have been kind enough to point out most helpfully, I am sure."

She smiled.

"By the way. Miss Ludlow told me of your intention to seek a place at the girls' school in St. Aldwyns. I had thought to inquire on your behalf the next time I traveled that way. But I suppose that is no longer necessary, as you have found employment here?"

Eagerly, she gestured for him to wait, then sat down at Mrs. Hinkley's desk. Promising herself to reimburse the housekeeper out of her first wages, Olivia picked up a sheet of paper and wrote as concise a letter as she could.

Dear Madam,

My mother, Mrs. Dorothea Keene, recommended I contact you about a possible situation.

I have taken a temporary post at Brightwell Court, but if you have a position available after February 4th, kindly write to me here.

Also, should my mother call upon you, kindly inform her (and her alone, if you please) of my whereabouts.

Most gratefully,
Miss Olivia Keene

She folded the letter, rose, and was about to hand it to Mr. Tugwell when the parlor door opened and Lord Bradley strode in, suspicion evident in the set lines of his face.

"Ah, Edward," Mr. Tugwell said. "I had just called in to see how Miss Keene fares."

"So I heard." But Lord Bradley's gaze rested not on the vicar, but on the folded paper in Olivia's hand.

Mr. Tugwell followed the direction of his stare. "Oh. I have offered to deliver a note for Miss Keene when next I call in St. Aldwyns. She was bound for the girls' school there when her, um, mishap occurred. How good of you to offer her a post here instead."

Lord Bradley made no answer to this but instead pinned Olivia with a challenging glare.

The vicar held out his hand, but the note felt suddenly like a six-stone sack in Olivia's hand. She remembered Lord Bradley saying that she was allowed to post no letters without his approval and knew she was breaking that rule in asking the vicar to deliver a note. But did he really think she would divulge his secret in a letter to a schoolmistress . . . and through a man of God in the bargain?

Seeing the steely warning in his gaze, she swallowed.

Evidently he did.

She stepped forward and handed the letter to Lord Bradley instead. He unfolded it and began reading.

The vicar frowned. "Really, Edward, is that quite necessary?"

He made no answer to that either.

After skimming the hastily written lines, he looked up at her from over the top of the paper. "Do you really expect to gain a post with such a vague letter? With no offer of a character reference, nor even your qualifictions?"

She hesitated, then nodded.

He pulled a grimace. "Did you honestly come here on the faint hope of securing a post at a school where you don't even know the name of the proprietress, or even *if* they have a situation available?"

She stubbornly lifted her chin and nodded again.

He shook his head. "Incredible. And what is this about your

mother? She has such confidence in the power of her recommendation that she has no doubt of finding you happily employed at the school whenever she happens to call?"

Olivia lifted a shrug.

"Why not write another letter to your mother directly? Let her know you have taken a post here instead. I shall approve it."

She hesitated, then slowly shook her head.

His pale blue eyes flicked over her clasped hands and hopefully benign expression before returning to the letter once more. "I wonder, *Miss Olivia Keene*—what are you hiding?"

She forced herself to hold his critical gaze without wavering.

He refolded the letter. "Thank you, Charles. But I shall have Hodges post this directly. No need to trouble yourself." He looked at her once again. "But I would not hold my breath awaiting a reply, were I you. Nor, of course, are you free to leave for another post until I give you leave."

Mr. Tugwell objected. "Edward, really. I don't see—"

He held up a halting hand. "Never mind, Charles. Miss Keene *does* see." He narrowed his eyes at her. "Does she not?"

She narrowed her own eyes in return, but nodded for the vicar's benefit.

"Very well. I shall leave the two of you to complete your visit." Lord Bradley turned on his heel and left the room as abruptly as he had entered it.

After an awkward pause, the parson picked up his hat from the settee. "Well, I had better take my leave and allow you to return to your duties." He hesitated, circling his hat by its brim. "I hope it will not make you uncomfortable if I tell you I am still praying for you, Miss Keene." He looked from her to the closed door and back again. "I sense there are things in your life that are not as they should be. I am asking God to 'work all things together for good,' as the Scripture says He will, for those who love Him and are called according to His purpose. Do you, Miss Keene?" he asked gently. "Do you love Him? Trust and serve Him?"

She stared, flummoxed. A man she hardly knew, posing such personal questions? She did not know whether to be touched or offended. His softly lined face blurred before her, and she was embarrassed to find tears once more filling her eyes and falling down her cheeks.

No . . . She shook her head. *I do not trust and serve God,* she thought. *Love him? Sometimes. Is my life as it should be? Am I? No, and again, no.*

He took her hand in his. "I shall pray for that as well."

❧

A few days later, Olivia offered to help Becky give the nursery carpets a good beating. As she struggled to carry out one of the heavy carpets, Johnny Ross jogged over from the stables to the laundry yard.

"Might I help you with that, miss?" the groom asked. "It is no trouble."

She allowed him to help her hang the carpet on a line and in return gave him what she hoped was a grateful smile.

His smile widened. "I was wonderin' when you get your half day," he began. "If it is Sunday afternoon, like mine, might we walk into the village together?"

Slowly, she shook her head.

"No half day?"

She shook her head again.

"Good. Well, not good, but at least you ain't sayin' no to me in general. You ain't, are you?"

Olivia shook her head. But not wanting to encourage him, she began swatting the carpet with the paddle Nurse Peale had provided. She felt his brown eyes on her figure as she worked, but he must have given up, for when she glanced over her shoulder he was gone.

A few minutes later, she sensed a presence behind her once

more. With a reproving smile, she turned around, expecting to see Johnny again. The smile fell from her lips.

"Expecting your admirer?" Lord Bradley sneered.

Olivia glanced around and realized they were shielded from the house by the hanging carpet. Perhaps he saw his opportunity to reinforce his threat without being seen with her and without the children present. She wished for the smiling Lord Bradley of the nursery and wondered where he had gone.

"I thought you understood you were not to talk with anyone."

Before she could respond, he continued, "From the smile on Ross's face, it seems you said a great deal with your eyes. Perhaps a promise for a later rendezvous?"

She shook her head.

"I hope not. If he is seen with you again, he might very well lose his position here."

She gasped. "That is not right!"

Her outburst surprised them both. Lord Bradley was momentarily stilled, but then continued evenly. "Your voice has returned, I see. What did you tell Ross?"

"Noth . . . ing," she rasped.

He stared at her, as though gauging her honesty. "Nor will you, until I give you leave."

She was indignant. "You cannot mean—" She swallowed, her throat dry and scratchy. "You cannot expect me to remain silent forever."

"You managed quite well at the Swan, when it was to your advantage."

"But I could not speak then," she argued hoarsely.

"Nor will you speak now."

"But for three months? Impossible!"

"For a woman I suppose it will be doubly difficult."

Olivia bit back a rebuke and instead reasoned, "It makes no sense. If I wanted to tell someone, I could"—she swallowed again—"all the while pretending to be mute before everyone else."

"Do you really think that in a household like this, word of your speaking would not reach me within minutes?"

She threw up her hands. "I promise you that I will not tell a soul what I heard."

"What is a promise from you worth?"

Olivia stared at him, feeling as though she'd been slapped.

He grimaced. "I am . . ." He rubbed the back of his neck. "I ought not to have said that. But—"

"If you think so poorly of my character," she said stiffly, "then why not send me away and have done?"

"Because I cannot risk having a loose tongue about." He added, as if to himself, "Especially now."

She wondered what that meant.

He straightened and continued briskly, "But in a few months, important matters should be settled. Perhaps then I can deal with the . . . the new information you overheard."

"But to pretend I cannot speak when I can, to deceive others . . . It is not right!"

"Neither is eavesdropping," he clipped, and stalked away.

If the weather be favourable, the children are taken out
by the assistant nurse for air and exercise.
The day should be devoted, in bad weather,
to such amusements as induce exercise,
of dancing, the skipping-rope, and dumb-bells. . . .

—SAMUEL & SARAH ADAMS, *THE COMPLETE SERVANT*

Chapter 10

*T*he housekeeper stood before Edward's desk. "The children
would like to walk in the wood to collect autumn leaves or some
such," Mrs. Hinkley began. "Might Livie take them?"

Miss Keene, Edward noticed, stood a respectful few steps
behind the housekeeper. Why had she enlisted Mrs. Hinkley's
help instead of writing another note? Did she guess he would refuse
her?

He thought back to his harsh words to her the day before,
regretting them yet again. But he did not regret his decision to
keep her at Brightwell Court and to keep her quiet. After all, it
was his future she held in her hands. His inheritance, his marriage
prospects, his father's dreams and plans for him. His very home.

Edward looked directly into Miss Keene's eyes. Could she read his suspicious thoughts? For indeed, he suspected she might use such an opportunity to flee.

"If she is to walk out of view of the house, she must take another with her. Nurse Peale or one of the maids."

"Nurse Peale stays indoors these days, my lord. She hasn't the stamina she had when you were a boy."

This surprised Edward. Miss Peale would always seem a paragon to him. But he was four and twenty now, and his old nurse must be nearing seventy. "Of course. I forget. A maid, then."

"It is really necessary, my lord?"

Unaccustomed to having his orders questioned, he narrowed his eyes at the housekeeper. She would never have questioned his father so. "It is."

At Mrs. Hinkley's inquisitive look, Edward met Miss Keene's eyes once more and said glibly, "She is new, you see, and might *inadvertently* lose her way."

❧

Wearing capes and gloves, Olivia and Doris followed behind as Andrew and Audrey tore down the path through the wood.

The autumn air was crisp, the wood a colorful fresco of flaming brown and orange beechwood trees, orange-red rowan trees, and the puckered berries of hawthorn. Leaves fell and twirled to the ground, revealing more of the pewter grey branches drop by drop. A pheasant skittered across their path, and from the direction of the river came a dipper's squeaking call.

As they walked, Dory kept up a cheerful prattle, unhindered by Olivia's lack of response.

Olivia was still thinking about Lord Bradley's reluctance to allow her to walk out of view of the manor alone. He had no way of knowing she had decided his estate afforded her a comfortable hideaway—until her mother came for her. She wondered if the schoolmistress at St. Aldwyns had yet received her letter.

A narrow track led from the main path to a clearing, where Olivia was surprised to see a snug stone cottage with a slate roof. A stack of chopped firewood, scratching chickens, penned pigs, and a wispy trail of chimney smoke declared the place lived in, while peeling paint, smeared windows, and one forgotten stocking swaying stiffly on a line bespoke recent neglect. Had they wandered outside the Brightwell estate?

Olivia paused and laid a hand on Dory's arm. Gesturing toward the place with her free hand, she gave the maid an inquisitive look.

"Oh. That's the gamekeeper's lodge," Dory said.

Olivia pointed to the frayed rope swing hanging listlessly from a tree.

"He hasn't any children, if that's what you mean. He lives alone out here and keeps to himself. Best place for him, I say."

Olivia lifted her brows expectantly.

Dory continued, "A rough old sod, from what I hear, though I have never spoken to the sourpuss. Looks as if he's lived on Tewksbury mustard his whole life." She shrugged. "Must be good at his post, though. Cook always has plenty of game. Though I grow tired of hare and snipes myself."

They walked on, quickening their pace to catch up with Audrey and Andrew.

"Stay to the path, dumplings!" Dory called ahead. To Olivia, she explained, "Never know where that man has laid his traps. And I for one don't wish to be caught in one."

Olivia shuddered. Neither did she.

❧

The weather being rough and cold the next morning, Olivia kept the children indoors. She sat with Audrey at the old pianoforte in the corner, helping her reach the correct fingerings, and running her own fingers along the score during the more complicated phrases. Andrew, meanwhile, would not cease running about the nursery, kicking a ball and knocking down Alexander's wooden horses, making the ten-month-old cry. After a sharp word from Nurse Peale, Andrew picked up a battledore from an umbrella stand in the corner and began swinging the racquet like a cricket bat. He hit a wooden ball across the room, and it clunked against the wall perilously close to Olivia's head.

Rising from the bench, Olivia walked across the room to Andrew and held out her hand. Looking chastened, he laid the battledore onto it. She went to the umbrella stand, but instead of replacing the racquet, she picked up a second and rummaged around until she found a serviceable shuttlecock. Turning back to the gloomy-faced little boy, she presented him with the racquet and, armed with her own, stood facing him, several yards away.

His face instantly brightened.

She tinged the shuttlecock with a gentle underarm hit that sent the feathered birdie into the air. Andrew swung his battledore so vigorously that he spun a full turn in place, missing the object completely.

"Good heavens," Nurse Peale grumbled good-naturedly. "I had better remove Master Alexander before he becomes the next poor 'birdie.' " She groaned as she bent over, scooped up the little boy, and took him into her own room.

Andrew picked up the shuttlecock and whacked it back, this time into the toy trunk. But after a few more tries, they were able to keep up a volley of two or three hits before having to stop and retrieve the bird. Audrey looked over at them with interest.

"May I play?"

Olivia nodded.

"Two against one won't be fair," Andrew complained.

"Then I shall have to join you." The deep voice startled Olivia. She had not even noticed Lord Bradley standing in the partially open doorway. She hoped their tromping about had not disturbed him. But she thought he looked pleased or at least amused.

"Have you another battledore?" he asked, removing his coat.

Olivia found two more racquets, handing Audrey the sound one and her cousin the one with two tears.

He regarded it with a dubious expression, but murmured only, "Perfect."

The game commenced with much whooping and chasing. Olivia could barely reconcile this smiling, playful man with the haughty Lord Bradley she usually encountered.

"My, my, does this not bring back memories."

Olivia turned. Mrs. Howe now stood in the threshold, arms crossed beneath her bosom, a dimple beside her pink lips.

"Hello, Judith." Lord Bradley gave her a little bow, rendered less ceremonious in shirt sleeves.

She shook her head, amusement and annoyance sparking in her round china-blue eyes. "George Linton called. Hodges could not find you."

Lord Bradley leapt to return one of Andrew's wild shots. "Sorry."

"You are not the least bit sorry, and you know it."

He reached high and managed to bring one down from near the ceiling. The man had the wingspan of a crane.

"Do you remember how you, Felix, and I used to play in this very room," Judith asked. "With George Linton or even your father making up the fourth?"

He nodded, distracted by the game.

One of Audrey's shots went wide to the wall, and in reaching it Olivia stepped near to Mrs. Howe. Impulsively, she held out the battledore and shuttlecock.

The woman hesitated, looking down at her black-and-white-striped walking dress. "No thank you, I am not really—"

"Oh, come, Jude," Lord Bradley teased. "You are not in your dotage yet."

"Play with us. Do!" Audrey urged.

Judith Howe grinned. "Oh, very well. But if I muss my hair, and Dubois scolds me, it shall be on your head."

"You are on my side, Mamma," Andrew called.

Olivia watched for a few moments, and felt an odd emptiness steal over her as the game commenced without her.

Olivia was crossing the entry hall Friday afternoon when a young man sailed through the front doors, removing his greatcoat.

"Take this for me, will you?"

Olivia looked around and, seeing no sign of Osborn or Mr. Hodges, gingerly took the heavy coat from him. Beneath it, he wore a coat of blue velvet over a brightly patterned waistcoat, pantaloons, and tall boots. The youthful dandy had light reddish gold hair. *Titian hair*, she believed it was called, and green eyes. Eyes which lit upon closer inspection of her person. "And who are you?" He smiled. "I am quite certain I have never seen you before."

Olivia craned her head around, but there was no one about to help her.

"What is wrong, my dear—speechless? I never knew I could be quite so intimidating. I find I rather like the notion."

He appeared to be younger than she was, perhaps only nineteen or twenty, but possessed confidence, or at least bravado, beyond his years.

"Not that intimidating you was my intention." He leaned near. "I make it my business to know all of the maids, and I should dearly like to know you. Your name, my sweet?"

Olivia looked at him, brows high.

"Quite right. How rude of me. I am Felix Bradley, Judith Howe's brother and Lord Brightwell's nephew. And you are . . . ?"

Olivia could barely believe this expressive, brightly clad young man was Lord Bradley's cousin. But then . . . She let the thought go unfinished. From her pocket, she withdrew the small card upon which she had written her name, for just such an occasion.

"Love notes already? How delightful." He squinted at her script. "Lydia?"

She shook her head, amused. She found his friendly smile and elfin green eyes charming.

He looked once more. "Lilly?"

She wiggled her hand, signaling, close enough. He straightened and smiled again. Olivia noticed he was tall and thin—not as tall as Lord Bradley but appearing so due to his narrow frame. His features were fine, patrician even.

"Mr. Bradley! I did not hear you arrive." Mrs. Hinkley bustled across the hall and discreetly put a hand on Olivia's back and nudged her toward the staircase. "Lord Brightwell is abroad, as you know. Shall I have Hodges announce you to Lord Bradley?"

"No need, Mrs. H. I shall just pop up and see my sister."

"Very good, sir. The Chinese room is ready for you as always."

Olivia walked toward the stairs as directed, feeling Mrs. Hinkley's actions were more protection than rebuke. She could still hear their conversation over the padding of her slippers on the marble floor.

"Who is the new girl? Most unusual."

"Oh," Mrs. Hinkley said with evident nonchalance, "that is Livie, new to us since your last visit."

"Livie. Ah."

"You realized she is mute, of course."

"Mute? Really?" He spoke casually, as though Olivia were already absent—or deaf.

She felt his eyes on her back as she climbed the stairs.

"Come to think of it, she did not speak a word. Yet I could have sworn she had the most beautiful voice."

Chapter 11

*L*ater that afternoon, Olivia sat beside Audrey as she read aloud from *Peter the Great*, following along and occasionally touching her fingertip to a word the girl had skipped over or mispronounced. If Audrey did not know the meaning of a word, Olivia would help her locate the definition in one of the volumes of Johnson's dictionary.

Bang. The nursery door hit the wall, startling them all. Andrew dropped his top and shouted, "Uncle Felix!"

Audrey squealed and jumped up from the settee, book forgotten. Both children ran to the man at the door.

"Hello, you ankle-biters," Felix Bradley teased. He patted his pockets and withdrew a peppermint for each of them. "Sweets for the sweet." His gaze sought and held Olivia's over their heads. He waved away their thanks. "I know my visits would not signify in the least were I not to bring you something."

He looked over at Olivia once more. "What is your new nurse tormenting you with?" He strolled to the settee and picked up the book. "Plague me. I remember this one. Devilish boring." He grinned at her censorious look. "Upon my soul, it was. Now. Who's for a game of hunt the slipper?"

His suggestion was met with cheers, and the children quickly cleared the toys from the worn circular carpet before the nursery hearth. Olivia rose to move the large wooden rocking horse, but Felix Bradley quickly came to her aid, stepping near and saying quietly, "Allow me, lovely Livie. And that is difficult to say, lovely Livie is, though I realize you shall have to take my word for it. I practiced saying it all the way up here."

She shook her head at his foolishness but could not help grinning.

Movement caught her eye, and she glanced over as a second figure appeared in the doorway. Lord Bradley stood, arms crossed, eyes narrowed. He looked from Felix to her and back again, seemingly annoyed to see his cousin standing so near to her. She felt defensive—she had not initiated the proximity. Still, she took a self-conscious step away.

"Felix. I am surprised to see you here."

"Are you? In the nursery, or in general?"

"Both, I suppose. Your term does not end for several weeks."

"That's right. Just before Christmas. I am only visiting. You do not mind, I trust?"

Lord Bradley regarded him speculatively, before his shoulders lifted slightly and his lips pulled down in a gesture of detached nonchalance.

"Come, Cousin Edward, do play with us," Audrey beseeched. "We haven't enough players for a proper game. And Nurse Peale says she is too old to sit on the floor."

"And what game are we playing?" he asked, eyes fixed on Felix.

"Hunt the slipper," Andrew answered. "Livie has never played it. Can you imagine?"

Lord Bradley feigned shock. "I cannot."

"Miss Livie, you are to stand in the center and try to guess which of us has the shoe," Audrey explained. "We shall use one of my doll shoes, for a real shoe would be too easily seen with so few players."

Andrew looked up at her soberly. "You are to say, 'Cobbler, cobbler, mend my shoe. Get it done by half past two.' But as you cannot speak, we shall say it for you."

Olivia dipped her head in appreciation.

"Whoever is caught with the slipper becomes the hunter, and pays a forfeit," Audrey explained. "One must sing a song, or dance, or tell a secret, or perform some trick."

"And, if anyone drops the slipper whilst passing it," Andrew added, "she must pay a forfeit as well."

"Why do you say 'she'?" Audrey demanded. "I shall not drop it."

"You always do."

"Do not."

While Olivia stood, the others sat on the floor—Audrey, Andrew, Becky, Felix, and Lord Bradley. She was surprised by his affability in joining the game. Evidently he was very fond of his young cousins.

The five sat, knees raised, in a boxy circle, and made a great show of passing the shoe under the tent of their bent legs. All fisted their hands and mimed the act of passing, trying to make the guessing more difficult. Still, they made a very small circle and Olivia was sure Andrew held the shoe, but then he passed it so quickly she could not be sure. A mischievous light gleamed in Felix's eyes.

She pointed to him with a suppressed smile.

He held forth empty hands and winked.

Olivia next guessed Audrey and, correct, was instructed to trade places with the girl—who had been seated directly beside Lord Bradley. Swallowing, Olivia sat down gingerly, careful to avoid grazing his knee with her own, and to keep her skirts tucked about her.

Audrey performed a pirouette for her forfeit, then lost no time in beginning another round, chanting, "Cobbler, cobbler, mend my shoe. Get it done by half past two."

Andrew passed the shoe to Lord Bradley, who reached for her hand to pass the shoe into hers. Olivia feared her palm would be damp with nerves at being so close to him. When his fingertips touched her palms she started, fumbled the shoe, and it fell to the floor.

"Now you've done it, Livie!" Felix said. "Got to pay your forfeit."

"Pay a forfeit, pay a forfeit!" Andrew chimed.

Olivia's heart pounded. She wiped her damp palms along the hem of her gown as it wrapped around her ankles. What should she do? What *could* she do?

She arose and stepped to the pianoforte and there played a few bars of one of Mozart's piano concertos, the festive "Turkish March" she had learnt at Miss Cresswell's. Afterward, she bowed with a flourish and reclaimed her spot on the floor.

Everybody clapped in delight except Lord Bradley. He merely stared. Had she overstepped by playing the pianoforte meant for the children's use?

Apparently she had, for he rose, smoothed his coat, and apologized to his cousins. "Forgive me, but I have forgotten an appointment with Father's clerk."

How foolish she felt, how chastened. The children groaned, but Felix watched him go as silently as she.

❧

Olivia awoke, cold. Her small room had no fire of its own, but drew warmth from the hearth in the adjacent sleeping chamber. And that fire had no doubt smoldered to ash hours ago. She pulled her bedclothes over her head, attempting to warm herself and return to sleep. She heard something and stilled, ceasing to even shiver as she listened. Her door creaked slowly open, and Olivia sat upright, heart pounding.

As her eyes adjusted to the dark, she saw a figure tiptoeing into her room. A small figure.

Andrew.

"I had a bad dream," he muttered and audibly shivered.

Olivia turned down her bedclothes, and he immediately climbed in beside her. She realized she should return him to his own bed and find him an extra blanket, or rouse Becky to stoke the fire and warm another bed stone. Instead, she pulled the blankets up under his chin and asked God to send him sweet dreams. Andrew curled into her side with a little sigh, falling to sleep within seconds. *Ah, well . . .* she would rise early and carry him back to his bed.

Stroking his hair, Olivia wondered if this was what it felt like to be someone's mother—to possess the sweet, satisfying power to comfort and console. She wondered, too, if she would ever have children of her own. Considering she was unmarried at nearly five and twenty, it seemed unlikely. She thought fleetingly of the sole young man who had ever courted her and squelched the icy doubts that followed. Instead, she put her arm around Andrew, relishing his warmth, his nearness, and the sunny smell of his freshly washed hair as she drifted to sleep.

❧

In the morning, Olivia awoke with Andrew still beside her and the discomfiting feeling of being watched.

She glanced toward her door and saw that it was still open from Andrew's entrance the night before. She gasped, startled to see Lord Bradley and Audrey in the threshold, peering at them. She jerked the bedclothes up over her thin nightdress.

"Forgive us," Lord Bradley murmured, averting his eyes. "Audrey was concerned when she could not find Andrew."

Olivia opened her mouth to defend herself, but remembered in time not to speak.

"Did he have a bad dream and ask to sleep with you?" Audrey asked.

Olivia nodded, realizing this was close enough to the truth and likely to assure their hastiest departure.

"There, Audrey, you see? Nothing to fear. Andrew is perfectly well."

He glanced at her, and Olivia felt her cheeks burn as she pulled the bedclothes higher.

Andrew opened his sleepy eyes and looked from Olivia to his sister and cousin, clearly confused to find himself in the under nurse's bed.

"You talked in your sleep, Miss Livie!" Andrew said, startling Olivia and their audience as well.

Olivia shook her head, but Andrew insisted, "You did! You said something about a comb and then, 'I should not have done it. I did not mean to.' You said that bit twice. What did you not mean to do?"

Olivia was dumbfounded and felt her face flush anew. She dared a glance up at Lord Bradley, knowing he would be displeased.

"Andrew, you must have been dreaming," Audrey said, stepping into the room. "Miss Keene cannot speak." She took Andrew's hand as he climbed out of bed and led him from the room. "You had another of your bad dreams last night, did you not?"

"I did, but—"

"See? That was all it was, then. Miss Keene talking in her sleep? What an imagination you have!"

After the children departed, Lord Bradley paused only long enough to nod curtly before pulling the door closed. Olivia sighed.

Next time, she could most definitely *not* let Andrew share her bed.

On Wednesday morning, Olivia delivered the children to the stable yard for their riding lessons. When she arrived, Lord Bradley was nowhere to be seen, so she and the children went to the far stall and watched Talbot shoe a horse and then looked on as Johnny saddled up the small horse and pony Audrey and Andrew would ride. When a quarter of an hour had passed, and Lord Bradley still had not appeared, Johnny took pity on the antsy children.

"What say you, Miss Livie. These two beasts are raring to go. The horses too." He winked. "Why don't I lead them about the yard until Lord Bradley comes?"

Olivia nodded gratefully.

Smiling, Johnny put the horse and pony on leads. The children mounted, all enthusiasm, and the groom led them around the yard in a wide circle. Not as exciting as a ride with their cousin, but at least they were not sitting idle.

A few minutes later, Lord Bradley strode into the stables with the merest glance in Olivia's direction. He walked to one of the stalls and, over its gate, stroked the long muzzle of his tall black horse.

"Have you and the children been waiting long?" he asked, his gaze still on the horse. She was surprised he would initiate conversation with her.

Since no one was within earshot, Olivia answered quietly, "Not so long."

He nodded. And as no groom offered to do so for him, he opened the gate and began bridling the horse himself.

She waited, but when he did not scold her for speaking to him, she asked, "Pray what is his name, this beauty of a horse?" *That once nearly trampled me to death*, she added to herself.

"Guess." He pressed the bit between the horse's large teeth, then lifted the leather straps over the regal head and ears.

"Hmm . . ." she mused. "Considering his color, and your general demeanor, I would guess . . . *Black.*"

"You wound me. Do you think me completely without imagination?"

"It is one's first impression." What was she thinking to tease him as she might tease Johnny? Was she so desperate for adult conversation?

Finished with the task, he narrowed his eyes at her. "Would you like to know what I am imagining right now?"

Throttling me? she thought, but whispered only, "No. Definitely not."

After the riding lesson, Olivia found herself in the uncomfortable position of walking back to the house beside Lord Bradley as the children, as was their wont, ran ahead. She slowed her pace to fall a respectful distance behind him, as befitted her station. He made no further conversation, and of course, neither did she.

She was startled when Croome rounded the corner of the manor. Evidently, Lord Bradley was startled as well, for he drew up sharply and she nearly collided with him.

"Ah . . . Mr. Croome." Lord Bradley's voice seemed suddenly unnatural and unsure. He turned to follow the man's hard gaze and for a moment, both men regarded her critically. Prompted to fill the awkward silence, Lord Bradley said, "This is . . . that is, you may recall Miss Keene."

"I recall," Croome muttered. "I recall I caught 'er snooping where she had no business."

"Yes, well. She has entered into service now. Helping with my young cousins."

Croome scorched her with a glare, but she doused it with an icy one of her own. For she remembered him as well, somewhere *he* had no business.

He looked away first and turned to Lord Bradley. "There's a polecat lurkin' about the place. I plan to set a trap for him, unless you prefer to leave him be. Keep the rats down, polecats do, but terrible destructive for game."

"I see. Well, whatever you think best, Mr. Croome. Father has always trusted your wisdom in these affairs."

Olivia studied Lord Bradley, perplexed. He was like a nervous schoolboy before an exacting headmaster.

Croome nodded and lurched away in his slightly limping gait, and they both turned to watch as the gamekeeper disappeared into the wood.

"You are still afraid of him," Olivia ventured quietly. "Has he ever harmed you?"

"No." He expelled a puff of breath. "Foolish, is it not? I think it has to do with my father. When I was a lad, he always seemed to stand closer to me whenever Croome was about."

How odd, Olivia thought. Aloud she said, "I wonder if Lord Brightwell knows something unsavory about the man's character." To herself she added, *Or about his dealings with poachers?*

"I don't know," Lord Bradley admitted. "But perhaps I shall ask him when he returns."

She was once again tempted to tell Lord Bradley where she had first seen Croome, but hesitated. She knew it would lead to more questions she was not prepared to answer.

❧

Late in the afternoon, when Olivia went down to the kitchen for the nursery dinner tray, the kitchen maids were sitting on low stools, plucking feathers from a basketful of small birds. Seeing her stare, Mrs. Moore explained. "Grouse from the gamekeeper. Grouse pie will make for a nice change, will it not? Our neighbor George Linton filled our larder with partridges from his estate, and everyone is sick to death of them."

Mrs. Moore added a dish of suet dumplings to the nursery tray, then looked up at Olivia. "Have you met our Mr. Croome?"

Olivia gave a slight nod, which traveled into her shoulders as a shudder.

"Afraid of the man, are you? I shouldn't wonder. Looks a fright most days, doesn't he?"

Olivia nodded her agreement.

Mrs. Moore clucked her tongue. "He's as thin as I've ever seen him. What must he eat, I wonder? I doubt he's had a decent meal in years."

Olivia wondered at the sympathy in her tone. Of course she had been at Brightwell Court long enough to realize Mrs. Moore could not stand the thought of anyone going hungry.

"And too proud to take a meal with us," one of the kitchen maids piped up.

"Hush, Edith, and keep to your plucking," Mrs. Moore said. "Has his own house and fire ring, hasn't he? Not in service like the rest of us."

Mrs. Moore sighed. "And me with two perfectly good partridge pasties and no one to eat them." She lifted woeful eyes from the pasties to Olivia and back again.

No . . . Olivia thought, and slowly, emphatically, shook her head.

Sukey accompanied her as far as the narrow track but refused to go further. Swallowing, Olivia gripped the packet more tightly and stepped into the clearing.

Croome sat on the lodge stoop, stroking a long knife over a sharpening stone. When she stepped into the clearing, he jerked his head up.

"What do you want?" Croome's wiry brows formed an angry V over narrowed eyes. "Nothing to snoop around here for."

She recalled Mrs. Moore's admonition. *"Don't let him see your fear. Worse than the predators he keeps out of the wood, he is, when he smells weakness."*

He stared at her, and it was all she could do not to look away from the venom in his eyes.

Suddenly his gaze targeted the packet in her hands. "Whatever that is, you can take it right back with you. I don't need yer charity."

She lifted her chin and held out the paper-wrapped package upon which Mrs. Moore had written its contents: *Hashed Partridge Pasty.*

His scowl deepened to one of disgust, and Olivia was stunned when he rose and snatched the packet from her and threw it maliciously into the pigpen. The packet split open and the pasties spilled out, soon surrounded and disappearing under the grunting work of pigs.

She cringed, feeling the sting of her offering being rejected, even if Mrs. Moore had been the one to suggest it. Hashed partridge was considered a delicacy—a rare treat for any man. How ungrateful he was. How rude.

She had kept his secret and, against her better judgment, had allowed Mrs. Moore to persuade her to offer a gift. Well, she had done all she would to repay him for her rescue. All the way back to the manor, she fumed. She was done with the man. Croome could starve to death, and good riddance!

Avoid as much as possible being alone with the other sex:
as the greatest mischiefs happen from small circumstances.

—SAMUEL & SARAH ADAMS, *THE COMPLETE SERVANT*

Chapter 12

The next morning, Olivia went downstairs to find Mrs. Hinkley, bearing a note Nurse Peale had dictated while she'd had her hands full with Alexander. The note requested the procurement of an ivory ring, and in the meantime, a crust of stale bread for the fussy, teething child to chew.

Olivia found the housekeeper sitting at the small desk in her parlor, bent over a lined book. She looked up when Olivia entered, and groaned. "I have spent the better part of three hours on the household accounts and cannot balance this ledger. Mr. Walters will want an accounting of every shilling tomorrow, and I cannot find where I have gone wrong."

Olivia bit her lip. Dared she offer? She touched a finger to her chest.

"You want to give it a go?" Mrs. Hinkley huffed a laugh. "Do you know anything about household accounts?"

Olivia lifted her shoulders, fluttered a hand.

Mrs. Hinkley rose. "Well, I suppose there is nothing confidential about how many rashers of bacon and pounds of sugar we buy or how much we pay the coal merchant."

She hovered behind the chair until Olivia shooed her gently away.

"Oh, very well. But if you don't find my error in half an hour, I shall have to try again."

Ten minutes later, Olivia rapped her knuckles against the desk. Mrs. Hinkley rose sprightly from the settee and hurried over. "Did you find something?"

Olivia nodded and pointed to an incorrect subtotal. She lifted a scrap of paper with the reworked sum.

"Bless me, you're right! How did I miss it?"

Olivia smiled and rose from the chair.

Still staring at the figures and shaking her head, Mrs. Hinkley said, "Sometimes a pair of fresh eyes is all that is needed, I suppose." Then she looked up at Olivia once more. "If you would not mind keeping this between us . . . ?"

Olivia nodded. She had no desire to tell a soul. She did not want anyone asking her how she came to know so much about account books.

She belatedly handed over Nurse Peale's note. Mrs. Hinkley skimmed it and sent Olivia down to the kitchen for the bread, promising to purchase the ring as soon as possible. Several minutes later, Olivia returned to the nursery with the crust of bread, only to have Miss Peale look at it blankly and say she was not hungry.

❧

That afternoon, Edward was meeting in the study with his father's clerk when movement out on the lawn drew his attention.

He paused in his dictation to Walters to look out the window. Miss Keene was outside, a red scarf tied across her eyes and bonnet, her arms outstretched in a game of hoodman blind. His young cousins, bundled head to toe, ran around her, evading her grasp. The children were laughing and calling out. Miss Keene was turning, her skirts and cape twirling about her, a wide smile lighting her face. He felt his own mouth turn up in response. He knew he should not find her attractive, but he did. He wished he knew if he could trust her. He thought of Sybil Harrington, whom his father hoped he would marry, with her classic features and rich dowry. She was more beautiful than any under nurse, surely.

Andrew ran too close, and Miss Keene grabbed him around his middle and lifted him, spinning him around and around until his hat flew to the ground. Andrew laughed with glee, the sound of it carrying through the glass. Miss Keene set him down and pulled down the blindfold. She mussed Andrew's hair affectionately before picking up his hat and replacing it on his head. Audrey joined them, sliding her gloved hand into Miss Keene's.

"Shall I repeat the last sentence, my lord?" the clerk asked.

"Hmm?" Edward murmured, returning to the business at hand. "Oh, yes please, Walters, if you would."

❧

Olivia stuffed the red scarf into her cape pocket. She covered her eyes with her hands, then pointed toward the outbuildings.

"She wants to play hide-and-seek!" Andrew shouted.

Olivia nodded with a wry grin. She was becoming quite adept at charades.

"I am weary of childish games," Audrey grumbled.

"Come on, Aud," her brother urged. "I'll even seek first. Ready, steady, go!"

Giving in, Audrey ran off in the direction of the garden.

Olivia followed more sedately, too self-conscious to run without the children at her side.

While Andrew counted, Olivia searched this way and that for a new hiding spot.

Johnny Ross stepped out of the stables, polish and brush in hand. "Here!" he called, waving her over. "I know a place those ankle-biters will never find you."

She hurried toward the groom, and when she smiled at him, his fair face broke into a blushing grin. "This way, miss."

Olivia followed him into the stables. There, he pushed at a section of wood walling that was actually a well-hidden door to a small closet.

"Don't use this anymore, not since the tack room was added."

Olivia stepped into the dark room, expecting Johnny to close the door from the outside. Instead, he stepped in after her and pulled the door shut against his back.

She felt suddenly ill at ease. She took a step toward the door, but he moved as well, blocking her path.

"You're a prime article," he whispered, gripping her waist. "A real beauty."

Olivia tried to pry his hands away. His grasp remained firm. By slim shafts of light filtering through cracks in the wall, she saw him lean his face toward hers. She turned her head so that his damp lips found only a bit of cheek and ear.

"Livie!" Andrew called from somewhere nearby. "Come out, come out, wherever you are!"

Olivia pushed Johnny away with all her strength and hurried out the door and into the stable yard, wincing in the bright sunlight. In a moment she could see, but dreaded what she saw.

Mrs. Hinkley.

The housekeeper's eyes slowly assessed her burning face.

Olivia looked away first.

Andrew, unaware of the awkward scene, explained. "Mrs.

Hinkley came looking for you, so I said she could help me find you."

"I appreciate your assistance, Master Andrew," Mrs. Hinkley said dryly.

Johnny stepped out from the dim stables. Olivia darted a glance at him, then at Mrs. Hinkley. The older woman looked from one to the other. Olivia knew the shrewd housekeeper would not miss their guilty expressions.

"Might I steal you from your game, Livie?" she asked, all placid nonchalance. "Lord Bradley would like a word."

Olivia swallowed, but a ball of dread seemed lodged in her throat as she silently followed.

Lord Bradley sat behind his desk in a blue coat and white cravat, his golden hair brushed neatly forward. The strong lines of his face were set. His pale blue eyes stared, unwavering.

Once Mrs. Hinkley had closed the study door and her footfalls had retreated down the corridor, Olivia said stiffly, "You wanted to see me?"

"Yes. Please sit down," Lord Bradley's voice was formal and firm. He entwined his long fingers on the polished desktop. "I have learnt of your recent activities and must say I am surprised."

"It was nothing, really," she stammered, cheeks heating at the thought of being caught coming out of a closet with the groom. "Nothing happened."

"Nothing? Come, Miss Keene, the whole staff is talking about it. Why, I witnessed your activities myself this morning from this very window."

Olivia's stomach dropped. "Did you indeed?"

"Quite. Mrs. Howe is very impressed, and I must say I am as well." He paused. "I see I am making you uncomfortable." His tone softened; his eyes as well. "I simply asked you here to thank you for taking on the care of the children so admirably—going far beyond the duties of an under nurse. It is much appreciated, especially as

117

they are without a governess at present." He picked up a letter from his desk and handed it to her. "And, to give you this."

The letter was addressed to her, and she was surprised to find the seal unbroken—he had not read it. She unfolded the single page and skimmed its contents. The brief letter was written in the arthritic hand of an older woman.

> *Miss Keene,*
>
> *We are not seeking to hire anyone at this time. Nor has anyone called here inquiring after you.*
>
> > *Sincerely,*
> > *Miss Kirby, Proprietress*
> > *The Girls' Seminary,*
> > *St. Aldwyns*

The curt reply held no warm remembrance or even acknowledgment of a former friendship with her mother. Had her mother put too much stock in the acquaintance?

"Any offer of a post?" he asked with apparent unconcern.

She shook her head.

"And have they told your mother where to find you?"

Again she shook her head, wondering what had delayed her mother.

"Perhaps it is just as well." He cleared his throat. "I have asked Mrs. Hinkley to give you a half day off per week—though I must still ask you to remain on the estate. I realize there is not much for a young woman to do here, especially this time of year, but—"

"I don't mind," Olivia interrupted, mustering a smile. "I could walk alone on the grounds or stay in my room and do a bit of reading. There are several books in the schoolroom—that is, if you do not mind."

He nodded. "By all means."

"Thank you, my lord." She straightened her shoulders and inhaled deeply. "I shall look forward to it. When is my half day to be? Sunday?"

His smile tightened. "Ross's half day is on Sunday, is it not?"
She hesitated, then nodded.
"Then yours shall be on Wednesday."

Taking the children for a turn around the shrubbery on Monday,
Olivia glimpsed Lord Bradley walk past the stone gardening shed,
then disappear behind a timber-framed outbuilding beside it. She
would have liked to ask the children what the building was, but as
she could not, she led the children toward it.

They turned the corner and saw Lord Bradley climb the two
steps to the stoop and run his finger along a crack in the building's
solitary window, then reach for the door handle. Seeing them, he
abruptly drew his hand away and stood with his back to the closed
door.

For once there was no welcoming smile for his young cousins.
"Hello, Andrew. Audrey."

He did not address her, nor offer any explanation of why he
stood there or what he was about.

"The gardener has just discovered a pure white cat living under
the woodshed," he said to the children. "It has one green eye and
one blue. If you hurry, he will no doubt show you."

Audrey and Andrew needed no further prodding and quickly
ran off.

Olivia waited one moment more, wondering if he would say
anything once the children were out of earshot. Instead, he just
stood there, arms crossed, staring down at her in cool challenge.

"Had you not better follow your charges?"

Piqued, she turned and walked back in the direction she had
come. Just as she turned the corner, she glanced back over her
shoulder and saw Lord Bradley slip inside the building and shut
the door firmly behind him. The message was clear. They were
not welcome there. What was he doing within? Was he alone? She

was tempted to peer in the window like the spy he already believed her to be, but recalling the challenge in his eyes, she resisted the impulse.

❧

The next day, when Olivia delivered the children to the stables for their riding lessons, Lord Bradley had yet to return from his morning ride, so Johnny once again led the children around the yard on leads.

A few minutes later, Lord Bradley cantered in on his black horse. He reined in, swung his leg over to dismount, then tied the horse to the rail.

His eyes scanned the stable yard. "What is Ross about? This horse needs a good rubdown."

"Perhaps you could show me how it is done?"

One sardonic brow rose. "Protecting your lover again?"

Ignoring this, she said earnestly, "Actually, I dread the thought of going indoors on such a perfect autumn day. I would love to stay out here and give it a go."

He hesitated. "Have you ever done so?"

"No. But you shall not find a quicker student."

"Very well." He stepped into the tack room and returned directly. He laid a brush onto her waiting palm, tightening the strap over the back of her hand. Resting his free palm on the horse's damp withers, he lifted her equipped hand with his own and began guiding her through the brush strokes until she felt mesmerized by the rhythm and the firm hold of his hand on hers. She could almost feel the warmth of his body standing behind her, though he touched only her hand.

He cleared his throat. "There, I believe you have mastered the motion."

He stepped away, and the perfect autumn day felt suddenly quite chilly.

Lord Bradley leaned against the stable wall and gave her a shrewd look. He rapped his knuckles on the hidden door, producing a hollow knock. "I understand you have discovered the secret room here."

She looked up at him sharply.

"Yes, I know of it. I was underfoot as a lad when our old steward built it. I imagine he wanted a closet to nap in, or perhaps for some private assignation. It is perfectly suited for it, do you not think?"

He watched her closely. No doubt saw the blush warming her cheeks.

"Andrew mentioned last night that you hid in the stables with the groom. You were in here together, were you not?"

"Only for a moment," she whispered, wondering if he would retract his offer of a half day.

"And what, pray, did you do during that moment alone, in the dark?"

"Nothing."

"Why do I doubt that?"

"Perhaps you assume I share your own ill-intentions."

"Touché." He held up a consolatory hand. "Forgive me, Miss Keene. I meant no harm."

"I had better return to the nursery." Dropping the brush, she turned and strode away, chilled and flushed at once.

The estate carpenter frequently made toys for the children in the nursery, furniture for the house, as well as carrying out repairs.

—UPSTAIRS & DOWNSTAIRS, LIFE IN AN ENGLISH COUNTRY HOUSE

Chapter 13

On the first Wednesday afternoon in December, Olivia left the children under the care of Becky and Nurse Peale, donned her cape and gloves, and let herself out the rear door. Though the early December day was cold, the sun shone invitingly.

Walking around the manor toward the gardens, she saw Lord Bradley in coat and hat disappear once again behind the outbuilding near the gardening shed. Curiosity tugged at her, and she followed him around the building.

There Lord Bradley stood beside a tradesman as he packed his bag of tools. Both men stood for a moment, eyes trained on a small clear window as though a work of art. Then the tradesman lifted a hand in farewell and turned to go. The new window was certainly in better condition than the rest of the timber-framed structure, whatever it was. Wondering how she would be received this time, she whispered, "My lord."

He looked at her with mild surprise. "Miss Keene. What is it? The children all right?"

"Yes, my lord. It is my half day."

"Ah." He nodded. "That was the glazier just here. Replacing this window." He stepped to the door.

"What is this place?" she asked.

He hesitated at the threshold, then looked at her over his shoulder. "Come in and see for yourself."

She wondered if it was proper, but curiosity—and the longing to speak with the only person with whom she was allowed to do so—overrode her sense of propriety. She followed him inside.

"It is just a little carpentry shop," he said. "A workroom."

Sun shone in through the new window, illuminating a one-room interior of unfinished wood. A lamp glowed on the worktable, which held a large drape-covered object atop it. A small stove in the corner heated the space. Tools hung neatly from pegs on the walls, and planks of various sizes were stacked beneath. A chair, mid-repair, sat in one corner. The place smelled of wood shavings, smoke, and him, and she thought the fragrance quite pleasant.

Lord Bradley removed his coat and hung it on a peg. She was further surprised when he tied a leather apron around his waist.

"Our former steward did quite a bit of carpentry." Lord Bradley looked about him. "I used to come out here with him as a lad and tag along as he went about his duties. I had a small part—and many slivers—in the outbuildings, the arbor, and of course, the present stables of which you are so fond."

He gave her a knowing look, but she quickly averted her gaze.

He sighed. "Then Matthews died and I went away to school, and the place fell into disuse."

"It does not appear abandoned."

"I have cleaned it out and made repairs." He picked up a

carpenter's plane and began stroking it across a pale piece of wood. "Matthews's tools were still here . . . like buried treasure for a man like me."

"What are you making?"

He shrugged. "Christmas gifts. A cricket bat for Andrew. Blocks for Alexander. Though a couple seem to have gone missing." He nodded toward the drape-covered object. "And something for Audrey. Attempting it, anyway. It must remain our secret, if you please, for I am dreadfully out of practice, and I don't wish to disappoint them if unsuccessful."

Another secret to keep . . . She looked with interest at the draped project. "Might I at least peek?"

He started to shake his head, then hesitated, regarding her with a gleam in his blue eyes. "You know, I could use an accomplice."

"An accomplice?" she said, her voice a little sharper than she intended, suspecting another reference to her "crime."

He held up one hand in entreaty. "Poor choice of words. But . . . you were a little girl once, were you not?"

"I should think so, yes." A little bubble of excitement rose in her chest.

"And you do sew?"

Her spirits quickly flagged. "You want me to *sew*?"

"Never mind."

She sighed. "Forgive me. It is only that I have a fair amount of sewing most evenings as it is, helping Becky keep the children's clothes repaired—especially Andrew's stockings and the knees of his breeches. But if you need something mended . . ."

"Not mended. Created."

"What?" She glanced at the chair in the corner. "A cushion for your chair, or . . ."

He followed her gaze. "Not a bad idea. But not for that chair." He pinched an inch of air between his thumb and finger. "Could you make one say, this big?"

She looked doubtful. "For a mouse?"

He cocked his head to the side. "You disappoint me, Miss Keene." His blue eyes twinkled as he pulled off the dustcloth from the large object on the worktable. "Have you *no* imagination?"

He revealed a three-story doll's house, a scale model of a manor very like Brightwell Court. Olivia drew in a breath of wonder. "*You* built this?"

"Your confidence astounds me."

"It is magnificent, truly."

"Do you think Audrey will like it?"

"How could she not?" Olivia said, though in truth, she wondered if Audrey was growing a little old for dolls. Still, she believed any girl would marvel at such a gift.

She pulled out a drawing peeking out from under the house and unfolded the thick paper to reveal the whole—a detailed drawing of the doll's house with measurements to scale. "You drew this as well?"

"Yes. So . . . will you?"

She dragged her gaze from the impressively drawn plan. "Hmm?"

"Help me make some draperies and cushions and bedclothes and such?"

She looked up at him, bewildered and touched that he would devote such time to amusing and delighting children who were not his own. "With pleasure, my lord."

He smiled down at her, his lips softening as his gaze seemed to fix on her mouth. She drew in a breath and turned away toward the doll's house. "Here is the nursery," she said quickly. "But you have not included my room, though you have been there." Her cheeks heated as she realized what she had said.

He stood beside her, bending near as they both pretended to study his handiwork. She felt his gaze on her profile, knew their faces were only inches apart.

A long curl of her hair came loose, a curtain falling between them. He slowly ran his finger along her temple and tucked the curl behind her ear. Her heart raced and her skin tingled at his touch. If she angled toward him, just a little, her lips might brush his. Did she want that? Did he?

The carpentry shop door creaked open and Olivia started. Beside her, Lord Bradley jerked upright. Croome stood framed in the threshold, eyes narrowed suspiciously, fowling piece in hand.

"Yes? What is it?" Bradley asked, somewhat defensively.

The man looked from Lord Bradley to Olivia. "I seen the door open to this ol' place and thought a raccoon or a tramp must have got inside." He pinned Olivia with a pointed look.

Lord Bradley replied, "As you can see, that is not the case."

Croome glared at Olivia a moment longer, then slowly lifted his gaze to survey the room. "You using ol' Matthews's shop again?"

"Yes, as you see."

Croome looked about at the neatly arranged tools, the sawdust, the work in progress.

"Have you some reason to object, Mr. Croome?" Lord Bradley asked with asperity.

The wiry brows rose. "Not my business, is it."

"Precisely."

"I'm setting rat traps in the outbuildings. Want one here as well?"

"Thank you, Mr. Croome."

He trained his eyes on Olivia once more. "Mind you don't get caught in it."

When Miss Keene left the shop, Edward took a deep breath and attempted to regain his composure. He should not, would not, be attracted to her. He brought Miss Harrington's image to mind once again, reminding himself that he would no doubt be seeing her at Christmas.

Christmas . . . His gifts would never be ready in time if he kept making a fool of himself over an under nurse. He was becoming as bad as Felix. He forced himself to return his attention to the blocks for Alexander. He had made ten of them, he was sure, with the numbers 1 through 10 rather crudely carved into one side and the letters A through J on the opposite. What had he done with blocks 1 and 2? They seemed to be missing. Being in close quarters with the woman had made sawdust of his brains. How had he mislaid them?

At that moment, Osborn knocked and announced that George Linton had just arrived. "Is my lord at home for callers?"

Stifling a groan, Edward untied his apron. The work—and the search—would have to wait.

That evening, Judith looked across the table at him as she cut her capon. She initiated their dinner conversation, as she often did, commenting on the exceptionally fine weather they had been having and could he believe December was already upon them?

Pushing away thoughts of Miss Keene, Edward murmured his agreement but knew himself to be distracted. He still found it strange to dine with only Judith, now that his parents were away and Felix had returned to Oxford. He supposed he should be used to Judith's company. She had lived with them since Dominick's funeral more than a year before. Judith's mother, who lived in a small townhouse in Swindon, had suggested the arrangement, and Lord Brightwell had quickly agreed, graciously offering a home to his then-expecting niece and her two stepchildren.

"I spoke with George Linton when he called for you," Judith said. "What did he want?"

"To boast about his new hunter." Edward guessed the call was only a ruse to lay eyes on Judith, whom George had admired in vain since boyhood.

She tried another topic. "Dominick's mother has written to ask if I have engaged a new governess for Audrey and Andrew." She paused to sip her wine. "I suppose I must, though I do so dread the prospect. Bringing in another creature like Miss Dowdle, who believes herself superior to me in education and my equal in station, were it not for her diminished means. Wanting to take meals with us, attend parties, and tempt the males of the family." She placed a dainty piece of capon in her mouth. "You saw how it was with Felix. I was never so relieved as when Miss Dowdle left—and not only because she was so stern with Audrey and Andrew. Even had the gall to lecture me on the proper manner of raising children."

Edward did not argue. He, too, had found Miss Dowdle most disagreeable and had worried where Felix's flirtation might lead.

Realizing he had left Judith to fend for herself in the conversation long enough, he wiped his mouth on a linen serviette and began a topic of his own. "What shall we do about Christmas?"

Picking at a sweetmeat, Judith said thoughtfully, "I suppose we must celebrate in some fashion, for the children's sake."

"I agree. But let us entertain modestly this year."

Judith nodded her assent.

Conscious of Lord and Lady Brightwell's absence, they together planned a smaller gathering than usual. No distant relations. No friends down from London. They would have only their neighbors—George Linton, his sister, Charity, and their parents—the vicar and his sister, and Admiral Harrington and his daughter. Edward would also invite his father's sisters, though he doubted their spinster-aunts would make the trip from the coast this time of year. And Judith would invite her mother, though she believed Mrs. Bradley planned to spend Christmas with friends in Bath.

"But Felix will come, of course," Judith added.

Edward nodded. "When does he arrive?"

"Who can say with Felix? But he shan't miss Mrs. Moore's mincemeat pie, nor the opportunity to wear out his welcome at Brightwell Court—that I do know."

Inwardly, Edward sighed. That was what he was afraid of.

I have been busily employed in preparing for passing Christmas worthily. My beef and mincemeat are ready (of which, my poor neighbors will partake), and my holly and mistletoe gathered.

—LETTER FROM "A WIFE, A MOTHER, AND
AN ENGLISHWOMAN," *EXAMINER*, 1818

Chapter 14

*O*livia witnessed the transformation of Brightwell Court with awe and delight. Mrs. Hinkley, with help from the housemaids and hall boy, dressed the mantels, windows, and doorframes with entwined greens of rosemary, bay, ivy, and yew. The housekeeper then twisted a long garland of holly down the stately staircase. "In remembrance of His crown of thorns," she whispered reverently. Soon, the entire manor was imbued with the spicy scent of greenery.

Doris, ever scheming, hung a kissing bow and a bunch of mistletoe above the threshold of the servants' hall. Mrs. Hinkley forbade that decoration in any of the public rooms upstairs, fearing the vicar would frown upon the pagan tradition.

In the nursery, Olivia guided the children in the cutting of silk and gold paper into stars and streamers with which they festooned their own hearth and walls. She wished she might purchase small gifts for her charges, and for Mrs. Moore besides. *Perhaps next year*, she thought and quickly chastised herself. She would not be at Brightwell Court next year. Her mother would come looking for her any day and only the Lord knew where they would be by next Christmas.

In her spare moments, when the children were otherwise occupied or sleeping, Olivia cut, pinned, and stitched in secret, creating miniature bedclothes, cushions, and pillows for the doll's house. She crafted a tiny embroidery hoop from a small strip of balsa wood, and wound miniature skeins of mending wool from embroidery floss. She painted several miniature landscapes with the supplies in the schoolroom and framed them in old shoe buckles. She even involved Audrey unknowingly, providing her with a tiny piece of canvas and suggesting she try to copy one of the prints on the nursery wall in miniature. Audrey had spent a pleasant afternoon doing so, none the wiser.

When the weather allowed, Olivia bore these small offerings out to the carpentry shop in her cape pocket and left them where Lord Bradley would discover them, both relieved and disappointed when he was not there to receive them in person. She hoped he would be pleased, and imagined the crooked smile that would lift one side of his mouth if he was.

One morning, she had that pleasure. She knocked softly and entered to find him examining one of the wooden blocks he had made for Alexander.

"Ah, Miss Keene," he said. "I was just thinking of you."

Her nerves tingled to attention. Thinking well of her, or . . . ?

"I seem to be missing a few of the blocks I made for Alexander. Have you seen any about?"

"No." She answered easily. Then she noticed he still studied her, as if testing her sincerity. The notion rankled. "Surely you do not accuse me of—"

He raised a placating hand. "I only thought you might have seen where I had mislaid them, or inadvertently picked a few up with a reel of cotton or some such."

"I did not."

He nodded, but he was still searching about the shop, distracted.

Disappointed, she set down the miniature paintings and carpets she had made and turned to go.

His voice stopped her at the door. "These are excellent, Miss Keene. Truly charming. And the cushions fit the settee perfectly. Well done."

She bowed her head in acknowledgment, but felt her pleasure dimmed by the nagging feeling that he had instantly assumed her—trespasser, eavesdropper, thief—responsible for the missing blocks.

❧

On the morning of Christmas Eve, once Olivia had made her bed, washed and dressed, she opened her drawer and, from under a handkerchief, drew forth her mother's small purse. She sat on her bed and opened it on her lap. She picked up the sealed letter and held it up to the weak morning sunlight coming through her window. Nothing was discernable. She looked once more at the script on the outside and ran her fingers over her mother's fine hand. Replacing it, she picked up the old newspaper clipping. She realized this was the announcement of his father's wedding, not the current Lord Bradley's as she had originally guessed. Evidently, *Lord Bradley* was the title the eldest son used until his father died, and then that son became the next earl, the next *Lord Brightwell*. She wondered again why her mother had kept the clipping.

Someone scratched on her door and swung it open before Olivia could react. She quickly closed the purse and looked up to find Mrs. Howe regarding her with a lift of her brow.

Olivia rose, heart pounding. Now what had she done?

She belatedly saw the gown Judith Howe held over her arm. No doubt she needed a lace mended or seam sewn.

"Good morning, Miss Keene."

Olivia wondered again why her mistress addressed her so, but was pleased by this apparent sign of respect.

"I've noticed that you have only the one dress."

Olivia felt her lips part. She looked down, hoping to hide the blush heating her cheeks. Had she embarrassed the family?

Mrs. Howe continued, "As it is Christmas, I thought to give you one of mine."

A cast-off dress? Olivia's pride rebelled.

Her mistress lifted the dark blue gown on her arm. "I shall never again wear this. Once my mourning has passed, I shall need a whole new wardrobe."

The reserved gown certainly befitted Olivia's station. She could hardly imagine Mrs. Howe choosing to wear something so prim and plain before her mourning. Olivia's pride once more urged her to refuse it, but her practical nature compelled her to accept. It was Christmas, after all. And had not it stung when Croome refused her offering? She gave Mrs. Howe a quick smile and curtsy and held forth her hands to receive the gift.

❧

Later that afternoon, Olivia paused at a tall window in the entry hall, drawn by the sounds of horse hooves and carriage wheels outside. It was not the Brightwell carriage, but rather a traveling coach. She watched as a liveried footman handed down an elegant young lady with a large ornate hat and fur-trimmed cloak. Behind her, a meek-looking woman followed, straightening the woman's cloak as she went. Her abigail, no doubt. Who was the lady? Someone invited to celebrate Christmas with the family of course, but who?

She had overheard Judith explain to Audrey plans for a more subdued Christmas this year. Lord Bradley would host in his father's stead while Judith, Olivia guessed, would act the part of hostess.

Someone grabbed her arm, and Olivia started, but it was only Doris, feather duster in hand.

"Come on, love," she whispered. "They don't want you greetin' their guest."

She pulled Olivia into a nearby closet, just as Hodges swept into the hall and opened the front doors. Dory closed the closet door, but for a few inches, and through it peered into the hall where the guest was being received.

With a sinking feeling, Olivia watched over Dory's shoulder as the elegant young lady slowly unfastened her cloak. The tall, graceful woman had caramel-brown hair, fine features, and large brown eyes.

The cape unfastened, Hodges took it from her. Her ivory gown shone with beadwork around a low-cut bodice. A large cameo necklace hung at her throat and sparkling gems encircled her gloved wrists.

Olivia almost whispered, "Who is she?" But before she slipped, Doris said in hushed tones, "That is Miss Harrington. Beautiful, is she not? Her father is an admiral and very wealthy. They say Lord Bradley will marry her for her dowry, even though she is beneath him."

Rich and beautiful . . . The thought pinched like a tight shoe. Olivia fidgeted behind the door. Perhaps Miss Harrington was the important matter Lord Bradley had mentioned, the one that ought to be settled soon—a matter that might be complicated by rumors and threats of exposure.

Suddenly Hodges opened the closet door and Olivia stifled a gasp. Dory put a finger to her lips. The man looked mildly startled to find them there, but as Doris and Olivia flattened themselves against the wall, he moved past them to hang up the lady's cloak.

He then backed from the closet and shut the door without a word. They would be reprimanded later, no doubt.

"Don't worry, ducky," Doris whispered. "You're not in for it. Maids are supposed to make themselves invisible."

Doris cracked open the door again, and Olivia saw that Lord Bradley had joined Miss Harrington in the hall. He bowed before her, then took her hands in his.

"Where is the admiral?" he asked.

"Spending a few days with an ailing uncle, but he insisted I come as planned without him."

"I am very glad you did," Lord Bradley smiled warmly, and Olivia's stomach knotted. He offered Miss Harrington his arm and escorted her from view.

Watching them go, Doris said on a sigh, "A shame she's vain as an alabaster bust." She smirked. "And about as softhearted."

Olivia knew she should hope it wasn't true.

Soon after, the Tugwell family and the Lintons arrived to share in an evening of fireside festivities. When Olivia ushered Audrey and Andrew down to the drawing room, she paused in the threshold to admire the room. The walls were hung with gilt-framed portraits over panels of crimson and green silk. The high windows wore matching draperies, and the chairs and settees were upholstered in rich, apple green velvet. Candles and a crystal chandelier glowed and reflected in the large looking glass over the marble chimney-piece. The Tugwell boys sat clustered around a card-playing table and were beginning a game of oranges and limes while the adults took tea before a roaring fire. Mr. Tugwell smiled warmly at Olivia from across the room, but his sister's cool glance spoilt the pleasure of the moment.

Olivia recognized the elder Mr. Linton as the master of the hunt, and his stout son George as the taunting roan rider, but knew it unlikely that either man would recognize her. She turned to go, but Judith Howe asked her to stay to accompany the children on the pianoforte.

Mr. Tugwell's eldest son, Amos, was home from school, and he led his four younger brothers in a sweet harmonized performance of "Adeste Fideles," which brought tears to Olivia's eyes as she played. Audrey and Andrew, dressed smartly for the occasion, sang "While Shepherds Watched Their Flocks by Night." They matched the Tugwells' enthusiasm, if not their talent.

Afterward, Osborn brought in a tray laid with Christmas fare— widgeon, preserved ginger, black butter, sandwiches, and tarts. The adults sipped spiced cider and toddies, while the children drank milk punch and syllabub. Olivia could almost taste her mother's thick, sweet syllabub, though none was offered her now.

Olivia's Christmases at home had been much quieter affairs, but still, Olivia missed the warm comfort of Christmases past, of sitting beside the hearth with her mother and father, roasting chestnuts, talking, and opening small gifts. Her father had usually remained with them all night, rarely taking himself to the Crown and Crow on that holy eve. Sometimes he would give in to Mother's urging and sing "Adeste Fideles," and Olivia never ceased to be amazed at his sweet, haunting voice. If only all of their days could have been as pleasant.

Audrey begged for a Christmas ball, saying they had danced last year and could they not do so again?

Finally the adults roused themselves to the task. Lord Bradley, Felix, George Linton, and Mr. Tugwell made quick work of moving aside the heavy armchairs and rolling up the carpet, not wishing to give the servants extra work on Christmas Eve. Again, Olivia was asked to play. They made five couples, Edward and Miss Harrington, Felix and homely Miss Charity Linton, Mr. Tugwell and his sister, Augusta, George Linton and his mother, Amos Tugwell and Audrey. Judith, claiming her widowhood, and the elder Mr. Linton his gout, contented themselves to watch.

Andrew and the younger Tugwell boys went back to their game of wind the jack.

Olivia wished her playing was better than it was. She had never played for a real ball before, only for the school's dancing master at Miss Cresswell's. She played a country dance and the heel-toe rigadoon, but then Miss Tugwell approached the pianoforte and said, "It would be so much easier to dance were the meter regular and the notes sharp. I shall relieve you, if you please."

Ears and cheeks heating, Olivia rose and dipped a brief curtsy and turned toward the door, hoping to make a quick escape. Mr. Tugwell's voice stopped her. "Miss Keene. Will you dance?"

An under nurse asked to dance with the family? Even she knew such a thing was not done. An awkward silence swelled. Olivia shook her head, her whole face burning now.

"But my partner has deserted me. Do have pity on me."

Several in the party exchanged scandalized glances, Miss Harrington among them.

Augusta Tugwell clanged a few sharp notes by way of introduction. "Do not be ridiculous, Charles."

"Oh, I shall take pity on you, Mr. Tugwell," Judith Howe said, rising. She gave Olivia a quick look of understanding, which eased Olivia's embarrassment. Mrs. Howe addressed the vicar once more. "That is, if you do not think it improper?"

"Not at all, madam. You are not so recent a widow." He bowed.

A widow and a widower, Olivia thought fleetingly, but could not envision the two as future husband and wife.

The next dance commenced with Miss Tugwell playing a vigorous and precise Scottish reel. Its militant pace put Olivia in mind of soldiers marching off to war.

Dismissed and feeling lonely, Olivia stole downstairs, hoping to find Mrs. Moore and share a glass of cider with the friendly woman by the warm kitchen hearth. As she passed the servants' hall, a figure shot out from the doorway and clasped her about the shoulders. Startled, she shrieked, just as Johnny kissed her full on the mouth.

He smiled impishly and looked above her head. "Yer under the kissin' bow, Livie. So don't slap me, like I see in yer eyes a mind to."

Her hand itched to do just that, but she resisted.

He frowned suddenly. "Did you make a sound just now?"

Oh, no . . . She hesitated, lifting a shrug.

He grinned. "Kissing you has made me addlepated, that's all." He leaned in to kiss her again, but she pulled away.

Shaking her head as she walked on, Olivia realized Johnny could not have known she would come belowstairs. For whom had he been lying in wait? Perhaps she should have slapped him after all.

Coming to the kitchen door, Olivia heard the hum of quiet voices. She paused to peek around the doorjamb. Mrs. Moore sat at a stool pulled up to the table, elbows resting atop it, hands around a large cup before her. Across from her sat Mr. Croome, taking the glass of cider Olivia had hoped for herself. She was stunned to see him there, head bowed, apparently listening to whatever Mrs. Moore was saying. Olivia's selfish disappointment gave way to a nobler emotion, and only the holy day could account for it. For she was glad the crusty hermit was not alone on Christmas Eve.

Suddenly the man flew to his feet, nearly toppling the stool he had so recently occupied. "I will thank you, madam, never to ask me again."

"Avery . . ." Mrs. Moore soothed, and in low tones attempted to cajole the man into sitting down once more. Olivia did not remain to see if she succeeded.

Giving up, Olivia climbed back upstairs. She wished nothing more than to go directly to her room and fall into bed, but knew she ought to check on the children. Returning to the withdrawing room, she peered in at the partially open doorway. The ball had apparently concluded. She heard only the hum of adult conversation and the occasional burst of youthful laughter. The adults were sitting once more before the fire, while at the table Audrey sat with the Tugwell boys, playing a game of dominoes. It was evident from her wide, adoring eyes that she thought Amos Tugwell a romantic figure.

But where was Andrew? Had he already gone upstairs?

Olivia turned back to the corridor and saw him. Curled up on the padded bench upon which the Tugwell boys had piled their coats, fast asleep. Poor lamb was exhausted. She lowered herself to her haunches before him. "Andrew?" she whispered, forgetting for a moment that she was not to speak. The boy didn't rouse. She gently stroked the brown hair from his forehead. She hated the thought of waking the child, but he was too heavy for her to carry up so many stairs.

"Shall I carry him?" a voice asked.

Startled, she looked up. Lord Bradley stood above her. She had not heard him step into the corridor. Had he heard her speak Andrew's name?

She nodded and silently mouthed, *Thank you.*

With gentle ease he bent and lifted the boy and carried him toward the stairs. Olivia followed.

On their way up to the nursery, Lord Bradley's breathing grew laboured, but he bore the child without pause. When they reached the sleeping chamber, Olivia hurried to assist, pulling back the bedclothes as he laid Andrew on his bed.

"Thank you," she whispered, this time aloud.

"A great many stairs, that," he said, unashamedly resting his hands on his knees to catch his breath.

"I am sorry. I should have tried—"

"No, of course you should not have. I am only sorry to be so woefully lathered. I shall have to take more regular exercise, I see."

Olivia removed Andrew's shoes, wondering where Becky was, but somehow glad the girl was not present just then.

She was surprised when Lord Bradley remained. "I shall see to him, my lord. I am sure you wish to return to your party."

He blew out a breath between his cheeks. "Not as much as I ought to."

He helped her remove Andrew's pantaloons and coat. His miniature neckcloth had long since been discarded somewhere. "Let us leave him sleep as he is," Lord Bradley whispered.

She nodded and loosened his shirt at the neck. The billowing white shirt, now untucked, resembled a nightdress at any rate. She pulled up the bedclothes under Andrew's chin. Still Lord Bradley lingered. He bent low and brushed the boy's forelock, much as she had done downstairs. How would it feel, she wondered, to be so gently touched by him? Or to stroke his fair hair with her fingers?

"He is very like his father," he said softly.

"Is he?"

"Yes. The dark hair, the cowlick, the impish face—all very like Dominick."

"You knew him well?"

"Fairly well, yes, though he was six or seven years older than I. Our London house was near to his, and we spent a great deal of time together during several seasons. Dominick was ever kind to me—even before he knew I had a beautiful cousin he might one day marry. He was in love with his Jeannette then and married her when he was still quite young. He was brought very low when she died. I admit I was surprised he rallied so quickly and married Judith only eighteen months later. I should not recover from such a loss so quickly."

Nor would I, she thought. "But then, he had two children who needed a mamma."

His expression darkened. "Yes." He hesitated, thought better of whatever he was about to say, and instead straightened. "I do appreciate the care you are giving my young cousins, Miss Keene. I am sure their stepmother does as well, if she has not said so."

"Thank you, my lord. It is my pleasure." She realized anew that Audrey and Andrew had lost both mother and father. Poor lambs! No wonder Lord Bradley felt so deeply for them.

He pursed his lips, then said quietly, "I find it interesting that you address me as 'my lord' when you know better."

Her heart pounded to hear him speak of the secret they never discussed. She said, "You call me Miss Keene."

He considered this. "A sign of respect, perhaps?"

She nodded, feeling warmth flood her body.

"How odd it is," he mused. "Carrying on . . . pretending everything is as it once was." He inhaled deeply, then stepped to the door. Once more he hesitated. "And for whatever it is worth, I thought your playing well. I am sorry you were so rudely dismissed."

She felt her ears heat at the recollection. "Think nothing of it. No doubt Miss Tugwell was right."

"Well, good night, Miss Keene. And happy Christmas."

A few minutes later, Olivia closed the door to the sleeping chamber quietly behind her, wondering how late Audrey would remain downstairs with the guests. Expecting the dark nursery to be empty, she started at the sight of a shadowy figure within. Had Lord Bradley not taken himself back down to his guests as she had thought?

But it was Felix's voice that rumbled through the darkness. "You know, Livie, when I came up here a few minutes ago, I could have sworn I heard two voices—in secret tête-à-tête. I waited in the shadows to see who would come out after my cousin and am confounded to find it was you."

Heart pounding, Olivia shrugged and shook her head.

"Not your voice?"

Olivia stared at him, nerves jangling.

Felix stepped closer. "Sticking to the mute bit, hmm?"

Olivia nodded.

His voice took on a silky sweetness. "So, if I were to, say, take your hands"—he pressed her hands in his—"you could not ask me to let you go?"

She stood stone-still, her whole body tensing.

"And if I wanted to hold you"—he pulled her against him, a surprisingly strong arm grasping her about the waist—"you could not refuse?"

She tried to pull free but could not break his grip.

"And if I were to kiss you . . . you could not protest?" He backed her against the wall, his voice a husky whisper now. "Don't protest, sweet Livie. Please. It is Christmas, after all." He leaned near, aiming for her mouth. She turned her face away, and he pressed a hard kiss against her neck. Olivia struggled, and finally, pulling one arm free, punched him in the eye.

Felix howled and cursed, releasing her to cover his face with his hands. "Livie!" he cried, incredulous.

She was already striding quickly from the room. His voice, calling after her, took on a pleading tone, "You needn't have done that. I was only teasing you. Don't go making a fuss!"

Was he afraid she would march straight to his cousin and report his behavior? Perhaps she should. She wondered briefly which man feared the other more. But who would believe her word against Felix's?

She would take Lord Bradley's secret to the grave, but if Felix Bradley dared touch her again, she would remain silent no longer.

We had 12 dances & 5, 6, or 7 couples. We then had a game of Hunt
the Slipper and ended the day with sandwiches and tarts . . .
I must not omit saying that the little ones dressed up as usual and
sang Christmas Carols.

—FANNY AUSTEN KNIGHT, CHRISTMAS EVE, 1808

Chapter 15

On Christmas morning, Olivia arose and ate a leisurely breakfast in her room while Becky, all apologies for disappearing the
night before, bathed and dressed the children on her own. Olivia
wondered where her mother was spending the day, and lifted her
teacup in a silent Christmas salute.

She again eyed the dark blue gown hanging on the back of
her door. She would wear it, she decided, and stood to dress. The
gown fit her well, though she was more slender than Mrs. Howe.
She guessed the woman had been thinner before her lying-in with
Alexander. To make the gown her own, Olivia wore her new lace
tippet—a Christmas present from Mrs. Moore—as a collar.

Stepping into the nursery, she saw Becky struggling to arrange
Audrey's hair, so Olivia brushed and pinned it herself. Audrey wore

a new long-sleeved pelisse over a printed muslin frock. Andrew wore his Sunday pantaloons, waistcoat, and new green coat.

Olivia escorted the children down to the breakfast room, where they were to join the adults before church.

After the tussle of the previous night, Olivia was relieved to find Felix conspicuously absent. Miss Harrington was not present either, though she was staying at Brightwell Court for several days.

Upon the sideboard rested a Christmas box for each child.

Opening it, Audrey's eyes grew as wide as the coins. "Two guineas."

"We are rich!" Andrew exclaimed, lifting his guineas high.

"Alexander has his as well," Judith explained. "But as he tried to eat them, I shall keep them until he is older."

Lord Bradley laid a hand on each child's head and added warmly, "From Lord and Lady Brightwell. Left especially for you before they departed."

"Ah . . . Christmas in Rome," Judith sighed. Then she turned to Olivia waiting by the door, the children's coats in her arms. She surveyed her figure, head to toe. "You look very well today, Miss Keene," she said.

Self-conscious, Olivia smiled and dipped a curtsy.

Lord Bradley surveyed her as well, but his expression was inscrutable. Olivia was relieved the woman did not announce to Lord Bradley and the hovering Osborn that Olivia wore one of her castoffs.

Felix stumbled in with rumpled hair and a hint of orange whiskers on his chin. The young man looked worse for drink from the night before. Olivia knew the look—greenish pale complexion, hollow eyes. She also noticed his bruised eyelid, which she could attribute to drink as well, at least indirectly.

Judith greeted her brother pleasantly. "Good morning, Felix. Mrs. Moore made mincemeat pie, your favorite."

"All I want is coffee."

"What happened to your eye, Felix?" Lord Bradley asked.

"Oh." Felix stole the briefest glance at Olivia. "I, uh, ran into an unexpected obstacle in the dark."

He poured coffee with less than steady hands. "I shall be my old self after coffee, a few more hours' sleep, a bath and shave. I won't manage church, I am afraid." He stirred sugar into his cup. "I would not wait for Miss Harrington either. To hear her father tell it, her little feet do not hit the floor until twelve most days."

Breakfast completed, Mrs. Howe, Lord Bradley, and the children rode in the carriage the short distance up the lane and around the high wall that separated Brightwell Court from St. Mary's. Glad to be allowed to attend, Olivia walked beside Doris along with the handful of other servants who could be spared from their duties.

Once inside the vestibule, Olivia followed Dory up into the gallery to sit with the other servants. She had never sat in a gallery before. At home, she and her mother sat on the main floor of the chapel with the small clutch of congregants who came out for Sunday services. Her father not among them.

Doris patted her knee and they settled in for the service. There was a feeling of camaraderie there in the gallery, the silent smiles shared among servants from different houses, who saw one another on occasional Sundays and rarely any other time. There were also winks and good-natured elbows in the side of a fellow groom or housemaid. Doris, she soon realized, attended only to flirt with menservants she would otherwise not see. The girl was fellow-mad.

Down below, on the second pew from the front, Olivia saw Lord Bradley, flanked by Audrey and Andrew. Beside Audrey, Judith stood in a black mantle and smart black hat with a half veil of silver gossamer lace. Alexander was too young to be quiet for church and had been left home with Nurse Peale. Olivia wondered how Andrew would manage to be still so long. How unlike his usual self he looked fidgeting in his Sunday coat, brown hair slicked down. Audrey, however, stood sedately and gracefully in her bonnet and gown, her gloved hand in Lord Bradley's. They looked like a family—husband, wife, children. Would they be one someday, once Judith's mourning was past?

Mr. Tugwell kept his sermon surprisingly brief, saying only thoughts of the sumptuous feast awaiting him could still his tongue on such a glorious day. He reminded the congregation that he and his good sister were once again holding an annual open hearth, and all were invited to drop in for a buffet meal.

At the close of service, Olivia stood and glanced once more down at Lord Bradley and the Howes, who were rising and gathering their things and smiling at their neighbors. Lord Bradley reached across the pew and shook hands with a man behind him. As the man turned, Olivia started. The man's profile struck her as familiar. She had seen him before. The man glanced up into the gallery, and Olivia quickly turned her head, hoping her bonnet would conceal her face. She did not wish to be recognized—could *not* be recognized. Who was the man? She wanted to look again, but dared not. Someone from home? Someone from Withington visiting family or friends? Someone who knew Lord Bradley. . . . Olivia's heart pounded, and she prayed the man would not be following them home for Christmas dinner.

Feigning a search for something in her reticule, Olivia waved Doris on and managed to be the last person to exit the gallery. As she hoped, the familiar gentleman—along with most everyone else—was gone.

At the door, Mr. Tugwell exchanged well wishes or a "Happy Christmas" with the last few members of his congregation as they filed out. Miss Tugwell stood at his elbow, handing out small bags tied in rag ribbon. How generous. She noticed Miss Tugwell eyeing each person as she offered a gift. When she surveyed Olivia's new gown she whispered, "You haven't use for wheat, I trust, Miss Keene?"

Thinking of Mr. Croome, Olivia nodded and held out her hand.

Augusta Tugwell ignored it. "Foolish notion in these times. When I think of the price of wheat!"

Mr. Tugwell glanced over, eyes flicking from Olivia's extended hand to the bag in his sister's clutches. "Sister, Miss Keene is awaiting her gift." He smiled at Olivia while Augusta Tugwell only sniffed and relinquished the bag.

❦

Edward found himself foolishly nervous while waiting for his young cousins to open their presents. He certainly hoped Miss Keene was correct and Audrey would like the doll's house, though she was not a little girl any longer.

"Mind your expectations," he said. "These are only things I made in the carpentry shop. Nothing new from the London shops, I am afraid."

Miss Harrington sat with perfect posture in the armchair beside his. She looked refreshed and elegant in a primrose gown with a white fichu tucked into the neckline. Felix sat slumped on the settee, more clear-eyed and certainly better groomed than he had been that morning. Judith perched on the settee's other end, little Alexander on the floor before her, sitting up of his own accord, but with his mamma nearby to catch him should he topple.

Judith set Edward's wrapped gift before the little boy, but Alexander seemed more interested in grabbing the silver buckles on his mother's slippers. Judith tore away the stiff paper for him, revealing the set of blocks, each carved with a letter, number, and animal.

"Look, Alexander. Cousin Edward has made such handsome blocks for you." She held one up. "What a charming fox, Edward. I am impressed. Look, Alexander, F for fox. And this one has a D on it and a very fine duckling."

Edward stared at the blocks as Judith fussed over them, still as confused as he had been when, two by two, they had reappeared in the shop. He had carved simple numbers and letters on each. But now they bore detailed images of animals as well.

Had Miss Keene carved the blocks as well as sewn all the cushions and draperies so skillfully? If so, she had never said a word. Somehow he could not imagine Miss Keene with a carving knife. But who else would have done so?

"Did you really make those yourself?" Miss Harrington asked.

Edward hesitated. "I had help with the carving."

Felix held up his hands. "Don't look at me."

"An anonymous Christmas elf," Edward said dryly.

Without waiting to be asked, Andrew ripped the paper from his elongated parcel. "Stab me!" he cried, mimicking his uncle Felix.

"Andrew, that is not polite," Judith admonished.

But the boy paid little heed. "A brand-new cricket bat! A ball too." He lifted the ball as if to give it a good whack.

Edward quickly stilled his small arms. "That is an outside gift, young man."

"Awww, but it is winter!"

"We shall bundle up tomorrow and see how it cracks, all right?"

Andrew dug the toe of his shoe into the carpet a bit sullenly. "All right . . ."

"Is it my turn?" Audrey asked quietly, looking up at her cousin with shy eyes.

Edward nodded, feeling his palms dampen as he watched the girl carefully begin to tug at the cloth covering her gift.

"I am afraid I hadn't enough paper for yours."

Slowly Audrey pulled the cover toward her.

"Just give it a good rip, Aud!" Andrew encouraged. "Shall I?"

"Leave your sister be, Andrew," Judith said.

Please let her like it, Edward thought. He almost wished sophisticated Sybil Harrington were not on hand to witness his failure, if failure it would be.

Audrey's eyes grew round and rather stunned as she took in the house, which came up nearly to her shoulders. "It is Brightwell Court," she breathed. She looked at him, uncertain.

His spirits fell. *She does not like it.*

"Is it really for me?" she asked.

"Yes, though if you are too old for dolls, I shall not be offend—"

"Look!" Audrey cried, kneeling before the open stories, the many chambers, and even a grand staircase. "There is the drawing room, where we are right now. And up there is the nursery!"

Edward felt the scrutiny of others and turned to find both Judith and Miss Harrington studying him with stunned incredulity.

"How long did it take you to build this?" Judith asked.

He waved aside her awe. "Oh, I have worked on it for several months, on and off, when I had the time."

Audrey looked up at her stepmother. "Look! It is the very settee you are seated upon. It even has a cushion!"

Judith's fair brows rose as she looked from the miniature piece of furniture to Edward. "If you tell me you made that as well, I shall not believe you."

"I had some help with the sewing and furnishings."

"The Christmas elf again?" Miss Harrington asked, one dark brow quirked high.

He thought it wiser not to mention any names.

Audrey looked up with wide eyes. "I painted this miniature landscape myself and never guessed what it was for!"

After several more minutes of exclaiming over favorite details, Audrey stood before him and made a graceful curtsy. "Thank you, Cousin Edward. It is the finest gift I have ever received."

Judith looked mildly offended, opened her pink lips, then shut them again.

Edward had not thought to outdo anybody. He simply wanted to please these children, these offspring of his friend, gone from this world. Did they not deserve some special happiness this day?

He bowed to Audrey in his best courtly manner, and then took her hand in his and pressed it. "You are most welcome, my dear Audrey."

When he looked up once more, Judith's expression had transformed into one of speculative approval. Miss Harrington looked from Judith to him, and appeared not pleased at all.

As the children began to play with the doll's house, Felix turned to him and asked, "Remember that raft you built, Edward?"

"Sink me, not that old yarn."

A mischievous sparkle lit Felix's green eyes. "You see, Miss Harrington, the great Noah here built us a fine raft when we were lads. Big enough to hold the two of us and that terrier—what was its name?"

"I don't recall."

"At all events, we put in near the Brightwell Bridge and the current bore us swiftly. Only when we passed the church, there where the river widens, did Edward realize he had neglected to fashion either rudder or oar!"

Self-conscious, Edward chuckled and shook his head.

"But the raft was seaworthy, I admit," Felix continued. "Took us all the way to the Arlington Mill and would have taken us further had Edward not grabbed hold of a low-lying branch and pulled us into the mill leat." He eyed his cousin. "Don't tell me you don't remember."

"I remember the miller was none too pleased. That I do recall."

"Whatever happened to that raft, I wonder?" Felix said. "I hope Andrew does not stumble upon it or we should never see that wag pirate again."

"Don't fear. I am sure that old thing has gone the way of most everything else I built in those days. Mother quietly disposed of it while I was at Oxford."

"Never say so! Such a work of art. Although after that excursion, I am quite sure you shan't have a career in shipbuilding."

"Nor would I want one."

Felix leaned back in his chair. "You have no need of a career, of course. It is only I who must find some way to eke out my existence."

"You make it sound as if you shall have to earn a living from the soil or some such," Miss Harrington said kindly. "Surely with a degree from Balliol it shall not come to that."

"No," he said. "I cannot fancy Felix Bradley, yeoman farmer."

"Nor I," Judith said.

"What will you take up?" Miss Harrington asked. "Have you decided?"

"I have not. I have no interest in the church. Detest the thought of fighting in a war. Haven't a head for the law. . . ."

"Come, now," Edward said. "You are as clever as the next fellow and will have your degree in due course. There must be something you are interested in."

"I am interested in a great many things. But none with prodigious remuneration. I suppose I had my heart set on remaining a gentleman, as my father and his father before him."

"And why not?" Judith said blithely.

"Because, as you well know, Jude, Father left us with very little but debts to live on. Uncle is generous indeed, but I cannot expect him to support a wife and children as well."

"Wife and children?" Judith straightened, suddenly alert. "My goodness, Felix, are you engaged? I had not the slightest notion you planned to marry soon."

Her brother flushed deeply. "No. Not engaged. No plans as yet. Only . . . hopes."

He smiled almost shyly at Miss Harrington. "I have not yet had the good fortune of meeting the perfect woman, as has Edward."

Miss Harrington's delicate complexion glowed pink while Edward grew uneasy.

Felix slapped Edward on the shoulder, then added with bravado, "But Edward won't be the only Bradley to marry well. Upon my soul he won't."

Olivia sneaked away to leave the bag of wheat on Croome's doorstep. As she turned to leave, she saw him bent low at the far edge of the clearing, laying a wreath of yew boughs on the ground. She wondered what he was about but, recalling his temper, decided not to interrupt him.

When she returned to the nursery, she was surprised to find Lord Bradley sitting on the settee beside Alexander and his new blocks.

He looked up when she entered. "I had no notion you could carve as well as sew, Miss Keene. Your talents are legion."

She frowned and, after glancing about to make certain no one else was in the nursery, whispered, "I am afraid you overestimate me, my lord. I carved nothing. I thought you did."

"I carved simple numbers and letters on each. And now they have animals carved into them as well. This H block has quite a detailed hound on it." He picked another block at random from the stack. "And the B has a bird of some type." He lifted the block toward her. "What do you make out?"

Olivia walked near and took the block from his outstretched hand, examining the skillful carving. To her, it looked very like a partridge.

The thought of animals brought the old gamekeeper to mind. "You don't think Mr. Croome . . . ?"

"I would be exceedingly surprised."

Olivia nodded. So would she.

Lord Bradley rose and cleared his throat. "Well, thank you

again for all your assistance." He withdrew a folded bank note and extended it toward her. "Here is a little something for your trouble."

She ought to have been grateful but instead felt oddly deflated to be offered payment for what had been an act of friendship. To be reminded once more of the true nature of their relationship—that she was simply another servant in his employ.

"No thank you," she said, and turned away.

Olivia spent the afternoon helping the children fill Christmas boxes for the servants, which they would disperse on Boxing Day tomorrow. Then she took Audrey and Andrew down to the dining room, where the family gathered for Christmas dinner at the early hour of four o'clock.

After the meal, all of the servants were invited in to share a glass and toast the season. How strange it felt to stand in the dining room with Mrs. Moore, Doris, Johnny, and the others, as invited guests. Croome was not among them. Nor did anyone seem to miss him.

Audrey and Andrew sang carols once more, this time without accompaniment. As they sang, Olivia felt Johnny's eyes on her but did not look his way. She did peek at Doris, who winked at her. Martha, she noticed, watched the children with tears in her eyes.

When they finished, the menservants dipped into their coat pockets, and the women into their apron pockets, and the children collected the proffered coins. Perhaps seeing her confusion, Mrs. Moore leaned close and explained in a whisper that this money would later be given to the poor. Olivia wished she had known. She would have brought down one of her last remaining coins, still tacked inside the little purse. Olivia hoped her mother did not miss the money. Did her mother miss her?

This was the first Christmas the two of them had spent apart, but Olivia feared it only the beginning of many lonely Christmases to come.

Where was she?

Olivia lifted her glass to her mouth. She had no taste for wine, but she hoped the action would conceal the trembling of her lips.

Chapter 16

*T*welfth-night festivities over, guests gone, and the house quiet once more, Edward sat down to enjoy his coffee and newspaper in peace. Hodges came in as stealthily as ever and held the letter tray before him.

Edward picked up the single piece of post and thanked the butler, who disappeared as silently as he had come. Glancing at the letter, Edward recognized the handwriting and noted the unfamiliar postal markings. The ink was smeared, but he believed it read, *Roma*.

Across the table, Judith eyed the letter over her teacup. "How exotic-looking. Who is it from?"

"Father."

Nibbling daintily at her toasted muffin, Judith regarded him with eager eyes. "I do hope they are enjoying their time abroad."

He hoped it wasn't bad news. With hands suddenly damp and clumsy, he broke the sealing wax and unfolded the letter.

My dear Edward,

I am grieved to inform you that your mother has left us—left her suffering and this world for brighter shores. She died peacefully in her sleep, with me holding her hand. I am returning home directly and should arrive by the tenth, God and tides willing.

Your loving father
BRIGHTWELL

A spear of grief pierced him. His mother . . . gone. Had she been frightened of dying . . . or accepting of her fate? Thank God she had died peacefully, and with her husband by her side.

Some adolescent part of him was relieved to have been spared the sight of his mother's death, but the nobler part of his heart wished he had been there. To have heard any last words she might have said to him. To have told her he loved her. No matter the past. No matter what. To say, "Until we meet again."

He recalled their tender parting as she left for Italy. How glad he was that he had kissed her cheek and bid her a fond farewell, not guessing it would be their last. *Almighty God,* he prayed, *please comfort my father.*

"Edward?" Judith asked. "What is it?"

He swallowed the lump in his throat. "Lady Brightwell has died."

Judith's hand flew to her heart. "Oh, Edward! I am sorry." She leapt to her feet and stepped around the table, laying a hand on his shoulder. He reached up and pressed it with his own.

"Thank you."

After a moment, he stood and excused himself, wanting to be alone. He went upstairs, shut himself in his study and there read the letter once more. He noticed that his father had ended with his title. A title Edward had once thought would be his one day. And now it might all be gone. His future. His very name. But at the moment, he could not care. He laid his forehead on his fist and wept, for his mother, for his bereaved father, for himself—a lost boy losing the only mother he had ever known.

❦

News of Lady Brightwell's death spread quickly through the manor. Olivia ached over Lord Brightwell's loss of his wife. For Lord Bradley's loss as well. She wondered how he was. Wished she might somehow comfort him. If she were to receive such news of *her* mother, she knew she would be devastated indeed.

The following day dawned dreary and rainy, which seemed to echo the general mood of the house. In the afternoon, the melancholy children even succumbed to rare naps. Not allowed that luxury, Olivia searched the schoolroom for another book for Andrew. Finding none to suit, she wrote the title she sought on a piece of paper.

Mrs. Howe, dressed in dull black bombazine, entered the nursery, delivering Alexander back to Nurse Peale. Olivia politely held the note before her mistress with a questioning lift of her brows. Mrs. Howe assured her they'd had a copy of *The History of Little Goody Two-Shoes* in the nursery, but perhaps it had been returned to the library by an overzealous housemaid. Declaring her intention to return to her own room to nap as well, Judith stepped to the door.

"Has she your leave, then, to go into his lordship's library?" Nurse Peale asked.

"Yes, yes." Mrs. Howe waved her hand dismissively. "There is no one to disturb."

Lighting a candle lamp against the darkening rooms, Olivia made her way downstairs to the library. She knocked softly and, when no one answered, let herself in. The muted aromas of cigars, leather, and musty draperies greeted her.

Lifting her candle high, she surveyed the room. Tall bookcases were fitted between draped windows and across the entire rear wall. At the front of the room stood an impressive desk, and two high-backed chairs faced a dark fireplace.

Placing her candle on the table near the wall of books, Olivia began skimming the titles. She felt self-conscious and presumptuous about poking about the earl's library but reminded herself she was looking for a book for the children.

Suddenly the library door opened behind her, and Olivia whirled about. An older gentleman stumbled in with his own candle lamp, clearly exhausted and dressed in a rumpled suit of clothes. Setting down his lamp, he slumped into a chair and did not even seem aware that she was there. *Lord Brightwell*, she realized. For a long moment, Olivia found she could not move, could not take her eyes off the bent, blond-grey head, nor the agony etched in the wrinkled brow.

Remembered images filled her mind. She saw the earl holding his wife, comforting her with gentle words, tenderly stroking her cheek and kissing her. She had never known a husband could so love a wife, and now he had lost her.

Impulsively, Olivia ran to him. She knelt before his chair and gently took his limp hand in her own.

His eyes flew open in surprise.

"My lord," she whispered, all vows of silence forgotten. "I am so sorry." Tears blurred her vision, obscuring and then magnifying his reaction.

He squinted hard; then his eyes widened, and his mouth parted in shock. Olivia read his thunderstruck expression as revulsion that a servant should address him. Touch him.

She released his hand, her face growing hot, and lowered her eyes. "I am sorry," she whispered again, rising to her feet.

"Miss Keene!" came a stunned gasp. Judith Howe stood in the threshold, hand on the door latch. "What in the world are you doing? Return to the nursery at once!"

Head bowed, Olivia walked quickly toward the door, not missing the look of apologetic concern Judith gave Lord Brightwell. "I did not know you had returned, Uncle. I shall see that you are not disturbed further."

Olivia felt two sets of eyes follow her from the room.

When the summons came the next morning, Olivia stiffened, but was not surprised. She had been expecting it. *I acted on impulse,* she silently defended herself. *I meant no harm.* What would Lord Bradley be angrier about, she fretted, as she took the stairs down. That she had dared speak with his father, or that she had spoken at all?

She entered the study as bid, shut the door, and stood rigidly before his desk.

Lord Bradley rose. "I wish to speak to you about my father," he began evenly.

Olivia lifted her chin, holding her head high.

"Miss Keene?"

She met his gaze coolly, making a great effort to show no emotion.

"Though one might never guess it from looking at you," he said wryly, "my father seems to think you are quite a compassionate young woman. What did you say to him last night?"

She stared at him, bewildered.

"Yes, he told us you spoke to him. Judith assured him he must have been distraught—imagined it—because you are a *dumb mute.*"

He pronounced the final words with relish.

"Tell me what you said to make such an impression."

Olivia felt her brow furrow, as perplexed by the earl's supposed reaction as Lord Bradley clearly was.

"All I said was how sorry I was."

He raised a brow. "What else?"

"Nothing." Her mind scrambled to recall further details.

An odd light crept into his eyes. "Then what did you *do*? Show me. Show me what you did, what you said, and how you said it."

She huffed in frustration. "But I cannot! He walked in and caught me unawares. The grief on his face was so devastating, his love for your mother so obvious, I was *moved* to act. It was an impulse. I did not think—"

He stepped around the desk and leaned back against it, arms crossed. "Show me."

"But you are not—" She stopped suddenly as a swift ache swelled in her chest. How could she be worried about defending herself when his mother had just died? The only mother he had ever known. She knew what it was like to love and miss a mother. It was ever-present pain.

Unbidden, tears filled her eyes. The man before her was pretending to be so hard, so aloof, but inside he was a boy who had just lost his mamma.

Edward saw the transformation cross her countenance and stared, mesmerized. When her eyes filled with tears, his chest tightened and his own eyes burned. He watched silently as she approached and stood before him, eyes wide, face pale and pained. She placed her slim fingers on his hand and drew it into both of hers, enveloping it in her warm grasp.

Edward drew in a shaky breath.

"I am sorry, my lord," she whispered, gaze locked into his. "I am so sorry."

Edward sank into her vivid blue eyes, finding beauty and empathy there, solace and peace. For a moment, he forgot his father, forgot his mother, forgot everything.

When he did not move or speak, Miss Keene laid her soft cheek against his hand. As Edward gazed down at her lovely profile, his free hand lifted of its own accord, as if to stroke her hair. He barely resisted the impulse.

"It must be so hard to lose your mother," she murmured.

He tensed immediately. This had been no ploy to seek her sympathy. He did not need a servant's pity or attentions, no matter how lovely she was.

He straightened and said sternly, "We were not speaking of me."

She quickly dropped his hand and stepped back, unable to meet his eyes, clearly embarrassed to find herself in such an intimate position—a position she had initiated.

He would not reveal how her nearness affected him. Would not be overcome as his father had been. "I must say," he began, hoping his voice would not waver and betray him. "I am very impressed with your acting ability. You might have a future in the theatre if you like. I can see why Father was taken with you, a woman half his age throwing herself at him."

"It was not like that."

"And you spoke to him!"

"I could not help it, I—"

"How many others have you spoken to?" Edward felt his anger rising but knew it had little to do with the fact that Miss Keene had spoken a few words to his father. It was his father's reaction to her that annoyed him. And if he were honest with himself, his own reaction as well.

"I am sorry—truly I am. But as Mrs. Howe said, your father was distraught. He may not remember clearly the events of last evening. He need never see me again and the whole business shall be forgotten."

"Au contraire," Edward drawled. "He wishes to see you tomorrow afternoon."

The undertaker would provide professional mourners or "mutes"
dressed in black to stand about and lend dignity to the affair.

—DANIEL POOLE, WHAT JANE AUSTEN ATE AND CHARLES DICKENS KNEW

Chapter 17

$\mathscr{O}$livia smoothed the bodice of the dark blue dress with trembling fingers as she walked downstairs and across the hall to the library the next afternoon. Becky had taken the children outside for her, and Olivia would much rather have been with them than on her way to this appointed meeting with the Earl of Brightwell. What could the earl want with her? Certainly there was nothing to Lord Bradley's innuendo. She shuddered. No. It could not be. He could not have so misread her sympathy.

She took a deep breath and knocked.

"Come in."

She stepped in and closed the door behind her, heart pounding. Would he reprimand her, or worse?

The earl was sitting in one of the high-backed chairs near the fire, but he rose when she entered. "Please," he beckoned. "Come here, child. You have nothing to fear from me."

Olivia swallowed and walked forward. As she approached, Lord Brightwell watched her closely, his face wearing that same stunned expression of the first night. Had he not asked to see her?

He quietly bid, "Do sit down."

She complied and clasped damp palms in her lap.

He cleared his throat. "Miss Keene, my son has told me of the circumstances of your arrival. You need not keep silent with me." His voice was gentle, and she noticed his gracious choice of words.

She felt a new stab of regret. "My lord, it was not my intention to eavesdrop."

He lifted a hand. "That is not why I asked you here. And though I am not certain I approve of his actions, I know Edward has the family's best interests at heart. Miss Keene, when you spoke with me the other night—"

"I apologize for my familiarity, my lord."

"Do not apologize, please!" His vehemence surprised her. "My own family has been treating me like a leper. Yours was the only true warmth I received all day."

Olivia felt tentative pleasure at his words and studied her clasped hands. Feeling his gaze upon her profile, she looked up to find him studying her.

"We have not met?" he asked softly.

"No, my lord. I saw you and your wife from a distance the night I . . . the night before you left, but that is all."

"May I ask where you come from?"

She hesitated. "To the north and west of here. Near Cheltenham."

He watched her, slowly shaking his head in disbelief or some unfathomable wonder. Leaning forward, he rested his elbows on his knees and made a poor attempt to sound casual. "Miss Keene, may I ask about your . . . your family?"

She felt the old pain in her stomach, and twisted on her chair. "What would you like to know?"

"What your parents are like, where they are from . . . ?"

She latched on to the first part of his question. "My mother is a wonderful woman."

The earl's face brightened. "Yes?"

"She is kind and lovely. Intelligent and patient. She loves to laugh. . . ." Olivia hesitated, trying to remember the last time she had heard her mother laugh.

Lord Brightwell nodded, clearly eager for more information. *But why?* Olivia wondered.

"Go on."

But tears had filled her eyes and she bit her lip to hold them back.

The earl said quietly, "You miss her."

"Very much," Olivia whispered.

"And your father?"

She swallowed, lowering her gaze. "He is clever in his own way. Quick with numbers. Ambitious. Forthright."

"But?" he prompted.

She took a shaky breath. "He is . . . changeable. Often angry."

"Does he . . . ill-use you, my dear?"

"No, never."

"Your mother?"

She looked down at her hands. "He sometimes lashes out at her with harsh words—accusations and threats. But never with his hands, until . . ."

"Until?"

She looked away from his earnest eyes and changed the subject. "He was not always so. But now . . . now I am afraid there is not much warmth between us."

"I am sorry to hear it."

"Still, I never meant—" She stopped herself.

"Never meant what, Miss Keene?"

She saw the compassion in his eyes and was tempted to tell him the whole story. "Never mind."

He handed her his handkerchief. "Pray forgive me, Miss Keene. I did not mean to upset you."

"There is nothing to forgive," she said, wiping her eyes. "You are the one suffering the deepest loss."

Tears brightened his eyes. "Yes, a great loss. My wife was dear to me indeed. But there was a time when there was not much warmth between us either."

She wiped her eyes. "I struggle to credit it."

"It is true, but I confide it only to give you hope. Perhaps your father may warm to you in time, Miss— May I ask your Christian name? I am quite certain Edward never told me."

"My given name is Olivia, but most people here call me—"

"Olivia?" he breathed, visibly stunned.

"I know. I suppose it is rather lofty for a girl in service."

"Olivia . . ." he repeated. His eyes held both triumph and anguish. "Your mother, she . . ." He faltered. "Is her name . . . Dorothea Hawthorn?"

Olivia stared at him dumbly. "No." She slowly shook her head. "It is Dorothea Keene."

They stared into one another's eyes until Olivia whispered, "How do you know my mother?"

He shook his head in wonder. "I thought it must be so when first I saw you. I thought I was seeing a ghost. Or an angel. Dorothea's daughter. I can hardly believe it. How is she? When did you last see her?"

"It is above two months now."

He nodded. "Were you still under your parents' roof before you came here, or did you have a situation elsewhere?"

"I had a position, but I lived at home."

"Then, may I ask, why did you leave? Did something happen, or did you merely come seeking a situation?"

She hesitated. "I . . . I cannot tell you, my lord. You must forgive me."

Concern shone from his face. "But . . . she is well, I trust?"

Tears burned in her eyes once more. Her whisper was as hoarse as when her voice had first returned. "I do not know."

"Do you wish to return home? Edward would allow it, if I—"

She shook her head. "I cannot go back." Anxious to divert the conversation, Olivia asked again, "How are you acquainted with her? You never said."

"Do you not know?" Lord Brightwell's pale eyes twinkled. "She had a post here herself."

Olivia shook her head.

"Dorothea was governess to my half sisters—much younger than I. She was all the things you said—lovely, kind, clever." He looked as if he were about to say something else, then hesitated.

"I would like to talk further with you. But . . . considering the unfortunate circumstances, perhaps that discussion should wait."

Thinking of the funeral to come, Olivia nodded her solemn agreement. Questions trembled on her lips, but she held them back. She was not perfectly certain she wished to know the answers.

❧

A dark cloud hung over Brightwell Court over the next days, rendering the place bright no longer. Judith Howe returned to full mourning attire of dull black bombazine and crepe. A horde of men in black coats, black hats, and armbands descended on the place like a flock of crows. Mr. Tugwell called in several times as well, pressing hands and murmuring condolences to family and servants alike.

In preparation for mourning, Judith Howe ordered a new black frock for Audrey from Miss Ludlow's shop. In the meantime, Olivia added several inches of black lace around the hem of

Audrey's sole black dress, to accommodate the girl's added height since her father's death. She also removed the shiny buckles from Andrew's black shoes and replaced the gilt buttons on his dark coat with simple black ones.

The children would not be attending the funeral itself, but were asked to join the assembled company beforehand. When Olivia led the children downstairs to deliver them to the drawing room, she heard the low rumble of somber conversation from within, where mourners ate cold meat and pie and shared remembrances of the past and wonderings about the future.

In the corridor, Felix stood, wearing the black gloves and scarf of a pallbearer. He greeted her and the children with a solemn bow, his flirtations and winks for once blessedly absent. From Nurse Peale, Olivia had learned that Felix and Judith had spent a great deal of time at Brightwell Court as children—though their parents had not—and it was clear he felt the loss of his aunt keenly. The tentative, woebegone expression he wore made him look very like the little boy he must once have been.

Olivia, of course, would attend neither the service at the church nor the funeral. But from the nursery window, she watched the slow cortege of hearse and mourners make its way to St. Mary's and, afterward, the long procession of mourning carriages pulled by horses draped in black velvet, with black feathers on their heads, leave the drive on their way to the Estcourt family vault.

Olivia heard the church bells toll six times—to indicate the passing of a woman. Then after a pause, one peal for each year of Lady Brightwell's life. The slow regular succession of peals struck Olivia's heart, and she prayed comfort for Lord Brightwell and Lord Bradley long after the last echo died away.

When one of the maids was found to be pregnant,
although Parson Woodforde did not re-engage her at the end
of her annual hiring, he gave her an extra 4s. "on going away,"
to supplement her wages.

—PAMELA HORN, INTRODUCTION TO *THE COMPLETE SERVANT*

Chapter 18

*S*itting with his father in the library on a quiet January evening, Edward once more read the brief, threatening note his father had first shown him on the eve of the ill-fated trip to Italy.

I know your secret. Tell him, or I shall.

The hand was fine, neat. Perhaps purposely ordinary and unadorned? *Who wrote it?* he wondered for the thousandth time. Not to mention the excruciating hours he'd spent pondering its ramifications.

He had been waiting for the proper time to raise the issue once again. And now that his father was home, and the funeral a week past, he thought the moment might be right.

He looked up when his father mumbled over some bit of parliamentary news in the *Morning Post*. Folding up the paper, the earl said, "Your mother's health being what it was this last year, I had no trouble receiving a leave for this session. How glad I am of that now."

Lord Brightwell rose and poured himself a glass of port. "I also appreciate your taking over the running of things here, Edward. During my absence and now. I own I am still not fit for it."

Edward nodded his understanding as his father flopped down in his favorite chair near the fire.

"Someday you will take my seat in parliament as well. How I wish I might be there when you receive your Writ of Summons, hear you read the oath, and see you sign the Test Roll. . . ." Lord Brightwell raised his glass in mock toast, then continued, "A young man with your mind, Edward, why, it is such a waste you must wait to serve your country until after I am dead and buried."

"At this point, it does not look as though I shall be taking your seat at all."

"Never say so, my boy. We are not undone yet. It was only one letter, and a vague one at that. Suspicions at best."

"Perhaps, but true nonetheless."

Lord Brightwell made no reply but only stared into the fire.

Seizing the lull, Edward took a deep breath and asked quietly, "Are you ready to tell me about it?"

"Tell you about what?"

"Everything. Where I came from. Who my mother was. My fa—"

The older man huffed, eyes still focused on the flames. "Your mother was Marian Estcourt Bradley, Lady Brightwell. The woman who *bore* you was an agreeable girl of humble birth."

"And my father . . . ? And do not say, 'Oliver Stanton Bradley,' for you have already admitted I am not your son."

"Of course you are."

"Are you telling me you are my father after all? Some poor dairymaid bore your child?"

"No. I was faithful to your mother. But you *are* my son— perhaps not legally speaking, not 'heirs-male of the body' and all that, but in every other way you are."

Edward slammed his fist on the desk. "Not good enough! Who am I? Who is my father? Who is the woman who bore me?"

"Do you really want to know, my boy? It does not signi—"

"Does not signify? Faith! Of course it does." Edward paced the room.

"You know I do not hold to all this fiddle-faddle about noble birth and blood. You have been raised by me; you are mine. You are just as much a Bradley as I am."

"Few in England would agree with you, sir. None in the peerage, I assure you." Edward dropped into the armchair beside his father's and leaned forward. "Who was she? What was her name?"

Lord Brightwell ran an agitated hand through his fair, thinning hair. "She was a modest, God-fearing young woman. Her father, a trusted man of . . . trade."

"How did you know her?"

He threw up his hand. "She was engaged as a kitchen maid. Happy? Or perhaps a housemaid. At any rate, I barely knew her."

Edward groaned. It was as he feared. He shook his head as though his brain refused the information. "My mother was a servant. And my father? Let me guess. The footboy? The coal monger? A poacher?"

"No." The earl clenched his jaw. "I am afraid it is worse than that."

Edward stared at him, stunned. But no matter how hard Edward pressed him, Lord Brightwell would tell him no more. "In due time" was all he would say.

❧

Mrs. Hinkley stood at the study door, twisting her hands. "My lord, might I have a word?"

"Of course, Mrs. Hinkley, come in." Edward waited until she closed the door and approached his desk. "What is it?"

"It is about the maid. Martha. You said to ask after Christmas what was to be done about her. But then with Lady Brightwell passing and all . . ."

"Yes, I understand." Inwardly, Edward sighed under the burden of responsibility; the earl still insisted on delegating such decisions to him. "Has she told you who the father is?"

"No, my lord. She's too frightened to tell."

"Frightened, why?"

"She said if she tells, she shall have to leave and has no place to go. I told her if she *did* tell, perhaps you could make the man take responsibility, but she insists she can only stay if she does *not* tell."

Edward felt his brow wrinkle, wondering why on earth the girl would think such a thing and who might have given her that assurance. One of the menservants? Felix?

He looked up from his thoughts to see Mrs. Hinkley eyeing him speculatively.

"Now, Mrs. Hinkley. You know better than to suppose—"

"Of course not, my lord. The girl is just being foolish, no doubt."

"Foolish indeed. Does she think this an orphan asylum? A home for unwed mothers?"

Mrs. Hinkley dropped her head. "Am I to put her out then, my lord?" she asked, her voice reedy with fear. "It is what is done, I know."

Edward winced. How easily he would have done so only a few months before. He sat quietly for a moment and then exhaled a deep breath. "No, Mrs. Hinkley. You are not to put her out. Tell her she may stay as long as you are satisfied with her work, until the delivery of her child. If she can find someone to mind the child, she may return to her post in due time. Otherwise, she may leave with a reference. But, Mrs. Hinkley, assure the girl that her refusal to name the father had nothing to do with my decision. Is that clear?"

"Yes, my lord." Mrs. Hinkley expelled a rush of air and relief. "Thank you, my lord." She beamed at him as she backed toward the door. He realized he had never before seen her smile so warmly.

It was not until several weeks after the funeral that Lord Brightwell sent Osborn to once again ask Olivia to join him in the library at her earliest convenience.

Waiting only long enough to finish plaiting Audrey's hair and hand Andrew a book, she left the children with Becky and Nurse Peale and made her way downstairs. When she entered the hall, Osborn came forward from his post and opened the library door, but did not bother to announce her.

Stepping inside, she found the earl sitting at his desk, bent over a ledger. So focused was he that he did not look up when she entered. "Dash it," he muttered. "I cannot make out these figures."

She waited until Osborn had shut the door behind her, shielding her from his too-curious eyes and ears.

Lord Brightwell looked up when the door latched. "Ah, Olivia, my dear."

She approached his desk and offered quietly, "Might I help, my lord?"

He waved his hand dismissively over the ledger. "My eyesight is failing, and there is not a blind thing I can do about it."

"Except make bad puns?"

He chuckled. "At least my sense of humor is not failing me. Can you make this out?"

She peered over his shoulder. "Two thousand seventy-nine."

"And the profits from those acres last year?" He pointed at a figure in the adjoining column.

"One thousand nine hundred sixty-two. For a sum of four thousand forty-one."

"You ciphered that in your head?"

She shrugged. "I was always good with figures."

"Your mother taught you, I suppose. She was an excellent teacher, I recall."

Olivia did not say the ability had been honed by her father, nor in what manner. It would mortify her to speak of it to Lord Brightwell.

"Well, I did not ask you here to balance my accounts." He rose and indicated the two armchairs near the fire. "Please. Be seated."

She complied and looked up from smoothing her skirts to find him studying her.

"I find your presence quite comforting, Olivia. I suppose it is because you are so like your mother. And she was once a dear friend to me."

He looked down at his hands. "In fact, there was a time I had hoped to marry her. But my father would not allow it. In the end, I suppose he was correct, for Marian and I dealt well enough together over the years. But at the time, I was sorely vexed to have to give up Dorothea." He shook his head, chuckling at some scene in his memory. "Dorothea and I had even discussed names for our imagined children. Our son would be Stanton, after my grandfather, and our daughter would be Olivia, after me. Vain, I know." Lord Brightwell stopped, eyes distant.

"After you?" Olivia felt her brow pucker.

He glanced at her. "My name is Oliver, did you not know it?"

She drew in a sharp breath. Mutely shook her head.

"Oliver Stanton Bradley, Lord Brightwell."

What is he saying? she wondered. *Might he mean . . . ?* She could not voice such incredible questions. Instead she made a tremulous attempt at levity. "It appears you changed your mind, my lord, for your son is not named Stanton."

But he did not smile or rejoinder with an amusing anecdote of his wife trumping his chosen name with a favorite of her own. Instead his brow wrinkled and he murmured, "No. Edward was not my choice."

His somber tone invited no further inquiry. The earl looked away from her, through the rain-splattered window to the memories beyond.

Olivia sat staring into the fire, seeing her own memories. *What if . . . ?* Entertaining such thoughts of her mother, of herself, brought heat to Olivia's ears and shame to her heart. Still, it might certainly explain her father's coldness. And if he had only learned of it later, might it not account for the destruction of the bond they had shared in her youngest days? Or did he simply despise her for losing that odious contest? For losing his money and respect, as she had long thought? Yes, that was far easier to believe. For even if her mother had named her in honor of a former love, that did not necessarily mean . . . anything else.

For several moments, they both sat as they were, silent and lost in thought. But soon, doubts broke in on Olivia's mind like pounding waves. "How long ago, my lord, did you, ah, last see my mother?"

Lord Brightwell thought, "Dear me . . . Can it already be six and twenty years? Yes, it must be that or more."

Olivia felt equal portions of relief, vindication, and reluctance when she whispered, "I am not yet five and twenty."

He nodded thoughtfully. "Of course I may have summed the years incorrectly. My memory is not what it used to be. Nor my ciphering." He gazed at her intently and gave her a shaky smile. "You are so like her, my dear."

Olivia's eyes filled with answering tears that slipped down her cheeks. She grasped his hand in hers.

Edward gave the door a sharp rap and, not waiting for an answer, swung it open and strode in. He faltered, startled to see his father and Miss Keene sitting in intimate conversation, holding hands. Edward's heart sank while his anger rose.

"Sorry to interrupt your tête-à-tête, Father," he said acrimoniously. To himself he added, *And so soon after Mother's death!*

"Edward, you will never guess—"

"Try me," he snapped.

He noticed Miss Keene squeeze the earl's hand to gain his attention, her gaze pleading. His father lifted a brow, and she shook her head, *no.*

Edward witnessed their secretive exchange with disdain. "What?" he growled.

The earl hesitated and then said, "Miss Keene and I have discovered a mutual acquaintance."

"Really?" Edward doubted such a thing, if true, would bring about such fervent hand-holding. When neither offered to enlighten him, he said curtly, "Walters is ready to review the ledgers, Father. Would now be . . . inconvenient?"

"Actually I was enjoying my time with Olivia."

Olivia . . . ? He did not like the sound of her name on his father's lips.

Lord Brightwell sighed and straightened. "But if it cannot wait . . ."

"I should be returning to the nursery at all events, my lord," Miss Keene said, rising.

"But—" The earl started to protest but, seeing her expression, ceased. "Very well, Olivia. Um, Miss Keene."

The two shared a meaningful smile that filled Edward's gut with bile. Surely his father held no inappropriate interest in the girl. True, lords had been seducing maids for centuries, but he did not think his father such a man. He recalled his recent conversation with Mrs. Hinkley about one of the maids and felt a renewed rush of anger. Another emotion surged within him, but he did not stop to contemplate it.

*Unprotected by her own family the governess
was vulnerable to sexual approaches.*

—KATHRYN HUGHES, *THE VICTORIAN GOVERNESS*

Chapter 19

*O*n her next half day, Olivia crunched through the newly fallen
snow on the path through the wood. There was not enough snow
for the children to play in, only a dusting on the ground and a thick
coat of sugar icing on the branches, bushes, and berries. Tufts of
grass and red and yellow leaves shone through the white glaze,
reminding Olivia of an iced cake of dried fruits and nuts.

She walked further along the wooded trail—in the opposite
direction from Croome's lodge—and then, drawn by the slurry
whisper of running water, strayed from the path and followed the
sound. She saw two dippers on the riverbank, bobbing and dipping
their heads in characteristic style. A woodcock, disturbed by her
arrival, beat the air with panicked wings and whirred away.

Olivia brushed snow from a fallen log near the river's edge

and sat down. How peaceful it was. Tipping her head back, she relished the unseasonably warm sun, which would melt away the snow far too soon.

As she sat there, Olivia realized she had reached the end of her three-month trial. Lord Bradley would allow her to go now, his father had said. Yet somehow the thought of leaving did not bring relief, but rather uncertainty. *Almighty God, show me what to do. . . .* She longed to know where her mother was and how she fared, but she had begged Olivia *not* to return—insisted that she would find *her* when it was safe to do so. But why had her mother not come? Had something happened to her, or had she stayed away for fear of leading the constable—or Simon Keene—to Olivia's door?

Another thought struck her then. Would Lord Bradley even allow her to stay longer? Suddenly she very much hoped so. At least then she would have a place to live while she waited, or until she found another post.

Edward walked through the wood, a gun held casually at his side. He had been scouting the far wood for wild dogs and poachers and now, on his return, paused at his favorite spot along the river. Looking up through the whitewashed canopy of branches, he saw a goose high overhead, flying alone. He found himself wondering how the creature had become separated from his flock. Where was it going? Would he find his way? There, surrounded by snow and silence, the sight filled Edward with a stinging loneliness.

He sensed movement nearby and tensed, searching the wood instead of the sky. Leaves crackled, and a woodcock took to flight, scattering snow in its wake. Surely there were no dogs this close to the house.

Then Miss Keene stepped into view on the far bank. She was humming quietly to herself and sat on a fallen log near the river. For several moments she simply tilted her head to the sunshine, eyes closed, dark curls framing her oval face. She was not as elegant as Miss Harrington or Judith, though of course she had neither cosmetics, fine gowns, nor a lady's maid, as they did. Still, Miss Keene was beautiful and—as Judith often alluded to—had a quiet nobility about her, a ladylike grace. He wondered again about the nature of his father's interest in the girl.

She stretched her legs out before her, and Edward glimpsed a sliver of stocking and tapered ankle. He averted his gaze. He was not a man to sneak a look at a woman's leg. He repeated this sentiment to himself once more. And then again.

Little flurries of snow began to fall, twirling and floating in the air like blossoms from a bird cherry tree. Returning his gaze to Miss Keene's face, he saw her open her mouth and hold forth her pink tongue, trying to catch snowflakes on it like a schoolgirl. He found himself smiling and had the urge to splash across the shallow river to join her. He wanted to share a smile with her, to share much more. But obstacles greater than an icy river stood between them. *I am a fool*, he admonished himself. *She would be mortified if she saw me and knew I had been watching her.*

He stayed where he was, reminding himself that his father had every intention of staying the course. He *would be* the next Earl of Brightwell and marry accordingly.

Miss Keene sat a moment longer, then rose from the log and turned from the river, brushing off her bottom with gloved hands as she went. Edward decided he would head back as well, and see if he might meet up with her at the Brightwell Bridge.

Olivia was surprised to see Johnny Ross sitting on the wooden bench at the top of the rise. She opened her mouth to admonish him, but remembered her charade just in time and quickly clamped her lips shut.

He looked up, rose, and came bounding down the path. "I surprised you, didn't I?" He laughed, putting his hands under her elbows. "I've been hoping to find you alone for days."

Olivia shook her head, gently pushing his hands away and heading up the frosted hill. They were so close to the manor. If someone saw them out there together, they would assume she and Johnny were . . . And if Lord Bradley saw them, Johnny would lose his place.

"Aw, come on," he urged, jogging to catch up with her. "At least sit with me on the bench a bit. I brushed the snow off."

Taking her arm, he pulled her down onto the bench beside him. She moved to its edge and took a deep breath. She didn't want to hurt his feelings, but nor did she wish to encourage him.

"Livie, you know I'm mad for you, do you not? Will you not give me a sign of affection?"

Oh, how frustrating! How could she explain without speaking? A simple shake of her head seemed so insufficient.

Johnny took her hesitation as his cue to convince her. He clutched her awkwardly by the shoulders and leaned forward to kiss her.

Turning her face away, Olivia glimpsed Lord Bradley on the path, and her immediate embarrassment flamed into irritation as she took in his arrogant stance. For a moment she was tempted to turn and kiss Johnny, show the haughty lord she was not intimidated by him. But she knew it would be unfair to use Johnny that way. For the briefest instant, she held Lord Bradley's cold gaze over Johnny's shoulder, unwilling to lower her eyes first. She had done nothing to be ashamed of.

Johnny pulled her closer, murmuring, "Come on, Livie. Just one kiss. You don't have to say a word. . . ." His razor-stubbled chin scraped her cheek as he pushed his face close.

Olivia held her tongue by the thinnest thread of self-will. She tried to pull away, but the groom was strong indeed. Would Lord Bradley just stand there? Was he no gentleman at all?

She thought, *I don't have to say a word, do I? Well, I am about to.* Olivia twisted in his grasp and opened her mouth to make very plain her ill-opinion of them both.

A gunshot exploded in the air. Johnny flew to his feet, sending Olivia tumbling from the bench onto the ground. His face went white as he whirled and saw Lord Bradley standing a few yards away, gun against his hip.

He strode toward them purposely, his face hard. "Back to the stables, Ross," he ordered as he bent toward Olivia and extended his hand to help her up. She ignored it and scrambled to her feet on her own, cheeks burning in indignation.

Johnny hesitated only long enough to glance her way without meeting her eyes and mumble a weak, "Sorry, miss." Then he all but ran up the path and out of sight.

As soon as he was out of earshot, Olivia hissed, "You needn't have done that. I could have managed on my own."

"That is not how it appeared."

"Perhaps you judged incorrectly. Perhaps I am sorry you interrupted us." She saw him hesitate, his jaw clench.

He said coldly, "Then you must excuse me. If you and your lover want privacy, I suggest you find a less public rendezvous. If Hodges had witnessed that little scene, Ross would be packing his bags as we speak. In the meantime, you ought to return to the house. It is not safe for you to be out in the wood alone."

"I am perfectly safe."

"Wild dogs have been spotted near Barnsley, Miss Keene. There is no guarantee they will not come here as well."

"You are only trying to frighten me."

"You should be frightened. You haven't your stick with you this time."

She stared, mildly stunned by his reference to their first meeting. So he did remember her from the hunt. Good. Maybe he would remember how rudely he and his friends had treated her.

"I appreciate your concern," she said coolly. "But I am certain you have more important things to do than protect me."

"You are correct. Therefore, I repeat—return to the house. Now."

"I have not finished my walk."

"Walk all you want in view of the house."

"I shall walk where I please."

"You forget your place."

"And you forget your promise of a half day to spend as I like. And your duty as a gentleman to treat me as a human being."

"Albeit a trespasser."

"You shall never let me forget my mistake, will you? *Forgive* and *forget* are not in your vocabulary. I am guilty of many things, but for the last time, I am neither spy nor thief. I foolishly trespassed upon your land, yes, but I would rather be a trespasser than an arrogant, unfeeling, ungentlemanly person like you!"

She turned her back on him, unwilling to allow him to see her tears.

"Miss Keene," he reprimanded.

She felt his gaze spear the back of her head but refused to turn around.

He raised his voice. "Miss Keene!"

She glanced at him over her shoulder. "I am not deaf, sir," she retorted. "Simply mute." And with that she lifted her skirts and ran down the path, deeper into the wood, choking back sobs as she ran.

Edward watched her go and realized with a prickling chill that it was the first time she had failed to address him by his courtesy title.

He sat down on the bench with a heavy sigh and held his head in his hands. Her words ricocheted inside his head and his stomach churned.

Well, she is wrong about one thing, he thought. *I am not unfeeling. I feel. I feel indeed.*

When Edward had spied her with Ross, he had been angry— but knew the emotion had little to do with the fact that fraternizing among servants was frowned upon. Hodges had let go more than one amorous footman and housemaid in the past.

In truth, he had been shot through with jealously, illogical though it was. Jealous . . . over attentions paid to an under nurse? He had never been attracted to one of the servants before, not even for a light flirtation as Felix often was. *Oh, how the mighty have fallen.*

When Ross had leaned forward to kiss Miss Keene, Edward's gut had clenched within him. He knew he should turn and quietly go—let Hodges deal with the groom later.

But I refuse to feel guilty, he thought. *Did she not spy on me?*

But instead of meeting Ross's kiss, Miss Keene had turned away. The flash of her eyes over Ross's shoulder told him she had seen him there and was not pleased. Still, he was relieved she had avoided the man's kiss.

Remorse filled him now as he replayed their recent exchange in his mind. *What am I doing?* He sat there trying to make sense of his turbulent thoughts and emotions. He knew he had no right to keep her there any longer, and no honest way to guarantee her silence. He ought to let her go.

In more ways than one.

He heard a sharp scream in the distance and knew instantly whom the voice belonged to. He jumped up, grabbed his gun, and flew down the path.

"Go! Be gone! Help . . . Edward!"

At her panicked cries, his legs flew faster. Branches cracked as he pushed his way through the underbrush in the direction of her voice. The sound of barking and growling reached him, chilling his blood. *Wild dogs . . .* He sprinted on, trying to load his gun as he ran.

Rounding a bend, his eyes registered the scene in an instant. Three dogs. One in a crouch, preparing to lunge. Edward snapped the gun chamber closed and raised the piece. *Too late . . .* The dog was midair, teeth bared. The moment slowed to a slogging dream. He saw a flash, heard a sharp report, and the dog's blazing eyes faded to grey, to emptiness, as the cur fell limply to the ground.

But Edward had yet to fire a shot.

Turning his head, he glimpsed Croome standing within a web of branches, arm outstretched and steady, fowling piece still smoking. Before Edward could respond, the second dog coiled to lunge. *Crack!* His own shot shuddered through the dog as it leapt. Olivia screamed as it landed in a heap at her feet. Before Edward could reload, the third dog flew forward and sunk its teeth into her skirts and gave a great jerk, pulling her feet out from under her, her head hitting the ground sharply as she fell. He saw Croome lift his fowling piece again and their eyes met. Croome did not shoot again. Why did the man not shoot? Fearing his own shot might miss its mark and hit Miss Keene, Edward charged forward, striking the dog with the butt of his gun. He shouted unintelligibly and struck again. Finally the dog unclamped its hold and scampered away. Croome's shot chased it into the wood.

Edward ran to where Olivia lay, silent and still.

"Miss Keene? Are you all right? Miss Keene?"

No response. He pressed trembling fingers to her neck and found a pulse. He gently rolled her by one shoulder to examine the back of her head where she had fallen. A jagged rock lay beneath her, smeared with blood.

Looking up, his gaze fell on the nearest dead dog. The dog's blank eyes were rheumy. Its tongue swollen. Foamy drool puddled beneath its mouth. Edward's heart thundered, ice formed in his stomach. He prayed the cur that escaped had only bitten her skirts, not her flesh. Jerking off his coat and bunching it to cushion her head, he rolled her gently back down. He was vaguely aware of Croome dragging the carcasses out of the way. Crawling to Miss Keene's feet, Edward pushed up her skirts only as far as necessary. He winced. Just below her knee, blood trickled red through her stocking. *God, no . . .*

He recalled too well his father's stories of the rampage of rabies through London in the days of his youth, when livestock and people died by the hundreds and lads earned five shillings for every dog they killed. The attacks of rabid dogs and foxes had become less common in recent years, but the disease—and dread of it—had never left England.

Edward rolled down the stocking and regarded the wound. The bite did not appear deep; the thickness of her skirts had no doubt hindered the cur's goal. Tossing aside her shoe, he yanked the stocking from that leg and wound it around the top of her calf, tying it tight. Croome reappeared, surveying his actions with wordless concurrence. The old man pulled his hunting knife from its sheath, uncorked his flask and poured some of the brandy over the blade, then handed the flask to him. Edward splashed the wound with the amber liquid. Croome offered him the knife, but when Edward hesitated, the man groaned to his knees and unceremoniously sliced the wound site. Olivia moaned but did not awaken. As the bleeding quickened, Edward rinsed it away with more of the brandy. He did not know if these actions would help, but it was all he knew to try. Once more he met Croome's eyes, deep in his skull beneath wiry grey eyebrows. The man's ever-present scowl offered him little hope.

Edward lifted Olivia in his arms and carried her as fast as he could up the path. Croome did not follow. When he reached the lawns, he saw Talbot and Johnny working a new horse in the gates.

"Talbot!" he yelled. "Send Ross on your fastest horse for Dr. Sutton. Miss Keene has been wounded!"

"Wounded?" Johnny's anxious eyes met his.

"Mad dogs," he gritted.

The young man paled and flew to his task.

To marry a member of one's household, even from its upper strata,
was considered an appalling social misdemeanor.

—MARK GIROUARD, *LIFE IN THE ENGLISH COUNTRY HOUSE*

Chapter 20

*D*r. Sutton arrived within the hour. With Mrs. Hinkley's assistance, he irrigated the wound with soap and warm water, then with diluted muriatic acid. When he commended Edward for his quick thinking with the knife and brandy, Edward credited his gamekeeper for knowing what to do.

"Avery Croome did this?" Sutton raised his brows and his lower lip protruded, but whether impressed or merely surprised, Edward did not know.

Dr. Sutton also bathed and bandaged Olivia's head wound, which he cited as the cause of her unconscious state—a bite, he said, even from a rabid dog, would not account for it.

"How long until we know if she has been infected?"

Sutton shrugged and pushed up his spectacles. "Symptoms may not appear for a week or more."

"What should we look for?" Mrs. Hinkley asked.

"Pain and itching at the wound site, headache, insomnia, nausea, refusal to eat or drink, agitation, aggression . . ."

Edward shuddered. "And if symptoms appear?"

"Then there is nothing we can do for her but keep her from passing the disease to others. Once symptoms are in full force, victims usually perish within the week."

A dull ache of dread pounded through Edward's body. "How long will she remain unconscious?"

"Only God knows. Head wounds are mysterious indeed. I shall arrange for a chamber nurse, shall I?"

"And I shall share that duty, if you don't mind," Mrs. Hinkley offered. "Even a chamber nurse needs rest from time to time."

Edward nodded his agreement and murmured dull thanks to them both.

Dr. Sutton continued his extensive irrigation of the wound, explaining that the best course was to do all in one's power to prevent the dog's saliva from making its way through the victim's body.

For the disease had no cure.

❧

Edward returned to the sickroom later that night to ask the hired nurse if she would like a respite. He was surprised to find the earl sitting beside Miss Keene, and felt a renewed pinch of grief to see his father sitting at another sickbed so soon after his mother's death. The matronly chamber nurse sat off in the corner, working some embroidery by the light of a candle lamp.

"Any change?" Edward whispered, surveying Olivia's form shrouded by bedclothes.

"She grows restless," the older man answered softly.

As if hearing the words, Miss Keene's forehead puckered and she turned her face away from them, then back once more.

Edward recalled the list of symptoms the doctor had described and felt fear prick his gut. "I would be restless too, lying about all day," he said in mock confidence.

His father looked at him, then away. "No sign of nausea. Or"—he attempted a grin—"insomnia. And Nurse Jones here has got her to swallow some water. Another good sign, is it not?"

"I hope so," Edward answered.

As if sensing his son's discomfort, Lord Brightwell asked Nurse Jones to give them a few moments alone, suggesting she take herself down to the kitchen for some tea.

"Don't mind if I do, my lord." She rose stiffly and left them.

After a few moments of silence, Edward confessed, "It was my fault she ran into the wood."

The earl's eyebrows rose, but he didn't press Edward. "The important thing is that she get well."

"Yes. I am afraid I have much to apologize for."

"More than you know," the earl said, his eyes growing tender as he looked at Olivia's pale face.

"What do you mean?" Edward asked. His father's warm tone and mysterious words brought leaden dread to his stomach. Certainly his father had no designs on the girl.

When their gazes met, the older man's eyes were bright with unshed tears. "I think Olivia may be my daughter."

"What?" Edward thundered.

"Shh . . ." the earl admonished, and both turned their eyes back to Miss Keene's unconscious form.

"Olivia favours her mother a great deal," his father whispered with reverence. "It is why I was so startled when first I saw her. Her looks, her intelligence and warmth—so very like Dorothea."

"Who is Dorothea?" Edward demanded, a dark cloud building inside of him.

"She was governess to my half sisters, your aunts Margery

and Phillipa." The earl frowned suddenly. "Do sit down, my boy. My neck grows stiff."

Edward complied, sitting in the last remaining chair, its hard wooden slats digging into his spine. Who had designed the torturous thing?

"Olivia's hair is darker, but still the resemblance is striking."

"And this Dorothea was . . . your mistress?"

The earl winced. "It was not as tawdry as all that. We fancied ourselves in love. I wanted to marry her, but as you might guess, my father would not hear of it."

Lord Brightwell rose and went to stand near the window, looking out at the moon pouring its waxy light over the white world below. "My father urged me to marry your mother, the Estcourts being such a well-connected and wealthy family." He sighed. "Of course none of us could have guessed that he would die before the year was out. In any case, I had barely agreed when the banns were read and the wedding set for three weeks hence. As soon as Dorothea heard, she resigned her post and left with no word of her destination. I never imagined she was with child, though perhaps I should have guessed. How irresponsible and selfish I was . . . how weak. I like to think I would have acted differently had I known. I did try to find her, but I own it was a halfhearted attempt at best. Even her family did not know where she was."

"Olivia," Edward whispered to himself, suddenly realizing the significance.

"Yes," the earl whispered.

Edward scowled. "Is she pushing for this, or are you?"

"I am. She doesn't want a shilling from me, if that is what you think."

"I did not think that," Edward muttered, though the thought had crossed his mind.

"I have not told Olivia outright what I suspect, though as intelligent as she is—and as *subtle* as I was—I believe she guessed. Being genteel, she is no doubt repulsed by the notion of being baseborn, as you can imagine."

"Yes, I can well imagine," Edward echoed wryly.

Lord Brightwell shot him a look. "You must know, Edward, Olivia is not convinced. My recollection of the timing and her age do not reconcile."

Edward shrugged. "Easily changed. No doubt many illegitimate children celebrate their first birthday a few months later than fact." Edward wondered for the first time what his real birth date might be.

The earl abruptly stood. "Dorothea would want to know. She would want to be here with her daughter. Did Olivia give you any direction beyond 'near Cheltenham'?"

Edward shook his head.

"Nor me. I wonder why. . . ."

The next day, Edward was just returning from the stables after exercising his horse when the shrill summons startled him.

"Master Edward! Come quickly!" Mrs. Hinkley stood at the garden door, waving wildly to him, her voice panicked. "It is Olivia. She is thrashing about and . . . and talking!"

She held the door for him as he strode toward her, pulling off his riding gloves and hat as he came. "Send for the doctor, Mrs. Hinkley. I shall go up and see what I can do."

"Yes, my lord," she answered, clearly relieved to have him take charge of the situation.

Tossing his things on a bench in the corridor, Edward took the stairs three at a time. He hurried into the sickroom, shutting the door behind him. Olivia's face was flushed, and she twisted about, the sheets and a long nightdress trapping her slender form. Her mouth twitched and her brows furrowed. Then she began muttering aloud, though her eyes remained closed.

"No! Be gone! Edward! Edward!"

His heart banged in his chest. He had never before heard her speak his Christian name. She was calling to him, no doubt reliving that horrible scene with the dogs.

Stepping to the bedside table, he wrung excess water from a cloth and then sat on the chair beside the bed. He held her face with one hand and with the other, gently touched the cool cloth to her cheeks and lips and brow. He murmured, "Shh . . . It is all right. I am here. The dogs are gone. You are safe now, Olivia. Perfectly safe."

She quieted almost immediately. He smoothed the cloth down her straight nose, dabbed her scratched chin, and then softly soothed the hot skin of her neck. Eventually he returned the cloth to the basin, and took one of her small hands in his own. He stroked her delicate fingers and spoke to her softly. "You are going to be all right, Olivia," he said, knowing his words were as much to reassure himself as her. He recalled the sound of her voice calling out his name. Not *my lord*, not *Lord Bradley*. Just *Edward*. He longed to hear her say it again, well and awake.

When Dr. Sutton came an hour later, he gave her chamomile and valerian to calm her and ordered she be helped to swallow more fluids. "It might just be a slight fever and not rabies, but it is too early to tell," he said. "There is little else to be done but wait."

Edward nodded. He would wait. But he would also pray. He sent Osborn with a note for Charles Tugwell, asking the man of God to join him.

Whenever you give any living creature cause to depend on you,
be careful on no account to disappoint it.

—Sarah Trimmer, *Fabulous Histories*
Designed for the Instruction of Children, 1786

Chapter 21

When his cousin entered the sickroom, Edward was sitting in the armchair by the window, reading an old volume of Chaucer. Nurse Jones had taken herself belowstairs for dinner and Olivia slept quietly in bed.

"How is she?" Judith whispered.

"She grew restless several hours ago but has been quiet since."

Judith took several steps forward but did not draw near the bed, as though afraid to get too close. She looked down at Miss Keene, an inscrutable expression on her pretty face. "I was just speaking with your father. He seems quite concerned about her."

Edward shrugged uneasily. "He is . . . taken with her."

"Which I find a bit odd." She tilted her head to look at him. "Do you not?"

Uncomfortable, Edward only shrugged.

She studied him thoughtfully. "And here you sit like a faithful hound at her side. Are you not afraid of contracting rabies?"

He shook his head. "The doctor thinks it only a fever."

"Does it not concern you?"

"Of course, but Sutton—"

"I do not mean the fever," she interrupted. "I meant, does it not concern you that your father has developed a *tendre* for our under nurse?"

When Edward didn't respond, Judith asked, "And what did Mrs. Hinkley mean when she said, 'Is it not a miracle?' "

"Excuse me?"

"When I passed her just now, she said, 'Is it not a miracle about Olivia?' "

Edward nodded. "I suppose she means that Miss Keene has been talking in her sleep."

Judith's plump lips parted. "Has she indeed?" Her eyes flashed in triumph. "Did I not tell you she might be pretending to muteness?"

Edward felt annoyance rising. Yet had he not suspected the same at first?

"What does she say?" Judith asked eagerly.

Edward felt suddenly self-conscious. "Hmm . . . ?" he murmured, deliberately obtuse.

"What does Miss Keene say when she talks in her sleep?" Judith pressed.

He hesitated, not wanting to divulge the truth, but his eyes must have given something away.

Judith's fair brows rose, and the corners of her mouth twitched with humor. "Do *not* tell me she calls out for you."

Edward felt his neck heat. "She . . . mutters a good deal of nonsense—that is all."

His cousin's gaze was all too knowing, and disconcerted, Edward looked away.

Olivia opened her eyes and looked about her, quite bewildered to find herself in an unfamiliar room. A candle lamp burned on the bedside table and a fire in the hearth. A woman she did not recognize sat nodding off in an armchair near the fire, a wad of needlework in her lap.

Slowly, Olivia pulled herself into a sitting position, concerned to find the act quite taxing. Why was she so weak? At the movement, the bed ropes creaked and the unfamiliar woman roused herself and gaped at Olivia, eyes wide.

"Miss Keene? Are you . . . well?"

Olivia nodded, the memories of the attack slowly coming to mind.

The woman toddled to the bedside. "I am Mrs. Jones, chamber nurse. Do you need anything? Will you take some water?" Mrs. Jones brought the glass to her lips, but Olivia gently took the vessel from her and sipped from it herself. The nurse beamed at her as though she had just performed an amazing feat.

"You wait right there," she said. "The others will want to know you've come back to us."

Olivia wondered how long she had been abed and if she was fit for company. She looked down at herself, oddly touched to find herself clothed in a fine and modest nightdress. *Whose?* she wondered. Moments later, a voice rang out somewhere in the manor and echoed down the stairs and corridor.

"She's awake! She's awake!"

Doris, Olivia mused, and sat waiting. A few minutes later, the door opened and Doris poked her head inside the room. "Hello, love! Feeling well enough for visitors?"

Olivia nodded, feeling weak and a bit dazed, but otherwise well. Doris entered, followed by Mrs. Hinkley, both of them all eager expectation, which mildly confused her.

Doris fluffed two pillows behind her and straightened the

bedclothes. "You've been asleep for two days, Livie. Did you know?"

Olivia shook her head.

Mrs. Hinkley smiled down at her. "You spoke in your sleep, my dear. I heard you myself."

Stunned, Olivia's mind reeled behind a stiff smile. What would Lord Bradley say? What had *she* said?

"You said a lot of balmy things, I hear," Doris chimed in. "I'd a paid two bob to hear 'em myself."

"Can you speak now?" Mrs. Hinkley's tone was gentle.

Olivia hesitated; they were both looking at her so expectantly. Lord Bradley slipped into the room behind them and held her gaze. He gave her a slight nod.

"I . . . ye-yes," Olivia stammered. "I believe I can."

"Ohh!" Doris exclaimed. "And don't she speak fine—just like a lady! Say my name won't you, love?"

"And mine?" Mrs. Hinkley added shyly.

Olivia chuckled. "My friend, Doris McGovern . . . and dear Mrs. Hinkley." Her eyes met those of the last person in the room, his expression inscrutable. She swallowed. "And . . . my lord Bradley."

A small smile curved his lips.

Doris and Mrs. Hinkley, suddenly self-conscious, murmured "Excuse me" and "God bless you" and hurriedly left the room.

"Perhaps she could speak all the time and didn't know it," Olivia heard Doris venture as the two women walked away down the corridor.

"Maybe so," Mrs. Hinkley agreed. "Or perhaps the sickness made her well."

❧

When Olivia stepped into the nursery after her absence of several days, Andrew bounded across the room and threw his arms around her. Still weak and wobbly from her recent indisposition, Olivia had to grip the doorjamb to keep from falling backward.

"Hello, Miss Livie. Are you well now?"

"I am."

His little mouth dropped open. "Say that again."

Olivia smiled. "I am. I am well."

Audrey approached cautiously and Olivia held out a hand. The girl hurried forward then, biting back her shy smile. "Hello, Miss Keene," she said. "We have missed you."

"And I, you."

"I told you she could talk!" Andrew said. "I did hear her talk in her sleep, but you wouldn't believe me!"

"Perhaps I did, Andrew," Olivia soothed, "but did not realize I *could* speak while awake."

"I must say I am disappointed in you, Miss Keene."

Olivia looked up, disconcerted to see Judith Howe standing in the sleeping chamber doorway, little Alexander on one hip.

"I am sorry, madam. I don't—"

Judith glanced down and then up again. "You see, I had imagined you to speak with a Prussian accent, or German, perhaps. As would befit a foreign princess fleeing her home."

Olivia forced a laugh. "I am sorry to disappoint you."

Judith straightened. "You did not run away from a tyrannical father, forcing you into a despicable marriage?"

Olivia's mouth was dry. "No . . . forced marriage, no."

The woman sighed theatrically. "Ah, well. So be it."

Lord Brightwell knocked and stepped into the nursery. "Full house today."

"Hello, Uncle," Judith said. "Our under nurse is well, you see, but fails to be the foreign princess I had hoped for."

He patted his niece's shoulder, amused. "Life is full of such little disappointments, my dear." His eyes twinkled. "Though Miss Keene may surprise you yet."

"What does that mean?" Judith asked sharply.

Olivia tried to signal the earl, but Judith caught her shaking her head. Mrs. Howe looked from one to the other with mounting suspicion. "What is going on?"

"Not a thing, my dear. You must forgive the foolishness of an old man."

"Must I?"

Fearing Mrs. Howe might come to a more *imaginative* conclusion on her own, Olivia explained, "Lord Brightwell means only that he has realized my mother was once governess to his younger sisters."

"Indeed?" Judith Howe said, surprised. She nodded slowly and chewed her full lower lip as the news sunk in. She was clearly still considering the notion as she let herself from the room.

❧

That night, when Olivia put the children to bed, they begged her to read to them and she happily obliged. She read Psalm 46, her favorite, and another chapter in *The History of Robins*.

Once more, Audrey leaned her head on Olivia's shoulder, while Andrew curled into her side, lifting Olivia's arm and draping it around himself like a human cloak.

"When the mother-bird arrived at the ivy wall, she stopt at the entrance of the nest, with a palpitating heart; but seeing her brood all safe and well, she hastened to take them under her wings. . . ."

"I like your voice, Miss Keene," Audrey said.

"Me too," Andrew murmured, on the verge of sleep. "Is that what our *mamma's* voice sounded like?"

And from the reverence with which he spoke the word, Olivia knew he referred to their first mother. Olivia felt the tremble pass through Audrey's frame and rested her cheek atop the girl's head.

"I don't remember," Audrey whispered. "But I think it must be."

Olivia's throat tightened, and she could read no more.

*Wanted, a Governess—a comfortable home, but without salary,
is offered to any lady wishing for a situation
to instruct two [children] in music, drawing and English.*
—ADVERTISEMENT IN THE *TIMES*, 1847

Chapter 22

When Olivia stepped into the kitchen for the first time since the attack, Mrs. Moore opened wide her arms and enfolded Olivia in an embrace as sweet as the confections she prepared.

"Livie, my love, how I have been praying for you. I cannot tell you how good it is to see you up and about and in my kitchen once more. Now sit yourself down and I will pour you a cup of chocolate and we shall have ourselves a chat."

Olivia smiled and felt her insides warm before one sip of the hot drink had passed her lips.

Mrs. Moore bustled about, then set the cup of warm chocolate before her, and a buttery scone as well. She lifted her thin brows, eyes wide in expectation. "Well?"

"Well what, Mrs. Moore?"

"Ewww! I have been waitin' to hear you say my name. Say something else."

"Mrs. Moore, you embarrass me. I feel as though I am called before my French master, there to impress him with my command of a new language."

"Ahh!" She clapped her hands. "Doris said you spoke like a real lady, and bless me, but she was right."

Olivia laughed. "Is it so strange to hear me speak?"

"Strange and wonderful, my girl. Strange and wonderful."

A knock sounded on the kitchen door and Mrs. Moore rose. "You stay as you are and drink your chocolate. I shall return directly."

Olivia watched in silence as Mrs. Moore opened the door to the outside stairwell and accepted three hares from Mr. Croome. Over the mottled grey fur, the gamekeeper snared Olivia's gaze, gave one curt nod, then pivoted on his heel without a word of farewell.

"Thank you, Avery," Mrs. Moore called after him.

Without turning, the old man merely raised a hand in acknowledgment as he climbed back up the stairs.

Laying the hares in a basket beside the worktable, Mrs. Moore glanced at Olivia. "You know, he asked about you, while you were ill."

"Did he?"

Mrs. Moore nodded. "You really needn't be afraid of Mr. Croome, Livie. He's not so bad. Had a rough life, poor rogue."

Olivia tented her brows. "You are the first I've heard speak of him with any sympathy."

"How could I not? Lost his wife. My own sister, she was."

Olivia was stunned. For a moment she just sat there, staring at the woman. Then she reached out and laid her hand on Mrs. Moore's. "He was married to your sister?" Olivia could not imagine a hard, angry man like Croome deserving a woman anything like warm and kind Nell Moore. But then, did Simon Keene deserve Dorothea Hawthorn?

Mrs. Moore nodded. "But she died long ago. Lies in the churchyard now, she does." Tears misted the cook's eyes in spite of the passage of years. "They . . . oh, never mind me." She sniffed and forcibly brightened. "We are celebrating your return—from the sickbed and silence." Mrs. Moore squeezed her hand. "A very happy day indeed."

Olivia smiled and sipped her chocolate. "Do you know, Lord Bradley told me that Mr. Croome shot one of the dogs before it could attack me."

"Did he? Never said a word to me."

"I wonder if I ought to thank him."

Mrs. Moore's thin brows rose again, all innocence. "Do you think so?"

Olivia did not miss the twinkle in her eye. "I don't suppose you have any tidbits left over you cannot bear to waste?"

Olivia found Croome chopping wood and shivered at the sight of him wielding a sharp axe. At his feet, a grey bird with mottled orange-brown wings showed no such fear. It shadowed Croome as he set another hunk of wood on the tree stump and split it cleanly in two. *Clunk, chunk.*

He hesitated when he saw her. "What are ya doin' here, girl?"

"G-good day, Mr. Croome. I am Olivia Keene, as you may recall."

"I recall. The girl I caught snooping about where she had no business."

Clunk, chunk.

She remembered Mrs. Moore's admonition. *"Mind you give it right back to him."* Olivia steeled her voice. "And I recall you, Mr. Croome, where you had no business. In Chedworth Wood with an . . . interesting . . . group of acquaintances."

He let his axe fall to his side and split her with a sharp look. Even the bird's proud, roosterlike face seemed to sneer at her.

"What I do when I'm away from here is none of yer concern, nor no one else's either."

"Very well."

He riveted his eyes on hers, and she forced herself to meet the glowering glare.

He bent and picked up another piece of wood. "Thought you'd tell the master 'bout that."

"I did not."

His eyes narrowed. "And why not?"

"Whatever else you be, you rescued me that night in the wood."

He lifted the axe again, but hesitated. " 'Course I did. Young girl, at the mercy of a vile, debauched man . . ." He brought the axe down with a vicious blow, and she wondered if he spoke of Borcher alone.

She added, "And now, I understand, you have helped rescue me once again. This time from four-legged curs in this very wood."

He shrugged. "Only doin' my job, wasn't I?" He tossed the split logs onto the pile.

"Even so, I am grateful. I am afraid I do not recollect the events of that day very clearly, but Lord Bradley speaks highly of your quick actions."

Croome halted, peering at her. "Does he?" For a moment his expression cleared, but then his eyes alighted on the covered jar in her hands. He scowled once more.

"I told you before. I don' need yer charity."

"I am glad to hear it, for I have nothing to offer you. This is from Mrs. Moore. Jugged hare, I believe she said. She made more than can be used in the manor, and said if you were too mule-stubborn to accept it, you might feed it to your pigs again. It matters not to her."

"Said that, did she?" The faintest hint of a smile teased his lips, then fled to a tremor in his hand. "Sounds like Nell. Bossy bird."

"Will you take it, or shall I dump it in the wood on my way back? I for one hate to hurt her feelings."

"No call fer wastin' it. Shouldn't ha' brought it, but I do hate waste as well she knows, scheming woman. Leave it. I have dogs as well as pigs. Between us, we shall see it put to use."

"Very well." She set the jar on the stoop and turned without another word, holding her chin high as she marched away.

But it was several minutes before her heart beat normally once more.

❧

At breakfast, Edward drank coffee while Judith took tea. His father had yet to join them. Hodges brought in the letter tray—bills for him, a letter from Swindon for Judith.

Setting down her teacup, Judith peeled open her letter and, after skimming a few sentences, said, "A letter from my mother. It seems my *dear* mother-in-law, Mrs. Howe, has written to her about the fact that the children have no governess at present. Meddlesome creature!"

She paused to sip her tea, then peered at the letter again. Edward guessed his cousin needed spectacles but she was too vain to admit it.

"Good heavens!" Judith's cheeks flushed. "Mamma offers—I'd say threatens—to engage my old governess if I am unable to find one on my own. The cheek!"

"I am sure my aunt Bradley only wishes to be of kind help to you."

"Kind!" Judith directed her stunned gaze at him. "Do you not *remember* Miss Ripley? I am sure you met her several times."

"I am afraid I do not recall that pleasure."

"She frightened me to death with her harsh ways and exacting nature. Miss Dowdle was a paragon next to *the Rip*. There was no pleasing the woman. I shudder at the thought of bringing such a creature under our . . . that is, your roof."

"Brightwell Court is your home now, Judith. You know that. For as long as you like."

"Thank you, but I should not presume—"

"Of course you must tend to the education of your children."

"But they are not my children."

"Judith"—his voice held mild reprimand and cajolery—"they are yours now. You know Dominick would want you to treat them as your own."

"I suppose. If his mother's gout were not so bad, I imagine she'd insist on raising them herself." Judith sighed. "Such a pity girls' seminaries have fallen out of fashion among persons of quality."

"But Audrey is still young. I hate the thought of sending her away at such a tender age."

"Do you?" Judith's eyes softened.

Edward looked away from her melting gaze. "Andrew will need be sent to school eventually, but I do hope it will not be too soon."

"How kind you are, Edward. Most men would not appreciate having another man's children underfoot."

"Judith, they are very welcome, as well you know."

She wrinkled her fair brow in thought. "There is a girls' boarding school in St. Aldwyns, I understand. Audrey would not be so very far away."

"Tugwell and I recently discussed that very place," he said dryly, but did not explain why. "Still, how much better to educate her here at home."

"It gives me such pleasure to hear you say that, Edward," Judith said, a slight blush in her cheeks.

Edward nodded, but felt uncomfortable under her praise. It was his father's generosity that housed them all. Not his.

Judith pensively studied the letter once more. "I don't suppose . . . No, I doubt it would be quite the thing."

"What?"

"I wonder . . . What about Miss Keene?"

"Miss Keene?"

"She is wonderful with the children and has none of the superiority and pretense I so despise in governesses."

Edward stared at her, rather taken aback and not sure if he should welcome or forbid such a course. He knew Miss Keene's "sentence" was over and he had no right to keep her any longer if she wished to leave. Might such a post entice her to stay on?

Judith continued, becoming more animated as she warmed to the notion. "I am already acquainted with her, as are the children. And she is very educated, you know. She has a fine hand and she speaks or at least writes French and Italian. And she plays. Well, a little."

He could not resist teasing her. "Are you so disappointed she turned out not to be a foreign princess that you shall make her governess instead?"

She wrinkled her nose at him, the expression reminding him of their days as childhood playmates.

He asked, "Has she ever been a governess before?"

"I don't believe so, but her mother was governess to Aunt Margery and Aunt Phillipa. And when I pressed her, she admitted she taught in a girls' school somewhere. I forget where. If they would provide a character reference for her, I should be well satisfied."

He studied her, perplexed. "Why are you doing this, Judith? Do you really so revile governesses in general, or have you some other reason for wanting Miss Keene in the post?"

"Many reasons. She is clearly an intelligent, patient young woman who adores children. Who adores *my* children. She has already taken it upon herself to begin teaching them their sums and to improve their reading. All the while performing her other duties quite admirably. What are the chances of finding some stranger who can do as well, and who would fit so well into our household? I own, the change would require a few adjustments.

For one, we shall all of us have to call her Miss Keene, instead of her Christian name."

"You and I do so already."

Judith nodded. "I have never been comfortable using her Christian name," she said breezily. "There is such an air of the lady in her countenance. I am afraid she shall turn out to be nobility yet, and I want nothing to answer for." Her dimple showed. "But beyond that, I see no great obstacles."

"I must say, Judith. I am impressed . . . I can almost believe you care for the girl."

She shrugged. "Not a fig. I simply relish the thought of amusing my friends with tales of our once-silent governess."

Edward slowly shook his head and felt a grin stealing over his features. "I don't suppose a month's trial can lead to any harm. We can always engage another governess should Miss Keene not suit. Shall I have Mrs. Hinkley speak with her, or would you prefer to do the honours yourself?"

❧

Olivia hesitated. "Governess? Good gracious. I don't know what to say. . . ." Was this an answer to her prayer for guidance? Or should she leave now that she could and risk going home, even though her mother had begged her not to return?

Sitting together in the housekeeper's parlor, Mrs. Hinkley handed Olivia a cup of tea. "I don't blame you, Olivia. It would mean quite a change for you. No more fraternizing with the servants, no tea and biscuits in the kitchen with Mrs. Moore . . ."

"But why?"

"My dear, are you not familiar with a governess's plight?"

"No." Her own mother had spoken little of those days.

"A governess is neither a servant, nor a member of the family. She must not socialize with either set. She is limited to the society of her pupils and the briefest contact with the children's parents, only as necessary to report any problems that arise."

"I do not presume myself part of the family, Mrs. Hinkley." The irony of that statement echoed in her ears. "But are you really telling me that, should I accept this situation, my dear friend Mrs. Moore will refuse to talk with me? That you would as well?"

Mrs. Hinkley fidgeted in her chair. "It is not that we would refuse outright, or be intentionally rude, but a very real wall will rise between us.

"I do not say this to discourage you from accepting, for you are no doubt doing those children more good than Miss Dowdle ever did, and I know you deserve the higher wages . . . but nor do I wish you to accept the situation unaware of what it will mean. We will very much lose you, my dear. And I for one will be sorry for it."

Olivia reached out and pressed Mrs. Hinkley's hand. "You are very kind to warn me. But I have always wanted to teach. I wish what you are saying were not true. For I shall be very lonely without all of you."

"Yes, my dear. I am afraid you most certainly will be." For a moment longer, the housekeeper regarded her with a gaze almost mournful. Then she drew herself up as sharply as if she had clapped her hands. "Well, if you have your heart set upon it, there is only one more thing to do."

Mrs. Hinkley rose and fetched quill, ink, and paper from her small desk. "Mrs. Howe would like to write to that school where you assisted and request a character reference."

Olivia's heart began to pound dully within her chest. Her brief joy fell away. She ought to have anticipated this. It was one thing to hire her without a character as a lowly under nurse, but as governess? Responsible for the education of two children?

"So, if you will just write down the direction, I will give it to Mrs. Howe."

She handed Olivia the quill and paper.

Blood roared in Olivia's ears. Dared she? She had no doubt

Miss Cresswell would write a fair and complimentary assessment—at least she would have been certain before recent events. Had Miss Cresswell heard what she had done? When she received the letter, Miss Cresswell would learn where Olivia was living. Would she feel obliged to share this information with her father, if he lived—or the constable, if he did not?

She thought once more of the silent schoolroom high in Brightwell Court, lying fallow as an unplanted field, just waiting to be brought to useful life once more. Nerves quaking, Olivia lifted the quill and dipped it in the ink. With trembling hands, she wrote the name and direction. Creating a connection with loops of mere ink that might one day form a noose.

Who as I scanned the letter'd page
Took pity on my tender age,
And made the hardest task engage?
My Governess

—WILLIAM UPTON, *MY GOVERNESS*, 1812

Chapter 23

The aromas grew stronger as Olivia descended the stairs to the kitchen. Something spicy, sweet, and tangy, like autumn, which seemed so long ago now.

"What is that delicious smell?" she asked Mrs. Moore, who was busy filling jars with quartered apples.

"Hello, Olivia. Just preserving the last of the apples in ginger syrup. My dear, I have heard the news and must congratulate you."

"It is not official yet, Mrs. Moore. We still await a reference from my former schoolmistress."

"And she'll write nothing but the highest praise, I don't doubt."

"I hope you are right."

"Of course I am. Clever, kind young lady like you. No skeletons in your brief past, I shouldn't say."

"I don't know about that."

Mrs. Moore eyed her closely. "Then you and I would have something in common, love."

Olivia wanted to ask her what she meant, but the woman began bustling about in her usual way, bringing teacups and filling a plate with lemon biscuits. Her face while she worked was impassive and welcomed no inquiry.

"We shall sit and have ourselves a memorial tea, shall we? One last hurrah." Mrs. Moore sat beside her on a stool pulled up to the worktable. "Though I for one will be sorry for it."

Olivia could hardly believe she would no longer be welcome in Mrs. Moore's kitchen. Bravely, she sipped her tea and tasted the biscuit. "Delicious!"

Mrs. Moore smiled, but the expression did not quite reach her eyes.

"May I ask," Olivia ventured, "how long ago your sister passed on?"

The woman nodded as though she had expected the question, as though the topic had already been in her thoughts. "Must be eight and twenty years now. Alice was just fourteen."

"Alice? Is she . . . their daughter?"

Mrs. Moore nodded. "They had only the one child. What a dear girl she was, Alice. Never knew the kinder. Called me Aunt Nellie, though everybody else called me plain Nell. I can still hear her sweet voice and feel her arms around my neck. . . ." Mrs. Moore's eyes shone with tears once more, and she dug into her apron pocket for a handkerchief. "Avery was a different man then, I can tell you. What with Maggie to keep him fed and Allie to keep him tender." She smiled tremulously through her tears.

Olivia felt answering tears fill her own eyes. Fearing she already knew the answer, she asked quietly, "What became of Alice?"

Mrs. Moore sniffed and looked down at her hands. "They say

she run off with a young man when she were eighteen, but . . ." She glanced up at Olivia, then away. "But between you and me," she whispered, "I know better."

"Have you never heard from her?"

Mrs. Moore shook her head, staring at some unseen point beyond the high windows. "She's with Maggie now, she is. I suppose that is some comfort."

"Poor Mr. Croome," Olivia breathed.

"Poor Mr. Croome, indeed." Mrs. Moore sighed, then straightened. "Well, that is enough of that. What a sorry last hurrah this is! But I will miss you, my girl, upon my soul, I will."

"And I you."

Olivia squeezed her friend's hand—too tightly she realized when the woman grimaced, but she could not help herself. Its impression had to last.

As she left the kitchen, Olivia crossed paths with Johnny Ross outside the servants' hall. His broad shoulders all but blocked the narrow passage, giving her little choice but to pause before him.

He shoved his hands into his pockets and stuck out his chin. "Governess, ey? I suppose that means you'll have no use for the likes o' me. Fancy yourself above me now, I'll wager."

"No, Mr. Ross, I don't—"

"Mr. Ross, is it? And I must call you Miss Keene now, and never more kiss you."

Glancing about and hoping no one was near, she whispered tersely, "Which you ought not to have done at any rate."

"Never said so before."

"I could not speak at the time, if you will recall."

His lip curled. "How high and mighty you've become already. I told the others that was how it would be."

She gaped. "Thank you very little. I prefer you not speak of me at all. What have I done to deserve your cruelty?"

"Me, cruel? It's you what used me ill."

She frowned. "How did I ever?"

"By throwing me over. You're too good for me now."

She shook her head. She had never thought of Johnny as a serious suitor. If she were honest with herself, she had always thought herself a little above him but could not admit such a thing now. He would never believe her rise in station was not what had come between them.

Doris scuttled toward them down the passage, laundry basket on her hip. She said tartly, "Let her be, Johnny. I'll have ya if she won't."

Doris winked at Olivia as she passed by.

※

Less than a week after Olivia had provided Miss Cresswell's direction, Judith Howe marched past her in the corridor, a letter in hand. "A glowing recommendation, Miss Keene." She waved the letter. "As I was certain it would be. I have wonderful instincts about people." Mrs. Howe headed for the stairs, to share the news with Lord Bradley, she guessed.

Olivia was relieved. She was also curious about Miss Cresswell's letter and wished she might read it herself. Would it contain any clue about what was happening at home?

She decided she would write to Miss Cresswell herself and ask. Now that she had revealed her whereabouts to her, what could it hurt? She wondered if she was still obligated to ask Lord Bradley to approve her letters now that her trial period was over.

While awaiting the reference, Olivia had prepared for her post as best as she could. There were several volumes in the schoolroom for use in instruction as well as books of advice, like: *Hints to Governesses* and *The Plan for the Conduct of Female Education*. The advice she read was often contradictory. Was a governess supposed to focus on making her pupil a "finished" lady, or a knowledgeable one?

Olivia did not wrestle with this issue for long and soon began developing her plans to help Andrew improve his reading, as well as introducing literature, poetry, French, Italian (it was the language of music after all), geography, the sciences, religion, and of course, arithmetic. According to the advice books, she must also teach Audrey plain and ornamental needlework, dancing, and drawing, as well as continuing the girl's lessons on the pianoforte. Later, a music master ought to be brought in, as well as a dancing master.

The list seemed endless. But instead of growing weary at the thought of the overwhelming work ahead of her, Olivia felt more alive and purposeful than ever before. She could hardly believe she would be instructing pupils in the very room where her mother had once taught. She hoped she might be half as good a teacher.

※

Olivia was both excited and nervous that first morning in the schoolroom. More nervous than she would have been, because Judith Howe joined them, saying she wanted to see how things got on. Audrey sat at attention at the table, hands clasped before her, posture erect. Andrew slumped beside her, eyeing Olivia warily, as if unsure about this new creature who looked a great deal like his under nurse but who now stood so officiously before them, iterating the rules of the schoolroom.

Mrs. Howe said in a loud whisper, "Do sit up straight, Andrew."

Olivia continued with the rules, much as Miss Cresswell had begun every term.

Judith Howe interrupted to say, "I do not allow any physical discipline, Miss Keene—just so we are clear. My own governess was a fiend, and I shall not have Dominick's children subjected to such."

Olivia nodded. She did not condone harsh tactics, but some form of discipline would likely be required, and she feared Mrs. Howe had already done a good deal to undermine her authority.

Rules dispensed with, Olivia decided to begin with the topic with which she was most comfortable. Arithmetic. She began by writing a few simple addition equations on Andrew's slate, and a few somewhat more difficult problems on Audrey's.

Audrey began to figure her answers speedily, but Andrew only sat, chalk still.

Judith walked over and stood beside him. "Andrew, those are so simple! You are not even trying."

"I am, Mamma, I am. You make me nervous. I wish you were not watching me."

Olivia wished it as well.

Andrew furrowed his little brow, his tongue protruding as he pressed the chalk hard on the slate, figuring one answer, then hesitating on the second. Olivia glimpsed Audrey writing a tiny number in the corner of her slate and tapping it lightly to draw his attention to it. No doubt she could have finished her equations already, but instead she was trying to help her brother. Olivia knew she ought to reprimand the girl but did not. She saw what Audrey was doing—trying to help her brother please a critical parent. For though generally kind to the children, Mrs. Howe did reprimand the boy a good deal more than she did Audrey.

Unbidden, Olivia was reminded of herself as a girl—of the time she let that Harrow boy win to spare him humiliation. Tears pricked her eyes, both at the pain of the memory and the pang of affection she felt for Audrey, trying to protect her brother. Olivia determined to do all in her power to fill the gaps in young Andrew's education . . . and in the attention paid him.

Eventually Mrs. Howe became bored and excused herself, telling Olivia with a flourish of her pale hand to "carry on."

When the door closed behind her, Olivia took a deep breath. Audrey and Andrew did the same.

Knowing the children were not used to attending for hours on end, Olivia declared a recess in lessons at two. She would have liked to take the children out of doors, but the weather was very rough—freezing rain *speck-speck*ed against the windowpanes.

So, instead, Olivia instigated a game of puss in the corner and felt her own spirits rise as she attempted to amuse her pupils.

Becky, who now filled the role of under nurse as well as nursery-maid, went downstairs to bring up the dinner tray. Olivia surprised the children by speaking French throughout the meal, encouraging them to repeat the names of simple objects, *"fourchette, poulet, pomme de terre,"* and to ask for things to be passed with *"si'l vous plaît,"* and *"merci."* Audrey took to the game immediately, but Andrew groused, wanting plain old chicken and potatoes and to eat with his fork and not his *fourchette.*

Olivia did not reprimand him. She understood how difficult it was to exercise one's brain all day when ill-used to doing so. She felt fatigued herself. After dinner, she allowed him to skip rope, while Audrey learned a few new dance steps.

That night, after Becky helped the children into their night-clothes, Olivia went into the sleeping chamber to hear their prayers. Because Audrey and Andrew had spent the day in the schoolroom, with much of that time devoted to reading, Olivia thought they might prefer to skip bedtime reading. Both insisted vociferously that this was not the case. Olivia was heartened that the children wished to continue their bedtime ritual even though she was now their governess. She remembered all too well what they—or at least Andrew—had said about their last governess.

Chapter 24

*B*efore Olivia had a chance to write a letter to Miss Cresswell, she received one herself, which Becky brought upstairs to her at the request of Mr. Hodges. Apparently, Lord Bradley had no wish to review her incoming post. Accepting the letter, Olivia instantly recognized Miss Cresswell's fine decorative script and excused herself from the children to read the letter in private.

Dear Olivia,

I was pleased to write a reference to a Mrs. Judith Howe describing your superior suitability as a governess. I hope it will secure a situation for you that will be mutually beneficial to you and your pupils. I confess I was relieved to hear word of you, my dear, since you left so suddenly. I desponded of losing contact with you as well. Do you know

And there a word—*where*, she believed—was crossed out, quite unlike Miss Cresswell's normally exacting hand. The sentence continued

when you might visit us?

That is odd, Olivia thought. Perfectly polite, but not one mention of her father's fate, nor of her mother, though she and Miss Cresswell were longtime friends. Had Lydia Cresswell no reaction to her mother's leaving? Or had she not left after all? At least if her mother *were* still at home, Miss Cresswell was sure to tell her about the reference request, and her mother would learn of Olivia's whereabouts that way. When would she come?

At all events, Olivia was relieved the letter bore no word of condolence or censure. Surely Miss Cresswell would not write such a brief, polite letter had the worst happened.

❧

Olivia began the afternoon lessons by posing questions from Mangnall's *Historical and Miscellaneous Questions, for the Use of Young People*. Miss Cresswell had used the text a great deal in her classes, and Olivia had been relieved to find a copy on the schoolroom bookshelf.

"Now, Andrew, you will not know these answers yet, but do attend just the same please." She cleared her throat and read, " 'Name the significant events of the first century.' "

"I am afraid I don't know either, Miss Keene," Audrey said.

"Very well. Let us consider some of them." But before she could begin, Lord Bradley's deep voice filled the void.

" 'The foundation of London by the Romans,' " he began,

leaning against the back wall of the schoolroom. " 'Rome burnt in the reign of Nero, and the Christians first persecuted by him.' "

Olivia watched him, lips parted.

" 'Jerusalem destroyed by Titus, and the New Testament written.' "

"Bravo, my lord," Olivia acknowledged. "High honours for you. You forgot Britain's persecution of the druids, but, still, excellent."

He bowed.

Distracted from her course, and disconcerted by his blue eyes studying her impassively, she returned her gaze to the book and read another. " 'Name some celebrated characters of the sixteenth century.' "

"Oh!" Audrey said. "I know. Christopher Columbus and . . . Martin Luther."

"Very good, Audrey."

Lord Bradley did not look as pleased. "But what about reformers Calvin, Melancthon, and Knox. Or the great naviga-tors Bartholomew Gosnold and Sebastian Cabot, for whom Uncle Sebastian was named. And what of the astronomers Tycho Brahe and Copernicus?"

Olivia was beginning to feel piqued. "Well done, my lord, but you are not one of my pupils."

"Indeed I am not, and gratefully so. Might I have a word with you?"

She stared at him, uncertain.

"Alone?" he added.

She swallowed. "Andrew, please write the alphabet, and Audrey, as many first-century events as you can remember."

She followed Lord Bradley into the nursery, but Nurse Peale was snoring softly in her rocking chair, so he led the way out to the corridor instead.

"Miss Keene, are you trying to educate my young cousins or bore them to death?"

She gasped. "What do you mean?"

"*Mangnall's Questions*? That is nothing but rote memory. You've got to teach them to *think*, Miss Keene, to develop their logic and discernment."

"I plan to do that as well, my lord, but certain facts are essential and lay a foundation for future learning of politics, history . . . And Audrey is at a perfect age for memorizing facts. She is like a sponge."

"And Andrew like a dried bone."

"He is young, I admit, but I do give him other assignments that are more suited to his age."

"I should hope so. A boy of his energies cannot sit all day listening to you and his sister rattle off fact after fact about dead men and advanced concepts that are so much Latin to him."

"I understand your concerns. And, speaking of Latin, you will wish to engage a tutor for him soon. I do not claim to be an expert. Perhaps Mr. Tugwell?"

"Andrew is a bit young yet, do you not think?"

"Not if Mrs. Howe plans to have him educated at Harrow or Eton or the like."

"I do not believe she has any definite plans as yet, Miss Keene. I rely on you to educate him yourself, to the best of your ability. For now."

"I shall do my best, my lord, with what I have."

He studied her. "What is it you lack?"

"Texts suited to his age, a blackboard for geography . . ."

"A blackboard?"

"A wall-mounted slate. The invention of a Scots headmaster, I understand. Though I imagine large pieces of slate must be in short supply."

His mouth lifted sardonically. "Anything else?"

"A bit of patience on your part would be most welcome, I assure you."

"That too is in short supply." He gave her a long look, then turned on his heel, nearly colliding with Felix as he came up the corridor. She had not known he was again visiting for the weekend. Lord Bradley passed him without a word.

Felix watched him go, brows high, then turned to look at her. "He must think highly of you, Miss Keene, or he wouldn't push you so."

So Felix had heard Lord Bradley's reproof. She doubted his interpretation.

"It is true," Felix insisted. "My sister says you are an excellent teacher and very clever. Yes, I believe those were her words. Edward must see your potential and that is why he pushes you." He added good-naturedly, "And why he basically ignores me."

This caught her interest. "Does he?"

"Oh, do not mistake me. He is good to me. Just never satisfied. He is a dreadful perfectionist, as you must have realized by now. I have tried to dislike him but cannot quite stick to it. I should be terribly envious of him, and I suppose I am in some ways. . . . But I feel sorry for him at the same time. He has never really fit in, nor seemed happy. Not at Harrow, not at Oxford, not in London. Do you ever see him laugh?"

Olivia thought. "Sometimes, I think . . . with the children."

"If so, then it is only with them. At all events, when that green bug bites me, I say, Felix, which would you rather be? Unhappy heir to an earldom, or a jolly untitled man with decent means and an endless stack of invitations?"

Olivia smiled at him, touched by the vulnerability in his eyes.

"Ahh, Miss Keene. What a gem you are, listening to me prattle on. You know it is quite unusual for a man to take a governess into his confidence. Into his bed, yes, but not into his confidence. Not that you wouldn't be welcome in my bed—that is if you wanted to, which of course you don't. Do you?"

Olivia shook her head firmly, embarrassed. But she could not bring herself to be too angry at a suggestion so humbly presented.

"Ah well, never hurts to ask, as they say." He extracted a cigar from his coat pocket. "Now, you must excuse me. This cigar is demanding to be smoked, but my sister forbids me to do so indoors." He turned, then paused to add, "It has been a pleasure as always, Miss Keene, though I fear I dominated the conversation just as abominably as I did when you were mute."

The next morning, Edward gestured Miss Keene into his study and closed the door behind her. He began quietly, "Miss Keene, do be careful about my cousin."

"Mrs. Howe?"

He frowned. "I meant Felix. I have noticed the way the two of you . . . talk . . . together."

She lifted her chin. "I am allowed to talk now, am I not?"

He pursed his lips. "Yes, and you have obviously made quite an impression on him, but . . . " He took a step closer and lowered his voice. "Take no offense, Miss Keene, but you are not the first governess he has . . . shown interest in."

She lifted her stubborn chin. "Never fear, I did not flatter myself that I was. At all events, he seems a pleasant enough young man." She hesitated. "Most of the time. You might treat him more kindly."

"Kindly? Felix and I get on perfectly well."

"He thinks you disapprove of him."

"Disapprove of him?" Edward frowned. "He told you that?"

She nodded. "Though I ought not to have broken his confidence."

Edward admitted, "Some of his habits and manners are not to my liking. But I don't disapprove of him as a person."

When she didn't respond, he looked up and found her regarding him thoughtfully. "What?"

"Are you unhappy?"

Edward felt irritation surge. "Why would you ask that? Did Felix suggest it?"

She shrugged.

Edward detested the thought of Felix and Miss Keene discussing his character. And finding it lacking. "I may be a bit dour of late, what with . . . everything."

"But even before . . . everything . . . were you really happy?"

He thought for a moment and felt a wave of pain threaten to spill into consciousness. He pushed it away. "What an odd question, Miss Keene. And quite inappropriate, do you not think?"

He realized he was doing it again, referring to her status to put her in her place, to stop her provoking questions. He saw the quick look of hurt replaced by sparks of anger and, yes, disappointment in her eyes. She didn't say "hypocrite," but he heard it anyway and could not argue.

❧

At the end of her first week as governess, Olivia made her way belowstairs in hopes of seeing Mrs. Moore, even though she knew she ought not do so. Doris and the hall boy stood in the passage, and Olivia heard the pleasant chatter of teasing voices and girlish giggles. Approaching them, Olivia saw kitchen maids Sukey and Edith in the stillroom, and realized the four of them were together enjoying a respite from their work.

"Careful, girls, there's a lady among us," Edith warned.

"Oh, shut up, Edie," Doris said. "She's only doing what any of us would do, given the chance."

"Wouldn't see me with my nose in the air, no matter."

Not knowing what else to do, Olivia walked past without a word.

"If she is standoffish, I don't blame her," Doris hissed. "She don't make the rules. How would you have liked it if that last governess, that sour-faced Miss Dowdle, had tried to join in with the lot of us belowstairs?"

"Not at all, but she was a regular governess. A right snob."

Dory's attempted whisper followed Olivia down the passage. "But Miss Livie is one too now. A governess, I mean, not a snob. And it isn't done, is it? She cannot have it both ways."

Though thankful for Dory's championing of her character, Olivia was relieved to enter the sanctuary of the kitchen.

There Mrs. Moore looked up from her receipt book and straightened. "Liv—Miss Keene. I am surprised to see you."

Olivia sighed. "I was afraid you would not be happy to see me. No one is, it seems."

"Now, now, love. No need to play the martyr. I am happy enough to see you, but governesses usually don't venture belowstairs."

"But I am not a usual governess, am I?"

"Certainly not. Never knew one so clever nor so kind." Mrs. Moore's eyes twinkled.

Olivia smiled. "Would you mind if I sat with you for a few minutes?"

Mrs. Moore patted the stool beside her. "A lonely life, is it? With only the young ones and Nurse Peale about."

Olivia nodded. "Nurse Peale isn't much for talking. When she does, she mostly repeats remembrances of the past. Tales of Lord Bradley from his nursery days."

"Not diverting?"

"A little. But not the same as talking with you." She squeezed the dear woman's plump hand.

Mrs. Moore winked. "What you won't say to get one of my lemon biscuits."

On her way back upstairs, Olivia walked directly into the path of Judith Howe. The woman looked from the door through which Olivia had just emerged to Olivia's no-doubt-telling red face.

"Miss Keene. I know you were one of the servants for a brief time, but I had hoped the experience had not affected you to a marked degree. I realize you have never been a governess before, so allow me to enlighten you on the proprieties. . . ."

Olivia swallowed as she listened, realizing she had paid her last visit to dear Mrs. Moore.

The lower lake is now all alive with skaters,
and by ladies driven onward by them in their ice-cars.
Mercury, surely, was the first maker of skates. . . .

—S. T. COLERIDGE, *THE FRIEND*, 1809

Chapter 25

*O*ne afternoon in February, Edward stepped into the school-room only to find Miss Keene and the children about to step out, bundled in coats, caps, mufflers, and gloves.

"Where are you all bound for?"

"We are going ice-skating," Audrey said. "Do come along!"

"Ice-skating? I have not strapped on skates in years."

Andrew tugged his hand. "Come along, Cousin Edward, do."

"I haven't the foggiest notion where my old skates might be."

Miss Keene pulled the largest blades from the trunk with a flourish and held them before him.

"How . . . fortunate," he grumbled.

A few minutes later, cocooned in his beaver hat, coat, and gloves, much like the children, Edward led the way as the small troupe tromped through the snow into the village, then along a well-trod path to the mill. He explained that the miller diverted water from the mill leat every year to fill a skating pond behind the mill.

"Very obliging of him," Miss Keene said.

Edward considered this. "I suppose it is. I have never thought of it before."

Using an old millstone as a makeshift bench, Miss Keene helped Audrey strap skates to her half boots while Edward assisted Andrew with the same.

"Wait for me, Andrew, and I shall come out and help you," Miss Keene called, tightening Audrey's final strap.

Edward eyed the blades still lying on the millstone. "Are you not skating, Miss Keene?"

"Oh no, my lord. I don't think it would be proper. I only brought that pair in case one of you tore a strap." She glanced around at the few skaters on the pond. "Besides, I shall be more surefooted in my boots, and more able to lend a steadying hand."

"Not fair of you at all," he said in mock sternness. "Insist I come, then sit out yourself? Come, now. What may not be proper in London or in your prim girls' school is perfectly proper here."

"I . . . Oh, very well. I shall give it a go."

"That is more like it."

She strapped on her skates before he finished his own, and hurried onto the ice to assist Audrey, who was flailing her thin arms and appeared about to fall. Andrew was busy chop-chopping the ice as he marched along, not falling, but not really skating either.

"Glide, Andrew, glide!" she called.

Edward skated to Andrew's side and held his mittened hand. Miss Keene took Audrey's arm and attempted to steady her while quietly instructing her on proper technique. Suddenly the girl's arms flailed again—her feet flew out before her and she fell back, taking Miss Keene down with her. They both slammed hard against the ice. Edward gave an empathetic wince and skated quickly over, leaving Andrew to his own devices. He crouched over their prone forms. "Are you all right?"

"Mortified and sore, nothing more," Miss Keene quipped, sitting up.

"I am sorry, miss," Audrey said, scrambling to her feet and wearing a pained expression.

"Never mind, Audrey. You shall master it by and by."

Edward offered Miss Keene his hand and, when she took it, gave a hard tug to pull her to her feet. The lurch propelled him backward, causing him to lose his balance and fall back. And as Miss Keene's hand was still captured in his, he pulled her forward with him before he could think to release her. He hit the ice first, and Miss Keene fell onto his chest, knocking the air from his lungs.

Edward opened his eyes, squinting at the blinding sunlight reflecting off snow, and at the disconcerting experience of having the governess draped over his body. If he could but breathe, he thought, the sensation would not be unpleasant in the least. Her blue eyes, wide with shock, met his. For a moment, they simply stared at one another.

Then Audrey giggled and Andrew laughed out loud, breaking the spell that held them. Miss Keene's face blushed deep pink and she averted her gaze, quickly pushing herself up and finding her feet with less than her usual grace.

Andrew, oblivious to their discomfort, continued to laugh.

"It is not kind to laugh at the misfortunes of others," Edward grumbled, pinning Andrew with a look of mock severity, which only sent his young cousin into a convulsion of guffaws.

A quarter of an hour later, Lord Bradley skated beside her. "I see you fooled us all by falling at the outset. You are quite graceful on the ice, Miss Keene."

"Thank you, my lord." Olivia had not skated since girlhood, and could still hear Miss Cresswell saying that in her day *ladies* did not participate in such sport. Pushed in an ice-car, perhaps, but skating . . . ?

The Tugwell boys arrived, waving and calling greetings. They invited Andrew to join them in a game which involved hitting a ball about the ice with brooms and sticks.

Audrey sat on a millstone beside George Linton's niece, who was near her own age, and soon the bonneted heads were close in confidences and chatter.

The children pleasantly occupied, Lord Bradley and Olivia continued to skate. She relished the gliding freedom, the crisp air, and the rare moment of no demands upon her person.

"I am glad to see you enjoying yourself, Miss Keene," he said.

She smiled up at him.

"Are we paying you for this?" he teased.

"Very little."

"Ah. Good."

"And you, my lord. Are you enjoying yourself?" she asked.

"I believe I am. The experience has become somewhat infrequent of late, but yes, I believe I recognize this emotion as enjoyment."

She shook her head and laughed. "Take no offense, my lord, but what else have you to do but enjoy yourself?"

He grimaced.

Realizing that she had annoyed him, she quickly changed the subject. "You are very involved with the children, more so than many *fathers* are, and they so enjoy your attention, but—"

"But it appears strange to you?"

"I am only curious, not criticizing in the least."

He nodded. "Their father was a good friend, as I mentioned, older though he was. A mentor, of sorts."

"You feel an . . . obligation, then?"

He lifted his shoulders as if to shrug off an uncomfortable garment. "Not directly, no. Though how can one help but feel some duty toward children who have lost both father and mother?"

"I think many 'help it' with ease. Look at the foundling homes."

He sighed. "You will think me stranger than you no doubt already do."

"Impossible," she teased.

He looked at her, as though to be sure she was jesting. "Well, nothing to lose, then. You see, when I was a boy of eleven, I made a promise to myself. Wrote it down even."

When he hesitated, she looked up expectantly.

"I know you admire my father, Miss Keene, and I do not deny he has always been exceedingly kind and generous. He is a good man, and I take nothing from him—do not mistake me."

"But?" She skated to the edge of the pond and stopped to give him her full attention.

He stopped beside her. "But he was away in London a great deal. As a member of parliament, he was obliged to spend January through June or even July there. Six or seven months a year. Sometimes longer. My mother and I did spend several seasons in London with him—it was there I first made the acquaintance of Dominick Howe—but still, we rarely saw Father. Even when he was in the townhouse with us, he was always busy with bills or correspondence or what have you. Mother soon grew weary of town life. I think her health was not very good even then. So we stayed home more and more. And even when Father returned to Brightwell Court, he spent more time with his clerk than with me." He held up his hand. "I am not criticizing, nor seeking pity, Miss Keene, merely showing the situation that inspired me to write a promise to my future adult self."

She nodded, and could not help compare his father to hers. He had spent many hours with her, though few of them idyllic—testing her in arithmetic, showing her how to balance the books, how to figure odds, and all those hours at the races and the Crown and Crow. . . .

"I can still see myself, a boy of nine, perhaps," Lord Bradley continued, "then a boy of ten, then finally eleven, standing with my fishing pole, waiting at the garden door for my father, who had promised yet again to take me fishing—'tomorrow,' 'tomorrow.' "

"He never did?"

Edward shook his head. "Hunting a few times, a game of chess now and again, but never fishing. I remember Croome came upon me waiting there, pole in hand, when my father finally came out—but only to tell me that he just could not get away. Croome offered to take me. But my father dismissed his offer. I remember feeling oddly sorry for the gamekeeper, though I had never felt anything but fear of the man before"—he grimaced—"or since."

Poor Mr. Croome, Olivia thought. An outcast even then.

"Forgive me. I am going on as endlessly as Mr. Tugwell. All this to say, after that I ran upstairs to the schoolroom, found paper and quill, and wrote myself a promise—to remember what it was like to be eleven years old, to remember what summertime was for, and when I had a boy of my own, to dashed well take him fishing." He glanced at her sheepishly. "I may have said something stronger, but you take my meaning."

She grinned. "Vividly."

"I know Audrey and Andrew are not my children, but they are under my roof without a father of their own."

"I think it wonderful," she said, and began skating again.

He skated after her. "Not every woman of my acquaintance would agree with you."

She guessed he referred to Miss Harrington.

"Have you?" she asked.

"Hmm?"

"Taken them fishing?"

He expelled a breath bordering on a groan. "Everything but

that. I confess I never learnt how." Clearly uncomfortable, he quickly changed the subject. "And your father, Miss Keene? Did he take you fishing, or whatever the girlhood equivalent is?"

Olivia doubted horse races and taverns were the girlhood equivalent to anything as wholesome as fishing. "I had not really realized it until you described your own childhood, that while my father has many faults, he did spend time with me. Still, my father was . . ." She caught herself. "Is very different from yours. Were I you, I would be grateful indeed for such a father as Lord Brightwell."

"I am. But do not idealize him. You know him as he is now, the benevolent grandfatherly sort he has mellowed into."

"Are you saying he was once cruel?"

"No, never cruel. Just . . . imperious, busy, absent. And yours?"

She decided to risk telling him, realizing he might otherwise think she disapproved of her father for no very good reason. "He took me with him to the local public house and there had me display my arithmetic skills to entertain the other patrons."

"He was evidently proud of you. Wanted all the gents to know what a clever girl he had."

She bit her lip. That much was true.

"He also took me with him to horse races. Even to the Bibury Course, not far from here, I understand."

"Did he indeed? As a boy, I would have loved such an outing with my father above all things."

He was turning everything around on her. Confusing her. "He brought his clerking work home and had *me* balance the accounts for him. . . ."

"Astounding! Do you realize how rare a thing it is for a man to educate his daughter in his own profession? A son, yes. My father has groomed me to take over for him one day, so this is something our fathers have in common."

She felt her ire and incredulity rising. "Did the *Earl of Brightwell* teach you to accept wagers and take a handsome portion of men's winnings? Did he drink too much and throw things when angry?" She stopped herself. Did he not understand what kind of man Simon Keene was?

"No. That he did not do. Though he did take me to gentlemen's clubs in London where I was exposed to much the same."

Andrew skated between them, grasping a hand of each, and the conversation was abandoned.

Later, on the walk home, the children ran ahead, tossing snowballs at one another. Though Olivia had never told anyone the story of that most significant of wagers in the Crown and Crow, she felt compelled to do so now. Compelled to have another person judge the situation more objectively than she ever could. Had she really wronged her father? Or had he treated her unfairly? Lord Bradley listened with interest as she relayed the tale, doing her best to tell him the facts without coloring the story to put herself in better light, nor her father in worse. But Lord Bradley did not react as she might have guessed, or would have liked.

"The young man was a Harrow lad, you say?"

She shrugged. "Herbert something."

His eyes brightened. "Herbert? Herbert Fitzpatrick?"

"I never heard a surname. Nor his father's name at all." The name Fitzpatrick did seem mildly familiar, though she did not know why.

"I'd wager it was my old school chum Herbert." He laughed. "Boy never could conquer arithmetic. Pale boy. The blackest hair. How he would perspire during examinations! We teased him mercilessly."

"I cannot credit it. From London, was he?"

"You know, I just saw his father in church on Christmas. Visiting a sister or some such."

That was the man she had seen from the church gallery at Christmas?—the man she thought familiar but could not place?

"He lives in Cheltenham, I believe. But he mentioned Herbert is managing one of his interests in the north somewhere."

Olivia frowned, thinking back to what she remembered of the gentleman and his son. "I am not certain it can be the same Herbert. I distinctly remember they were merely passing through on their way home to Harrow and London."

"If memory serves, they moved to the Cheltenham area a year or two ago."

She did not respond to this, and after several minutes of silence, he said quietly, "It was not fair of your father to put you in such a position, Miss Keene. But do you not see what confidence he had in you? What pride? But he ought to have realized what you were about in allowing poor Herbert to win and been proud of you for that as well. It was very noble of you, especially for one so young."

"He was not in the least proud."

Lord Bradley looked at her, eyes soft in understanding. "I see that you did not have a typical upbringing, nor a typical father, Miss Keene. But as you have caused me to appreciate my father's qualities anew, I hope you will allow yourself to admit that your father has his good qualities as well."

"I don't want to admit it."

He looked at her, surprised. "Why? What do you risk in doing so?"

"More than you know." For if she admitted the good along with the bad, then how could she live with herself, knowing what she had done to him?

She did not tell him the most condemning charge against her father—what he had done, or at least tried to do, to her mother. She was too ashamed to form the words.

Rebuked and saddened, I resigned myself with no good grace
to my routine of instruction.
Where were all the romantic fancies and proud anticipations
with which I had accepted the position of governess . . . ?
—ANNA LEONOWENS, *THE ENGLISH GOVERNESS AT THE SIAMESE COURT*

Chapter 26

All that night, Miss Keene's words echoed over and over again in Edward's mind. *"What else have you to do but enjoy yourself?"*

The question goaded more than it should have.

Edward regarded himself in the looking glass above his washbasin. The face he always saw stared back at him, his fair hair darkening to a bronze in the long side whiskers, golden stubble glinting on his cheeks in the candlelight. His blond brows, a shade lighter than his hair. The pale blue eyes, so prevalent in the Bradley family, which he supposed was an ironic gift of fate. The nose, with the slight angle at its tip—a "gift" from Felix when they were boys and his cousin had rammed a sled right into his face. The snow had turned as bright red as cherry ice.

Edward had always assumed his looks came from his father.

People had even commented on how Edward favoured Lord Brightwell—in looks, if not in character or temperament. His father had always been sanguine—an easygoing man who did not demand perfection in himself or others. He was at his ease in company, smiled often, and everybody liked him.

Edward, however, was not easily given to smiles. His neutral expression was intense, he knew, always seeming to waver on displeasure or disapproval. Why, he could not say. As Miss Keene had remarked so flippantly, what had he to do but enjoy life? At least until recently, he'd had no real reason not to smile throughout his days of blessing and ease. Yet, he had not. It was as if every minute he had been waiting for the fairy tale to end, for someone to disappoint him, to take it all away and destroy the grand illusion. But no, he could not factor recent revelations into a character formed over four and twenty years when he'd had not one inkling that he wasn't his father's boy. His mother's son.

His mother had known, however, and Edward found himself wondering if her awareness of his low birth had colored her perception, made her suspect his behavior and abilities were not all they should be. If she had sometimes been critical—*surely he might be further along in Latin,* and *what did he mean he had no ear for the Italian?* How his laugh *grated on her nerves* and his *table manners were low indeed.* Might not any mother have the same irritations with a son—boys being what they were, especially when young? Still, he knew she had loved him in her way. And he had loved her. Tears pricked his eyes at the thought. He would always miss her.

Perhaps he was more like his mother in temperament. More critical of others, never satisfied with his own performance. After all, he had spent more time in her company than in his father's, who was occupied with parliament so much of the year.

Parliament. Edward had known from boyhood that he would take his father's seat one day. He thought he might be good at lawmaking, since he tended to see things in black and white. Right or wrong. Good or bad. A person of quality or not. Educated or uneducated. Master or servant. But now . . . ? What sort of person was he?

If his secret was exposed, what then of his career in parliament, his marriage to Miss Harrington, his future as an earl? It was all at risk now. And if it all disappeared tomorrow . . . ? What then? What would he do with his life?

❧

Olivia sat at the library table on Sunday afternoon, playing chess with Lord Brightwell. Winter sun spilled in through the library window through which she had first laid eyes on the earl and his wife. How long ago that seemed. Dust motes floated on the shaft of sunlight, which illuminated the ornate pieces and inlaid chessboard of the rosewood table. The earl seemed preoccupied, whether with his next move or something of greater import she did not know.

Lifting his queen, Lord Brightwell began, "Olivia, I must tell you something about your mother."

Olivia dropped her chess piece. "You have news of my mother?"

He nodded gravely. "I sent a man to search for her when you were ill. I thought she would want to know."

"A search?"

"You had been quite vague in your direction, if you will recall, something about 'near Cheltenham.' "

Olivia blushed.

"I am afraid he returned unsuccessful. When you finally named your village—for the school reference—I sent Talbot once again on horseback. Winter roads being what they are, he would never have made it in a carriage. As it was, he barely got through. In Withington, he located the constable, who was able to direct him to the home of Simon and Dorothea Keene."

Olivia nodded. "The cottage with the green door, just past the cobblers and beside the churchyard."

"Not any longer," he said quietly.

Olivia started to say Talbot must have missed it. It was a small cottage after all, but something in the earl's eyes stilled her tongue.

"He found the house, my dear, but no one was there."

Olivia swallowed, her mind working. "My father . . . was perhaps away at his work, and my mother gone. . . ."

"My dear, I do not mean that no one was home at that moment. I mean that no one had lived there for some time. The place was deserted. A neighbor confirmed it."

Olivia flinched. Was it as she feared, her mother gone and her father dead? But if her mother had left, why had she not gone to the school in St. Aldwyns and been directed to Brightwell Court? Or learnt her whereabouts from Miss Cresswell and come directly to find her?

Lord Brightwell scooted his chair closer to hers and held her hands in his. "Talbot spoke with several neighbors. While no one claimed personal knowledge, the rumor is that Simon Keene has fled the village to avoid arrest, and that your mother . . ."

Father is alive. I did not kill him. Her brain barely had time to register relief at this confirmation before a new fear swept in to take its place. "Yes?" she urged.

"There is a new grave in the churchyard, Olivia. I am deeply sorry to have to tell you that Dorothea Keene is believed dead."

Olivia stared with unseeing eyes. Her heart felt as if it had burst within her, and throbbed with the pain of it. Had her father lived only to end her mother's life?

"The constable would neither confirm nor deny anything. He told Talbot if he wanted to know who was buried in the churchyard, he would have to ask the church warden. That man referred him to the local midwife. A Miss . . ."

"Miss Atkins."

"That was it. But she would tell Talbot little. Seemed very suspicious of him and said she was under no compulsion to tell a stranger anything. When Talbot asked if she knew where Dorothea Keene was, the only answer she made was, 'She won't be coming back.'"

"I don't understand," Olivia said, voice trembling. "There must be some mistake. Miss Atkins would tell me everything. I know she would." Olivia leapt to her feet. "I shall have to go home."

His expression deeply apologetic, the earl said, "My dear, the roads are quite impassable at present after the recent snows. You shall have to wait for a thaw."

She bit her lip and blinked back tears. "At the first opportunity, then." She strode to the door, then forced herself to turn back, adding woodenly, "Thank you for telling me."

❧

Edward found Miss Keene a short while later, sitting on the fallen log beside the river, crying into her hands. Scooping aside the wet snow, he sat down next to her on the log.

She looked up with red-rimmed eyes. "Did Lord Brightwell send you to find me? I am sorry to have troubled you."

"He did not send me, Miss Keene," Edward said gently. "But he is concerned about you. As am I."

She drew in a shaky breath. "I thank you, but I shall be well presently."

He tilted his head to regard her more closely. "Good. But I should like to stay with you, if I may."

"Have wild dogs been seen again?"

"No."

She nodded, tears trailing down her cheeks. Edward longed

to touch her face, to wipe the tears from her eyes. But she turned away from him toward the river.

He said, "Lord Brightwell briefly described to me what Talbot learnt, and the rumors of your father's hand in your mother's disappearance. If true, how I regret defending him that day on the ice." Edward hesitated. "Do you . . . think such a thing possible?"

She inhaled. "A year ago I would not have believed it. But now . . . yes, it is possible, though I pray I am wrong."

He lifted her cold hand and placed it onto his palm. She had neglected to wear gloves. When she didn't stiffen, he began to softly stroke her knuckles with his free hand.

"I know," he murmured. "I know."

"Yes," she whispered, "you must know. You have lost two mothers yourself."

For the first time, he allowed himself to acknowledge that truth. "Yes, I suppose I have."

They sat in silence for a long moment.

Edward hesitated. "I am sorry I kept you here. Kept you from returning home."

She shook her head. "I could not have gone home then in any case. And now . . . if what Talbot discovered is true . . . there is nothing to go home for."

He didn't know how to respond. Simply held her hand.

After a moment she said, "Mr. Tugwell once told me he was praying that God would work 'all things together for good.' But I do not see how that can be so now."

Nor I, Edward thought, but forbore to say so.

I sit alone in the evening, in the schoolroom.
Really I should be very glad of some society,
it would be such an enjoyment.

—MISS ELLEN WEETON, *JOURNAL OF A GOVERNESS* 1811–1825

Chapter 27

Tamping down her sadness, Olivia did her best to keep to a schedule, knowing children thrived under order and regularity. Bedtime promptly at eight was the rule, although Mrs. Howe often disturbed their routine, coming in after the wicks were extinguished to kiss Alexander "just once more."

While she was there, she would bid Audrey and Andrew "good night" or "sweet dreams," and how they, the boy, especially, would beam up at her. Now and then Judith would stop by his bed and lay her hand on Andrew's head, much as Lord Bradley often did, and ruffle his hair. The look of pleasure on the boy's face always pricked Olivia's heart. Did the woman not see the power she held to wield joy or pain?

Seeing how much these nighttime visits delighted her charges,

Olivia did not think to complain about them, even had she dared.

And so they passed the next few weeks of winter in relative peace and tranquility, Olivia's uncertainty over her mother's fate wavering from grief to hope and back again. She kept busy, finding new and more active ways to teach Andrew, while Audrey continued to advance in her studies by the methods that had proved so effective at Miss Cresswell's.

Still, Olivia had never spent so much time alone in her life. When the children ate suppers with the family, and each evening after they were in their beds, Olivia spent time alone in the school-room, since it was larger and warmer than her room, and more private than the nursery, which was clearly Nurse Peale's domain. There, she read or sewed by candlelight. She thought back to the fine needlework her mother had done for Mrs. Meacham, the wife of her father's former employer, and more recently, for the wife of his new employer as well. Olivia had not such fine skills with the needle, nor such patience for the craft, but she could repair hems and darn socks, and that passed the time better than nothing.

She remembered with fondness the small cushions and bed-clothes she had fashioned for the doll's house Lord Bradley had made. How she had enjoyed working on that clandestine project with him.

Lord Brightwell had extended an open invitation for her to sit with him in the library of an evening, but this she did but rarely, loath as she was to cause gossip among the servants.

In bed at night, the doubts would come, torturing her with endless scenarios of what might have happened after she left home. Feeding her worries over her mother's fate . . . and her own. And where was her father? A part of her longed for the roads to clear quickly, while another part dreaded the confirmation of her worst fears.

In the meantime, she arose each morning eager to return to the schoolroom, to lose herself and her worries to teaching once more.

She even began teaching Becky to read and write whenever the maid's heavy workload allowed. She took great satisfaction from this. She thought Nurse Peale, who sometimes hovered nearby to watch when Becky bent her head over her slate or a simple book, would complain. But she did not.

On a day in early March, Olivia was listening to Becky read aloud from one of Andrew's books, helping her whenever she stumbled over a word. The two women froze when Lord Bradley strode into the nursery without knocking. He drew up short at seeing the two of them huddled together near the hearth, a candle lamp between them, for the evening was dark and rainy.

"A new pupil, Miss Keene?" he asked, and she could not tell if he was angry or simply curious.

She rose. "Yes, my lord. Becky is coming along nicely with her reading. But we only have lessons when Becky's duties are done, and Andrew and Audrey are with you or their stepmother."

"Where are they now? I have just returned from Northleach and can find no one about the place."

"Mrs. Howe took the children to visit their grandmother Howe."

"Dominick's mother? Good. And my father?"

"I am afraid I do not know."

"Well, the roads are finally becoming passable. Perhaps he has gone on some long-neglected errand or some such."

Olivia thought of the promised trip to Withington, once the roads had cleared. Surely he had not gone without her.

"Would you join me in the study, Miss Keene? When you are through here, of course."

"Certainly, my lord."

Becky looked at her apologetically, as though it was her fault

Olivia was about to be reprimanded. She smiled at the girl, hoping to reassure her.

When Olivia stepped through the open study door a few minutes later, Lord Bradley rose from his chair near the fire.

"Please, be seated."

If she were about to be called to account, she would rather stand. "Do you not approve of my teaching Becky? As I said, I only do so when the both of us are—"

He lifted a hand to silence her. "I do not disapprove, Miss Keene. That would be rather hypocritical of me, would it not? But do be warned that Mrs. Howe might not be as liberal minded as I have recently become."

"Very well."

"Please sit down," he repeated. "I would ring for tea, but well, I think . . ."

She sat in the facing chair. "No, thank you, my lord. Nothing for me." She understood perfectly that a servant bringing tea to the young lord and the governess would set tongues to wagging in a hurry.

He sat down again as well. "I am curious, Miss Keene. I would think after teaching all day, taking on another pupil would be the last thing you would want to do."

She chuckled. "I believe it is the other way round. Becky is so exhausted by day's end, she can barely keep her eyes open to read."

He leaned back, steepling his fingers. "Do you really enjoy it so much?"

Olivia shrugged. "I know it may sound strange. But I believe God made me to teach, or at least gave me abilities that lend themselves to the calling. I have wanted to be a teacher—like my mother before me—since I was a little girl."

Tears pricked her eyes, and she quickly changed the subject. "What was it you wanted to be as a boy?" She studied his face as though the answer might be written there.

He looked away, uncomfortable. "Be? I wanted to be who I *thought* I was."

"Do, then. What did you want to do?"

It was his turn to shrug. "Gentlemen are not expected to work at much of anything. I was not born with a burning desire to accomplish something great *soli deo gloria*, like Bach or Beethoven, Rembrandt or Copernicus." He paused, thinking. "I did look forward to being Earl of Brightwell someday—peer of the realm, member of parliament, and all that—though *why* I looked forward to it, I could not say. I suppose because it was what I always expected to do."

He repositioned himself on the chair. "May I ask. Before you came here, what were your plans? Were you really going to teach at that little school in St. Aldwyns?"

"I hoped to."

"That was the dream I have kept you from?"

"No, my lord. A stepping-stone at best."

He looked at her expectantly.

"You will laugh."

"I will not."

"Very well. My dream is to have a school of my own one day. Ideally, with my mother as partner, though I have always known it was unlikely my father would allow her to do so. And now . . ." She clasped and unclasped her hands, taking a deep breath to steady herself. "But even on my own, I believe I could be mistress of a school one day. And I would love nothing more than to open its doors to all girls, regardless of their ability to pay."

One corner of his mouth lifted. "Only girls?"

"There are many more schools for boys, and as someone has so kindly pointed out to me, teaching boys is not my forte."

"I am sorry I said that."

"You were quite correct. At the time. But I believe Andrew is getting on famously these days."

"I believe you are right. What would we have done without you, I wonder."

She felt her cheeks heat. She had not meant to praise her own abilities. "No doubt some other governess would be performing as well, if not better. Never fear, I do not think myself irreplaceable."

He looked at her intently. "Oh, but there are those who would argue that."

She did not ask if he were among them.

Once Miss Keene had taken her leave, Edward resumed his seat by the fire, staring at the orange embers and the occasional flame that tongued to life. What he had said to Miss Keene was true enough. He felt no burning desire to do anything specific. Yes, he would have enjoyed the prestige and privilege of being lord of the manor—the running of the estate, investing in the property, and seeing the rewards of careful management. But even then, he would actually *do* very little. A clerk and perhaps a new steward would manage the daily affairs, while his tenants, workmen, and servants accomplished the actual work.

He did not enjoy managing people, and tensed whenever Mrs. Hinkley or Walters brought to him some concern with a servant or tenant. He did not mind hearing the problem, nor offering solutions, but was uncomfortable with tears and excuses.

He took well to his new role as village magistrate, which had seemed good practice for his service in the House of Lords yet to come. He had also enjoyed reading law at Oxford, though as a gentleman and future earl, he had never considered taking up the law as a profession—nor any profession for that matter. But now?

Miss Keene had said that she knew she wanted to be a teacher like her mother since she was a little girl. Charles Tugwell, a clergyman like his father before him. Was it not natural that he had planned to follow in his father's footsteps as well?

The only actual work he had enjoyed as a boy was building things with Mr. Matthews. The old steward had not been keen on accounts, but could repair a carriage wheel or a window casing with equal aplomb. He had often given Edward and young Felix scraps of wood, bent nails, and wooden mallets and had let them build whatever they willed. Felix had turned out boards with bent nails. Edward, a bench which stood in the stable yard to this day and a humble three-tiered bookcase, which had graced his bedchamber for several years, then disappeared while he was away at school. Become so much kindling, no doubt.

Mr. Matthews had built with stone or wood. From a drawn plan or from a scheme in his mind. And Edward had found great satisfaction in assisting him, especially during those long months his father was away.

But Edward had only helped, and boasted few real skills to speak of. He had given it all up as a young man. Carpentry and building had no place at Oxford. Architecture, perhaps. But he had no lofty dreams of building cathedrals or palaces. And he could not go into trade—building benches, bookshelves, and doll's houses— could he? How his supposed friends, even the villagers and his tenants, would scoff at the thought of Edward Stanton Bradley in such a humble profession.

Were other men so directionless? Of his peers, decidedly so. But, he reminded himself, they were his peers no longer.

In every town you go through, you may see written in letters of gold,
"A Boarding-school for Young Ladies."

—CLARA REEVE, 1792

Chapter 28

The roads were slippery, muddy, and full of deep ruts. Olivia gripped the strap above the seat and hung on tightly as the carriage jerked and swayed. She had thought Lord Brightwell had been exaggerating the road conditions in order to put off this trip, to delay the inevitable disappointment he felt sure Olivia would suffer. Now she was suffering indeed on the tooth-jarring, stomach-churning journey, which seemed far longer than the sixteen miles it was. When Talbot stopped to water the horses, Johnny Ross let down the step so she and the earl might stretch their legs. Looking away from Johnny's cold glance, Olivia noted with dismay the mud-splattered coach and horses.

On their way once more, Olivia watched from the window as they passed through villages which became increasingly familiar with each mile. Fossebridge, Chedworth, and finally the outskirts of Withington itself, a grey-stone village on the river, sitting high on the Cotswold uplands. The closer they came, the closer her heartbeats seemed to sound until they were almost one atop the other in an erratic drumbeat. Beside her, Lord Brightwell squeezed her gloved hand.

When the carriage halted, Johnny once again lowered the step, opened the door, and gave her a hand down. She needed his assistance more than usual, for her legs felt suddenly weak and weightless. She looked about her and saw little had changed, except that the trees sported new buds where leaves of yellow and brown had been when she left. There stood the old mossy-roofed Mill Inn and, across the river, the Crown and Crow. And there the sleepy, slanting churchyard of St. Michael and All Angels.

Not ready to contemplate the churchyard, she quickly turned away. The cobbler's door was propped open to allow in the temperate breeze. And there, their low stone wall, her mother's bit of garden, their cottage of blond stone with its green door. The place looked much the same as ever, yet different somehow. Forlorn. No smoke rose from the chimneys, no welcoming light shone from the windows.

Olivia walked up the stone path and tried the door. Locked, as it rarely had been. She bracketed her eyes with gloved hands and, peering in the windows, saw that the place looked tidy but unlived in. No vase of early spring blooms graced the table, no kettle sat on the stove, no log glowed in the hearth. No . . . life. Her stomach twisted. Perhaps her mother really was dead.

"Have you a key?" Lord Brightwell asked. "Or perhaps a neighbor might?"

She shook her head. "Never mind." It was people she wanted to see, not empty rooms.

She crossed the lane and knocked on Muriel Atkins's door, but no one answered. Asking Lord Brightwell to wait for her, she walked across the village in hopes of seeing Miss Cresswell.

At the school, she let herself in and found the woman answering correspondence in her office. Olivia was relieved not to have to go looking about the schoolrooms for her. She was not ready to face her former pupils, nor to answer awkward questions.

"Olivia!" Miss Cresswell exclaimed upon seeing her. She rose quickly and hurried around the desk to embrace her. "My dear, how pleased I am to see you. I must tell you how relieved I was to receive that character request or I would never have known what became of you. Why did you leave so suddenly? I feared I had offended you somehow."

"Never, Miss Cresswell."

"You and your mother just seemed to disappear overnight!"

Olivia felt suddenly winded. "When did you last see her?"

"Not since you left in the fall. I thought . . . hoped . . . the two of you might have gone off together."

Olivia shook her head. So her mother had left . . . or been killed, right after Olivia fled?

Miss Cresswell's countenance dimmed, and she once more sat behind her desk, gesturing Olivia into the chair before it. "I was afraid to ask in my letter, not wanting to alarm you, in the event you did not know."

"Is it true what people are saying?" Olivia asked. "About the new grave in the churchyard?"

Miss Cresswell reached across the desk and touched her arm. "Oh, my dear. I had hoped you were spared that rumor. I avoided mentioning it when I wrote to you. The churchwarden will not say who is buried there. I believe Muriel may know, for she has been acting devilish queer for months, but she has told me nothing. You might ask her, but she is off attending a lying-in somewhere out in the country. I know not where."

"Where is my father now?"

Lydia Cresswell hesitated. "Have you not heard? There is a warrant out for his arrest."

Olivia swallowed. "For . . . murder?"

Her old mentor looked at her askance. "Murder? My dear, why would you think that? The specific charges have not been made public, but the rumor is embezzling."

"Embezzling?"

"That is what they are saying. Though some people still insist it relates to his part in your mother's disappearance, which I for one do not credit."

"I don't understand. . . ."

"You do know your father had been managing the spa Sir Fulke is developing near Cheltenham?"

Olivia shook her head. She knew her father clerked for a new employer, but not that he had been given such great responsibility. "I heard he fled the village to avoid arrest after he . . . after I left."

Lydia Cresswell pursed her lips in thought. "That was the rumor, but the warrant has only recently been issued. I believe he lived out at the construction site all winter. Though now . . . as he hasn't been seen there, nor here, for nearly a fortnight, he may very well have left to avoid whatever charges Sir Fulke is bringing against him."

Miss Cresswell interlaced her fingers on the desktop. "I gather Sir Fulke requested the charges be kept private, because if it is a case of mismanaged funds, and his investors hear of it, there will be a terrible scandal and they might all bail out."

Father, steal? Why could she not believe it, when she believed him guilty of far worse?

Olivia squeezed her eyes shut to clear the whirling confusion, then looked up at Miss Cresswell once more. "When you see Miss Atkins, will you ask her to write to me? With any word of my mother. Even . . . bad news?"

Lydia Cresswell squeezed her hand. "Very well, my dear. May I ask about your situation. It goes well?"

"Yes, I think so."

"And being a governess, it is to your liking?"

"I cannot say I would not prefer to be back in a school, but it is a satisfying, if sometimes lonely, post."

Miss Cresswell nodded. "I am afraid I have hired Mrs. Jennings, as you left with no word of returning, but if you are in need, perhaps—"

"Thank you, no, Miss Cresswell. You are very kind, but I am satisfied where I am. For now." She rose, and Miss Cresswell followed suit, promising to write and let Olivia know if she learnt anything new.

Olivia next visited the constable—ironmonger by trade. How strange to seek out one of the very men she had feared might come looking for her not long ago.

When she entered the shop, the tall bald man looked up from the nails he was sorting. "Miss Keene! It's glad I am to see you. We was worried some dire fate befell you as well."

"As well, Mr. Smith?"

He looked sheepishly troubled and pushed paint-stained hands into his pockets.

Olivia pressed her lips together. "I am well as you see, Mr. Smith, I thank you. But I am looking for my mother. Have you seen her?"

He shook his glistening head. "You ain't the only one. Several folks were here askin' after her last fall. Your own father amongst 'em. Devilish sorry to tell you he is a wanted man, miss. Did you know it?"

"I have just heard. Who else has been trying to find my mother?"

"Oh, there was a liveried man here some time ago, inquiring on behalf of a Lord somebody I never heard of, or so he said. I sent 'im on his way sharp-like. Sir Fulke asked after 'er as well. Seems yer mum did sewing for his missus or some-like. Took a hard fall down the stairs he did. Ears still ring fierce, I gather."

"I am sorry to hear it."

"Are you? Never liked the man myself. Surprised you would, after what he did to you and yer father."

"Do you mean, accusing Father of . . . some crime?"

"That too, but—do you not remember? In the Crown and Crow, that wager twixt you and his Harrow boy?"

"*That* was Sir Fulke?"

"Aye. Sir Fulke Fitzpatrick. Did you not know it?"

Fitzpatrick . . . Lord Bradley had been right. "We never learnt the gentleman's name at the time, and I have had little cause to see the new owner of Meacham's estate. He must not have recognized my father or he never would have kept him on as clerk."

"Oh, 'twas his steward what kept 'im on. Sir Fulke hasn't much to do with the day-to-day running of things."

"And his son, Herbert. Is he here as well?"

"He comes to visit his mother every month proper, but lives to the north somewhere, managing some interest of his father's."

Lord Bradley had been right again.

"I see." But Olivia didn't see. Her mind was whirling. Could it really be? That snobbish gentleman and his son who passed through the village more than ten years ago, had returned to the area, purchased Mr. Meacham's estate where her father worked, and kept him on as clerk, never knowing he was the same man he had humiliated before his peers? Accused as a cheat?

Had her father not recognized him? Surely they would have crossed paths at some point, even if the steward hired him. A chill prickled up Olivia's neck and scalp. Had her father recognized the gentleman all along, and kept the knowledge to himself, planning his revenge in the form of financial ruin? As logical as it sounded, something within Olivia rebelled at the thought.

"And Miss Cresswell was lookin' for you as well. Seemed fiendish odd that you would up and leave town without a word to yer father or your employer."

"I . . . needed to leave quickly."

His brows rose. "And why was that?"

Ignoring his question, she asked, "Did my mother . . . disappear . . . the same day?"

"I couldn't say, as I don't exactly know when you left or when she left, only that yer father first reported you both missing on—" he stepped to a corner desk and consulted a grimy notebook—"the second of November."

Olivia had left on the eve of the first, if she remembered correctly. "Morning or afternoon?"

"Evening, though I don't recollect the specific time. I gather he came home the night before and fell asleep, not knowing the house was already empty. He did not see either of you next morning, but thought maybe you'd gone out. And since he had to hurry to his post, he did not report the two of you missing until that evening. Sober as a puritan he was too. I remarked upon it at the time."

"Did you verify that—that he spent the day at his post?"

He narrowed his eyes. "Why would ya ask that? Suspect yer old man of having somethin' to do with yer mum's disappearance?"

Did she not? She shrugged. "Is not a spouse always suspect?"

He slowly shook his head, dark eyes glittering. "The man loves yer mother. I for one cannot imagine 'im harming her. You ought to have seen 'is face when he come and reported the two of you missing. Devilish white-faced, he were. Worried some evil had befallen the both of you."

Had Simon Keene been shaken to find his wife missing? Or because of what he had done to her?

"Yer tellin' me the two of you did not leave together?" Smith asked.

"No, sir," Olivia said. "She was still at home when I left."

"You still haven't told me why you had to leave."

Dare she tell him the whole truth? Would she be in trouble if she confessed striking her father in defense of her mother, even though she had not killed him as she once feared? Her father was already a wanted man. Did she really want to be responsible for suggesting him guilty of worse? To be responsible for his hanging?

When she had not witnessed anything more than assault? When, in fact, Simon Keene had lain unconscious on the ground when last she saw him?

"I left for a post, sir. My mother thought I might obtain a place in a school she was familiar with in St. Aldwyns."

"That where you are presently?"

"No. But nearby."

"With that gentleman who accompanied you into the village?"

He evidently saw her surprised look. "Ah yes. I have eyes and ears everywhere, I do, miss. Had them that night as well."

What was he implying? That he knew or guessed her part in that night's violence? Or that he knew something else?

"Yes. He is my employer."

He proffered his notebook. "If you would be so good as to give me 'is name and direction? In case I have any further questions or hear anything about Mrs. Keene?"

Olivia swallowed, but complied. What had she been thinking in returning to Withington? Now her whereabouts would be common knowledge. But did it matter anymore? The constable was not trying to find her, nor, it seemed, was her father.

"And if you hear from either of your venerable parents, especially Mr. Keene, I trust you will be good enough to send me word?"

Olivia's throat seemed impossibly dry. She nodded wordlessly and took her leave.

The return journey to Brightwell Court was an exceedingly quiet one.

Few governesses could expect to obtain situations
after the age of forty.

—RUTH BRANDON, GOVERNESS, *THE LIVES AND TIMES OF*
THE REAL JANE EYRES

Chapter 29

*T*he house had seemed empty while his father and Miss Keene were away, and Edward had been plagued with the notion that Miss Keene would not be returning to Brightwell Court. He was relieved to have been wrong.

His father confided the little he had learned from the venture, and Miss Keene, it appeared, had reverted to silence.

Three days after the trip, Edward was startled when Judith rushed into the study and took his arm. "Edward, do be a dear and come with me. My mother and mother-in-law are here—the both of them! I need moral support. A diversion. Reinforcements. Something."

He chuckled and rose. "I shall greet them, of course, but do not expect me to sit for hours of gossip, and talk of fashion, and I know not what."

He followed after her as she hurried out into the hall. She rushed to greet the ladies even before Hodges could escort them into the withdrawing room.

"Mamma! Mother Howe! What a surprise. I did not expect you. Certainly not at the same time. If I . . ." Judith hesitated, seemingly stunned to glimpse a third woman behind the first two.

Following her gaze, the elder Mrs. Howe said, "Your mother was kind enough to help me locate your own former governess."

Judith nodded stiffly to a plain, exceedingly thin woman in her mid to late forties. "Miss Ripley," she murmured, then quickly turned back to her mother. "But did you not get my letter, Mamma? I have engaged a new governess just as you suggested. It was not necessary to bring Miss Ripley here."

"Well, we are all here now," Judith's mother said. "Are we to be invited in, or shall we stand here in the hall?"

"Of course. Do come into the drawing room. I shall order tea."

While Osborn and Hodges took their wraps, Edward stood awkwardly, awaiting an opening to greet the women. Judith seemed to suddenly remember his presence, which a moment before had seemed so imperative. "You remember Lord Bradley, our cousin?"

"Indeed I do," the elder Mrs. Howe said. "A great friend to my poor Dominick, God rest his soul. How are you, dear boy?"

Edward pressed the woman's hand. "I am well, Mrs. Howe. Delighted to see you again. You are well, I trust?"

"Gouty leg, I fear. Otherwise quite well."

"And Aunt Bradley. What a pleasure." He kissed his aunt's powdered cheek.

"Upon my soul," Judith's mother said. "You look more like your father than ever."

"Indeed?" Edward hesitated. "I . . . thank you. You are very welcome here, ladies. I hope you have a pleasant visit."

"Will you not join us for tea?" Judith asked, her smile strained.

"Thank you, no. I must take my leave of you."

He bowed to the ladies, ignoring Judith's panicked expression. He would not be trapped in a room with this gaggle of females. Not for the world.

❦

Osborn, breathing hard, beckoned Olivia to come down to the withdrawing room directly, explaining that Mrs. Howe and her guests desired her to attend them.

When Olivia entered a few minutes later, she quickly took in the scene. Judith Howe, hands fluttering nervously, stood beside the mantel. Two matronly women in their late fifties sat perfectly erect on the settee. One shabby, stick-thin woman a decade their junior sat on a chair in the corner.

As Olivia crossed the room, Judith's gaze swept her person with approval, and Olivia was glad she had taken a moment to re-pin her hair and smooth her skirts.

"Mother, Mother Howe, may I present Miss Olivia Keene, our new governess."

Mrs. Howe, the older of the two matrons, narrowed her eyes. "That gown. I have seen it before. Is it not one I recommended for your *trousseau*?"

"I do not think so," Judith forced a little laugh. "But I have been wearing mourning so long I cannot recall my former gowns. At any rate, I doubt I shall fit into any of them after having a child."

"Endeavor to eat less, my dear," Mrs. Howe said. "For economy's sake in both food and clothing."

Judith's smile grew tight. "How kind of you to offer advice, madam, but really, why do you concern yourself? It is not your money that pays for my clothes, nor feeds me and the children."

The older woman stiffened. "If you should like to live with

me, Judith, you are welcome to do so. With economy, we should do well enough were we both to take in needlework."

"Thank you, no, madam. The children and I are quite comfortable here."

"For how long, I wonder?" The younger matron, Judith's mother, spoke up.

"What do you mean?" Judith asked.

"Lord Bradley is of an age, my girl. When he marries, the new mistress of the house may not look kindly upon sharing her husband's home, money, and . . . attentions . . . with you."

Mrs. Howe, continuing the previous topic, said, "Dear Jeannette, God rest her soul, went right back into her maiden gowns after Audrey was born."

"How nice for her," Judith said with acerbic sweetness.

Mrs. Bradley, still elegant and attractive as her daughter would no doubt remain, turned cool eyes back on Olivia. "Miss Keene, is it? From where do you hail? Would I know your family?"

"I would not think so, madam. I come from Withington."

"I do not know any Keenes. Has your family any connections to speak of?"

"I am not certain."

"And your father . . . what sort of gentleman is he?"

Olivia lifted her chin. "He is not a gentleman of any kind. He works as an estate clerk."

"A clerk? Really, Judith, where did you find this girl? What made you think her suitable?"

"She attended a very good school, Mamma. She reads and writes French, Italian, and I know not what."

"Does she indeed?"

"Yes, madam," Olivia answered for herself. "I attended Miss Cresswell's School for Girls. And after, Miss Cresswell was good enough to make me her assistant."

"Never heard of a Miss Cresswell," Judith's mother-in-law murmured, pulling a loose thread from her sleeve.

"And your mother, Miss Keene?" Mrs. Bradley asked. "I suppose it is too much to hope that she is a woman of gentle birth?"

"Indeed she was," the earl announced from the doorway. The ladies started. "Forgive me, ladies, but I could not help overhearing your, mmm, interview with Miss Keene."

"Lord Brightwell!" his sister-in-law exclaimed. "We did not intend to disturb you."

"You do disturb me, madam, if you question Miss Keene's suitability. Not only is she extremely clever and accomplished in her own right, but her mother is of the Cirencester Hawthorns, with whom I believe you are some acquainted."

"The Hawthorns?" the elder Mrs. Howe said. "Why, we have not seen that family in years, not since Thomas Hawthorn died and his wife and daughters moved away."

"Did your sisters not have a governess by the name of Hawthorn?" his brother's wife asked.

"Indeed, madam. Dorothea Hawthorn is Miss Keene's mother, and a finer governess I have never known."

His sister-in-law's brow puckered. "I seem to remember something about that governess. Now what was it? She left without notice, I believe. But there was something else. . . ."

The earl's warning look did not match his words. "What a keen memory you have, Mrs. Bradley."

"Do you know, I remember something of that family as well," the elder Mrs. Howe said, eyes alighting on the tea tray Osborn carried in, laden with cakes and tarts. "Of course they lost their home when Mr. Hawthorn died and the estate was entailed onto some cousin or other. But one of the sisters made an excellent match. Married a gentleman of means, a Mr. Crenshaw of Faringdon, and Mrs. Hawthorn, I understand, lives with her daughter on Crenshaw's estate."

Mrs. Bradley gestured for Osborn to lay the tea things on the table before her, as though mistress herself, then returned a cool gaze to Olivia. "While the other sister, your mother, married a . . . clerk?"

"Miss Keene," Lord Brightwell interjected, "if you have finished your visit with these fine *Christian* ladies, I wonder if you might join me in the library. I have hit another snag in the estate records and am in need of your skilled eye and mathematical prowess."

Olivia guessed he had fabricated the latter for the benefit of his hearers, but did not mind the pretense. In fact, she felt like kissing his hand.

After stopping briefly in Lord Brightwell's library for the requisite look at the records—in which she found a small error within a matter of minutes—Olivia excused herself, wishing to return to Audrey and Andrew. In the corridor, she found Miss Ripley sitting alone on a bench near the drawing room door. From within came the sounds of conversation and the musical ting of china, as the other ladies took tea together. Miss Ripley made a piteous figure, and Olivia, who had tasted a small sampling of a governess's lot, felt sorry for her.

"Miss Ripley. Would you care to join me in the schoolroom?"

The woman's drawn face brightened, then fell once more. "Thank you, miss, but you do not want me."

"Indeed I do. Did I not ask you?"

Compelled by Olivia's response, delivered more tartly than she had intended, the woman roused herself and followed Olivia up the many pairs of stairs to the schoolroom. Olivia opened the door with a flourish, secretly proud of the organization of the room. While Olivia added more coal to the stove, Miss Ripley surveyed the neat desk and table, maps and globe, easels and hung landscapes, books and slates with apparent approbation.

Rubbing skeletal fingers over the books on Olivia's desk, she asked, "What texts are you using?"

"*Mangnall's Questions*, primarily, as well as—"

"Excellent. Nothing better. And discipline, Miss Keene? Have you instilled proper discipline in your pupils?"

"I do not know. I own I sometimes struggle to command their attention."

"Never say so! You must rule with an iron fist—or rod, Miss Keene. A good boxing of the ears never goes awry either."

"I do not think . . ." Olivia decided nothing would be gained by voicing disagreement and said instead, "I am sure Mrs. Howe would never allow it."

"Miss Judith tasted her share of discipline as a girl, I can tell you, and it did her a world of good. I shall talk to her before I take my leave. Encourage her to be more stern with the children and allow you to be as well."

"Th-thank you, Miss Ripley. But that is not necessary. That is, I am finding my way."

"You shall never find your way without discipline, Miss Keene. Do not make the mistake of trying to befriend your pupils. You are not their friend; you are their governess, and so you must govern. They will not like you. Do not expect it. Expect them to show neither warmth nor appreciation, and you will not be disappointed."

Olivia stared at the older woman and saw a brittle façade formed by years of rejection and ill treatment. She said quietly, "It is a lonely way to live, is it not?"

"Of course it is. But any governess worth her salt knows so going in and expects no more."

"But . . . without friends, or warmth, or appreciation?"

The older woman looked at her then, as if for the first time. "It is our lot."

Olivia touched the woman's arm, and Miss Ripley jumped as if burned. "Would you take tea with me, Miss Ripley?"

The older woman's eyes glistened. "Thank you."

Becky brought them tea and a plate of Mrs. Moore's ginger biscuits, and the two governesses sat together at the schoolroom table.

"I was prepared to hate you, Miss Keene," Miss Ripley admitted over her teacup. "The inexperienced youth taking the post I wished for myself. I need a place, you see. No one wants a governess quite so old as I am, it seems."

Miss Ripley took a ladylike sip, then regarded Olivia earnestly. "I was not the only person surprised by your youth, Miss Keene. Before the ladies dismissed me, Mrs. Bradley commented on it to Miss Judith. She said you were altogether too young and pretty to be trusted. I gather she is concerned you will turn Lord Brightwell's head."

"Lord Brightwell?" Olivia assumed she had misheard.

"Yes." Miss Ripley took a delicate nibble of her biscuit. If she were not so homely, she might have been elegant. "Miss Judith asked her mother if she meant Lord Bradley, Lord Brightwell's son, but Mrs. Bradley was quite adamant. Then she realized I was listening and said no more."

"How strange. Lord Brightwell is old enough to be my . . ." The word stuck in Olivia's throat. "I assure you, Miss Ripley, that there is nothing of that sort going on."

Miss Ripley lifted one thin shoulder, her small smile a knowing one. "I would not blame you if there were. We must do what we can to secure our futures, I say."

Olivia gratefully took up this change of topic. "And what will you do now, Miss Ripley? Return home?"

"I haven't a home, Miss Keene. I have lived in other people's homes for more than twenty years. Sharing chambers with boys in nightdresses and curls, boys who have long since died in wars or had children of their own. Few remember me, and none fondly. I met a governess once—a Miss Hayes, who was so adored by her charges that she moved with them into adulthood, serving as governess for their children and then, when she was too old to work, lived with the family as a beloved friend. I have heard only one such story. More common are tales of governesses too old to work, or at least too old to be pleasant to look at and so not hired, begging menial work, living in a small rented room, and then on the streets, slowly starving to death." She took another bite of her biscuit. "No one is governess by choice, Miss Keene. It is a role of necessity. Of survival. A gentlewoman's only real means of putting a roof over her head and keeping herself clothed and fed."

Miss Ripley surveyed Olivia head to skirts. "I know what circumstances compelled me to enter the profession all those years ago, but I wonder at yours. I suppose your father could not, or would not, support you. But you are too pretty not to have offers of marriage, and you might have taught at a girls' school instead. May I ask what has driven you to this?"

Olivia stared at the woman, taken aback by her long and forthright speech. When was the last time Miss Ripley had had another adult to talk to, as an equal?

"I did assist in a girls' school," Olivia acknowledged, "but circumstances, as you say, compelled me here." Her father *had* supported her financially. Olivia could not say otherwise. But nor did she feel compelled to defend the man. He was a great part of the reason she was here after all.

Chapter 30

After Judith's mother, mother-in-law, and former governess had taken their leave, Judith cornered Edward in the billiards room, where he was enjoying a solitary game.

"Did I not tell you?" she exclaimed. "Miss Keene is granddaughter of a landed gentleman!"

"Hardly a Prussian princess, Judith."

"Still. I knew there was more to her than met the eye."

"Why are you elated? Are not most governesses gentlewomen of reduced circumstances?"

"Come, Edward, admit it. You thought her no better than a charwoman when she first arrived."

He shrugged. "Her grandfather might have been gentry and

her mother of gentle birth, but as her mother married a clerk, Miss Keene is not even a gentleman's daughter."

"What a snob you are, Edward. Really, it is quite surprising."

He stilled. "What is?"

"Hmm?" Judith said, idly twirling a cue ball on the felt.

"You said it is quite surprising. What is? That I am a snob or that Miss Keene should be daughter of a clerk?"

There was laughter in her eyes and a touch of pique. "Both, I suppose." She turned and flounced from the room.

That evening, Olivia sat on her narrow bed and once again turned over the sealed letter she had found in her mother's purse. Should she open it? If her mother was dead, as a part of her feared, did not the brief directive inscribed upon it bid her to do so? And if she was not dead, as Olivia still hoped and prayed might be the case, then might whatever was inside help Olivia find her? She wondered yet again if she should have opened the letter sooner. Guilt and indecision pulled her this way and that. *Almighty God, what should I do? What is right? I wish to honour her request, but I want to help her if she needs me. . . .*

Hands trembling, she slid a fingernail under the seal and pried it open. She unfolded it only to find another letter within, this one sealed as well. It looked like an ordinary letter, directed to a *"Mrs. Elizabeth (or Georgiana) Hawthorn."* The surname rang in her memory. Had not Mrs. Howe and Mrs. Bradley discussed the Hawthorns as her mother's family? Her mother had said almost nothing about having family over the years, except to say that all ties had been cut between them. Now her mother was writing to them, but a letter meant to be delivered only after her death?

She would not open a letter directed to another. Nor could she post it in good conscience without knowing her mother's fate.

Needing counsel, she sought out Lord Brightwell and found

him on the garden bench, smoking a cigar amid the budding trees and daffodils of an early springtime evening. She showed him both the outer and inner letters.

"You have had these all along?" He studied the outer letter more closely. "She must have feared something would happen to her. Forgive me, my dear—of course we still hope and pray that she is alive and well."

While Lord Brightwell considered the situation, Olivia prayed for wisdom for them both. After several moments, he set down the letters. "Well, there is nothing for it. You must go to Faringdon and see them."

Olivia's heart began to beat faster. "Will they receive me, do you think?"

"I do not know. But I hope they shall. You, after all, cannot help your mother's unfortunate marriage."

The words bit hard. She did not like to hear him say so, true though it was.

"Shall I accompany you?" Lord Brightwell asked.

"I don't wish to inconvenience you, my lord."

"It might be wise if I went along. At the risk of sounding proud, you may be better received."

❧

Taking Lord Brightwell's card, the Crenshaws' footman went to ascertain if Mrs. Hawthorn was "at home" to visitors. Olivia's pulse raced and her hands grew damp within her gloves. She had taken extra time with her appearance, wearing half boots and a new spencer jacket, purchased from Miss Ludlow, over her dark blue gown, hoping it would give her the confidence she needed for the meeting ahead. She expected no warm reception from this woman, grandmother though she may be, since she apparently disowned her own daughter years before. Olivia took a deep and shaky breath, relieved Lord Brightwell had insisted on accompanying her.

They were shown into a formal drawing room. A dainty woman in her midsixties rose to greet them, and Olivia felt a start of recognition. The woman's nose was somewhat hawkish and her face lined but attractive. Lord Brightwell bowed and the woman gave a shallow curtsy, whether because of stiff limbs or lack of due respect Olivia did not know.

"Lord Brightwell, how do you do."

Olivia wondered if she might acknowledge that her daughter Dorothea had once had a situation with his family, but she did not.

"Mrs. Hawthorn. Thank you for seeing us."

At the word "us," Mrs. Hawthorn glanced at her. Olivia's heart lurched. Yes, there was a definite resemblance to her mother, in the eyes and high cheekbones. Was it her imagination, or did the woman falter as well?

"May I present Miss Olivia Keene," Lord Brightwell said.

Olivia dipped a low curtsy, and when she rose again, the woman had not moved, but was studying her. And not with a smile.

"I have not met Miss Keene, I do not think?"

"No, madam," Olivia said quietly.

"Do be seated." Mrs. Hawthorn regained her seat.

Lord Brightwell sat in a chair across the low table, while Olivia sat near the woman's left.

"Now, to what do I owe this visit?"

With fingers suddenly thick and clumsy, Olivia withdrew the inner letter from her reticule and handed it to the woman.

"What is this?" The woman's thin, kohl-darkened eyebrows rose. Then she squinted at the writing and Olivia wondered if her eyesight was poor. She turned it over, saw the seal. "Who has written this? I take it you know?"

Olivia nodded, somewhat surprised and disappointed that the woman had not recognized the hand. "Dorothea," she answered simply.

Whatever reaction she had expected, it was not this. The

woman threw down the letter as if a venomous spider clung to it. "After all this time? She writes a letter and has *strangers* deliver it?"

Olivia withdrew the outer envelope and handed it to the woman. "It was sealed in this," she said quietly.

The woman stared at it, then brought it close to her face, until it touched her brow. When she lowered it again, Olivia saw tears in the woman's eyes. She grimaced and said bitterly, "I should have known. After more than twenty-five years, she would not contact me otherwise."

"We are not certain Dorothea is . . . has died," Lord Brightwell said. "But she has disappeared and we fear the worst. We are hoping that if we are wrong, something within might help us find her."

Still the woman hesitated.

"Please, madam." Olivia retrieved the rejected letter and handed it to her once more.

The woman swallowed, a bony ball moving within her thin, withered neck. She accepted the letter, eyeing Olivia once more before returning her gaze to the seal. She broke it with stiff fingers and unfolded the single sheet within.

Olivia waited, anxiety rising. What possible good could come from this? It had been a mistake to come here.

She felt Mrs. Hawthorn's penetrating look and forced herself to meet the woman's eyes.

"You are this Olivia. Her daughter?"

Olivia nodded.

Mrs. Hawthorn fixed her eyes on her a moment longer, then refolded the letter. Olivia fought to keep her face impassive. How she wanted to read it—any words her mother had written!

"I am afraid there is nothing here to help you," the woman said.

"Nothing?" Olivia asked, and in her own ears her voice sounded like that of a petulant child.

Mrs. Hawthorn laid the folded letter on the chair beside her and crossed her arms as though chilled. As though to protect herself. Did she fear Olivia had come to ask for money, or to be taken in like a poor destitute foundling?

"I want nothing from you, madam," Olivia said softly, "save any information about my mother. I had hoped she might have come to you when she . . . disappeared . . . and could not find me."

"She did not."

When the woman offered no more, Olivia rose and said somewhat frostily, "We shall trespass upon your time no longer."

The earl stood as well.

"I think it highly unlikely Dorothea would contact me," Mrs. Hawthorn said. "But if I am wrong, do I understand that you are . . . staying . . . at Brightwell Court?" She looked from Olivia to Lord Brightwell.

Lord Brightwell, perhaps roused to defend Olivia, to step in with a warm gesture when her maternal grandmother had not, said, "Yes, Miss Keene is living under my protection, and that of my son."

Olivia wondered why he had mentioned his son. Did he fear Mrs. Hawthorn might assume an inappropriate relationship between himself and her, had he not? She very well might, Olivia realized.

"It does not appear that you are friendless, after all," Mrs. Hawthorn said, leaving Olivia to wonder once more just what her mother had written, and concluding from the woman's words that she felt relieved of any obligation to aid or even contact her ever again.

Mrs. Hawthorn added, in an offhanded manner, "It might interest you to know . . . a man came here several weeks ago now, asking for Dorothea. I refused to see him and had my man send him away, though he did not go quietly."

Father? Olivia wondered. *The constable?* "What . . . sort of man?"

"A gentleman, by appearances, though certainly not by behavior. I own I glanced from the window and saw him as he swore at my footman and climbed back into his chaise. I did not see his face."

Not the constable. Her father, perhaps, in new clothes and a hired chaise? It seemed unlikely, but who else could it have been?

A chain of gold ye shall not lack, Nor braid to bind your hair;
Nor mettled hound, nor managed hawk, Nor palfrey fresh and fair.

—Sir Walter Scott, "Jock O'Hazeldean"

Chapter 31

On a misty March morning, a basket over one arm, Olivia led the children through the wood. As they went, she pointed out primroses, wood anemones, and the last of the snowdrops with their modest, bowed heads. She identified many birds as well—flitting yellowhammers, jackdaws building nests, and a chain of rooks flying over the budding treetops.

When they neared the gamekeeper's lodge and stepped into the clearing, they found Croome slopping his pigs.

"What is it this time?" he asked in a long-suffering manner, as though it were a trial indeed to be given delicacies from the best cook in the borough.

Olivia lifted the basket on her arm. "Rump steak pie and canary pudding."

One wiry brow rose.

She chuckled at his scandalized expression. "There are no canaries in it, sir."

He reached for the basket, but Olivia turned as though she had not noticed. "We are learning about animals today, Mr. Croome," Olivia said. "And I thought you might be able to help us."

"What? Me do yer job fer you?"

"Who better? Who knows more about animals than you do?"

"I only know game, and cows and pigs and chickens and the like. And o' course all manner o' land fowl and waterfowl."

"And predators, Mr. Croome?"

"Oh, aye. A gamekeeper has to know his enemy, doesn't he? The owl, the raven, the wildcat, and weasel. But I'm no teacher. Never have been and never will be."

Olivia sighed. "Very well. Children, is a partridge a land fowl or waterfowl?"

"A bird?" Audrey guessed.

"A pigeon!" Andrew exclaimed.

Mr. Croome shook his head, not taking the bait.

"And what do wildcats eat?"

"Milk?" Audrey guessed.

"Pigeon!" Andrew exclaimed.

Croome threw up his bony hands in disgust. "Boy, have you ever seen a wildcat?"

Andrew shook his head.

"If you had, you'd know such a greedy beast would not bother with a tiny bird when the wood is filled with hares. That's his favorite, mind. Though he'll eat pheasant or partridge and all manner o' fowl if need be. It's why I keep Bob inside at night."

"Who's Bob?" Andrew asked.

When the man hesitated, Olivia sweetly supplied, "I believe he is Mr. Croome's pet partridge."

She was rewarded with a barbed glare.

"You keep a pet partridge?" Audrey asked in awe.

"I do, and don't be mockin' me."

"No, sir!" Andrew said. "May we see him?"

Audrey added, "May we feed him?"

Croome leveled a long look at Olivia, resentment fading to resignation. "Oh, very well, you rogues. I'll bring him out and show ya."

From the basket, Olivia lifted the stack of two covered plates. Croome reached for them, but Olivia held fast. "Mrs. Moore will need these returned. Have you something we might transfer the food into?"

His brows dropped darkly, but she thought she saw the faintest flash of humor in the silvery blue eyes. "You don't fool me, girl. Just want to nose about my place, don't ya?"

She only shrugged. "These dishes do grow heavy. . . ."

"Oh, come on, then. Wipe yer boots, Master Andrew—it isn't a pigpen."

Inside, Croome slid the pie and the lemon yellow pudding into basins of his own while the children fawned over Bob, who followed Croome about like a devoted hound. Olivia walked slowly about the room, taking in the dust, the cobwebs, a humble bookcase, and two colorful paintings on the wall, displayed in fine beech-wood frames as though in a portrait gallery. She bent closer to peer at them. Though the paper was coarse, the paintings themselves were surprisingly good. The first showed a man from the waist up, head tilted to look at a small bird in his hand. The man wore a hint of a smile as if he knew he was being observed. The artist had captured a put-out, though tolerant, expression.

"Why, this is you!" Olivia exclaimed. She had barely recognized Mr. Croome with a smile.

He scowled at her over his shoulder. "Stop yer pokin' about. I wouldn't keep a likeness o' me in plain sight, but Alice done it. Painted it, framed it, and hung it there. It pleased her, so I leave it. Now, leave it be."

Ignoring him, Olivia studied the second painting. It was of a woman—head and shoulders—surrounded by a border of colorful flowers and cherubim. Her face was not as clear as Mr. Croome's likeness, but held a vague, ethereal beauty.

"Is this your wife?" Olivia asked.

"Aye. That's my Maggie." Croome left the children feeding flies to Bob and joined her at the wall. "A decent likeness, though Alice painted it from memory after her mother was gone."

"She is beautiful."

He nodded. "I recollect she was even lovelier. Though I would think it."

"I am sorry for your loss," Olivia said. She would have liked to ask about Alice but did not dare.

"Not as sorry as I am." He stepped back to the table. "All right. Here's Nell's dishes. Now, quit yer meddling."

❧

Edward strolled leisurely through the wood, intent on visiting his favorite spot near the river. The air was fresh and smelled of new grass and recent rain. Robins sang *twiddle-oo, twiddle-eedee* in a cheerful chorus around him. Into this chorus joined children's voices, and Edward paused. He heard laughter and an odd *fwwt, smack* sound. What in the world? Was Miss Keene in the wood with the children on one of her "nature expeditions"?

He followed the sound, at first eagerly, but then slowed as he realized it was leading him to the gamekeeper's lodge.

Approaching the clearing, he paused and looked through the trees at an unexpected scene.

Miss Keene sat on a stump. Audrey swung like a lazy pendulum on an old rope swing. Mr. Croome was helping Andrew position a bow on his small shoulder and showing him how to align the arrow on the bowstring. The boy released the arrow and it flew in a weak arc, landing shy of the straw-backed target across the clearing.

"Aww . . . it's too hard," Andrew moaned. "Why bother with arrows when you have your fowling piece, Mr. Croome? Let me get my hands on that, and I could shoot dead on, I know I could."

"Guns has their place, young man. But so does the bow and arrow."

"I don't see how. Why not just blast the game and be done?"

"Use yer head, boy. Blast the gun once and all the county knows it. All the game take off running or fly away. But with the bow and arrow, you have stealth, boy. You can bag a hare or down a buck before its neighbor is any the wiser."

"Ohh . . ."

"Now, try again, Master Andrew, and this time, pull back with every muscle God gave ya."

Andrew nodded and lifted the bow once more. Croome helped him level the arrow, whispered some direction in his ear, then placed his fingers over the boy's, helping him pull the cord further back.

"You can do it, Andrew," Miss Keene encouraged.

"Don't forget to aim," Audrey added.

Man and boy released the arrow. *Fwwt, smack.* The arrow pierced the outer ring of the paper target and shuddered into the straw barricade behind it.

Audrey and Miss Keene cheered. Croome slapped Andrew on his slight shoulder, causing the boy to jerk forward, but Andrew's smile only grew the wider. Edward felt conflicting emotions, remembering his father's long-ago warnings about their game-keeper. Edward had even shared those concerns with Miss Keene, yet still she felt it safe, wise, to bring the children here?

Croome noticed him first. He darted a sharp look over his shoulder—his old ears evidently still keen, alert to approaching prey and predator alike. Which was he? Edward stepped forward, and the children rushed to greet him.

"I hit the target, Cousin Edward. Did you see?" Andrew asked.

"I did. Well done."

Audrey pouted. "You missed my turn. I hit the target once too, even closer to the center than Andrew did."

"I am sorry to have missed it. Perhaps you might try again?"

"Perhaps Lord Bradley would take a turn first, and show us how it is done?" Miss Keene suggested, blue eyes twinkling.

He narrowed his eyes at her. "You are too kind to offer, but I do not wish to interrupt the children's education, or whatever this is."

"It is sport. Good for the body and mind."

"Come, Cousin Edward. Do try," Andrew urged. "You cannot do any worse than Miss Keene did. She hit Mr. Croome's house!"

Miss Keene's cheeks pinked. Mr. Croome looked away and scratched the back of his neck.

"Did she indeed?" Edward said, barely suppressing a grin.

"Are we going to shoot or gad about all day?" Croome asked. "I've lines to set and eggs to hatch."

Edward swallowed. "Very well, I shall give it a go."

Croome handed him a second, larger bow, and then an arrow, his narrowed eyes fixed on Edward's face with disconcerting scrutiny. "Never done this before, have you?"

Was it so obvious? "No, sir."

Croome nodded and said in a low voice, "Place the arrow there and keep 'er level, both eyes open; pull back to your right shoulder, aim, then release."

Edward did so, the cord scraping his cheek as it released. The arrow smacked into the target, not far from Andrew's.

"Not bad for a first shot," Croome said. He eyed Edward's smarting cheek. "You'll live."

"Perhaps, Mr. Croome," Olivia said, "you might show us how it is done, for none of us has the way of it yet, I fear."

"Practice is all that's needed."

"We would like to see you shoot, Mr. Croome," Audrey said. "Are you very good?"

"Not bad, but don't like to make a coxcomb of myself either."

"We don't mind. We want to see," Andrew said. "Please?"

Croome gave Edward a glance, as if for his approval, which surprised him.

"By all means, Mr. Croome," he said.

"Do! Do!"

"Oh, very well, you little rogues, if only to still yer yappin' and give me peace."

Croome took up the stance and positioned the arrow in one smooth movement. He pulled the cord taut with practiced ease and sighted his target. *Fwwt, smack.* Dead center.

Edward decided he would not want this man for an enemy.

He was surprised when a bird came strutting across the clearing toward them, its grey neck stretched high and its broad belly balanced on peg legs, like a snobbish, well-fed footman. While not an experienced fowler, Edward guessed it a partridge.

Andrew, who was once again sighting the target, suddenly veered to the side, aiming at the partridge, making a mock *fwwt* sound between puffed cheeks.

Croome caught his arm in a blurred, razor-fast grab. "No, Master Andrew. Don't even pretend it."

Edward felt instantly defensive on his cousin's behalf, not liking the man's rough treatment of the boy. Over a game bird?

Andrew looked sheepish. "I am sorry, Mr. Croome. I was only fooling. I would never shoot Bob. Never."

Bob? The man had a pet partridge named *Bob*?

Perhaps he wasn't as fearsome as Edward had been led to believe.

Chapter 32

That evening, Edward stood in the doorway, amused by the scene in the drawing room. The carpets had been rolled back and some dancing master's text lay open on the floor. Andrew stood on a straight-back chair, face-to-face with the governess, who stood on the floor before him, hands in his. Audrey stood beside Miss Keene, an impish grin on her face. At Miss Keene's instruction, Andrew lifted one hand high, but before Miss Keene could turn beneath it, Audrey reached up and tickled him under his arm. Andrew doubled over and giggled.

Miss Keene sighed. It was clearly not the first time this had occurred.

Edward could not resist. He crossed the room to them, bowed, and asked formally, "May I cut in?"

With of whoop of relief, Andrew jumped from the chair and—after a running start—slid several yards across the polished floor in his stocking feet.

Shaking his head, Edward returned his gaze to Miss Keene and found her dubiously eyeing his offered hand.

She said, "I was only trying to demonstrate the nine positions of the German and French waltz."

"So I saw. Shall we continue?"

"You need not . . . That is, I am sure my lord is much too busy to—"

"Not at all. It is for the children's benefit, is it not? Their education?"

She opened her mouth to protest further, but before she could, Audrey said, "Show us position four, Cousin Edward. For neither Andrew nor I can master it."

Edward wondered if Audrey Howe fostered as many romantic fancies as did her stepmother. But he did not complain.

"You were doing fine, Audrey," Miss Keene said. "It was difficult without a proper partner. I am not very good at being the man."

Edward felt his brows rise.

"Please?" Audrey begged her governess.

Miss Keene sighed once more. "Very well. I shall be you, Audrey." She turned to Edward. "And you shall be the man."

He said dryly, "I can but try."

Edward raised his left arm over his head, and she, reluctantly, did the same. He grasped her uplifted hand in his own, creating an arch above them. "Position four requires, I believe, the woman to place her hand about the man's waist. And the man—that is me—to place his about hers. Is that not correct?"

She swallowed. "Yes."

Edward relished circling his arm around her and drawing her close to his side. Regarding her under the arch of their upraised arms, he noticed her pink, averted face. "To stand so close and yet ignore one's partner, Miss Keene? That will never do."

She tried to meet his gaze, but was clearly too self-conscious to do so.

Audrey dashed to the pianoforte and exclaimed, "I shall play and you two dance! I know I shall understand if I see the positions performed."

Little schemer, Edward thought, and felt his fondness for his young cousin grow.

Audrey began banging out a piece in three-quarter time, with none of the stately decorum the composer had intended.

Miss Keene gave him an apologetic look. "You need not. I—"

"Nonsense." He put both hands around her small waist— *Position seven or eight?* He did not care, only wanted to hold her close—and propelled her forward before she could object.

She grasped his upper arms and hung on desperately tight as he spun her around the room. He maneuvered her to his side— *position five?*—and whirled them both around, then lifted one arm and twirled her beneath it just as Audrey pounded out the final notes.

Still holding one of her hands, he bowed to her, the room spinning slightly. She seemed about to curtsy but instead swayed. He grasped both of her elbows to steady her. How desirable she was with her high color and coils of dark hair falling around her. Not to mention their entwined limbs. Standing this close to her, his face bent near hers, he wanted very badly to kiss her. Of course, he could not. Would not.

"Are you well?" he quietly asked.

"Besides breathless, dizzy, and embarrassed?"

He nodded.

"Perfectly."

Chuckling, his gaze roved her features—her bright blue eyes and parted lips, the rapid rise and fall of her chest—taking in every detail, but with none of the detachment his friend Dr. Sutton might have shown. He lifted her hand, still in his. She wore no gloves, and he felt an irrational urge to press his lips to her warm, bare skin.

"What is it?" she asked, concerned as he continued to inspect her fingers. "Is something wrong?" She tried to pull her hand away, but he held fast.

"I was only looking to see if your knuckles were white. You were holding my arms with impressive force."

Her mouth formed an O, and her blush deepened. He found her reaction quite charming.

"I am sure their impression will last several hours," he said, lifting one corner of his mouth in a half grin. "At least, I hope so."

He gave in to his impulse then and kissed the back of her hand. Warm and soft, as he'd imagined.

Audrey clapped, and Andrew came to a sliding stop beside them. "Is that a part of the dance too?" he asked.

"Perhaps," Edward said, reluctantly releasing Miss Keene. "When you are much older."

❧

Audrey sat on a little stool in the garden, easel and watercolors before her, tongue poking between her lips as she concentrated. While the girl worked on a likeness of the arbor, Olivia walked back and forth a few feet behind her, Latin text in hand, now and again pausing to offer encouragement or suggestion.

Andrew sat cross-legged on the grass, capturing beetles in his hand and listening idly to Olivia as she attempted a Latin lesson.

A door in the churchyard wall squealed open, and Olivia started. Mr. Tugwell appeared in the narrow arched doorway. "Good day, ladies. Master Andrew." He bowed. "Was that you I heard declining Latin verbs, Miss Keene?"

Olivia's face suffused with heat. "I am sure my grasp of Latin is nothing to yours, Mr. Tugwell. I hope I did not disturb you."

"By no means. You have a lovely speaking voice. You know, I remarked upon it to Bradley when first you came. For I had met you once before that unfortunate . . . mmm, mishap stole your powers of speech. And from our brief meeting I knew you must be a woman of education and refinement."

"Did you indeed? Then I thank you. Lord Bradley, it seems, did not credit your assessment."

"No. He is a man to draw his own conclusions, and sometimes, I fear, all too quickly."

She grinned. "I believe he might say the same of you."

"You are no doubt right. Though I may be too quick to judge charitably and he harshly, I think mine the lesser flaw, if I do say so myself." His eyes twinkled.

"I quite agree with you. But to hear Lord Bradley tell it, you have often paid a high price for believing the best of people." She tilted her head and asked, "Perhaps you might relay such an instance?"

Mr. Tugwell tucked his chin. "Ah, you will join him in mocking me, I see."

"Not at all, sir. But it does arouse one's curiosity, naturally."

"Very well. If you consent to take a turn with me about the garden, I shall."

Olivia smiled and rose, encouraging Audrey to keep on with her painting and assuring both children she would return in a few minutes.

"I do hope such a tale will not discourage you from trusting people, Miss Keene," he began.

"I shall endeavor to keep an open mind."

"Good. Now, how shall I choose but one instance? Let me see . . . Of course I have had the odd problem at the almshouse. I thought the old gent on crutches really was a former soldier down on his luck. Stole every stick of furniture from his room and left only his crutches behind to spite me!"

Olivia laughed and quickly pressed a hand over her mouth.

"Then there was that young maid—a pretty lass, so Edward warned me especially against her. But I did trust her and there went a twelvemonth's worth of wine for the sacrament. Then, of course, there is my sister, but it would not be charitable to continue." He winked at her in a most unparsonlike manner.

Olivia grinned. They took another turn around the garden, Audrey and Andrew ever in view at its center, and Olivia asked the vicar more questions. As Charles Tugwell shared about his work at the almshouse, Olivia felt drawn to help. Might it not make some small amends for her failings, bring good from all the bad that had brought her to this place?

＊

In his study, Edward stared at Miss Keene incredulously. "You would like to spend your half day *where?*"

"In the almshouse. Mr. Tugwell said I might be of use."

"Mr. Tugwell invited you?"

"Yes. Surely you could have no objection? I understand the two of you are friends."

An unfair but clever tact, he thought as she continued.

"You do trust Mr. Tugwell, do you not?"

Did he? Trust Tugwell with his secret? Perhaps. Trust him with Miss Keene? The man had fathered five children in six years. No, he did not trust Charles Tugwell with Miss Keene.

"I thought his sister assisted him."

"She does what she can, but with the boys and a house to manage, she hasn't much time. Miss Ludlow helps as well, when she can get away from her shop. But there is always more to do. Your mother, I understand, was quite a patroness of the place."

"Yes, she was." Feeling a lingering ache over her loss,

Edward stared off into the distance and said no more for several moments.

"You might . . . come along if you like," Miss Keene said.

He swiveled his head sharply and studied her face. Her cheeks were tinged with pink.

"To oversee my behavior, I mean," she hurried to amend. "Make sure I do not say or do anything I ought not."

With his secret, he wondered, or with Tugwell?

"You admire the man?"

Her eyes widened. Her lips parted, closed, then parted again. "I . . . I certainly have a great deal of respect for such a selfless clergyman. And he has been very kind to me since I arrived."

Far kinder than I have been, Edward thought with remorse.

"It is not as though I keep you prisoner here," he said. *Any longer.* "You attend services now and see the man every Sabbath. Are you certain there is not some other way you would like to spend your half day? Perhaps visiting a friend, or even the market in Cirencester?"

"You would give me leave to do so?"

He swallowed. Took a deep breath. "I believe I would. I would send someone to accompany you, of course. Just to see you return safely. Perhaps even I, should no one else be available."

She stared up at him with those mesmerizing blue eyes, and he felt as ensnared as a polecat in one of Croome's traps. His gaze caressed the curves of her face, her smooth fair cheek, and pointed chin.

Her voice was hushed and warm. "I should very much like to go to the market in Cirencester, if you, or someone, might accompany me."

He tried to nod but could not tear his gaze from hers. "I shall take you." He was tempted, sorely tempted, to tell her how beautiful she was. How sorry he was for the way he had treated her. To ask her to forgive him. To ask her to—

"There are several things I should like to buy for the almshouse," she continued brightly. "Mr. Tugwell mentioned a wheel of cheese would not go amiss and perhaps new gloves for the residents."

Hang the almshouse and hang Tugwell, Edward thought. The spell broken, he nodded curtly and stepped back. "Talbot can take you," he said, and strode away.

The real discomfort of a governess's position
arises from the fact that it is undefined.
She is not a relation, not a guest, not a mistress, not a servant—
but something made up of all.
No one knows exactly how to treat her.

—M. JEANNE PETERSON, *SUFFER AND BE STILL*

Chapter 33

On her way to church that Sunday, Olivia walked a short distance behind the family, as was proper. As she entered the church behind the Bradleys and Howes, she noticed that many people smiled and quietly greeted them, while they ignored her.

Eliza Ludlow, however, grinned and patted the pew next to her. Gratefully, Olivia sat next to the woman.

Here it was again—she was not family and could not sit with them, but nor was her place in the gallery with the servants, though she would have been more comfortable there. As if sensing her unease, Miss Ludlow squeezed her gloved hand in one of hers and offered to share a prayer book with the other. What a dear she was.

After the service, Miss Ludlow walked down the aisle beside her.

"That spencer looks well on you, Miss Keene."

"Thank you. I like this maroon kerseymere you suggested. Much nicer than the puce I wanted."

"I am glad you are pleased with it." Eliza Ludlow smiled and took Olivia's arm. "I understand we may be seeing one another at the almshouse on Wednesdays?"

"Yes, if I can be of any use."

"I am sure of it. Mr. Tugwell speaks very highly of your generosity and willingness."

Olivia's heart sank to see the look of raw longing on the kind woman's face as she gazed across the chapel at the vicar, already shaking hands with his departing flock at the door. When they reached him, he smiled briefly at Miss Ludlow and then shifted his cherubic gaze to Olivia.

He took her hand in his. "Miss Keene. You are well, I trust?"

"I am, sir. I thank you."

Olivia did not miss Miss Ludlow's doe-eyed look swivel from Mr. Tugwell to her, nor the slight pinching of her smile as she registered the attention he paid the relative newcomer and the lingering press of hands. Was the man blind? Or did he choose to ignore Miss Ludlow, not realizing the worth of such a woman?

For her part, Olivia thought Eliza Ludlow a treasure. She had brown eyes, dimples, and a cheery, if mildly crooked, smile. Her dark hair was pulled back with a soft height, framing her face in a most attractive light. Eliza had not the across-the-room arresting beauty of a Judith Howe or Sybil Harrington, but a natural, sweet appeal. Miss Ludlow was also gentle, intelligent, charitable, and at ease with people. She would make a wonderful parson's wife. What did Mr. Tugwell find lacking in Eliza to so completely overlook her? Olivia hoped with all her heart that Mr. Tugwell's passing interest in her would not put a wedge between Miss Ludlow and herself. Friends were hard to come by in her position.

"Perhaps you might join me for tea on Wednesday," Miss Ludlow invited as they parted ways, "after our work at the almshouse?"

Olivia smiled. "I would be honoured."

A treasure indeed.

❧

The Jesus Almshouse.

Olivia regarded the sign on the low white building with interest, taking in the engraved words and a fair likeness of a dove.

"Lady Brightwell commissioned that plaque," Charles Tugwell said, crossing the vicarage garden to join her. "I find it ironic, really. The almshouse was founded by a yeoman farmer who made his money dealing in land and property. He acquired quite a dubious reputation in the bargain. I wonder if he thought his good deed would make up for all his foul."

"You do not esteem good deeds?" She shifted the basket handle to both hands, just as a cool breeze blew a bonnet string across her face.

"My dear Miss Keene, what would the world be without them?" He brushed the string from her cheek. "Are we not admonished to be doers and not merely hearers of His word? Yet not on a mountain of good deeds can we climb our way to heaven."

She was confused by his words. Nothing she could do about her foul deeds? This was not what she wanted to hear. "You surprise me. If good deeds cannot move God to forgiveness, what will, then?"

"Not a thing. Which is why I find the name of this place so fitting. *We* cannot redeem our dark deeds, Miss Keene. Only the Lord can—and already has. All we can do is accept the merciful salvation He purchased for us on the cross long ago. But"—he smiled and rubbed his palms together eagerly—"we can serve our fellow creatures and delight our heavenly Father's heart in so doing."

She found herself frowning. "Can one truly delight God? I own I do not think of Him that way."

"No? How do you think of Him?"

She shrugged, again shifting the heavy basket. "A God of wrath and judgment, I suppose. Cold and angry in the face of our wrongdoings."

He looked at her thoughtfully. "My dear Miss Keene. Is it possible you endow your creator with the attributes of your earthly father?"

The thought stilled her. Did she? But was it not natural to do so?

"God is holy and just, yes," Mr. Tugwell continued. "But He is infinitely loving and merciful as well. He loves you, Olivia, no matter what you do or fail to do."

If only her father could have loved in that manner. Did God truly love her—after what she had done?

"He does," Mr. Tugwell said, as if reading her thoughts.

She smiled feebly, touched yet unsure. He made it sound so simple. Could it really be so? She looked up to see him regarding her sheepishly.

"Now you shan't have to attend this week's service, having suffered through one of my sermons already! Do forgive me, Miss Keene."

She dipped her head. "There is nothing to forgive."

He eyed her basket. "May I ask what you have brought? Dare I hope for one of Mrs. Moore's seedcakes, perhaps?"

"I am afraid not, sir. Only cheese and gloves for the poor."

He heaved a shuddering breath. "You shall be good for me, Miss Keene. I have become too spoilt by widows plying me with cakes and sweets. We shall pour our energies into relieving the pangs of the poor, and not our earthly wants, shall we?"

She found his final statement mildly disconcerting. When she glanced up, he looked away, a boyish blush on his face, as though just realizing the implication of his words.

Inside, Olivia found Miss Ludlow sitting on the worn settee in the almshouse parlor, surrounded by yards of fabric.

"What are we working on today?" Olivia asked.

"New draperies for the parlor window. The old ones have grown shabby indeed. What think you of this corded muslin?"

"Lovely. So much lighter and cheerier than the present draperies."

Eliza smiled, dimples blazing. "I hoped you would like it."

Olivia helped Miss Ludlow take down the dusty old draperies and from them form a pattern to cut the new ones. Miss Ludlow announced that she would be more comfortable doing the sewing in her own home and reiterated her invitation to tea.

Mr. Tugwell was just bidding farewell to an elderly resident as the two ladies took their leave. All politeness, Miss Ludlow invited Mr. Tugwell to join them as well, and seemed surprised when he accepted. Olivia hoped he was not accepting on her account.

A short time later, ensconced in Miss Ludlow's sitting room, Charles Tugwell picked up his teacup and asked, "How goes governessing, Miss Keene?"

"Well, sir, I thank you. I still miss teaching in a school, but there is much to commend the profession."

"That reminds me. I called in at the school in St. Aldwyns last week, to see how the Miss Kirbys were getting on. I did inquire on your behalf, but it seems they have all the help they need at present."

"That's all right, Mr. Tugwell," Olivia said, resisting thoughts of her mother. "I am content where I am at present."

He nodded thoughtfully. "You know, I have an old friend—a friend of my late wife's, actually—who has a very successful girls' school in Kent. If you ever want a change, I should be happy to introduce you."

"Thank you. I shall keep that in mind."

The vicar studied Olivia over the tray of tea things. "You are what, Miss Keene, five and twenty?" he asked.

Olivia nodded. Her twenty-fifth birthday had recently passed with no one to recollect the date but herself.

"And not married?"

Self-conscious, Olivia shook her head. He must know this already. Did he think she was keeping a husband hidden along with her other secrets?

"It is a wonder a woman like you has not been swept off her feet by some worthy man long ago."

Olivia smiled weakly and nibbled her cake.

"Never been in love?"

She shrugged, increasingly uncomfortable with his line of questioning, especially under the vulnerable, watchful eyes of Eliza Ludlow.

"Surely you have been courted at least," he persisted.

She hesitated. "There was one young man who admired me," Olivia began, hoping to put off questions yet more personal. "He was kind and charming in his way, yet I could not fancy myself married to him. He worked as a panhand in a brushmaker's shop, hair-sorting and bundling bristles. He was proud of his pay, I recall. 'Twenty knots a penny-fourpence, halfpenny per good broom.'"

Miss Ludlow smiled encouragingly. The gesture brought the youth's image to mind—dark hair and warm brown eyes, a boy's impish smile. "He was the one young man in the village who did not mind my bluestocking speech and endless reading, although he had no interest in reading anything beyond the newspaper. We had so little in common."

Olivia thought back to how she had daily witnessed the frustration, the resentment, even the falsely awkward peace of a marriage between unsuited people. She'd had no wish to enter into one of her own.

Shaking her head, Olivia inhaled deeply and finished her tale. "I suppose the village girls were right. Perhaps I did think of myself too highly." *For who was I, after all?* she thought. *Merely the daughter of a clerk and a gentlewoman of reduced circumstances.*

Mr. Tugwell nodded his understanding but did not comment.

His attention had suddenly shifted to Miss Ludlow as though he'd just remembered she was there. "And why did you never marry, Miss Eliza?"

Miss Ludlow tucked her chin, cheeks quickly reddening. "I don't know," she murmured with a lame little laugh.

"We all thought you would marry the miller," Mr. Tugwell said kindly. "A wealthy and influential man as ever there was."

"Perhaps I should have." Miss Ludlow's tone was nearly bitter, and Olivia's heart went out to her. The vicar had made her ill at ease with his awkward questions. Had he truly no idea how she felt about him?

His brows rose. "He offered marriage, then?"

Miss Ludlow gave a jerk of a nod.

"Forgive me, Miss Eliza. I did not intend to embarrass you. I own a parson's natural curiosity and concern for his flock. I am only surprised you did not marry."

She raised wounded brown eyes to his. "I did not love him."

"Ah . . ." He nodded thoughtfully, looking down into his teacup. "Never been in love . . . a good reason for remaining single."

She looked at him levelly. "I did not say that, sir."

He seemed unsure of her meaning but was finally aware that he had waded into murky, discomfiting waters. He finished his tea and straightened. "Well, thank you for tea, Miss Eliza. I shall trespass upon your hospitality no longer." He rose and bowed. "Good day, ladies." He avoided the eyes of both women as he stood and donned his hat.

Chapter 34

Charles Tugwell paid a morning call, and as was his habit, timed his visit to partake of a Brightwell breakfast. Hodges led him to the breakfast room, where Edward was sitting with coffee and newspaper.

The parson eyed the sideboard as if it were a lost soul. "Ah, my old friends crumpet and curd, how I have missed you."

Edward rolled his eyes with tolerant amusement. "Yes, I am well. Thank you, vicar."

"Do forgive me, Bradley. How are you? Look a bit tired, I will say."

"I am well enough." Edward flipped a page. "Now that you've dispatched with the niceties, do help yourself to breakfast."

"Don't mind if I do."

A few minutes later, Hodges returned with the tray and offered Edward his post. Ignoring his friend's moans of gourmand delight, Edward opened the first letter.

And froze.

His body broke out in a cold sweat. The script blurred and then focused once more.

> *Lady Brightwell has never borne a living child.*
> *You may be innocent, but your father has knowingly*
> *deceived the world at the cost of another. Where is justice?*

"My friend, what is it?" Mr. Tugwell asked around a bit of crumpet. "You look very ill."

Edward threw down his serviette and rose abruptly, toppling his chair in his wake and preparing to bolt from the room.

Tugwell rose as well. "Edward, wait!"

Edward pressed his eyes closed and took a deep breath.

"What is it? My dear friend, I have never seen you thus. You have come undone."

Panic rising, Edward paced the room liked a caged animal. "Exactly so. Undone, unwoven, unstrung."

"Edward, you alarm me! Do tell me what has happened."

"Have I your promise of secrecy?"

"Need you ask?"

Edward tossed him the letter, which the vicar read and read again, sitting slowly back down as he did so.

"Is it true?" he whispered, eyes wide.

Edward's pulse pounded in his ears. "I would not be this upset over a rumor."

"Lord Brightwell . . . ?"

"Admits it. This letter is not the first."

"I am sorry, my friend."

"You are sorry?" Edward bit back his frustration and lowered his voice. "Yes, well, so am I."

"Has he told you who or how . . . ?"

"Only that I was a foundling, taken in by them."

"Generous."

"Generosity was not the primary motivation. Rather, a determination that my uncle Sebastian never lay his hands on Brightwell Court."

"But he is dead now, is that not so?"

"Yes, which leaves Felix."

"Do you think—?"

"I don't know what to think." Edward raked agitated fingers through his hair. "Or who to blame."

Charles Tugwell stared at the letter once more. "And when this gets out . . . ?"

"*If* it gets out, I am ruined. My reputation . . . shot—baseborn nobody. Title, gone. Peerage to Felix. Political future . . . dead. Why do you think I was so determined to keep Miss Keene cloistered here?"

"She knows?"

"Yes. She overheard—the night she was arrested."

"Ahh . . ." The vicar slowly shook his head, eyes alight in deeper understanding.

"I stand to lose everything. My inheritance. My home. My very identity."

Charles set aside the letter and stood. "No, Edward. That you will not lose." He clasped Edward's shoulder. "Dear friend, whatever happens, you will always be God's child. 'And if children, then heirs; heirs of God, and joint-heirs with Christ.' "

Edward ran a weary hand over his face. "Cold comfort, Charles, when I believed myself heir to an earldom."

After Charles Tugwell took his leave, Edward sought his father in the library. Finding him at his desk, Edward carefully closed the door behind him and flopped down in a nearby chair. His father raised his eyes, taking in Edward's disheveled state.

"So much for parliament," Edward began.

"What are you talking about? Of course you will be summoned to take my seat after I am gone. It is what is done."

"Not in every instance, and certainly not in this."

"What has brought this on? You are my heir apparent—the next Earl of Brightwell. No one can take that from you."

"Are you sure about that, Father?" Edward tossed the note onto the desk.

"What is this? Hand me my spectacles."

Edward rose to deliver the wire frames and then watched as his father read the brief note. Lord Brightwell removed the spectacles and rubbed his eyes with thumb and forefinger. He sighed deeply. "When did this come?"

"This morning." Instead of resuming his seat, Edward resumed pacing.

"Have there been others?"

"This is the first directed to me. Have you received others?"

"Not since that first one before your mother and I departed for Italy."

"Who could have written this?"

"I don't know. I have never told anyone. I cannot speak for your mother, of course. I suppose it is possible she confided in someone—a friend or someone from her family." The earl looked far off for an answer. "Devil take it, who would do such a thing?"

He pulled the first letter from a desk drawer and laid both side by side. Edward looked over his shoulder and studied the handwriting.

His father asked, "Were both written by the same person, do you think?"

"I assume so. But it is difficult to tell—the first was so brief."

Lord Brightwell held the most recent letter at arm's length and regarded it, chin tucked. "Looks like a woman's hand to me."

Edward straightened. "But Felix is the obvious suspect."

"Felix? Felix can barely plan his attire, let alone a scheme like this." His father returned the letter to him.

"He has the most to gain."

"Not at present. Do not forget, Edward, the courtesy title you use is mine. Even if you *were* to give it up, Felix cannot use it in your stead. He would only be my heir presumptive, with no title and no inheritance until after my death."

Edward nodded and began pacing once more. "It may not change the present, but certainly his prospects for the future."

"I suppose you are right. Still I cannot credit it. From where was it posted?"

Edward turned the letter over. "Cirencester." The word echoed in his mind, and he recalled Miss Keene's recent trip there to "purchase cheese for the almshouse." Edward frowned. Just a coincidence surely.

"From so near!" Lord Brightwell said.

Should he tell his father? But no, it couldn't be Miss Keene . . . could it? He decided not to reveal, for the present, the fact of her being in Cirencester a few days ago.

"Is not Felix back at Oxford?" his father asked.

"Yes. But it is not so long a journey, if he wanted to throw us off the scent."

❦

Restless and unable to focus on the accounts, Edward tucked the estate ledger under his arm and went to return it to Walters. When he could not locate the clerk, Edward took himself upstairs instead. He felt the need to see Miss Keene, to somehow reassure himself of her innocence.

Ledger still under his arm, Edward silently let himself in and stood at the back of the schoolroom. Audrey and Andrew, eyes forward, did not even notice him enter. Miss Keene did, however, and faltered in the lesson she was delivering. She glanced expectantly at him, but when he did not speak, she continued the Latin lesson, though clearly distracted by his presence.

" 'Terms Seldom Englished,' " she read from the text. " '*Viva voce*, meaning by word of mouth. *Inter nos*, between ourselves.' "

Did she choose those terms for my benefit? Edward wondered. He thought back to the days when he alone heard Miss Keene's voice.

" '*Argumentum ad ignorantiam*, a foolish argument.' "

Oh yes, they'd had a few of those. Crossing his arms, Edward leaned against the wall, watching her closely.

" '*Alias*, otherwise.' "

Edward raised his brows. Had he not once accused her of giving an alias instead of her real name? Was it his imagination, or was a flush creeping up her neck?

" '*Alibi*, being in another place.' " She glanced up at him—guiltily, he thought. Had she need of an alibi? In his current state of mind, every word she spoke had some latent meaning, and seemed to accuse her. But she was innocent, was she not?

She cleared her throat, then continued, " '*Bona fide*, without fraud or deceit.' "

Was Miss Keene without deceit? His father believed she was. And Edward very much hoped he was right. But she *was* hiding something. She had never really explained how she had come to be at Brightwell Court with no belongings and no plans other than the name of a school, nor why she had initially concealed where she was from. No doubt it had something to do with her foul-tempered father. But even so, it did not mean she had anything to do with the letters. *Merciful Lord, let her have nothing to do with the letters.* . . .

" '*Extortus*, meaning extortion.' " Miss Keene glanced at him once more, clearly self-conscious, then closed the book.

Why was she so nervous?

"Well, I believe that is enough Latin for today. Let us move on to arithmetic. Your slates please, children."

She was turning to the shelter of the subject she knew best, he realized, recalling her tale of the public-house contest. Suddenly curious, he raised his hand. "May I pose a question?"

The children turned to smile at him, but Miss Keene looked anything but pleased. "Very well."

He opened the ledger and referred to one of the equations written in Walter's neat hand. "What is 4,119 multiplied by 4, then divided by 12?"

For a brief moment, she stared at something over his head. "It is 1,373. Why?"

He stared back, stunned. "I wonder . . . just how clever are you?"

Is it not the great end of religion . . .
to extinguish the malignant passions,
to curb the violence, to control the appetites,
and to smooth the asperities of man . . . ?

—WILLIAM WILBERFORCE

Chapter 35

*O*livia had been sound asleep when her father's shout startled her awake. Had she really heard it, or merely had a nightmare? She listened, heart pounding. There it came again. All too real.

How did he find me? she frantically wondered. *Did Miss Cresswell tell him? Surely not the constable, when Father is a wanted man!*

Dare she pull the covers over her head and hope he would go away?

At a third shout, Olivia scrambled from bed, padded to her window, and looked down, but could not see the main doors from this angle. She unlatched the window and pushed it open. Through it, she could hear his voice more clearly—and hear him banging on the door as though to break it down.

"Dorothea! Dorothea . . ." It was half-rant, half-sob, and

Olivia's heart seized to hear it, even as her mind clouded, cleared, and clouded again. He was not calling for her at all. If he was trying to find his wife, then he must believe her to be alive—had not knowingly brought about her end.

"Dorothea!"

Should she go down to him? Did he know she had been the one who struck him?

"Open up! I want to see my wife!" His voice was uncontrolled, slurred. She knew that tone, that cadence. He was foxed.

She heard the sound of a gun cocking and froze. Croome—she knew it instantly.

"On yer way, mister. Before I send you on yer way in a pine box."

Lord Bradley's voice joined in, though Olivia had not heard a door open. "Whom do you seek at this ungodly hour, man?" He had probably come out by one of the side doors and was likely bearing a pistol himself.

"I told you. Dorothea. My wife. She is here. I know she is."

"There is no one here by that name. Upon my honour, there is not."

"Who are you?"

"Lord Bradley."

"No . . . not Bradley. I want Brightwell."

"Lord Brightwell is my father."

"Your father? But you are so . . . grown. He must be old as I am and serves him right. Gone back to him, has she?" His voice rose again. "I mean her no harm. But I must see her. I must!"

"Do lower your voice, my good man. I promise you, my father has no woman here. He is in mourning for his own wife, only recently passed on."

"A widower, is he? How kind fate is to them! There is no hope for me, then. I have lost her. Well and truly lost her."

How defeated he sounded. How lost. Olivia steeled her heart.

This is remorse talking. And guilt. And perhaps fear of consequences. I must not forget—I saw him with his hands around her throat.

But she could not fully reconcile this argument with the broken man she heard below.

Olivia threw her cape over her nightdress and ran down the stairs, suddenly determined to speak with him, to push confession or explanation from him, knowing she would be safe in the company of Mr. Croome and Lord Bradley.

But when she reached the front hall, she found Hodges and Osborn huddled at the door, holding it fast.

Mrs. Hinkley pulled the curtain aside from the long-view windows. "He is gone."

All expelled a collective sigh of relief.

Even Olivia. He would not have given her trustworthy answers, she decided, foxed as he was. And with his passions so out of control, who knew how he might react to finding her there, in his enemy's abode? For clearly he did know of her mother's relationship with Lord Brightwell, long past though it was.

❧

Even though it was not yet her half day off, Olivia left the children with Becky and Nurse Peale, donned her bonnet, and hurried up the lane and across the street to the almshouse. She was still unsettled from the late-night visit from her father and hoped a visit with calm Mr. Tugwell or cheerful Eliza Ludlow would soothe her. When she stepped inside and hung her bonnet, she saw no sign of Miss Ludlow. Hers was the lone article of feminine apparel on the pegs near the door. The parlor door was open and, hearing Mr. Tugwell's voice within, she went to greet him. She crossed the threshold and froze.

Charles Tugwell sat talking earnestly to Simon Keene, who was hunched in an armchair, head bowed, elbows on his knees. She was stunned to see him. It was such a collision of her old world and new . . . that for a moment she just stood there, stupefied.

Mr. Tugwell noticed her first and rose. "Miss Keene."

Her father's head jerked up. "Livie!" His hair, dark like hers, was in need of cutting. Stubble shadowed his cheeks. His suit of clothes was surprisingly fine, though somewhat rumpled.

He stood and took a step forward, as though to . . . what? A part of her longed to flee before she found out, but she felt rooted to the spot, as in a dream where one cannot run from danger. He stood where he was, staring at her. For a long moment she could not find her voice. When she remained silent, the light in his brown eyes faded and he sank back into the chair, thin mouth turned down.

Tugwell asked her quietly, "Shall I leave you?"

"Please stay."

"Come to rail at me?" her father asked. "I know I was a fool last night. I can hardly blame you for not coming to the door."

Mr. Tugwell said apologetically, "I am afraid I let it slip you were in residence."

Olivia lifted a stiff shrug, keeping her eyes on her father. "You did not ask for me."

"I would have, had I known. Thank God you are well."

He did not know, she realized, that she was the one who had struck him. All this time, living in fear . . .

He kneaded his hands as though they ached. "Your mother is . . . well, I trust?"

Olivia felt her brow furrow. *How could he ask such a thing, when he . . . ?*

"I have no idea," she said, more bitterly than she intended. "But if she is well, it is no thanks to you."

She felt Tugwell's look of surprise but ignored him. She wanted no sermons on forgiveness now.

Her father bowed his head. When he looked up, he did not quite meet her eyes. "The parson here assured me Dorothea is not at Brightwell Court, but I own I did not quite believe him."

"She is not. I have not laid eyes on her since I left. I have feared her dead these last months."

"Dead? Why?"

"*You* ask that?"

He grimaced. "You have heard the rumors about the grave?"

She nodded.

"I admit I too feared the worst when I awoke that morning and found broken glass and even a smear of blood. Figured I had come home foxed and had a terrible row with Dorothea." He sighed. "I did not realize the two of you were gone until the next day. I went to see Miss Atkins, but she would not even allow me into her house. She told me you had left to find a situation, and that Dorothea was gone and not coming back. She would not tell me more."

Had he really no recollection of trying to strangle his wife, of being struck himself? Had he been so drunk? How did he explain the large gash or lump that must certainly have risen on the back of his head?

She asked, "But what of the blood you mentioned?"

"I don't know." He held up his hands, turning them over. "Thought I must have punched a wall again, or cut myself on the glass, but I found no cuts on my hands."

It was on the tip of her tongue to ask if his head had bled. But then she would have to explain how she knew he had been injured. She was not ready to tell him, not now, when he knew where to find her. He seemed so peaceable and remorseful—so sober—at present, but for how long?

"I too heard the whispers about the new grave in the church-yard," he said quietly. "But I knew better—knew I had driven her away at last. Back to the arms of her *Oliver*."

Oliver? It jolted her to hear the name on her father's lips. Just how much did he know about his wife's long-ago relationship with the earl?

"I tried to let her go. . . . Moved to the spa site to better man-age it, and to steer clear of that empty house and all the suspicious looks I was drawing about the village. All winter I was driven mad with missing her.

"Finally I could bear it no longer. I had to find her. It took some time to locate this man Oliver, for I had never known his surname. I tried to contact Dorothea's family, but they would not see me. Finally someone I asked knew an Oliver and directed me to Brightwell Court." He shook his head regretfully. "I should never have stopped off at the inn last night. 'Just one cup for courage,' I told myself. But one led to two, then three . . ."

He winced his eyes shut. "For so long, I have imagined her with him, and how it has eaten at my soul. If she is not there, where on earth is she?"

"I do not know," Olivia said. "I thought she would come to find me, but she has not. Perhaps she feared *you* might find her if she did."

He shook his head. "The way you look at me, girl . . . Do you hate me so?"

"You ask me that? When you could barely stand the sight of me all these years? Not since that contest in the Crown and Crow. How you hated me for losing."

Simon Keene frowned. "Hated losing that contest, but never you."

She expelled a puff of air and disbelief. "You have never treated me the same since that day. You cannot deny it."

"I don't deny it. But not because of that plagued contest. Don't you know? That was the very day I learnt that you . . . that I . . ." He grimaced in his effort to find the words. "That your mother named you for this Oliver fellow."

Olivia shook her head. "I don't recall that. . . ."

"Do you not? When the three of us rode into Chedworth together, earlier that same day?"

"To see the Roman ruins—that I remember."

"And do you recall that woman who came up and greeted your mother like a long-lost friend?"

"Vaguely."

"I remember it perfectly. Your mother introduced me by name and then said, 'And this is our daughter.' She gave my name, see, but not yours. So like a fool I said, 'This is our Olivia.'

" 'Olivia! After Oliver?' the woman says, then turned redder than a beetroot and tried to cover her tracks. Mumbled something like, 'Oh! Of course not. Only a coincidence, I am sure.'

"That's when I learnt the knob's name. *Oliver.* Dorothea denied the connection, said she had *always* liked the name Olivia. But what could she say? What more proof did I need?" His thin mouth twisted in disgust. "The cheek of her—naming the girl I fed and clothed after a man who never lifted a hand for either of you. It wasn't your fault, I know, but I could never look at you the same way again. Never look at myself the same. To think how idiotically proud of you I was when I had no right to be."

Olivia shot a glance at Mr. Tugwell, who seemed suddenly interested in the condition of his fingernails. If she had feared the parson admired her, this would certainly cure him of any lingering romantic notions.

Simon Keene shook his head again. "I knew she had a lover before I met her. And that she went to see the rake once, even after we were married. But then time went by, see, and we had a few good years, and I let myself think that maybe she had got over him—maybe she could love me after all. . . ." His voice broke. "Only to learn she had lied to me all those years. My own little girl, not mine after all. Named after the man she *really* loved, so she would never forget him."

An awkward silence followed, as her father tried to regain control of his emotions. Olivia felt torn between wanting to rail at him for attacking her mother, and confusion over his story. Her mind whirled, trying in vain to make it jibe with her own memories.

Simon rubbed a hand across his stubbled face. "It boiled my blood—and cut me deep, I own. How it galled me, the thought of her still pining for him. Still wishing she had never tied up with the likes of me."

Had this been behind his dark moods and fits of anger? Driven him to drink so heavily?

"Surely you know that is not why she left you," Olivia said. "I have never heard her speak of any other man, or seen anything that would make me think—"

"And why would you?" he interrupted. "Away at that school all day as you were? Your mother home alone, or so we thought. Did you never notice two glasses on the sideboard, or smell cigar smoke in the house?"

"Mother would never . . . " Olivia hesitated. Had she smelled cigar smoke? She could not be sure. Olivia *had* spent a great deal of each day and sometimes evenings at Miss Cresswell's. But to assume a caller was Lord Brightwell, after all these years? Ridiculous. "If someone was in the house, surely it was only a friend come to call," she said. "Or someone picking up needlework . . . or—"

"Then why would she not tell me who had called? Why did she act so nervous and secret-like? The more she lied about it, the angrier I got, until I thought I should explode!"

Had he snapped? Had his irrational jealousy led to that final act of violence?

The mantel clock struck the hour, and no one spoke while the bell chimed, then faded away.

The parlor door, which still stood ajar, opened a few inches further, and Lord Brightwell himself appeared in the gap. From his angle, Olivia realized, he could see only her, and perhaps Mr. Tugwell.

"Olivia, a puppeteer has arrived in the square and I thought the children might—" He pushed the door open further, and his gaze encompassed the entire parlor. "Oh, pardon me, I did not realize . . ."

Olivia panicked. These two men in the same room together? What dreadful timing! "Lord Brightwell. I . . ."

Simon Keene wiped his sleeve across his face and rose. "Speak of the devil. Oliver, is it?"

Mr. Tugwell laid a staying hand on her father's arm and in a low voice urged, "Steady . . ."

Olivia cleared her throat, finding it difficult to breathe in a room suddenly thick with tension. "Actually, it is Lord Brightwell. And this is Simon Keene, my . . ." Olivia swallowed, and before she could continue, the earl stepped to her side, assuming a protective stance.

Simon Keene looked from one to the other and slowly shook his head. "I see how it is." He shook off the vicar's hand and faced the earl squarely. "I will ask you, sir, man to man. Do you know where Dorothea is?"

Lord Brightwell stared coldly back. "And I will answer in all truth that I do not. But if I did, I should not tell you."

Olivia cringed, expecting her father to rage at this, to fly across the room and strike the earl . . . or strangle him.

But the fight seemed to have gone out of Simon Keene. "I see. Well." He picked up his hat and turned it in his hands. "I shall take my leave. Sorry to have bothered you."

Mr. Tugwell touched his arm once more. "Mr. Keene, wait. You are in no fair shape to sally forth. You are welcome to stay as long as you need."

The vicar glanced at the earl as though to gauge his reaction, but Lord Brightwell was looking at her. He offered his arm and together they exited the almshouse, leaving the two men where they were, Tugwell speaking gently to his visitor. Olivia guessed Simon Keene had never heeded a parson in his life, and doubted he would begin now.

It was only after she and Lord Brightwell had crossed the high street that Olivia realized she had not asked if her father knew he was a wanted man.

Those ladies, who from the misfortunes of their families
have been compelled to exchange happy homes and indulgent relations
for the society of strangers, are objects of peculiar sympathy.

—ADVICE TO GOVERNESSES, 1827

Chapter 36

For days, the meeting with her father revolved and replayed in her mind—what she should have said to him, the questions she ought to have asked, the truths she should have demanded. After torturing herself in this manner for several long, restless nights, Olivia decided to dwell on the positive aspect of the meeting. Simon Keene believed her mother alive. And Olivia would endeavor to believe it as well.

On her next half day, Olivia spent the afternoon keeping Eliza Ludlow company in her shop, and managed to enjoy herself quite convincingly.

She returned to Brightwell Court to find two letters awaiting her. One came with no return direction. The other bore the fine, artistic hand of Miss Cresswell. Olivia first opened the letter from her former teacher, feeling sixty percent eagerness and forty percent dread. Had Miss Cresswell heard from her mother? From Muriel Atkins, the midwife?

> *My dear Olivia,*
>
> *Muriel has finally returned. After the birth in the country, it seems she went directly to her niece in Brockworth, whose time came early. It was a long and difficult lying-in (twins—both live, praise God), and rarely have I seen Muriel so exhausted.*
>
> *When I told her of your visit, she said I was to tell you in confidence that your mother does not lie in the churchyard. Is that not good news? I am not to tell anyone but you. Muriel fears someone intends your mother harm, and if this person believes she might be, well, gone, then so much the better. She would not say who, but I am sure your guess is the same as mine. Sounds a desperate plan to me, when her own daughter is allowed to believe such a tragedy!*
>
> *I understand your mother fell ill and stayed with Muriel's sister for much of the winter, but she has since fully recovered. Still, Muriel insists she knows nothing about where your mother is now, nor how she fares. She only hopes the ruse may have spared your mother from real harm. But as no letter has come, she begins to fear this is not the case. Still she and I hope every day for word from our dear friend Dorothea.*
>
> *I am afraid my other news may be difficult for you to hear. Your father has been found and arrested. The specific charge has still not been made public, but rumors abound.*
>
> *Do write and let me know that you are well. I am praying God's peace for you during such uncertain times.*
>
> Miss Lydia Cresswell

Arrested? He must have gone directly to Withington from the almshouse. Again, Olivia wondered what her father was accused of doing, and whether or not he was guilty. She felt an overwhelming ebb and flow of emotions, from vindictive satisfaction (did he not deserve some retribution for his violent act?) to embarrassment at having a parent in prison, to unexpected pity when she thought of the broken state in which she had last seen him. How strangely unsettling it had been to hear him acknowledge that he was not her father. It ought to have been a relief—even more so now after Miss Cresswell's tidings. Instead, she felt empty. Emotionally bankrupt. She thought back to Mr. Tugwell's words about a person's inability to pay for his own foul deeds, and felt spiritually bankrupt as well. For had she not committed her own offenses?

Olivia studied the outside of the second letter, noting the elegant seal and the fine stationery. She did not recognize the hand. Who else could be writing to her? Mrs. Hawthorn crossed her mind, but she quickly chastised herself for the foolish hope.

She pried open the seal and unfolded the letter, immediately looking at the signature. It *was* from her grandmother.

Dear Miss Keene,

Please forgive the delay. This is my fifth attempt at composing this letter.

I have given your visit a great deal of thought. In fact, I can think of little else, save occasionally fretting over what may have befallen Dorothea. You may think it cold of me to think of you instead of mourning my daughter, but you see, I mourned her loss more than five-and-twenty years ago, when she wrote to tell me she had married a man I could never approve of, nor accept. She said she knew she could expect no further relations between us and decided to spare me the trouble of severing ties myself. Still, I confess I have always held out hope that she would contact me again one day, to let me know where she was living and, if nothing else, that she was all right. Receiving such a letter from your hand was quite a shock.

When my daughter Georgiana returned from her shopping trip, she found me sitting where you left me, that letter still in my hand. She drew from me the events of the day and was quite vexed with me for not having asked you to stay long enough that she might have met you herself.

*I regret not receiving you more warmly, my dear. Please, will
you do us the honour of calling again?*
                              Mrs. Elizabeth Hawthorn

Seeing the woman's name in her own hand caused Olivia's heart
to contract as it had not done before she had met Mrs. Hawthorn.
Elizabeth. Her own name was Olivia Elizabeth. Had her mother
named her for her father and grandmother?

Another script, this one free and loopy, wrote an addendum
beneath the precise formal hand:

> *Please do come, Olivia. Imagine! I have a niece!*
>   *Your Aunt,*
>   *Georgiana Crenshaw*
> *(Mr. Crenshaw says you are most welcome.)*

Olivia felt herself smiling, already drawn to this effervescent
aunt she had never met.

Edward and Lord Brightwell made their way to the drawing
room to greet Felix, who had returned to Brightwell for a weekend
visit. Judith had arrived before them, evidenced by her voice sifting
into the corridor from the open door.

"How go things at Oxford?" she asked.

Edward entered the room in time to see Felix shrug. He took
up the refrain. "Yes, Felix, how go the studies?"

"Studies? Oh, is that what I am to be about at Oxford? I thought
I was there for rowing and singing and impressing the ladies."

"Well, that too, of course," Edward said good-naturedly.

Felix selected a cigar from the wooden box on the sideboard
and slipped it into his coat pocket. Then he helped himself to the
decanter of port.

Lord Brightwell seated himself and asked Felix to pour him

a glass as well. "Felix, I am happy to sponsor you at my old *alma mater,* but I did hope you would apply yourself."

Felix sighed and handed the earl a glass. "I am afraid I must disappoint you, Uncle. It seems success is beyond my reach. I have a mind to quit the whole business."

"What?" Edward exclaimed, trying but failing to keep the edge from his voice.

Felix threw up his hands. "Does it really matter? No one has ever expected much of me. Don't tell me you depend upon my having a brilliant career in the law, or the church, or politics or some such thing. It is ridiculous."

"No, it is not," Edward said.

"Why?"

"Why?" Edward faltered and felt Judith's curious glance. "Because . . . well, you never know what the future might bring, and well . . ."

His father joined in, "And Bradleys have always excelled at university. Even your father."

Edward was surprised to hear Lord Brightwell mention his long-estranged brother.

"My, we are all feeling charitable today, are we not?" Felix said. "Even my father, who is never praised here in his childhood home, was more intelligent than I, it seems."

"Your father was clever indeed," Lord Brightwell said. "But this is not about intelligence. You have perfectly good brains, my boy, you just lack . . . well . . ."

"Self-discipline," Edward offered.

"Ambition," Judith added.

Acrimony dripped from Felix's lips. "Well, thank you all very much."

"How bad is it?" Lord Brightwell asked, with an anticipatory grimace.

One hand on the mantel, neck bowed, Felix stared at the fire.

"Not only will there be no honours, but I am on the cusp of failing out."

Lord Brightwell gaped. "Never say so!"

"I am afraid it is quite true, Uncle. I have come to grief at Oxford. I see no point in returning for the rest of the year and wasting more of your money."

Edward frowned. "You will not quit, Felix."

Felix stared at him, hard. "Why? Can't stand to see a blight on the Bradley pride?"

"What about *your* pride?" Edward said. "A man does not quit what he has begun. Now go back to Balliol, pass the examinations, and obtain your degree."

"To what purpose? I already told you I am not fit for the church or the law."

Edward felt Judith studying him, awaiting his answer just as her brother did.

"You have a bright future before you, Felix," he said, hedging. "I cannot say how it will come or what form it will take, but I would have you be prepared to rise to the occasion when it presents itself."

Brother and sister still stared at him, brows furrowed. Lord Brightwell stepped in to the unsettled void and slapped Felix on the back. "Come on, my boy. You can do it. We are all of us behind you."

When you set yourself on fire, people love to come and see you burn.
—JOHN WESLEY

Chapter 37

*T*he next morning, Olivia and the children played hide-and-seek amid a lifting grey fog and the hoarse call of ravens.

While Audrey covered her eyes and counted, Olivia stepped behind the carpentry shop. She was surprised Andrew had not followed and hidden near her as was his wont. Perhaps he had seen Johnny or Lord Bradley and had run off to join one of them.

Audrey made a great show of checking the garden and arbor, then ran across the lawn in her direction. Smiling, Olivia retreated behind the shop wall.

"I found you, miss. I found you!" Audrey happily announced.

Olivia smoothed a lock of hair from the girl's brow. "Yes, you did, my clever girl." Unexpected tears pricked her eyes, as thoughts of her father came unbidden. *"My clever girl"* had been his pet name for her in happier times.

"I am sorry I found you so quickly if it makes you sad," Audrey said, stricken.

"No, I am pleased you found me. Now, shall we go seek Andrew together?"

Audrey looked about her. "He isn't with you?"

"Not this time."

That was when Olivia heard it. The barked word "fire!" repeated again in a woman's shrill cry. "Fire! Fire in the stables!" The laundry maid, Olivia guessed, who worked near the stable yard.

Olivia's heart started. *The stables?* All that hay and straw. The poor horses! A dreadful thought struck Olivia's chest like an iron mallet. *Good Lord, no . . .*

"Andrew!" she cried, and ran headlong across the lawn. Audrey followed behind, shouting her little brother's name.

Reaching the stables, she called to the coachman, harried and single-handedly trying to herd the horses from harm.

"Mr. Talbot! Have you seen Andrew? We were hiding and—"

"No, miss. He isn't here."

Relief filled her. The coachman looped a rope around the neck of a grey gelding, and all but dragged the terrified animal from the stable. If only Lord Bradley would return from his morning ride!

"Audrey, run into the house and find Lord Brightwell," Olivia said. "And ask everyone you meet if they have seen Andrew."

The girl scurried to her bidding.

Johnny came on a run from the direction of the wood, a sheepish Martha trailing behind him.

"Have either of you seen Andrew?" Olivia called.

"No," Martha said, eyes wide. And she ran off to look for him while Johnny rushed to help Talbot with the horses.

Something compelled Olivia to stay where she was. She heard a terrified whinny and then another. *Bang!* The stable gate exploded outward, kicked hard by the rear hooves of a large black horse. Lord Bradley had not gone on his ride as she had thought. Where was he?

Instinctively, Olivia ran forward, skirting the horse's dangerous hind legs and stepping to its great head, trying to calm the horse as she had the day she had groomed it, with a firm hand and soothing words. The horse reared up and hit its head on the stable rafters, clearly disoriented by the smoke and too panicked to respond to her prodding.

Lord Bradley appeared through the smoke and whipped a hood over the horse's head in one deft throw. "Major, walk on!" And with a great heave, he pushed the stubborn horse through the broken gate and out into the yard.

Over his shoulder he called, "Miss Keene, get away from here!"

"Not until I know Andrew is safe. He was hiding and we have not found him. Have you seen him?"

Pulling the last of the horses free, Talbot scowled, "I told you he weren't here, miss. I checked the stables, the office, and the tack room." The coachman threw up his hands. "Now, get out the both of you before the roof falls down upon us."

Olivia and Lord Bradley swung around to look at each other, their gazes locking into place. The same thought—fear—in both of their minds. The little-known closet. What if Andrew had hidden there?

Olivia lurched forward, but Lord Bradley caught her by the arm. "Talbot, keep her back."

The coachman stepped forward and gripped her upper arms. Lord Bradley shrugged off his coat, bunched it over his nose and mouth, and disappeared into the smoke.

Olivia strained against Talbot. "Let me go!" Every maternal feeling swelled within her, overriding even her survival instinct.

A little boy, her charge, might even now be overcome with smoke. "Let me go to him. Let me go."

The coachman's wiry strength was unyielding, and she was no match for a man who controlled horses six or seven times his weight.

Oh, God, please. This is my fault. Oh, please, spare them both!

The smoke roiled black and grey. With a loud crack, the far wall and roof crumbled—the section where the hay and straw were stored. The flames shot through the aperture, and the smoke rose even higher. People were running from all directions now, Mr. Croome leading the charge. Behind him, Hodges, Osborn, Mrs. Moore, Mrs. Hinkley, the gardener, hall boy, and maids, all formed a water brigade from the garden well. Grim-faced people sloshed bucket after bucket of water at the ravenous mouth of the fire. But Olivia could see it was futile. She scanned the growing crowd but saw no dear little brown mop of hair. No wide brown eyes. Now Lord Brightwell ran out of the house. And there, Judith, pulled along by Audrey. The girl's face was wild with fear. Olivia's heart sped within her. No Andrew.

Lord Brightwell reached them first. "Are the horses all out? The groom?"

Behind her, Talbot said, "All accounted for, my lord."

The earl looked at the coachman, still holding her fast, then searched her face. "What is it, Olivia?"

Stretching out her hands, she gripped Lord Brightwell's arm as tightly as Talbot held hers. "I could not find Andrew. Edward went in to make sure . . ."

"I told him not to, my lord," Talbot said.

Craning her neck, she asked the coachman, "Did you check the closet? The hidden door between the tack room and the saddle rack?"

"There is no closet there."

"But there is!"

Rumble . . . crack! The roof collapsed like a snake of dominoes from right to left.

"Edward!" Lord Brightwell lunged forward, loosing Olivia's hand as though a child's grip.

Through the black smoke, a figure materialized, black against black, like a specter. A beam fell and struck the dark figure, and Olivia screamed.

Lord Bradley, a burden in his arms, stuttered to the side and crashed to his knees just ahead of the weight of the wreckage. Olivia jerked away from Talbot's stunned grip and ran forward on the earl's heels, passing him and reaching Edward first. She pulled the small coat-shrouded body from him, and relieved of his burden, his duty, he fell face forward. His father caught him as he dropped, cushioning his fall. Croome appeared beside the earl, face ashen. Together they each took an arm and dragged Lord Bradley from the flames.

Watching from a point of relative safety, Andrew in her arms, Olivia's heart pounded, and new tears pooled in her eyes for reasons too numerous to sum.

※

In the library that evening, Lord Brightwell and Judith Howe sat in high-backed chairs very much like thrones. Olivia stood before them, hands clasped behind her back and head bowed—the posture of a criminal awaiting judgment. She felt she deserved the moniker. And worse.

Audrey stood behind her stepmother's chair, eyes red-rimmed. Olivia wished the girl need not be on hand to witness her dismissal.

Olivia forced her head up. "I am very sorry, Mrs. Howe. Lord Brightwell. I should never have allowed Andrew to run off on his own."

Judith Howe played with the worked lace on the arm of the

chair. She looked up and said coldly, "I must say, Miss Keene, I am prodigiously disappointed in you."

"It was not her fault, Mamma," Audrey said. "We were only playing hide-and-seek. Miss Keene could not know a fire would start."

"How quick you are to defend your governess, Audrey," Mrs. Howe said. "You may leave us now."

Olivia's dear pupil gave her an apologetic glance and hurried from the room.

When the door closed behind Audrey, Mrs. Howe asked, "Are you in the habit of letting the children run wild about the estate, without supervision?"

"No, madam."

"Even that nurserymaid, who is little more than a girl herself, knows better. If anything had happened to Andrew . . ."

"I know. I know." Olivia pressed her eyes closed, miserable. "I would never have forgiven myself."

"Nor would you ever have the care of children again, had I anything to say about it." A new thought struck her mistress. "And why were *you* out with them instead of the girl?"

Olivia swallowed. "Becky has so much other work, and I enjoy playing with the children."

"It does not sound as if you were *with* them at all, but instead off on your own somewhere." She darted a glance at her uncle. "Perhaps meeting a lover?"

"No, madam. Nothing of—"

"Judith, please," Lord Brightwell admonished. "Such accusations are neither fair nor becoming."

Mrs. Howe gave him a sharp look. "Are you so quick to defend her as well?"

The earl spoke in moderating tones. "Of course I am. Miss Keene has been a marvelous addition to our household. I am sure she regrets this incident and will see that it does not happen again."

Judith looked from her uncle to Olivia and back again. "It seems, Uncle, that you would forgive her anything."

"It was an accident, Judith," he said. "And Dr. Sutton assures us Andrew will be fine. He did inhale a quantity of smoke and will cough for some days, but he is breathing well and will be his old mischievous self in no time."

Olivia dared ask, "And what of Lord Bradley?"

"He is badly injured," Mrs. Howe snapped. "Thanks to you."

"My dear Judith," Lord Brightwell said, "do you accuse her of starting the fire as well?"

Judith stubbornly lifted her chin but gave no answer.

"Judith, really! According to Talbot, there *were* two persons in the stables before the fire." He gave Judith a pointed look. "But neither was Miss Keene."

Mrs. Howe did not ask whom he meant, Olivia noticed. And wondered why.

After the interview, Olivia stepped into the sickroom. Andrew lay there, head raised on several pillows, eyes as red as the glass of berry ice he clutched in his hands.

Olivia felt her chest tighten. *Thank you for sparing him*, she breathed. "Hello, Master Andrew."

He smiled up at her, teeth and lips stained red. "Hello, Miss Livie."

"How are you feeling?"

"My eyes burn like the time I got Mamma's perfume in them. My throat hurts too, but Becky brought me an ice, which feels ever so good. Delicious too."

Olivia smiled. "I am very glad."

He scooped up another spoonful into his mouth, and several drips found their way onto his white nightgown.

"Might I help you with that?" she asked.

He shrugged good-naturedly and handed her the spoon as Olivia sat on the edge of the bed.

She gave him a spoonful and simply savored the sight and nearness of the dear little boy. A floorboard creaked and Olivia turned her head.

Judith Howe entered the dim room. "Miss Keene," she said officiously. "Why are you not in the schoolroom with Audrey? That is what Lord Brightwell is paying you for, I believe. I shall ask Mrs. Hinkley to sit with Andrew until the chamber nurse arrives."

Andrew's little brow furrowed, clearly hearing the restrained anger in his stepmother's voice. He asked, "Are you cross with Miss Livie, Mamma?"

"If I am, it is only because I am concerned about you, Andrew. You might have been killed in that fire."

"But *she* did not start the fire."

"She should not have allowed you to go into the stables alone."

Andrew shrugged his little shoulders again. "She did not 'low me, I just went. Saw Uncle Felix and wanted to talk to him."

"Did you? Still, she ought—"

"But he was already talking to Martha when I got there," Andrew continued. "So I just went into that hiding closet, like I seen Miss—"

"Saw."

"Saw Miss Keene coming out of that time."

Judith looked at her shrewdly. "Indeed?"

"I could see Uncle Felix and Martha through the cracks in the wall. He sounded angry, so I did not jump out and scare him as I planned to."

"Very wise," Judith murmured, distracted.

"He was smoking one of those cigars, Mamma—the ones you don't like? And he threw it down."

Judith darted a look at Olivia, then said agitatedly, "Yes, well, we cannot know if that is how . . . that is, you did not actually see the fire start?"

Again Andrew shrugged. "No. I went to look out the back of the closet to see if Audrey was coming to find me yet. I saw

Martha run off into the wood and Johnny run after her. I smelled smoke and thought Uncle Felix must still be near, but that is all I remember. . . ."

"Poor boy."

"I am *well*, Mamma." He bestowed another of his cherry red smiles.

"I am relieved to hear you say so. Well, I am away to visit my mother. Miss Keene, you will return to your duties in the schoolroom promptly, I trust?"

"Yes, madam."

"At least . . . your duties for the present." Mrs. Howe nodded curtly and left the room.

Andrew opened his mouth for another bite and Olivia hurried to oblige him. He asked as though of a great adventure, "Did Cousin Edward really rescue me?"

"Yes, he did," Olivia said, and the little boy looked happier than he had opening gifts on Christmas morn.

The governess ought never, under any possible circumstances,
to allow herself to be either the source of family contention,
or mixed up as a party in any domestic quarrel.
—THE GUIDE TO SERVICE, 1844

Chapter 38

Olivia met Lord Brightwell coming out of the room next to the study. She waited until he closed the door, then whispered, "My lord, how is Ed— Lord Bradley?"

The earl's face was grim with exhaustion, but he managed a small smile for her. "Dr. Sutton has every confidence in a full recovery. The beam struck Edward across the nose and both brows. He has suffered minor burns around his eyes, but Sutton does not expect any long-term effect to his vision. His left arm is also injured. And two of his fingers burned, though not severely."

"How dreadful."

"He is well, Olivia." He lifted his chin toward the door he had just exited. "I was just in to see him, and his only concerns were for Andrew's well-being and your own."

"I am so sorry, my lord," Olivia said over the lump in her throat.

"My dear, those children have been running amuck since they came here, and if Judith has led you to believe they were under a watchful eye every moment before your arrival, then she has given you a false impression." He looked at her fondly and patted her hand. "You have given those children more attention and supervision than Judith ever has. Assure her it will not happen again and all will be well."

Olivia shook her head. "I believe I ought take my leave of you. I am certain Mrs. Howe would prefer it, and I do not blame her."

"Olivia, you are innocent in this, and I will make Judith see reason. But if it comes down to it, she is my niece, but you are my—"

She pressed his arm. "Don't say it."

"Very well, but if she will not have you as governess, you are welcome to stay as my . . . ward."

Olivia shook her head. "I am five and twenty, my lord, and, I pray, no orphan; surely this disqualifies me as anybody's ward."

"We shall see about that."

"I am grateful that you still want this . . . after everything," she whispered. "But I beg you, put the thought from your mind."

❦

That night, once she had heard Audrey's prayers and kissed her brow, Olivia went downstairs to check on Andrew in the sickroom yet again. He lay so peacefully that for a moment she feared he did not breathe. She laid her ear close to his face, and feeling the warm breath on her cheek and seeing the gentle rise and fall of his chest, she kissed him and left the room. In the corridor, she noticed a door ajar—the door Lord Brightwell had indicated earlier.

She hesitated, knowing she should take herself upstairs and climb into bed. Yet she knew she would not, could not, sleep. Not without seeing Lord Bradley with her own eyes. To assure herself he was well, that he had all he needed, and that he did not blame her.

Surely Osborn was seeing to his every comfort—she was being foolish. Dr. Sutton had left half an hour ago and would have stayed were there any cause for alarm.

Then why did her heart beat so fast?

There was nothing for it. She stepped across the corridor, barely believing she was actually going to his bedchamber alone, at night. No, certainly she would *not* be alone. Lord Brightwell would be sitting at his bedside, Osborn at least.

She paused before the door, but heard nothing. Fearing to wake him should he be asleep, Olivia knocked softly. Receiving no response, she took a deep breath and opened the door several more inches. She would just look in on him. If he was asleep she would make sure he was breathing and then slip away. In and out. If Osborn was there, she would . . . what? Invent some excuse— Audrey could not sleep without first knowing if Lord Bradley was well? She hated to lie, but nor did she want every tongue in the servants' hall wagging by morning.

She hesitated in the threshold. Several lamps were lit, but she saw no one about. A black and gold Chinese screen stood in the middle of the room, blocking her view.

A giggle trickled down the corridor, and Olivia turned her head. At the far end of the dark passage, she saw snooty Osborn, footman and valet, pressing Doris against the wall and kissing her.

Quietly, Olivia slipped inside. As she began to pull the door, she saw the teakettle sitting beside the door and picked it up, then stepped gingerly into the room.

"Where the devil have you been, Osborn?" Lord Bradley mumbled dully.

Something in his voice worried her, and she walked quietly forward without identifying herself. Carrying the kettle—which

Osborn must have been delivering when waylaid by Doris—she peeked around the screen, assuming she would find him awaiting tea. Stifling a gasp, she stopped midstride.

He was in a bathtub, his head resting against its high back, a large bandage across his eyes. Remnants of dark soot lingered along the hard line of his jaw and in the laugh lines around his mouth. His left hand, also bandaged, hung over the edge of the tub, propped on a nearby chair clearly put there for that purpose.

Her gaze traveled up from his swathed hand to his muscled forearm, bicep, and shoulder. His broad chest glinted with golden hair. Olivia felt herself flush, her heart thudding like the deepest bass drum.

"Let me know when an hour has passed. I wish to have done with this foul poultice." His voice was uncharacteristically languid, and she wondered how much laudanum the doctor had given him. She was thankful his eyes were covered and that no one was there to witness the burning of her face.

He huffed. "If you still insist on washing my hair again, let's have done. I could sleep for a fortnight."

Olivia's mouth went dry.

His hair needed another washing—the normally fair hair still bore streaks of ashy grey. What would it feel like to wash his hair? To entwine her fingers in the smooth blond strands? Imagining it, she released a shaky breath.

He lifted his head, brow furrowed. "Osborn?"

Caught. She froze, expecting any moment the poultice to drop and him to glare at her in shocked disgust at the vulgar intrusion. Dread seizing her, she set down the kettle with a splash and hurried from the room.

❧

All the next morning Olivia berated herself. What had she been thinking to go into his bedchamber? From Audrey, she had learned

Lord Bradley was up and about already. That was good news at least. Still, it was late in the afternoon before she finally roused the courage to walk down to his study. If she did not, would he not think her most ungrateful and unconcerned about his welfare? Would her absence not seal any suspicions he might have of the identity of his silent visitor the previous night? Pressing a hand to her chest to calm her beating heart, she knocked on his study door.

"Enter."

Wiping damp palms on her skirts, she pushed the door open and stepped inside.

"Ah, Miss Keene . . ." Lord Bradley, seated at his desk, laid down the letter he was reading. His coat hung over one shoulder, his injured arm not within its sleeve.

"My lord." She made a shallow curtsy, detesting the heat she felt infusing her face. For though he was now fully dressed, she involuntarily envisioned him as she had seen him last.

"You wanted to . . . see me . . . again?" he asked. Was that a twinkle in his blue eyes, or was she imagining it?

She licked her dry lips. "I wanted to make certain you were all right."

"And now that you have seen me, all of me, what is your prognosis?"

She felt heat creeping up her neck, though she had not, she told herself yet again, *not* seen all of him. So he did know. Or was very confident he did. She would not give him the satisfaction of admitting it.

His eyes flitted over her burning face and twisting hands with apparent amusement.

She pressed her jittery hands to her sides and cleared her throat. "Yes, that is . . . I wanted to thank you for rescuing Andrew so courageously."

"You are prodigiously welcome," he said. Rising, he stepped around the desk and leaned back against it. "Though why you should feel the need to thank me, I do not quite grasp."

"You know I adore Andrew, and if anything were to happen to him . . . And of course, I feel dreadfully responsible, letting him run off alone."

He nodded. "It is unfortunate Andrew learnt of your secret hiding place, and that Talbot did not know to look there, or this"—he raised his wrapped and slung arm—"might have been avoided."

She lowered her head, ashamed.

"Then again, I would not have earned your gratitude."

She looked up at him, uncertain whether he was being sincere or sarcastic. "If you wish to dismiss me, I understand and shall go at once."

He crossed his arms, quickly winced, and let go. "I hardly think it necessary. Nor am I ready to part with you. Judith was vexed, I know, but any mother—even stepmother—would be. Some of the steam went out of her when she learnt her darling brother was likely responsible for the fire—though, of course, Felix does not admit it."

He sighed. "At all events, it was an accident. In the meantime, we shall stable the horses at the Lintons, who have kindly offered, and rebuild. I for one look forward to the project and plan a few improvements and enlargements, though I was sorry to see our old steward's handiwork destroyed."

She looked at him more closely. "Will you be able to, do you think? How are you getting on? Does your arm not pain you?"

"It is naught. Aches a bit, but it is not broken as Sutton originally feared. Fingers itch like the blazes from whatever foul potion he applied. But otherwise I am well."

"And your face?"

He grimaced. "You tell me. I dared look in the glass and thought myself ridiculous with these singed brows and swollen nose. The thing was bent as a boy, and now has been bent yet again."

"You look . . . well, I think." She hurried on. "And your eyes?"

"My vision seems unhindered, thank the Lord." He studied

her. "In fact, I believe I see more clearly now than I ever have before."

She swallowed. "Do you indeed?"

He held her gaze a moment longer, blue eyes to blue eyes, and his were alight with something inscrutable. "Indeed."

*Between a governess and a gentleman there was no easy courtesy,
attraction, or flirtation, because she was not his social equal.*

—M. JEANNE PETERSON, *SUFFER AND BE STILL*

Chapter 39

*O*n Monday afternoon, Edward went out to the carriage to
greet Judith, returning from another visit to her mother. She took
his good arm and they walked companionably across the courtyard together, their pace made languid by the invitingly warm
springtime air.

Miss Keene and the nurserymaid had brought the children
outside to greet their stepmother. As usual Judith had eyes only
for Alexander and took him from the maid, kissing and stroking
the child.

Smiling at Audrey and Andrew in her stead, Edward thanked
Miss Keene and then took his leave of his cousin, who broke off
her cooing only long enough to smile at him before returning her
gaze to her young son.

Edward returned to the library to see how his father was getting on. When he entered, he found the earl standing at the tall windows facing the lane. He did not turn when Edward entered.

"You are not thinking of marrying her, I trust?"

Edward stilled, instantly wary. "Why do you ask?"

"I have noticed the . . . change in your relationship of late. At least on her part."

Had she changed? Warmed to him? He had thought so, but wondered if he only imagined it.

"And if you are entertaining marriage, I must know."

Edward heard the concern in his father's voice. "You disapprove."

"Profoundly."

Irritation surged within Edward. "I am surprised, considering, well . . . everything." Had he not decided Olivia was his own daughter?

The earl looked out the window once more, rubbing his lip with thumb and forefinger. "I have my reasons."

"Even if she is related to you, I don't see how that signifies."

The earl turned to Edward, expression stern. "You don't see— that is exactly right. You don't. You must trust me in this, Edward. I have your best interests at heart. Hers as well."

"Her best interests? Which of us is beneath the other?"

"This is not about rank."

"But you think it in her best interests to have nothing to do with me?"

"Romantically speaking, yes."

Had *he* not loved Olivia's mother? "That is rich, coming from you, Father. You who have always been so *wise* in your love affairs."

"That is enough, Edward."

But Edward pressed on. "Even if she is who you think she is, I hardly think that raises her station of life beyond my own. Miss Keene is—"

"Miss Keene?" The earl eyed him speculatively, a strange stillness in his countenance.

"Were you speaking of someone else?" Edward asked, confused.

"Ah . . . well . . ." Lord Brightwell cleared his throat. "I am afraid you must excuse me. I spoke without thinking." The earl abruptly turned and strode across the room.

At the door, Lord Brightwell hesitated. "And you are quite right, Edward. I am not in the least qualified to give marital advice. You may disregard what I said."

Edward frowned, but his father—for there was no other way he could think of the man—was already out the door. Edward had the distinct impression he had not been worrying about Miss Keene at all. He replayed the exchange in his mind. If his father had not been speaking of Olivia, had he somehow been referring to Miss Harrington? But she was no relation of theirs. That left only Judith. And why should his father worry about her?

⁊

After the conversation with his father, Edward realized he had left things unsettled with Miss Harrington for too long. She might still be expecting an offer of marriage. How strange that an alliance he had recently contemplated with pleasure, or at least contentment, now filled him with misgiving.

Feeling restless, he asked Ross to saddle Major and took to the open road. His arm was still wrapped, but he no longer needed a sling. What he needed was to ride. To think.

He rode south and west, giving Major his head, then reined him to a pace the well-conditioned animal could sustain for a longer journey.

When he trotted up the tree-lined avenue to Oldwell Hall, a young groom hurried out, and Edward flipped the lad half-a-crown, directing him to feed and water his horse.

Oldwell Hall was a large manse barely more than a decade old, with a central two-story block and two recessed wings. To Edward, the boxy grey building looked more like a military fortress than a home.

He was relieved to see Miss Harrington taking a turn about the lawn, a parasol on her shoulder. Still unsure of what he would say, Edward strode across the avenue to meet her.

She must have seen him, for she turned and waited until he reached her. "Bradley, what a nice surprise," she said with a warm smile. "I am afraid Father is gone to Bristol."

"That is just as well, Miss Harrington, for I hoped to speak with you."

A knowing smile lifted one corner of her mouth.

"May I walk with you?" he asked.

"Of course."

Shifting the parasol to her other hand, she took Edward's arm. Together they strolled across the lawn, damp from recent rains. The landscape was stark; only a few shrubs and a massive fountain ornamented the grounds. The temperature was mild, and the sun shone at intervals between passing clouds.

He cleared his throat and began in what he hoped was a nonchalant tone. "Do you recall you once said you wished your father would not pressure you, that you might"—he hesitated to verbalize the word—"marry as you pleased?"

She dipped her chin coyly, tentatively drawing out her reply, "Ye-ess . . ."

"Would you wish to marry a man, Miss Harrington, were he not heir to a title and peerage?"

She lifted her head and grinned. "Would this 'man' still be rich?" She laughed, but soon quieted. "Bradley, I am only teasing you. Has someone suggested I am only interested in you to become a countess?"

"Perhaps."

Her brow puckered. "But . . . how could I not admire you? You are the future Lord Brightwell . . . as well as young and handsome and attentive."

"And were I not?"

"My dear Bradley, we shall all grow older and less attractive in time. Though I shall find it a tedious bore not to have heads turn whenever I enter a room. . . ." She laughed again and awaited his chivalrous assurance.

"I meant, were I not a future earl," he persisted.

A spring breeze fluttered the parasol ruffle. "Really, you are in a strange mood. You know perfectly well that you are your father's heir. And if you were not, I would most likely have never even met you."

"Some other fortunate chap would be walking beside you now?"

She grinned again. "Some other fortunate *aristocratic* chap."

He nodded and walked on in silence.

She sent him a sidelong glance. "Why are we playing this game? Has your cousin Judith been riddling you with doubts about me?"

"Judith? What has she to do with it?"

Miss Harrington expelled a puff of dry laughter. "She wants you for herself, of course. Do not tell me you have never guessed."

Edward drew in a deep breath. Had he? Had this been what his father was hinting about? Cousins married often enough, he knew, but Judith was almost like a sister to him.

Sybil Harrington gave him a discerning look. "Tired of your game, Bradley?"

He managed a weak smile. "Yes, I suppose I am." He looked at her, then sighed. "Tired of the whole charade."

"Good," she said, blithely. "Are we . . . that is, will you be going to town after Easter?"

He shook his head and said quietly, "I will not."

She twirled the parasol on her shoulder. "Being in mourning,

I did wonder. Still, what a bore to endure the season without you. Father hoped we might avoid it altogether this year, if . . . "

He knew what the "if" was. If he was going to propose marriage, then she need not go to London in hopes of securing a match.

As if suddenly aware of the change in him, she stopped walking and regarded him closely, cautiously. The earlier amusement faded from her brown eyes.

He turned to meet her somber gaze. "Miss Harrington, I think you should go. Enjoy yourself."

Her cheeks paled, but she masked her disappointment well. "Do you indeed?"

"Yes, in fact, I am convinced of it." He faced her earnestly. "Please. Do not forego anything on my account."

She smiled bravely, but he did not miss the trembling of her chin. "Very well, I shan't." She turned away and looked up at the cloudy sky. "Now, I am afraid I must return to the house. My slippers are soaked, and it looks very much like rain."

❧

That evening after the children were in bed, Olivia sat with Lord Brightwell in the library. Edward was gone, she had heard—off to visit the Harringtons—and how the thought depressed her.

Silently, the earl withdrew a velvet box from his pocket and handed it to her.

She was instantly uncomfortable. "My lord, you should not—"

"It is something I gave your mother long ago. Something she returned before she left. I want you to have it."

Swallowing, Olivia opened the hinged box and gazed at the lovely cameo necklace nestled within. "It is beautiful. Thank you."

He pressed her hand. "Olivia, I have thought about this. I

care about you, and your mother was a special person in my life. It would give me great joy to call you my daughter."

Olivia flushed and lowered her head. Then she closed the box and looked up at him earnestly. "But we are not at all certain, and now . . . now we may never know."

"I realize that, but I believe I owe it to your mother to care for you now that she is . . . gone."

Something like panic rose within her. "Pray take no offense, my lord, but I have little wish to be *anybody's* illegitimate daughter. Besides, I do not feel it would be right to proclaim I *am* your daughter, when that is far from definite."

He grinned. "A proclamation. Excellent notion. I shall proclaim my intention to adopt you as my ward. We need not mention the blood tie if you prefer."

"But . . . is not such a thing highly unusual?"

"Well, yes." The earl chuckled. "I can just hear the cronies talking now, 'gone and made a lovely young woman his ward, clever old fox.' "

"Oh!" Olivia exclaimed, flustered.

He leaned forward. "Olivia, should it matter what those old fools think? It matters not to me. We know the truth."

"But we don't," Olivia emphasized.

"Olivia . . ."

"Do not think me ungrateful. I am more thankful than I can say for your many kindnesses to me, but you need *not* recognize me."

"But I want to."

A part of Olivia was deeply moved to be so warmly cared for when her own father had become so cold. But another part of her recoiled. It was not right.

"But what would your family think?" she asked.

"I do not care what Judith and Felix think. Their father did far more scandalous things, I assure you."

"And your son? Do you not care for his opinion either?"

He nodded. "I do care what Edward thinks. When he returns, I shall have to ask him."

"Ask me what?" Edward said, striding into the room in time to hear his father's last sentence.

"Edward! You are returned early. We did not expect you."

Edward shrugged, not wishing to discuss the Harringtons in Miss Keene's presence.

"What did you want to ask me?" Edward repeated.

Miss Keene avoided his gaze and seemed to shrink in her seat as the earl explained his plan.

"You cannot be serious!" Edward exclaimed. "Why on earth would you? A ward, at her age?"

At his outburst, Miss Keene ducked her head, and his father reached over and grasped her hand. "Because, as I have told you, I believe she is my daughter."

"But it is madness—she is a grown woman!"

"I realize that."

Edward paced the library like a caged tiger. "Are you really so convinced she is your child?"

Lord Brightwell looked at Olivia's bowed head, before returning his gaze to Edward. "More so than Olivia is . . . but it does not matter to me if she is or not."

"How can it not matter?"

His father looked at him pointedly. Indeed, Edward already knew how little blood meant to the man.

Edward stewed in silence, his emotions quaking within him.

Miss Keene stood. "Pray excuse me," she said and turned toward the door.

"Very well, my dear," Lord Brightwell soothed. "We shall talk again tomorrow."

Edward rose, but Olivia refused to look at him as she swept past, cheeks mottled red and white.

When the door closed behind her, his father sighed. "That was badly done, Edward. Badly done indeed."

"I know." Edward hated that he had injured her feelings, but he had his reasons for objecting.

"Olivia was already reticent to accept my offer. In fact, eschews any public proclamation. Your little snit has not helped my cause."

Why would Olivia not want the protection, connections, and resources of the Earl of Brightwell? Edward wondered. Was she so loath to be thought illegitimate? If so, what must she think of him?

But he refused to voice the searing thought that caused his heart to lurch—for if Lord Brightwell acknowledged Olivia as his daughter, she and Edward would be half brother and sister in the eyes of the world.

Governesses had a way of coping with status incongruity.
This most often took place in a form of escape.
—Carissa Cluesman, *A Historical View of the Victorian Governess*

Chapter 40

At least, Olivia told herself, she had her answer to what Lord Bradley thought of her becoming the earl's ward. He thought her unworthy, would be ashamed of her—that seemed clear. She should not have been surprised, but witnessing his outburst had hurt more than she would have guessed, and she had blinked back tears all the way to the schoolroom.

She expected Lord Bradley to avoid her after that terrible clash. She certainly planned to avoid him. But two nights later, as she was writing a letter to the proprietress of the girls' school in Kent—the friend of Mrs. Tugwell—Lord Bradley threw back the schoolroom door.

It was difficult to say which startled her more, the thunderclap of door hitting the wall, or being caught writing a letter she meant to send in secret. She jumped, and reflexively covered the letter with Mangnall's text. The quill in her hand shook, and she quickly laid it down upon the desk.

His blue eyes darted from the quill to the book to her no-doubt-guilty face. His expression darkened. "Writing another already, I see."

He strode to the desk, face grim, eyes sparking dangerously. "'*Extortus*, meaning extortion,' hmm?" he sneered, parroting her Latin lesson back to her. "Did you really think you could get away with it?"

Confusion and dread filled her. "What are you talking about?"

He unfurled a letter clenched in his hand. "We received this note in the post, or so I thought. It bears no postal date stamp, and Hodges has no recollection of how it arrived."

"I wrote no note."

"Here. Perhaps this will jar your memory." He thrust the note toward her, and she took and read it. The harsh, vile words stunned her.

> You tryd to hide yer secret, but I know what you did.
> Leave 50 ginny in the pozy urn on Ezra Sackville's grave
> on olde Lady Day and none shall be the wizer.

"Oh . . ." Olivia breathed, feeling a smart punch to her stomach. She looked up into his face with concern, but at his contemptuous glare quickly angered.

"You don't believe I wrote this," she challenged, holding up the note.

"I don't want to believe it, but how can I ignore the evidence of my eyes?"

She sputtered, incredulous. "It is not even in my hand!"

"Easily disguised."

"And the abominable spelling . . ."

"Cleverly done, Miss Keene. I noticed that right off."

"I did not, could not, write such a thing."

"Your accomplice, then. The 'he' with poor spelling. For you are the only one who knew."

"Obviously not. Surely there were people who learnt of it at the time. Your birth mother or one of the staff or family."

"Someone who has held this information all these years only to reveal it now? I for one think that too great a coincidence."

"I admit it—"

"You admit it?" he roared.

"I admit it looks bad, but I did not do it."

He shook his head. "Has your time here been so intolerable? Is this your plan to exact revenge?"

"Revenge?" She shook her head in disbelief.

"Your motive. And why not pry a bit of coin from us in the bargain."

"Why indeed," she blustered. "But more than a bit of coin. A hundred guineas might do for starters."

He glared. "The letter says fifty."

She lifted her chin. "I have just raised the figure. A hundred guineas seems a small price to pay to keep the world from knowing what you *really* are."

He stared at her, momentarily stunned. He shook his head bleakly. "At long last speaks the true Olivia Keene. You really have made fools of us all."

His words stung deep, and her anger moldered into shame. She rose unsteadily.

"Forgive me," she choked out. "I had no right to say such a thing." Her voice grew haggard. "But I tell you, I have nothing to do with this, nor have I ever breathed one word of your secret to another soul. Give me leave to go and I shall be silent forever."

She abruptly turned and all but ran from the room.

Edward clomped back down the stairs, anger and suspicion giving way to regret and dejection. In truth, he had taken the extortion letter to the schoolroom not believing Miss Keene a party to it at all. But then he had seen her hide the letter she was writing and he'd jumped to conclusions.

He took himself to the library to join his father. Lord Brightwell was asleep in his favorite chair before the fire. He was startled awake when Edward closed the door.

"Hello, Edward," he said, straightening himself in the chair.

"Better remain seated," Edward advised. "We have had another letter."

The earl sighed wearily.

"From the hand, I assumed it was from a tradesman and opened it with the other estate correspondence, as you'd asked." Edward retrieved his father's spectacles and handed them and the note to him.

His father read, cursed under his breath, and dropped the letter to his knee, staring blindly at the fire.

"Who could have written this?" Edward asked. "I have accused Miss Keene, but—"

"Olivia? Are you serious? I cannot believe you!"

Edward squeezed his eyes shut. "I know, I know. I have made a muddle of it. I walked in while she was writing a letter—one she quickly hid from me. I suppose I snapped." He ran a hand through his hair. "All that plagued secrecy since she arrived. Her silence about her past and even where she lived. Is it any wonder I suspected her of some plot?" He shook his head. "I will apologize. I don't really believe she would do this. But who else knows? Perhaps someone who was there at the time?"

"It is possible. The girl's father knew, but he swore his secrecy. Nurse Peale attended your mother and must have known, though I don't recall her asking any questions."

"Loyal Nurse Peale. I cannot imagine her having anything to do with it."

"Nor I."

"Anyone else?"

"The physician and the midwife who told your mother she was unlikely to bear a living child must have suspected, but neither was actually present when I brought you here."

"When you switched a living infant for a stillborn, you mean? And passed me off as your own?"

"Yes. Do you judge us so harshly for it?"

Edward rubbed his eyes with his good hand and exhaled. "No. Forgive me. I am grateful you raised me as your son. But obviously, someone else is not."

❦

Edward spent a restless night, tossing to and fro in his bed, tortured by echoes of his unforgivable words to Olivia.

In the morning, he dressed without care, not bothering with a cravat, and struggled into his boots without calling on Osborn. He trudged downstairs to the empty breakfast room. The thought of food sickened him, and even the coffee he poured was too bitter to drink. He slumped into a chair and rested his head in his hands.

A soft scratch on the door roused Edward from a doubt-induced fog. "Come."

Mr. Tugwell stepped in, hat in hand.

"Hello, Charles," Edward said bleakly, not bothering to rise.

"I am returned to see how you fare," the parson began, closing the door behind him. "I have been concerned about you, my friend, since the fire and"—he lowered his voice—"the letter. I have been praying, of course. Is there nothing more I can do?"

"Nothing. Unless you can rewrite the past. Unless you can conjure a father who was actually wed to the woman who bore me. A peer, ideally, that I might take his seat in the Lords and fulfill my life's ambition."

His friend regarded him with drooping hound eyes. "There is no need to conjure a father. For He already calls you His own. And no mere earl or duke, no. The very King who reigns forever."

Edward sighed. "Thank you, Charles. I know you mean well, but I am not talking about religion—"

The vicar's voice rose. "Neither am I!"

"Faith in God will not change the facts of my past."

"No, but it could make all the difference to your future."

Edward leaned back in his chair. "What future?"

"Oh, really, Edward. I have had quite enough. You are behaving like a spoilt child. Lord Brightwell will not leave you penniless, will he?"

"No, but—"

"Where has God promised to fulfill our every whim according to the minutia of our earthly desires? Where has He promised to keep us from suffering or disappointment? Things He did not spare His own Son? You were raised in one of the finest manors in the borough, by a man and woman who could not have loved you better. You have been given the best education, the best of everything. You are sound of mind and limb, and yet you dare to rail at God? I for one grow weary of it. Now leave off simpering like an ungrateful brat and make something of this new life you've been given."

Edward stared. His old friend, the docile Charles, had utterly disappeared. The man before him was suddenly every inch the Reverend Mr. Tugwell, someone to be revered indeed.

Emotions wrestled for preeminence within Edward. He rose, wanting to strike the man, stalk off, or . . . laugh. Absurdly, the latter won out, and he felt a smile crack his scowl and he chuckled.

"What?" Charles said peevishly.

Edward laughed, bent over, and laid his hands on his knees as he did so.

The vicar frowned. "I fail to see what I said that has so amused you."

Edward placed a hand on his friend's shoulder. "I wish you could have seen your face just then. I wish your father might have seen. How it shone with righteous wrath! He would have been proud indeed."

"You are mocking me."

"Not at all. Everything you said was quite true." Edward slapped his friend's back and the smaller man jerked forward. "You have woken me from my stupor, Charles, and I am grateful to you." He put his arm around the vicar and turned him toward the door. "You really ought to deliver your sermons in such a manner. The old men would stay awake and how the widows would swoon."

Charles Tugwell took his leave, but Edward saw not his friend's retreating figure. Instead, other scenes filtered past his mind's eye, bits of memory and conversations with Olivia. Finding Andrew in her bed, grooming his horse together, working on the doll's house in stolen moments in Matthews's shop, ice-skating with the children, hearing her speak his name in her sleep, that delicious dance lesson . . .

What a fool he had been, what an irrational fool. And he realized, there and then, that he could not do it anymore, he would not hold on to what was not his. It was making him a defensive, suspicious lout, snarling at everyone, dreading that at every turn his secret would be revealed. It had to stop. It was not worth it.

Edward strode quickly down the corridor with an urgent sense of purpose, realizing there was one benefit to the new life Tugwell referred to, the one thrust upon him. He was free to marry without regard to rank and connection.

He took the stairs up to the nursery by threes, ignoring the wide-eyed stare of a young maid, who was slowly making her way down. He knocked on Olivia's door and, when there was no response, stepped quickly down the corridor and pushed open the schoolroom door. He was startled to find his father there, standing at the window, peering out.

"She is gone, Edward."

Edward's heart lurched. "Gone? Run away?"

"Not 'run away.' I was able to prevent that, if barely. Patching up after you is not an easy task."

"I was wrong, I know. Utterly, unforgivably wrong. Did you not tell her I never really believed her responsible for those letters? I was angry, irrational, I did not mean—"

His father lifted his hand. "Yes, yes, but she wished to leave anyway."

Edward ran a hand over his face. "Where is she?"

The earl sat at the schoolroom desk, looking older than his age for the first time in Edward's memory. "I think it best not to tell you at present," he said. "I believe it would be unwise of you to go charging after her now, when she wanted quite desperately to get away from here."

"Away from me."

"Well, yes. And can you blame her, after you accuse her of extortion, not to mention your less-than-enthusiastic response to the notion of making her my ward?"

Edward groaned. "She can be your ward. She can be your daughter as far as I am concerned. I am ready to end this charade. Felix can have it all. The title, the estate, the peerage. I just want—"

When he broke off, the earl raised his brow. "Yes?"

Edward pressed a hooked finger to his lip. "There will be time enough for what I want later, Lord willing. In the meantime, let us figure out a way to let the wind out of our adversary's sails."

Men . . . generally look with a jealous and malignant eye on a woman of great parts, and a cultivated understanding.

—JOHN GREGORY, *A FATHER'S LEGACY TO HIS DAUGHTERS*, 1774

Chapter 41

*W*alking briskly, Edward led his father to his favorite spot in the wood. A branch snapped, and through the trees, Edward glimpsed Croome kneeling on the ground in the distance—doing what, he could not tell. Croome rose and walked away, disappearing into the wood.

"Why do you drag me all the way out here?" Lord Brightwell asked, out of breath.

"Shh. The walls have ears, as they say. Or might." Edward glanced around. Satisfied they were alone, he said, "Now. I have been thinking about our greedy adversary."

"Of course we shall not gratify such vile demands."

"Oh, but we shall."

"What? And have the fiend ask for a hundred the next week and a thousand next year?"

Edward shook his head. "We shall bag up a few shillings and leave them in Sackville's urn as bait. We shall wait and see who comes for it and then have our man. Or woman."

"And what are we to do with the wretch once we have caught him, or her?"

"I have not the slightest notion. But at least we shall know whom we are up against."

❧

On the night of old Lady Day, Edward and his father slipped through the narrow door in the wall and into the churchyard. There, they positioned themselves on a granite bench behind the mausoleum of the second Lord Brightwell, a position which leant them a view of the Bradley and Sackville plots, across from a cluster of graves called the Bisley Piece.

"Do you see my mother's tomb, there?" the earl whispered. "And the flower urn beside it?"

Edward looked. "Yes?"

"That is where I buried our stillborn son."

Edward stared at the spot and felt a shiver run up his spine. It was eerie enough in the churchyard after dark without thoughts of late-night, clandestine burials.

"I bundled him well and buried him there beside his grandmother. I moved that urn over the spot to disguise the disruption of grass and soil."

Edward looked at the massive stone planter and could not imagine any man moving it. "Alone?"

"Yes . . . I was a younger man then, of course. And prodigious scared I would be caught."

They sat for several more minutes in silence, waiting, their eyes and ears alert for the extortioner's approach. An owl screeched and his father jerked. Edward laid a hand on his arm.

A cloud, masking the greater portion of the moon, rolled away on the wind whistling through the yew trees, and the moonlight illuminated Sackville's grave more clearly. A figure stood before it, though they had neither heard nor seen anyone enter the churchyard.

"What the devil . . ." his father whispered, but Edward shushed him with a squeeze to his arm.

They watched as the figure reached into the urn, but when he withdrew his hand, it held no white bag. His father made to rise, but Edward increased the pressure on his arm. "Wait."

Two things caused Edward to hesitate. First, he wanted to catch the person with bribe in hand to seal his guilt. And second, there was something familiar about the thin figure.

"It is Avery Croome," Edward whispered.

"What? I cannot believe it."

Surprisingly, Edward could not believe it either and sat where he was, deliberating.

Instead of reaching in again to try to find the money—perhaps they ought to have used a larger sack, as his father had suggested—or turning to leave, Croome crept around a carved, pre-Norman tombstone and disappeared.

"Where did he go? Is there another gate behind the Bisley Piece?"

"Not that I know of. Perhaps he is lying in wait?"

"For us? You think he knows we are here?"

"Shh . . ."

Footsteps approached through the churchyard gate, boot heels on the paving stones. Now who was coming? Edward feared it would be Charles Tugwell, come to pray, or worse yet the constable on his rounds. While the constable would no doubt be more adept at apprehending the extortioner, they did not want it done publicly.

The figure left the paved path and turned in their direction. Edward and his father sat utterly still, hidden by tombstones and shadows.

A bat flew low over them, brushing the hair on Edward's hatless head. He did not so much as flinch, so focused was he on the approaching figure. Whoever it was wore a hooded cape, as dark as the enveloping night. Beneath the black shadows of the hood, a crescent of face shone pale in the moonlight.

"Is it a woman?"

"Shh . . ."

Edward did not think it was a woman—the walk was a masculine lurch. *But it might be a ruse.*

The caped figure walked directly to Sackville's grave as if the way were familiar even in darkness. An arm lifted, and Edward saw the slight glimpse of a pale hand as it reached into the "pozy urn"—deeper, deeper . . .

Snap! A vicious metallic clang split the silence, and the figure screamed. For a second, Edward and his father sat frozen in shock. The perpetrator's hood fell back and Edward saw it was a white-haired man. Screaming again, the man snatched back his hand—and the steel trap which impaled it.

His father turned to him, eyes wide in the moonlight. "Did you . . . ?"

Rising, Edward shook his head. "Croome." He rushed forward, his bottled fury at this unseen enemy greatly deflated by the old man's pitiful cries. Croome reached the man before Edward did.

"Get it off me, get the fiend off me," the man begged.

"Tell me who sent you," Croome demanded in his gruff voice.

Did Croome know what was going on? How? Why did he assume the man was not acting on his own?

"For the love of Pete—get if off me! My arm's broke."

"Croome . . ." Edward quietly urged.

"Who told you to do this, Borcher?" Croome persisted. "Who?"

"Nobody."

Croome stuck a stake into the trap's release, but instead of springing it open, he levered up the pressure.

"Stop! All right!"

Croome lowered the stake.

"A woman come round," the man began breathlessly, "askin' questions 'bout Lady Brightwell's lyin'-ins, my missus bein' the midwife in those days, God rest her soul. I had not thought on it in years, until the lady put it into my head again. She let on that Lord Brightwell had a secret." He panted, perspiring profusely. "My boy Phineas figgered it might be worth a great deal to him to keep it quiet. He wrote the letter. Never learnt to write myself."

Croome released the trap. "Phineas Borcher. Figured he had somethin' to do with it."

Edward glimpsed the man's bleeding wound and dug into his pocket for a clean handkerchief. "Who was the lady who came to see you?" he asked.

"Oh, Lord Bradley! I . . ." The old man looked stricken to see him. "I don't know. She wore a black veil. I never saw 'er face."

Edward wordlessly handed him the handkerchief.

He pressed it to the wound. "I never meant you no harm. You—"

"Only me?" his father asked, coming to stand beside Edward.

The man's eyes widened even further. "Bless me. Lord Brightwell! I never meant to . . . I don't really know what it is all about."

Edward turned to Croome. "Did you overhear us in the wood?"

The gamekeeper gave a slight nod.

"Even so, how did you—"

Croome held up his hand. "Let's just say I have the misfortune o' being acquainted with this man's son. And I make it my business to know his. Heard him boastin' how he was gonna lighten yer purse, my lord."

"We didn't mean no harm," the man whined. "Phineas said we could get some blunt for nothing, and times is hard, you know."

Croome scowled. "And about to get worse."

My nurse was my confidante.
It was to her I poured out my many troubles.

—WINSTON CHURCHILL, *MY EARLY LIFE*

Chapter 42

Despite her regret over abandoning Audrey and Andrew and leaving without saying farewell to those she had come to love at Brightwell Court—and Miss Ludlow and Mr. Tugwell, besides— the time with her mother's family had proved more pleasant than Olivia would have guessed. She had fretted how Mr. Crenshaw might react to her, considering her mother's unsuitable marriage, disappearance—and the potential scandal—might all one day be revealed. But Mr. Crenshaw, a small, balding, cheery-faced man with dancing brown eyes, warmly assured her that he had "got quite used to taking in scandalous Hawthorns, forced from their homes and down on their luck—and should like it above all things to take in another." It had been too many years since he had done so, he added with a wink and a smile for his wife. Olivia could not help but smile as well.

As Olivia had expected from the few lines Georgiana Crenshaw had penned within her grandmother's note, she liked her aunt immediately. She was warm and amiable, with easy, unaffected manners. Perhaps it was the likeness to her mother, but Olivia felt as if she had known Georgiana for years.

Her grandmother was somewhat tentative and staid at first, asking questions about Olivia's childhood and education. She avoided asking about Mr. Keene, for which Olivia was relieved. Still, Olivia realized that her grandmother was making a sincere effort to welcome this granddaughter she barely knew, and Olivia could not help but be touched.

The Crenshaws urged her to stay for as long as she liked. Olivia hoped to begin teaching school in the autumn but gratefully accepted their invitation to spend the summer at Faringdon.

Olivia had been with her relatives for less than a week when the Crenshaws' footman announced Lord Brightwell and showed him into the morning room. Olivia rose, suddenly nervous in his presence, as she had not been in some time. Her anxiety was heightened by the fact that his usually placid countenance was strained.

"Are the children well?" she asked.

"Yes, though disappointed, of course, to learn of your . . . leave."

"Is Mrs. Howe very angry?"

He chuckled mirthlessly. "I think my niece smells another mystery in the air and longs to get to the bottom of it."

Olivia longed to know how Lord Bradley had reacted to her departure but would not ask. Remembering her manners, Olivia said, "Please. Do be seated." She settled back into her own chair, but he remained standing. He pulled something from his coat pocket.

"Olivia. I have something for you."

"Not another gift! You have given me too much already."

"No. Not this time." His sober voice chilled her.

"What is it?"

He unfolded a rectangle of thick paper and held it before her. She accepted it gingerly, as though it were a coiled snake. Angling the printed notice to better catch the light from the window, she read quickly, gasped, then read it again.

Olivia Keene
24 years old, dark hair, blue eyes
Anyone with information please contact the
Girls' Seminary, St. Aldwyns

"Where did you get this?" Olivia breathed.

"It was delivered by a paid messenger who did not know, or would not say, whom it was from."

Olivia felt a painful mixture of fear and hope. "It looks somewhat faded—and I am five and twenty now. Perhaps my father posted this before he came to Brightwell Court."

"Do you think so? But why would he go through a school?"

"Because he is clever. He knew I would assume my mother was trying to find me. Or it could be her doing," she acknowledged. "Maybe she has come to find me at last."

"But you sent a letter to the school, letting them know your whereabouts."

"I did. But that was several months ago. Perhaps the mistress did not recall." She looked up from the notice and found him watching her closely. She asked, "Will you take me to St. Aldwyns?"

He nodded. "The carriage is just outside."

❧

Asking Olivia to wait inside the closed carriage, Lord Brightwell strode the few feet from the lane to the seminary door. Peering discreetly from behind the curtained chaise window, Olivia watched as a thin, older woman came to the door. Lord Brightwell introduced himself, and the woman curtsied and identified herself as Miss Kirby, one of the mistresses of the seminary.

The earl pulled the notice from his pocket and held it before her. "I am here because of this."

She gave it a cursory glance. "Forgive me, my lord, but what has this to do with you?"

"Perhaps a great deal." He hesitated. "Can you tell me, are you acting on behalf of a family member?"

It was the woman's turn to hesitate. "I don't . . . that is, I am not at liberty to say."

"I would very much like to speak with this person."

"I am afraid my sister, who would know how to go about this better than I, is away at present. If you could return another time?" She began to close the door.

"Olivia will be disappointed," he said shrewdly, and the door opened once more.

The woman's face became animated. "You have seen her, my lord?"

"Yes. She has been at Brightwell Court these several months. I hope to make her my ward."

"She is there now?" Olivia heard the restrained excitement in the woman's voice.

Again the earl hesitated, likely not wanting to give away her location until he knew who was looking for her. "Not at present. But I know where she is."

"And she is well?"

Olivia missed the earl's reply.

"That is excellent news. I will pass along this information to . . . to the interested party."

"Thank you." The earl gave the woman his card.

"I think I should tell you, my lord," Miss Kirby said nervously, "that you are not the first person to inquire after Miss Keene."

A sense of foreboding filled Olivia as she listened. Had her father called at the seminary before he came to Brightwell Court?

"Oh? Who was it?" he asked.

"The woman did not give a name."

"A woman? How old? What did she look like?"

Hope and caution competed within Olivia. Had it been her mother, after all?

"I really could not say. She was heavily veiled. A well-to-do woman, I would guess. She had an upper-class voice at any rate. Not old, but not a girl either."

Was the veiled woman her mother? Disguising herself to avoid being recognized by Simon Keene, not knowing he had been arrested?

"What did she say?" the earl asked.

"She tried to persuade my sister to tell her who was looking for Miss Keene, and why. She said she would like to talk with this person on behalf of Miss Keene."

"You did not arrange such a meeting?"

"Sister was tempted. The woman seemed so sincere in her concern. But at the last minute sister felt it was not right."

"Thank the Lord for that."

"We expect the woman to return Friday at two."

"Then you may expect me Friday at one."

❧

Determined to conquer his lowness of spirits, Edward dragged his weary limbs up the many stairs to the nursery. He had not gone as often as late, and he knew the reason. But a visit with his young cousins might cheer him.

He found only Nurse Peale, sitting motionless on her rocking chair, staring vaguely ahead.

"Hello, Miss Peale," he said kindly. "How are you getting on?"

"Master Edward, my dear boy."

"Where are the children?"

"Becky took the older two outside. Alexander is down for his nap."

He nodded, then asked, "You were here when I was born, is that not right?"

She smiled, her eyes strangely bright and distant. "That I was. Monthly nurse for your poor mamma. How is Lady Brightwell? Still sad as ever?"

He hesitated. It struck him hard to realize the mind of his stalwart nurse was failing, but on impulse he decided not to remind her of recent events. "Quite so. Why is she sad, Miss Peale?"

"Foolish boy, because her babies died." She looked past him at some unseen object or memory.

His breath caught. "All of them, Miss Peale?"

She sighed. "All of them."

He gently asked, "Did you mind when they took me as their own?"

"Why should I? They said I could stay on as your nurse and at quite high wages in the bargain." She glanced up at him. "Do you know I earn more than Hodges? Mrs. Hinkley once remarked upon it." She cackled. "I would have stayed for less. I loved ya the moment I saw ya. So like Alexander."

"Yes," he murmured, trying to keep the concern from his expression and tone. "You were a very good nurse and have served our family well."

She nodded, her eyes clouding in confusion. Had she just realized she had admitted something she was never to divulge?

Another thought startled him. Could she have written the letters? Confused as she was? He realized he would not know her writing if he saw it. Had he ever seen it? But something Miss Keene once said whispered in his mind.

He said, "Yes, you were an excellent nurse, but you never learnt to read and write, did you?"

She shook her head. "I can't lie to you, Master Edward." She winced. "But pray don't tell. It has been my shameful secret all these years."

That secret she kept, he thought, somewhat cynically.

"What was my mother's name?" he asked, deciding to take advantage of her current state of mind.

Nurse Peale shook her head slowly, eyes far away again. "Poor Alice Croome . . ."

His heart jerked. *Croome? It cannot be.* Had Croome a wife? Daughter? Niece? He had not thought it.

"Is that her name?" he pressed. "Is my mother Alice Croome?"

Nurse Peale looked up sharply, mouth stern and a fire in her eyes that would have set him quaking as a lad. "Your mother is Lady Brightwell, of course," she snapped. " '*Who is my mother* . . . ?' What nonsense!"

The most fashionable [school] was Mrs. Devis's in Queen square,
where dancing masters, music masters and drawing masters
were much in evidence.

—RUTH BRANDON, GOVERNESS, THE LIVES AND TIMES OF
THE REAL JANE EYRES

Chapter 43

Olivia spent an anxious few days with her aunt and grandmother before Lord Brightwell came for the promised return to
St. Aldwyns.

When the carriage arrived at the school and Lord Brightwell
again went to the door alone, Miss Kirby seemed more agitated
and nervous than ever. "Oh! It is you, Lord Brightwell. I feared it
might be that veiled woman returning once more."

"She has already been here? It is not even one o'clock."

"She came early. And was very vexed when I would not tell her
what she wished to learn. You have only just missed her."

Olivia, still ensconced in the nearby carriage, looked out the
chaise's rear window and glimpsed a figure in a dark cape, hat, and

full veil step into a waiting carriage parked along the high street. Her stomach lurched. Had she just missed her mother?

"My sister has gone to pick up a new pupil from the afternoon coach," Miss Kirby said. "If you would care to return in, say, an hour's time?"

"Thank you. Might my ward and I tour the seminary while we wait?"

Hearing her cue, Olivia let herself down from the carriage.

Miss Kirby watched her approach with owl eyes. She faltered. "I don't . . . That is, this is not really a convenient time, my lord. My sister not being here, you understand. And I am wanted in class in three minutes' time. The dancing master departs at one sharp."

Olivia offered her hand to the woman. "I am Olivia Keene," she said.

Miss Kirby's mouth gaped as she accepted Olivia's hand. "Is it you?" She bit her lip. "If only . . . But my sister left strict instructions. If perhaps Miss Keene would care to wait alone?"

"Miss Keene stays with me, under my protection," Lord Brightwell said. "You understand."

"I don't think, that is . . . Oh, I really must go in. Here. If you will follow me, I will show you to the parlor. If you will remain there, I shall send my sister in to you the moment she returns."

"You are too kind, Miss Kirby."

The woman's head swiveled side to side as she led them into the school and down a short passageway to a small, tidy parlor. "Wait right here," she said and closed the door firmly behind her.

"Cautious lady, our Miss Kirby," the earl remarked.

"I noticed that as well."

"I do hope they are not delousing pupils or some such thing they don't wish visitors to witness."

Olivia made no reply but walked slowly about the room. "This is where I was bound, before I diverted to Brightwell Court," she said. "I had hoped they might want another teacher."

"You hope it still, I see."

"Do not think me ungrateful."

"I don't. You are your mother's daughter. Of course you want to teach. Whenever I see you with Audrey and Andrew, why, it is like seeing Dorothea all over again."

"About that, my lord—are you thinking what I am thinking? About the veiled woman, I mean?"

He frowned. "I doubt it."

"You do not think it was my mother, come in disguise to find me?"

"No, I do not," he said flatly, with no hesitation.

She was about to ask him to explain when muffled laughter seeped beneath the closed door.

Olivia swung to face Lord Brightwell, grabbing his forearms. "It is Mother!" she whispered. Excitement pulsed in her veins.

The earl's eyes shone with sympathy. He shook his head and pleaded, "Olivia . . ."

Olivia hurried to the door and carefully opened it several inches, listening. The laughter rang out again from somewhere in the seminary.

"It is her! I know it!" Olivia bolted from the room. True, it had been a long time since she had heard her mother laugh, but the sound connected with her soul. She pushed open the first door she came to.

"Mother?"

A girl of thirteen or fourteen looked up from her desk, startled.

"Forgive me," Olivia mumbled and backed out, feeling the most foolish creature alive.

Lord Brightwell stood in the parlor doorway, silently beckoning her back inside. But Olivia heard the laugh again, from somewhere above her. She ran to the nearby staircase and, lifting her skirts, rapidly ascended the stairs. She hurried down the passageway to an open door and looked within. A woman sat at a low table, her back to the door. Before her were two girls near Audrey's age, playing a game with French vocabulary cards. The girls saw Olivia first.

"What is it?" The woman turned her slim shoulders and sable-brown head, revealing an infinitely familiar profile.

Olivia's stomach flipped and nerves shot through her body.

The woman's eyes widened, and she leapt to her feet, hand pressed to her heart. Olivia and her mother stood staring at one another in stunned silence.

"Olivia!" Dorothea Keene opened her arms and pulled her daughter close.

"Oh, Mamma, we have been so worried," Olivia said, tears filling her eyes. "We thought you were dead!"

"Olivia. Let me look at you. Until a few days ago, it was I who thought you were lost to me forever." Her mother pulled her close again. Then Olivia felt her stiffen. "Oliver . . ." she breathed.

Olivia turned and saw Lord Brightwell standing in the threshold, visibly shocked.

"It was Mamma I heard," Olivia said, out of breath. "Did I not tell you?"

"Yes . . ." the earl murmured, not taking his eyes from Dorothea's face. "Hello, ah . . . Mrs. Keene."

"My lord." Her mother bowed a jerky curtsy that lacked her usual grace. "I asked after Olivia in Arlington, but the only newcomer described to me was a dumb mute."

Olivia looked at Lord Brightwell and chuckled sheepishly. "It is a long story, Mamma. . . ."

❧

Miss Kirby served them tea in the parlor, apologizing, but explaining that they had instructions to reveal Mrs. Keene's presence only to her daughter—and only if her daughter was alone.

"I am sorry I could not come sooner, Olivia," her mother said. "After you left, Muriel took me to her sister's in the country. I intended to stay only a few days while I recovered from my . . ." She darted a look at the others, then returned her gaze to Olivia. "But I am afraid I fell dangerously ill. Between that and impassable roads, I was forced to trespass upon her hospitality for several months. I only managed to come to St. Aldwyns in early March and posted the notices then." She smiled at Miss Kirby as the woman poured tea. "When I did not find you, the Miss Kirbys kindly offered me a situation here."

Olivia thought it a just fate that her mother had been given the post she herself had wanted. There was no one else more qualified or deserving.

"Did you send a copy of the notice to Lord Brightwell?" she asked.

She shook her head. "I had no reason to think you would go to Brightwell Court instead of here."

Politely, Olivia asked Miss Kirby if she recalled the letter she had sent, inquiring after a position, and giving her direction within, should her mother come looking for her.

The older woman winced in thought. "I vaguely recall Sister mentioning a letter from Brightwell Court some months ago, but nothing about Dorothea's daughter—that I would remember! Did you not mention your mother by name?"

"I am certain I mentioned Mrs. Keene."

"Ah! But you see, we knew her only as Miss Hawthorn. Sister no doubt failed to make the connection. We only learnt the name Keene upon your mother's arrival, and I suppose Sister had forgot all about the letter by then—her memory is not what it should be. Nor mine, I am afraid." She winced again. "I hope you will forgive us, my dear."

"Of course I shall."

When Miss Kirby left, the three of them began to fill in the details in an overlapping jumble of conversation.

"I sent a man to Withington a few months ago," Lord Brightwell explained. "But your neighbors led him to believe, or at least *allowed* him to believe, that you might very well occupy the new grave in the churchyard."

Dorothea nodded, shamefaced. "It was Muriel's idea. But I agreed. It was the only way I could think to escape him. I knew he would search for me otherwise."

Olivia blurted, "Father has been arrested. You are safe."

Instead of relief, her mother's face froze, then furrowed. "Your father?"

"Yes. At first we assumed he had been arrested for . . . bringing you harm, but Miss Cresswell—"

"Olivia, no," her mother interrupted. "Your father did not . . . Did you think it your father you struck that night?" Her face was white with shock.

Dread and confusion filled Olivia. "Yes."

"My dear. I don't deny your father has a violent temper and many faults. But he has never raised a hand against me. It never occurred to me you thought it was him."

"I . . . I know it was dark, but I saw glass smashed against the grate and his coat on the overturned chair. . . ."

Mrs. Keene shook her head, her expression pained and bewildered.

"Then . . . who was it, Mamma? Whom did I strike?"

Dorothea glanced at Lord Brightwell, and then down at her hands. "Perhaps we might discuss this later. We have only just been reunited. And . . . you say your father has been arrested?"

"Miss Cresswell thinks the charge embezzlement."

"Although others believe Mr. Keene responsible for your . . . disappearance," Lord Brightwell added. "Especially as he fled the village as if guilty."

Pain creased Dorothea's brow. "I could not bear it if he were punished for a crime he did not commit," she said. "Do you think any magistrate would convict him with no evidence?"

"Who *was* buried in the churchyard?" Olivia asked.

"A poor gypsy lady who died in childbirth, her infant with her. Miss Atkins knew the church warden would never allow such a woman to be buried in the churchyard if she asked permission. So she did not."

Olivia shook her head. Over and over again. "I have felt so guilty. So sickened. To think my own father . . ." Olivia paused, glanced from her mother to Lord Brightwell and back again. "*Is* Simon Keene my father?"

Her mother stared at her, uncomprehending. Then she looked at Lord Brightwell sitting beside her daughter, and understanding slowly dawned on her face. Still she hesitated.

"Lord Brightwell thought . . . that is, we . . ." Olivia stammered.

"We hoped," the earl added, taking Olivia's hand.

"Oh, Olivia." Uncertainty clouded Dorothea's features. "Miss Kirby told me Lord Brightwell had taken you under his protection, but I never dreamt—"

"You named her *Olivia*," the earl said, almost plaintively.

She winced as if in pain. "Very foolish, I know. But in truth I had always loved the name, and had planned it for my daughter since girlhood." She stole a sheepish glance at the earl. "And yes, I was fond of the name for other reasons as well."

Dorothea fixed her eyes on Olivia's hand clasped in Lord Brightwell's and her eyes filled with tears. "Good heavens . . ." She swallowed and ducked her head. "I had just learned I was with child when I left Brightwell Court," she quietly acknowledged, cheeks flushed. "And Simon married me, knowing it. I could think of no other alternative. My family would not, I knew, have anything to do with me if they learnt of my disgrace. I could not support myself, and moreover, I wanted my child to be born in wedlock. Legitimate." Dorothea looked into Oliver Bradley's eyes, and time seemed to slow down. "But I miscarried that child soon after the wedding."

"Then why did he despise me!" Olivia burst out, feeling suddenly very young indeed.

"Oh, Olivia. It was not your fault." Her mother's voice shook. "He was terribly jealous, and I made it worse by going back to

Brightwell Court after the miscarriage. I should not have done so. I went only to see with my own eyes that he was well and truly married, gone from me forever."

Dorothea addressed Oliver, tears in her eyes. "I saw the two of you in the garden. Saw you embrace her. Kiss her. That was all I needed. It killed me and set me free at once."

The earl's eyes glistened. "I never knew you were there."

Dorothea returned her gaze to Olivia. "I returned home the same day and threw myself in Simon's arms, determined to make a new start. But then someone told him I had been seen on the eastbound coach, and he accused me of meeting a lover that day." She inhaled. "I assured him I had not. And for a time, I thought he believed me."

"But even he thinks Lord Brightwell is my father!"

Tears glistened on Dorothea's cheeks. "If only we had not gone to the Roman ruins that day." She shook her head. "Ruins, indeed."

"I thought if it were true, it might explain . . ." Olivia began, but tears closed her throat.

Lord Brightwell added, "I asked Olivia to allow me to publicly claim her as my ward, even knowing we could not be certain she was my daughter. But Olivia steadfastly refused. She must have known somehow, in her heart."

"Oh, Olivia." Her mother shook her head, contrite. "This is why I did not reveal myself when Lord Brightwell first called here. I thought perhaps you would be happier with him, instead of reuniting with me and my sordid lot."

"Olivia has been heartbroken over you," Lord Brightwell said. "I could never take your place."

Olivia felt tears streaming silently down her face.

"I am sorry all of this has befallen you, Olivia. Sorry most of all that you should think so ill of your father." Her mother cupped her chin. "Life was not always so bad, was it? We all got on reasonably well at times, when your father was sober. . . ."

Olivia felt numb. Her mother continued to speak, but the words grew indistinct.

Instead she heard the clink of glasses, the low rumble of men's voices, and her father's deep voice saying, "That's my clever girl." She felt the warmth of his praise wash over her again. An opaque web clouded her vision, and her mother and Lord Brightwell blurred. How long had it been since she'd thought back on the evenings around the fire, number games at the kitchen table, or listening to her father sing? Too long. Yes, there had been bad times. And she had tallied them like figures in a column, not remembering to factor in the good. She had doctored the books.

Suddenly Olivia felt embarrassed at having presumed on the earl's kindness. Yes, she had told him her reasons for doubting. But she had let him hope, had let their relationship grow.

Beside her, Lord Brightwell still held her hand. If anything he held it tighter. But Olivia could feel herself pulling away. Edward's face appeared in her mind. His expression full of disdain. How pleased he would be to know she had no claim on the earl after all.

Olivia wiped her eyes, realizing she had another confession to make. "When we feared the worst, Mamma," she said, "I opened that letter in your little purse. Lord Brightwell and I delivered it to your mother and sister."

Dorothea's eyes widened, and her countenance paled. "I wish you had not done so."

"You needn't worry," Olivia assured her. "Your mother and sister have welcomed me into their home. Aunt Georgiana's husband as well. They are very kind, Mamma, and Grandmother regrets the long separation between you. I know they would welcome you as well."

"Do you think so?"

Olivia had rarely seen her mother so uncertain. "Will you return to the Crenshaws' with me? It will be quite a shock to them, I own, for we thought never to see you again, but a wonderful shock, I assure you."

"I don't know. . . . Perhaps you might break it to them, and if they still wish to see me . . . you could write and let me know?"

"Are you certain? You could come back with me now and see them in person."

Her mother shook her head. "It is all too sudden. And I have my pupils here now. Perhaps another time?"

"Then, might I stay with you tonight?" Olivia asked. "Do you think the sisters would mind? It seems wrong to leave you so soon after finding you again."

Dorothea smiled. "You may share my room. They cannot mind that."

Lord Brightwell stood and suggested, "Why do I not send the carriage for you tomorrow, Olivia, to take you back to Faringdon. Or if you decide to stay here longer, you might send Talbot with a message for your grandmother so she does not worry."

"Thank you, my lord." Olivia rose, as did her mother. "You are always so thoughtful."

Dorothea curtsied before Lord Brightwell. "I am truly grateful for your watch-care over my daughter."

The earl bowed in return, but his farewell smile did not quite reach his eyes.

Olivia walked the earl to the seminary gate and there gently pulled her hand from his.

"What will you do now, my dear?" he asked.

She chewed her lip, then answered, "Spend time with Mother, of course, and learn what I can about my father's situation. I have been invited to spend the summer with my aunt and grandmother, and after, I hope to take a teaching post in Kent."

"But, Olivia, must you go so far away? Your mother will miss you, and so will I. And Edward."

"Well," Olivia faltered, and then pushed the thought of Edward from her mind. "I shall miss you as well. But I long for a new start."

He shook his head. "I know this has been quite a blow for you, Olivia. But it changes nothing."

"My dear Lord Brightwell, I disagree. We can no longer feign a relationship that we now know to be false. Your kindness has been my greatest solace these last months, and I will always be deeply grateful to you. But I must not depend upon you further." She leaned close and kissed his cheek. "Thank you for everything." She quickly pulled away, fearing yet more tears.

"Olivia . . ."

"Please, tell no one of my plans."

He looked incredulous. "But why?"

"I have but a few months before I leave for Kent, assuming they offer me a post, and I wish to spend every moment with my family."

He winced, stung. Olivia felt the sting in her own heart and instantly regretted her choice of words.

He asked, "But will you not at least come to Brightwell Court and say good-bye to everyone?"

"Well . . . I . . ." Olivia could not bring herself to admit the truth: that she did not want to see Edward. The earl must have seen her awkwardness, and the reason for it evidently dawned on him.

"Edward will be away tomorrow morning," he said quietly. "You might call in then, before you return to the Crenshaws'."

Olivia looked into Lord Brightwell's eyes and saw mournful understanding there. Her throat tightened. She whispered hoarsely, "Yes. Tomorrow morning will do."

She waved as he climbed into the carriage, and the equipage drove away. Then she turned toward the seminary. As she did, a thought that had been lurking in the back of her mind darted to the forefront at last. She recalled her hope that the veiled woman had been her mother, come to find her. Now Olivia felt a chill creep up her spine like a slithery silverfish. Her mother had been within the seminary when they arrived. Who, then, was the veiled woman Olivia had seen . . . and what did she want?

Chapter 44

Edward found the gamekeeper on his stoop, sitting in a puddle of sunshine, pet partridge at his heels, whittling knife and wood in his hands.

"I have learnt some distressing news, Mr. Croome," Edward began somberly.

The old man shot him a hawk-eyed look. "I daresay I can guess who told ya. Whatever she said, I trust you'll hear my side o' the tale. Isn't as bad as it appears."

"She? Are you talking about Miss Keene?"

"Well, ain't you?"

"No. Should I be? What might Miss Keene have told me?"

Croome closed the knife with a snap. "You'll ask 'er now, so I'll tell ya myself, and you can put me out if ya have a mind to. She seen me once before she ever come here. With a bunch o' ne'er do wells in the Chedworth wood."

"Chedworth—? What was our gamekeeper doing there?"

"I take a day now and then. After more'n thirty years workin' for yer father and his before 'im, I have it comin', haven't I?"

"But what—?"

"These men be poachers, but not here, my lord. Not after I caught them the once. Netting partridges by the barrelful."

"When was this? I don't recall hearing of it. Did you take them in to the constable?"

"Long ago. And no I did not. One o' those men was no more'n a lad. Another had a new missus with 'er first babe on the way. I couldn't do it. So I struck up a bargain-like. They would never more set foot on Brightwell property, and I would not take them in."

"But to trust the word of poachers?"

"I don't say I trusted them. Not Borcher and that other scoundrel. Hard, uncouth dogs. So I followed them, see, and they none the wiser, all the way back to the Chedworth wood, where they camp."

Edward scratched the back of his head. "Are you telling me you happened upon Miss Keene the one time you went? Preposterous!"

"No. I go back every fortnight or so."

"Why? Are you in league with them? I cannot imagine another cause but profit to travel such distance."

"Can you not? I would have credited you with more imagination, lad. A man with a full belly is much less likely to poach, ain't he?"

Edward looked at the old gamekeeper sharply. Wanted to cut as he had been cut. "Who is Alice Croome?"

The man's face slackened, then stilled. A wary light came into his faded eyes. "What did yer father tell ya?"

"I don't know who my father is. Do you?" When Croome hesitated, Edward hissed, "Are you the man?"

The old man's eyes widened, and he gave a mirthless bark of laughter. "Seems you have imagination after all, be it twisted. If I knew who yer father was, I'd 'ave killed him long ago for what he did to my sweet Alice. But never would she tell me who used her ill. And her what never hurt a living soul."

"Alice was your . . ."

"My girl. My own daughter." His voice trembled. "The dearest creature God ever made."

Croome's daughter. From worse to worse. "Where is she now?"

"Where did Lord Brightwell tell you she were?"

"He told me nothing."

"Then how did you hear of her?"

Edward shook his head, snorted a laugh. "My old nurse. The venerable Nurse Peale forgets a great deal these days, but recalls things she was meant to forget."

Croome seemed deep in thought and nodded his under-standing.

Edward studied him. "Seems she is not the only one who knows, for we have received more than one threatening letter. You wouldn't know anything about that, would you?"

Croome scowled. "I know naught of threatening letters, save the one from Borcher. Do you think I would raise a hand to harm you? Me? When yer all I've left in this world to show for me and mine? And sure and why did I refuse Linton's offer at twice the wages? Or Sackville's, for half again as much, and a lodge what's not falling down about me in the bargain? Why do I stay here? Where naught but me cares for the wood nor game? Not a sportsman on the place since the fourth earl. Did I stay bidin' my time so I might one day write you a threatening letter? Never."

Listening, Edward felt rattled, disconcerted to hear laconic Mr. Croome speak so many words together.

"Forgive me. I did not think you were behind the other letters. But you still have not told me where my . . . where your daughter is." Edward could not say nor even think the word. Lady Brightwell was his mother and always would be.

Croome stared off at the westerly sun, shining between the trees like a golden clockface framed in wood. "They say she run off with her young man."

"They? Who is they?"

"They what don't want people askin' questions 'bout her and what become of her."

"And what do *you* say?"

Croome narrowed his eyes until they all but disappeared beneath overgrown brows. "I say the Lord knows, and the earl knows, and one of them'll have to be the one to tell ya."

❧

Olivia asked the coachman to first stop at the dress shop, where she bid an affectionate farewell to Eliza Ludlow. From there, she went to the vicarage, and found Mr. Tugwell in his garden.

"I have come to say good-bye."

He pressed her hand. "I heard you were leaving us. And very sorry I was too."

"Thank you." She hoped it was not obvious she had been crying and attempted a light tone. "Might I ask a favor, Mr. Tugwell?"

"Anything, Miss Keene."

"I have written to your late wife's friend—the mistress of the girls' school in Kent?"

He nodded.

"She has written back to offer me a post, on the condition you will provide a character reference. Will you?"

"Of course, my dear. Though I should very much dislike for you to move so far away."

She forced a smile. "No need to fear. Miss Ludlow will still be here. And the two of you deal very well together."

"At the almshouse, yes." He hesitated. "You have been . . . let go . . . from Brightwell Court?"

"Not exactly, but with all that has happened, I think it best I leave. In all truth, I miss a schoolroom full of pupils, the camaraderie of girls from near and far, the company of like-minds, the friendship of other teachers."

"As well you might. I have never envied the life of a governess. Such lonely hours. Betwixt and between the family and the servants. A school would be much more commodious. I confess I cannot abide being alone for more than a few hours. I become bored with my own company all too quickly."

Olivia shook her head, bemused and mildly frustrated. "I think you must be blind, Mr. Tugwell. Or only see what you wish to see."

His brow puckered. "What do you mean?"

What could one say to a parson? The vicar of prestigious St. Mary's? *Open your eyes, man. The woman loves you. If you don't make Eliza Ludlow the next Mrs. Tugwell, then you are foolish indeed.* It would not do. Men did not like to be pushed. She would need to appeal to his heart of faith. Speak his language. "I believe you ought to pray for Miss Ludlow."

"Oh?"

"Yes. I cannot divulge details, but there is cause to believe she shall soon marry, and she will need wisdom to choose her husband wisely."

"Choose? Do you mean to say she has more than one suitor? I did not know she had any."

"I cannot break a confidence, Mr. Tugwell. Only ask you to pray fervently for our dear Eliza and for God's will to be done in her life."

"I shall, of course." He looked pensive and disconcerted.

Olivia reckoned it a good sign.

Olivia felt a pang of regret as she made her rounds of the estate, saying farewell to one and all. She hugged Doris and held her close.

"I am ever so happy you found your mum," Doris said. "What about your nasty ol' papa?"

Olivia inhaled deeply. "I found that I had misjudged him. At least in part."

"Did you now—not a mean crust? A slip-gibbet scape-gallows?"

The words stilled Olivia. Might Mr. Tugwell not say they were *all* scapegallows? Escaping the penalty for their deeds only through God's grace? She swallowed. "I am not certain *what* he is, but I plan to find out."

Doris sighed. "I don't hold much hope for people changin' their ways, but I'd be glad to be proved wrong. And no matter what, you've got a mum who loves ya, and that's more than most of us have, and don't you forget it."

Olivia smiled. "How I shall miss you, Dory."

In the kitchen, Mrs. Moore crushed Olivia in a warm embrace. "We shall all miss you, love. Mr. Croome as well, though he would never admit it. Have you been to see him?"

"No, but I shall."

Mrs. Moore nodded and pressed a wrapped bundle of biscuits into her hand. "Take this, my dear," she said, eyes glistening. "A piece of my heart goes with it."

In the nursery, Andrew threw his arms about her waist. When he loosened his hold at last, Olivia knelt down to his eye level.

"Why are you going away again, Miss Livie?" Andrew asked with a pout. "You have been gone too long already."

Audrey stood apart, and Olivia held out a hand to her. The girl came forward, crestfallen.

"I will miss the both of you very much," Olivia whispered. "But I find I must go."

"But we need a teacher!" Andrew complained.

Olivia forced a bright tone over the lump in her throat. "You shall have kind Mr. Tugwell for your Latin, I understand."

"Ugh. He's nothing like you, Miss Livie. He talks a great deal but teaches very little."

Olivia did not doubt his words were true, but she bit back a smile. "Be respectful and attentive, Andrew. He might improve on you."

She pressed Audrey's hand. "And lovely Audrey will have another governess, or perhaps attend the Miss Kirbys' seminary and have the best teacher of all—my own mother."

"Your mother is a teacher there?"

"Indeed she is. You would enjoy having Dorothea Keene as your teacher. I know I did."

Andrew dug his toes into the carpet. "Aud reads from the *Robins* book every night. But it isn't the same as having you read it."

Eyes burning, Olivia embraced each of them again, holding them under her wing one last time.

On her way down the stairs, she paused before Edward's study. She wondered if she ought to leave a note. But what could she say? How would she even begin to write down how she felt? She put her hand on the doorknob, running her fingers along the cool, smooth surface. Then she turned and walked away.

On her way to the gamekeeper's lodge, a quiet voice whispered in her mind. On its impulse she stopped in the garden, where the kindly gardener helped her cut a handful of lily of the valley. How sweet the aroma.

She found Mr. Croome sitting at the edge of the clearing beside a slight grassy mound, his back against a tree. Seeing her, he gave a little lurch as though to rise, but sank back, apparently resigned to being found in such a humble pose.

Stepping near, she glimpsed several flat, lichen-encrusted stones on the mound, in the shape of a cross. She said nothing. Nor did she meet his challenging look. She hadn't the strength to spar with him that day.

She bent, laid the lily of the valley on his daughter's grave, and walked away.

Never keep servants, however excellent they may be in their stations,
whom you know to be guilty of immorality.

—SAMUEL & SARAH ADAMS, *THE COMPLETE SERVANT*

Chapter 45

Edward found Lord Brightwell in the garden, smoking one of his cigars. He slumped onto the bench beside him, blind to the beauty of the arbor, trees, and flowers.

"I spoke with my *grandfather* yesterday," Edward began.

The earl looked up sharply. "Devil take it. He swore—"

Edward cut him off with a dismissive hand. "He has never breathed a word. It was Nurse Peale. Her mind is slipping. Her tongue as well."

Lord Brightwell groaned.

"Is that why you never wanted me to be alone with the man?" Edward asked. "Afraid he might try to take me back? Faith! I grew up in terror of my own grandfather."

"I did worry. But you were never to know. He was never to *be* your *grandfather*. He agreed to the arrangement—wanted the best for you." Lord Brightwell inhaled and exhaled a long stream of smoke. "I had no idea what a difficult thing I was asking at the time. Now, when I think about how I would feel giving up a grandson forever, for another man to claim as his own? Impossible! But at the time, I was only thinking of your mother and myself. And I knew that only by absolute secrecy could we raise you as our own flesh and blood and rightful heir."

Edward huffed. "Well, we see how well *that* has worked out." He rose, restless. "How did you manage the exchange?"

"Croome came to me several months into your mother's third lying-in. Your mother had already suffered two miscarriages during the first few months of our marriage. After the second, both the physician and midwife examined her and concurred that she was unlikely to ever bear a living infant. Still, when she was soon once again with child, we hoped they were wrong, that this time would be different. At all events, Croome asked if I had any idea who was responsible for his daughter being with child. As she worked in my house, he assumed I might be in the way of knowing. He did not accuse me, for I gather his daughter was good enough to exonerate me, even as she refused to name the man responsible.

"I did what I thought best. Assured him we could handle things quietly—his daughter would give notice before her condition became evident, and I would not tell a soul. I gave her an extra quarter's wages on going away, then put her from my mind.

"Months passed and Marian's lying-in seemed to be going miraculously well—her longest yet. The physician ordered bed rest and all manner of dietary precautions, but I could tell he did not hold out much hope. We called in only the physician that time, for after Marian's first two experiences, she did not want the blunt, coarse midwife to attend her again."

He paused for breath. "When Marian was seven or eight months along, she went into early labour and we sent for the physician. He assured us it was only a false labour, but when he tried to find the infant's heartbeat, he could not and told us to prepare for a stillbirth. Marian was terrified.

"She began having pains again a few days later, but we assumed it was another false labour and did not send for the physician right away. By the time we did send for him, the labour was hard and fast. But the doctor had been called away somewhere. I wanted to send for the midwife, but your mother refused. Miss Peale was already here, installed as the doctor's monthly nurse. In the end, she alone attended the birth, as I mentioned. A stillborn . . .

"We were devastated, Marian and I." He shook his head at the painful memory. "I had never seen your mother laid so low. When she finally fell into a grief-exhausted slumber, I left her in Nurse Peale's care and went out of doors. I needed air. And . . . to ask Matthews to fashion a tiny coffin.

"But near the carpentry shop, I paused. I heard wild keening from the direction of the wood and feared mad dogs or worse. I followed the sound to the gamekeeper's lodge. The keening grew louder until I thought some animal was tearing Croome limb from limb. But as I ran near, I found only Croome sitting beside a mound of dirt just beyond the clearing. He was rocking himself and wailing in a way that echoed my own lament.

"Croome saw me and waved me away, barking at me to leave him alone. I wanted nothing more than to do just that. But then you cried. There from the little basket where he'd placed you. I could not bear to look upon the grief-mad father and so I looked at you. At your bald, misshapen head and red face. And thought I had never seen anything so, well, pitiful and irresistible all at once." Lord Brightwell chuckled.

"He buried his daughter there, in the wood?" Edward was incredulous.

"He said he could not bear to have his Alice taken from him. Wanted her near. I feared he was a bit unhinged, and I suppose that was part of the reason I always cautioned you against him."

Edward nodded, remembering the protective gestures, the

whispered warnings. But had they been justified? Would not any parent be as distraught, at least temporarily?

Lord Brightwell continued, "I wanted nothing more than to leave that makeshift grave, that scene of a parent's worst nightmare. But I realized I did not wish to leave alone. I asked him if a midwife had been called, if anyone else knew. He said only Mrs. Moore."

"Our cook? What on earth?"

"Croome's sister-in-law, I gather. Young Alice's aunt. I wonder if he blamed her."

"Blamed her? Why should he?"

"I take it she delivered the child the day before, when neither midwife nor doctor could be found. And when things went badly . . ." He lifted a hand expressively.

Edward nodded, his mind filling in the gruesome scene.

His father rose and went to stand beside the arbor, turning to face the sun. "I am not sure how rashly I behaved in insisting Croome not tell anyone his daughter had died. I suppose I thought, if people knew she died, they'd ask how. If they knew she died in childbirth, they'd want to know what became of the child."

The earl ran a hand over his face. "It was wrong of me to deny him his right to grieve openly. I was thinking only of my family. Me. I did not understand. I don't think I had ever loved anyone the way he loved his Alice. But all that changed in the course of days, hours even, once I held you."

"He agreed to give me to you?" Edward barely managed to keep the edge from the words. "Or did you pay him?"

"I own I asked if he required any remuneration, and I thought he would strike me down where I stood. He made it clear he was not 'selling the child,' but only giving you to me because he was not fit to raise you himself. He threatened me with violence if I ever mentioned money again." The earl shuddered. "I never did." He shook his head remembering. "I did ask if Mrs. Moore would feel the same way. How he glowered at me. He said, 'You leave her to me. She'll not say a word, she won't.' And to my knowledge she never has."

Edward's mind spun. Did Mrs. Moore know what became of the babe she delivered? How odd to think that his family's cook, and certainly their gamekeeper and his own nurse, had known the truth about him all these years, while he'd had not a clue. Had Mrs. Moore written the letters? He could not credit it. Why now, after so many years?

"And . . . Mother," Edward asked. "What did she think of it all?"

"She was hesitant at first. We would not have pursued such a course for many years, if ever, had opportunity—in this case, you—not landed in our laps. Providence, I say. There was little warmth between Marian and myself in the first year of our marriage, but we fell in love over you, my boy. And she did love you, Edward. Never doubt it. Though I admit she never liked your name."

Edward felt his brow rise in question.

"It was Croome's final word on the subject. He told me in his gruff voice, 'His name is Edward. *She* named him that. My father's name, and my second name as well. I'll not have you changing it.' " Lord Brightwell chuckled. "I did not dare."

Edward shook his head, failing to see the humor in the situation. *Edward* . . . How ironic. How strange. He had been named for his father's gamekeeper, a man he had spent his whole life avoiding.

❧

When Edward walked into the kitchen, Mrs. Moore looked up, mouth slack, eyes wide. He almost never came belowstairs, save for Christmas carol singing and the like a few times each year. Any directions for the cook were delivered through the housekeeper or butler.

Two young kitchen maids stared up at him, one blushing profusely, the other daring a saucy look.

Edward asked, "Mrs. Moore, might I have a private word?"

The woman swallowed, evidently expecting news of the worst sort. "Of course, my lord."

She directed him to the stillroom off the kitchen, with its floor-to-ceiling shelves of blue-and-white china, jarred pickles and ruby red preserves, and the sharp, tangy aromas of beehive and gooseberry vinegars.

Once inside, he closed the door behind them, startling her further.

"I have been speaking with Mr. Croome. . . ." he began.

"Oh dear," she interrupted. "What has the old fool been up to now?"

"Nothing to fret over, I assure you. I was asking him about his daughter, Alice."

She frowned, clearly troubled. "Were you? I am surprised you even know of her. She . . . left us . . . before you were born."

"Did she?"

Mrs. Moore squinted in thought. "One or two days before, I believe. It is so long ago."

He nodded. "You delivered her of a child, I understand." He added gently, "It is all right, Mrs. Moore. I know she died."

Her mouth puckered, her round cheeks paled. "Avery told you that?" She looked stricken indeed. "I know he has never forgiven me . . . but to tell you? After all these years? When he swore me to secrecy?"

"I don't think he blames you. I suppose at the time, in his grief . . ."

She shook her head. "He planned to send her north to his family to have the child, but never did. Never could bear to part with her. When her time came, he asked me to stay with Alice while he went to find the doctor or midwife. I was only to sit with her. But he didn't return for hours, and when he did, he was alone. He could find no one to deliver her. I understand your father had the same problem when your mother's time came soon after."

Edward nodded. "Nurse Peale attended my mother."

She squinted once more. "Yes, I do remember hearing that." Mrs. Moore grimaced. "I did what I could for Allie, but I knew so little. I had never even had a child of my own. I have never felt so helpless. My own dear niece, my sister's lass, and I couldn't save her." She shook her head, clearly reliving those mournful images once more. Tears filled her small hazel eyes and rolled up and over her round cheeks. "Avery has never forgiven me. He sent me back to the house soon after, as if he couldn't bear the sight of me."

Mrs. Moore swiped at her tears with the back of a fleshy hand. "And the child . . . a little boy. He never would tell me what became of him. I suppose he took him to kin in the north, or found some family to take him in. I was surprised he could part with him, all he had left of his Alice. But he was in no fit shape to raise wolves, let alone a child in those days." Her lips trembled as she spoke. "He was mad with grief, repulsed my every effort to comfort him. Refused to speak of it. To tell me where the boy was." Her voice broke. "The boy she died bringin' into the world."

"Mrs. Moore," he said gently. "You will not believe it, I fear. But Alice died bringing *me* into the world."

She stared at him, brows furrowed, lips tight. She looked angry or at least frustrated and confused.

"Mr. Croome did not take Alice's son to the north," Edward continued quietly. "He gave that child to Lord and Lady Brightwell. To raise as their own."

Her small mouth slowly drooped into a sloppy O. She looked nearly comical, and he bit his lip to stay a rogue grin.

"I said you would not believe me."

She peered up at him, shaking her head in wonder. "I never saw it," she breathed. "You are not very like her."

"Ironic, isn't it, how I look so much the Bradley."

"God's hand, I should say."

"I don't know about that." He ducked his head, giving way to a sheepish smile.

"There. I see a hint of her." Mrs. Moore's hazel eyes twinkled. "Something around your mouth, when you smile. I can't remember seeing you smile, not since you were a lad."

"I shall have to work on that."

Her mouth dropped open again as a new thought struck her. "That must be why it was all such a secret! Why he refused to say what became of you." She sucked in a long breath. "And why he stayed on, when we all thought he would leave. Why does he stay, I used to wonder, since he had family in the north that would care for him in his old age. What keeps him here now his Maggie is gone and Alice too?" She stared at Edward, slowly shaking her head in amazement. "He couldn't bear to leave *you*."

Edward's chest tightened, and his throat followed suit.

"I cannot believe it." Tears sprung anew into her eyes, but the desolation of moments before was replaced by apparent joy. "Allie's boy." She reached out to him, but quickly caught herself as she realized what she was about to do. "Forgive me."

He took both of her hands in his own. "There is nothing to forgive, Mrs. Moore. After all, you are my great-aunt, are you not?"

She laughed and beamed up at him, squeezing his hands. "I suppose I am." She bit her lip. "Though I suppose it is all still a great secret?"

He inhaled deeply. "At present, yes, if you don't mind. But not forever."

"How long have you known that you are not . . ." She let the question go unfinished.

"I only learnt of it when Miss Keene arrived, last autumn."

"Miss Keene? What has she to do with it?"

He pulled an apologetic face. "It is a long story, I fear."

As if sensing a dismissal, she withdrew her hands and

straightened. "I am sure you are quite busy, and I . . . well, supper will not cook itself."

She opened the stillroom door, but he stopped her with a gentle entreaty.

"Mrs. Moore. Please."

She hesitated in the threshold.

He stepped near, closing the gap between them. "I should very much like to tell you all, but another time. Perhaps we might take tea together some afternoon? Say, in the gamekeeper's lodge?"

She gave him a sidelong glance. "He won't like that."

"You might be surprised. And I think it would do him a world of good."

"Do you indeed?" Her eyes twinkled once more. "Then I should like that above all things."

On impulse, he leaned down and kissed her cheek.

As he turned, he heard the kitchen maids gasp, followed by giggles and frenzied whispers.

Mrs. Moore's officious voice followed him as he ascended the stairs. "He was only thanking me for my best plum cake, and had you ever tasted it, you would buss me as well. Now, haven't you garden peas to shell?"

Edward smiled.

❧

Edward Stanton Bradley knocked on the gamekeeper's lodge and held his breath, the tool case heavy in his hand.

After a long minute, Avery Croome opened the door, his silvery blue eyes narrow. "Hope you ain't come to ask me to break my word."

"I am asking you to break nothing, Mr. Croome," Edward said, feeling strangely buoyant. "I am here to repair what is already broken."

Croome's overgrown eyebrows rose. He looked from Edward's face to Matthews's tool case and back again. "You?"

Edward gestured toward one of the front windows, eyeing a deeply cracked pane. "I shall call out the glazier for that. Will Tuesday suit?"

Croome only peered at him, suspicion pinching his features.

"Now, let us take a look inside," Edward said, gesturing toward the door.

"Why?"

Edward said innocently, "Because I have it on good authority that the place is all but in ruins. I believe you spoke of wanting a lodge that is not falling down about you?"

Keeping his eye on Edward, Croome pushed open the door and stepped backward, as though not to turn his back on a potentially dangerous predator. He said, "I weren't expecting company, mind. Not since Miss Keene left. She's the only one what bothered to come out here."

"Was she indeed?"

"Up and left, ey?" Croome shook his head, mouth twisted in disapproval.

"I fear I am to blame," Edward confessed. "If it is any consolation, I miss her too."

Croome scowled. "Never said I missed her."

"Oh, and before I forget—" Edward pulled a wrapped bundle from the tool case—"Mrs. Moore sent along a slice of plum cake. Still warm."

Croome's eyes were mere slits now, and he gave his head a slow shake. "Got you in on it now, has she?"

Edward shrugged but bit back a grin when the old man accepted the bundle.

Edward followed him inside. A musty smell greeted him— damp, but not vile. The main room was relatively tidy, and only one dish and cup stood waiting to be washed on the sideboard.

"Does not look so bad," he said, surveying the room. "Where is the problem?"

Laying Mrs. Moore's offering on the table, Croome limped over to the far wall and pointed up to a ceiling water-stained and cracked.

Edward followed. Sinking to his haunches to lay the heavy tool case on the floor, he paused, his attention snagged by the bookcase standing against the wall.

His eyes roved over the three tiers crudely pieced and stained in his favorite shade. He had not laid eyes on it in a half-dozen years, but he knew it instantly.

Behind him, Croome muttered, "Saved it from the bonfire. Couldn't stand to see it wasted."

Edward nodded, chest tight.

"Well, let's get to it," Croome said brusquely. "I do hope yer skills 'ave improved since then."

The objects of the present life fill the human eye with a false magnification because of their immediacy.

—WILLIAM WILBERFORCE

Chapter 46

When the Crenshaws' footman held forth the silver letter tray, Olivia recognized Lord Brightwell's scrawl on a letter directed to her. Pleased to hear from him, she peeled open the seal and unfolded the single sheet. Her breath caught. For the words within were written in a different hand—a bold, masculine hand. His.

Her aunt Georgiana stepped into the room, pulling on her gloves. "Olivia my dear, are you ready?" she asked.

Olivia closed the note. "Forgive me, Aunt, but I have just received a letter. Would you mind very much if I stayed here? You go on without me."

"Are you certain, my dear?"

"Quite certain."

Reluctantly, her aunt agreed to pay morning calls without her.

Olivia hurried to her room and, with shaking fingers, unfolded the letter once more.

> *My dear Miss Keene,*
>
> *There is so very much to tell you, I barely know where to begin. Except to say how profoundly sorry I am for how I have treated you. For the foolish accusations, and for what must have seemed a rejection of yourself when I objected to my father's plans to acknowledge you as his daughter or at least his ward. Please know I hold only the deepest respect and admiration for you. Although the motives which governed me may appear insufficient, I had a very good, albeit selfish reason for not wanting the world to believe you my sister. I will say no more about this herein, except to ask you to forgive me if you can.*
>
> *I long to share with you, of all people, the facts which I have learnt since your departure. But I dare not do so in a letter, should it be misdirected. Therefore I write in vague terms which I know you, clever girl, will understand.*
>
> *I have not learnt all I wish to know, but a great deal has recently come to light. I hope I might one day be able to tell you all in person. In the meantime, I pray that all goes well with you.*
>
> *Again, I offer you my deepest apologies. And will only add, God bless you.*
>
> *Edward S. Bradley*

Her heart squeezed, even as questions began spinning through her mind. She read the signature once more and saw that his title was notably absent. What had he learned? What did it mean?

❧

Johnny Ross stood before the desk, hat in hand. Beside him stood the maid Mrs. Hinkley had told Edward about, now noticeably with child. Hodges and Mrs. Hinkley awaited his verdict at the back of the room. Lord Brightwell stood behind Edward, still content to leave such decisions to him.

"I know we are not to marry while in service, my lord," Ross said. "But Martha here is expecting, so . . . we did."

"Are you the father?" Edward asked and instantly regretted it. He had thought another man responsible, but it was none of his business, and he certainly had not meant to mortify the young woman. He obviously had, however, for she bowed her head, a blush creeping up her neck. Even Ross's face burned red.

Behind Edward, Lord Brightwell cleared his throat. Edward opened his mouth to retract the question, but Ross answered before he could.

"No, my lord. But I love her just the same."

Edward noticed the young woman surreptitiously take the groom's hand in hers.

Ross continued, "Mr. Hodges said I am to be dismissed, unless you say otherwise. I was wonderin', my lord, if you might see your way to givin' me a character. Otherwise another post will be awful hard to come by."

Edward stared at the groom, stunned by his unexpected nobility. "No."

Ross looked down at the floor.

"No, you shall not be dismissed," Edward clarified, turning toward the earl. "That is, unless you disapprove, Father?"

Lord Brightwell hesitated. "Ah . . . no, Edward. Whatever you think best."

Ross beamed. "Thank you, my lord. Thank you!"

Even Martha gave him a shy smile, and Edward could not help but think of Alice Croome and wonder what she had looked like while carrying him.

Once the details and lodging arrangements had been discussed, the staff took their leave.

Edward shut the door behind them and turned to face Lord

Brightwell with steely resolve. "Who was my father?" he asked quietly,

The earl began, "The girl never told anyone, so—"

"Who was he?" Edward persisted.

For a moment Lord Brightwell looked pugnacious, as if formulating another excuse, but then sighed. "I thought you might have guessed by now."

Frowning, Edward shook his head.

"Have I not always insisted you are a Bradley?"

Edward blinked and felt a chill run through his body. "Sebastian—*Uncle Bradley*—was my father?"

The earl nodded. "I believe so, yes."

Edward's mind whirled. He was a Bradley after all. Still illegitimate. Still rightful heir to nothing save shame and his adopted father's unmerited love.

He thought back to all he knew about Sebastian Bradley, dead these six or seven years.

He was aware, of course, of the long enmity between Lord Brightwell and his brother. Though Oliver was eldest and their father's heir, he had not left Sebastian to fend for himself, as perhaps he should have. He had set him up in a London house, furnished it, supplied him servants, a carriage, and horses. Most of which Sebastian had lost gaming or owed to debt collectors. Oliver, in turn, lost all respect for the younger man. Nor was uncontrolled gambling Sebastian's only sin. He had taken advantage of more than one young woman in his day, requiring sums to be paid and arrangements made.

The earl had confessed himself surprised when Sebastian announced his engagement to a respectable woman. He had even come to Oliver, hat in hand, and proclaimed himself a changed man. And Oliver had wanted to believe him.

Soon after his own marriage to Marian Estcourt, Oliver invited his brother and sister-in-law to visit Brightwell Court, which they did that summer and again in the fall, bringing with them their baby girl, Judith, and her nurse.

But that autumn visit was to prove the last for Sebastian. He was permitted at Brightwell Court no longer, though his wife and Judith, and eventually Felix, were still welcome. The reason was not specified. A falling out of sorts was assumed, some disagreement or one too many gaming debts to pay off . . . something.

Now Edward realized there was more to it than that.

"I came upon Sebastian one night, coming up from below-stairs," the earl began. "His face was scratched and his clothing disheveled. He seemed startled to see me, but quickly recovered. I asked what he was doing belowstairs, and he made an excuse about looking for something to eat, though he could easily have asked a servant to bring him a tray. I also asked about his face, and he said it must have gotten scratched in the wood or some such. I did not believe him.

"When he had taken himself up to bed, I went down to the kitchen, and there came upon Croome's daughter, sitting near the dying fire, face in her hands, thin shoulders quaking.

"I own I wanted nothing more than to turn back, but I was compelled by duty to speak to her. I hoped I was wrong in my sus-picions. That Sebastian really *had* scratched his face in the wood.

"The girl jumped when she saw me. When I asked her what the matter was, she only gaped at me, apparently stunned or shaken. I took a step closer, lifted my lamp to better see her face, and asked if she was unwell. How wide her eyes were, I remember, and through them, I thought I witnessed some inner struggle, though perhaps my memory is now colored by later revelations.

"Thinking to encourage her, I said that I was acquainted with her father—a most trusted man. But at the mention of Mr. Croome, new tears filled her eyes. She assured me she was well, that she *had* been sad over some trifling matter but was better now. It was not a very convincing performance.

"I left the kitchen with a heavy heart, telling myself I had done my duty, had given the girl every opportunity to accuse my brother, but she had not. Perhaps nothing so terrible had happened. If it had, why had she not told? Was she so frightened of her father—afraid he would blame *her* for any wrongdoing? Perhaps the girl was a known flirt.

"With these paltry justifications, I dismissed the scene from my mind. Only later, when Croome came to me—devastated by his daughter's fallen state—did I realize Sebastian was the person she had feared, for her father clearly doted on the girl and believed her the very picture of innocence. I wondered if Sebastian had threatened to have Croome sacked should she tell. Sebastian had no authority to do such a thing, but a maid would have no way of knowing that, would have no reason to think the lord of the manor would believe her over his own brother.

"But I would have. Experience had taught me not to trust Sebastian. I was infuriated with myself for opening my heart and home for more disappointment and debauchery. That was the end. Nevermore was Sebastian welcome at Brightwell Court—no matter that it had been his childhood home. It was his home no longer.

"I did not admit my suspicions to Croome. Saw no reason to. Croome would likely have killed Sebastian and ended in a hangman's noose, and then where would his daughter have been? Alone in the world with a by-blow to raise on her own. I needed to let the girl go, of course—no master kept on an expecting girl in those days, no matter his charitable leanings. I gave her a quarter's wages and raised Croome's salary on the sly, to help him provide for her.

"I knew my brother would not do anything for the girl. It was left to me to make recompense. As it always was."

When his father finished speaking, Edward asked, "You never told him?"

"That he fathered a child? Do you think he would have welcomed the news? Done his duty by your mother—had she lived—and by you? Never. There had been rumors of other illegitimate children, but none had tempted him to duty before."

"But you did not go about the country taking in his other whelps?" Edward asked dryly.

"No. I confess the thought never crossed my mind. But then, I had never met one of his victims personally, witnessed her devastation, and that of her father—a man I respected as my father had before me. I was untouched by those other faceless women and rumored offspring. But not this time.

"Still, I had no intention of claiming or even supporting the child when first I learnt of its coming. It wasn't until months later, when your mother had given birth to a stillborn son . . . and I remembered the verdict the physician and midwife had given us—no children. No son and heir . . ."

Edward said, "You would not have been the first peer to face that disappointment."

Lord Brightwell sighed. "Indeed not. But who would inherit in a son's stead? None other than my brother, Sebastian, who would no doubt lose everything and ruin Brightwell Court—sell off anything not nailed down or entailed. Let the place out to strangers and I shudder to think what all."

"But what of Felix?"

"There was no Felix when I made my decision to make you my son and heir. And even if there had been, Sebastian would have been heir before him. I doubt there would have been much left to inherit after Sebastian had been Earl of Brightwell for a few years."

"But now Sebastian is dead."

Lord Brightwell inhaled deeply. "Yes."

"And so Felix is your rightful heir."

"Felix is a fool. And with that Titian hair and green eyes, he is likely less a Bradley than you are. My sister-in-law had her revenge, I daresay, though in the end it does not signify. She and Sebastian were married at the time of his birth, so in the eyes of the law, Felix is legitimate, no matter what is whispered about his mother and a certain ginger-haired duke."

His face weary, Lord Brightwell pressed his fingers against his eyelids. "Forgive me, Edward. I have never before joined in the rumor-mongering and am ashamed to have done so now." He ran a hand over his face. "I am not myself at present."

Edward attempted a grin. "Neither am I."

Lord Brightwell shook his head. "Felix is young and irresponsible, and already shows every likelihood of following Sebastian's dissolute ways. Still, he isn't the scoundrel my brother was. At least not yet. I will see him provided for. And Judith and the children, of course."

"Hmm," Edward muttered, shaking his head. "It is ironic. Judith has often commented that she and I looked more alike than she and Felix. I wonder if she had any idea how close to the truth she was."

"I doubt it."

"Now I see why you warned me against her romantic notions."

"Yes. You see, my dear boy, you really are a Bradley. My only son, and your uncle's eldest son—at least, as far as we know."

"But the law . . ."

"Dash the law."

"No, Father. It doesn't change what I am. In the eyes of the law, I cannot be your heir."

"Then the eyes of the law need not see."

Edward grimly shook his head. "The veiled woman would not agree with you."

Women saw the governess as a threat to their happiness.

—M. JEANNE PETERSON, *SUFFER AND BE STILL*

Chapter 47

When the post came that day, Judith snatched a letter from Hodges and quickly took herself upstairs. Edward watched her go with fatalistic sadness.

A few minutes later, he stepped into Judith's private apartment for the first time in his adult life. And he did so without knocking.

Judith was seated at an elegant lady's writing table, bent over the missive.

"Hello, Judith. Another letter?"

She looked up sharply, searching his face. "Yes ... but it is only from Mamma." She fluttered her fingers dismissively and began to refold the single sheet.

"May I?" he asked, feigning nonchalance as he held out his

hand. Their gazes locked. When she did not release the letter to him, he pulled it from her grasp.

He removed the first threatening letter from his pocket and compared the two as if they were nothing more interesting than two newspaper accounts of the same story. "And how is *Mamma* keeping these days?" he asked idly.

She watched him, face stiff, eyes wary. She said in convincing disinterest, "She is well enough, I suppose."

"I imagine she is. Now that she has reason to believe her son will be heir to Brightwell Court."

"Will he be?" Judith asked, her voice revealingly high-pitched.

"It seems likely, as well you know. Here she says, and I find it most interesting, 'Do you see any sign of his giving way? Or need I write again?'"

Judith swallowed. "That could relate to any number of subjects."

Edward tucked both letters into his pocket. "How long have you known?"

She considered him with steady, round blue eyes. "We are not the ones who have done anything wrong, after all," she said, abandoning pretense.

"Nothing illegal, at any rate. Unless one counts your part in the extortion attempt."

Her fair brows rose high.

"Yes, the midwife's husband was inspired to attempt extortion after your visit, or was it your mother's?"

She shook her head, lips parted. "I would not have believed it. The doddering fool seemed barely to know his name when I called. He did recall his wife muttering about strange goings-on at Brightwell Court many years ago. Yes, it might have to do with a baby, but he could not say what it was." She lifted a shrug. "If I did hint at the secret, I certainly never suggested extortion."

"Still, I think the constable might find the connection most interesting. As magistrate, I know I do."

"I did not start this crusade," Judith defended. "Though I did insist Mamma leave off for a time after Lady Brightwell died."

She pushed back her chair and rose. "She says she and Father always suspected something. Doctor come and gone with no news of a birth. Everyone certain Lady Brightwell had suffered another 'mishap.' Then suddenly there appears a perfectly stout baby boy."

Judith walked languidly across the room. "It was only rumors, of course, and since you looked every inch a Bradley, nothing was done. But then your father took ill with the lung fever—when was that, seven, eight years ago? And my father thought the situation might bear looking into. He tried to locate the midwife, but she had already passed on. He next sought the doctor, but you know how physicians are, all gentlemanlike and professional and discreet. Too successful to be brought round by any small bribe my father might offer." She exhaled deeply. "So he let it lie again. And then died himself while your father fully recovered."

She turned and faced him. "But you see, Edward, your dear loyal nurse is getting on in years. Her mind is slipping. She prattles on about how my Alexander looks so like you at that age, and how can that be? I told her it was not surprising, considering you and I were cousins. 'Cousins?' said she, and laughed as though I had made a fine joke. The first time, I thought she was simply confused. Forgot that you and I were related, because of my married surname. But often she seems quite certain of herself. Quite clear."

"That is no proof, of course," Edward said, sounding, he believed, satisfactorily unconcerned.

"Do we need proof?" she asked rhetorically. "All we need do is pose the question to the House of Lords with enough circumstantial evidence that *they* ask your father. Would he lie to his countrymen? In deed, perhaps, but not in word, if asked directly."

Edward cringed at the thought of his father being publicly condemned by his peers.

"And then there is you, noble Edward. You would not take another man's rightful place, knowing as you now do that you have no claim to it."

"You flatter me, Judith. But can you think so highly of one of such low birth?"

"It is all in the rearing, I suppose."

"You sound like Father." Edward studied her, sadness stealing over him. "Why did you do it, Jude?"

She shrugged, said flippantly, "I was afraid of doing without. Of being embarrassed by reduced circumstances once more. You know I detested growing up with shopkeepers and bill collectors forever knocking on the door. My father gambled away all his money and then Mamma's, so that I could barely outfit myself for a proper coming out."

"You always looked well to me."

"Much good it did me. I married a dashing naval captain, sure he would make his fortune in the war. Instead I ended a widow with no fortune, and another woman's children to care for."

"But Father provides for you, does he not?"

"Yes, but for how long?"

He waited for her to explain. Now that she was talking, she seemed ready to reveal all.

"I admit a part of me was loath to learn of your base birth, for it fouled my plans. I had thought you and I might marry, once my mourning was past."

"Did you?"

She hurried on self-consciously, before he could confirm or deny having similar thoughts. "You are so fond of the children and, as a friend of Dominick's, felt some responsibility, I think."

"True."

She glanced at him, but then turned away once more. "But you *would* pursue Miss Harrington and even Miss Keene. If you were to marry another, your wife might not be so willing to have me under her roof and support the children. But if Felix were to become heir, as my brother, he would always be obliged to provide for me, would he not?"

"I am your brother, Judith. As much as Felix is."

She frowned. "What can you mean?"

"There is a reason Alexander resembles me. You do remember remarking how you and I favour one another more than you and Felix do? There is a reason for that."

She gaped at him, almost fearfully, he thought.

He continued evenly, "My mother was no one you would know. But you knew my father. For he was yours as well."

She stood perfectly still, as if holding her breath. Then her eyelids began to blink, a window shutter, opening and closing, trying to change the view or chop to pieces a hundred images of the past. But she did not try to refute it.

"Did he know?" she asked.

"Your father? I don't think so."

"I think he may have suspected it. . . . Perhaps that is the real reason he decided to let it lie."

Edward sighed, sick of the whole affair. "Well, it does not matter in the end, nor does it change anything. Does it, *dear* sister?"

She blinked again, this time to clear the tears at his biting tone. "Do you so despise me?"

He regarded her somberly. "I could never hate you, Judith. But I am disappointed. I had thought we were friends at least. You might have simply come to Father and me with what you had learned. There was no need for all this cloak-and-dagger business."

Edward stepped to Judith's wardrobe and opened its door casually, like a youth searching the cupboards for a late-night repast.

She lifted her chin. "He would never have admitted it, unless forced."

"You may be right. But I fear you may live to regret the cost of your little charade." He pulled down the veiled hat and tossed it on the dressing table. "The veiled woman, Judith? How gothic."

"It was Mother's idea. She thought Lord Brightwell's interest in Miss Keene might threaten our plans. When I showed her the notice from the seminary, she hoped we would discover something incriminating about her, which might sever their attachment."

"Why? Even if she had been his daughter, which she is not, she would inherit nothing, save perhaps a dowry or some small settlement."

She grimaced. "Daughter? We did not think that. We feared he might . . . that he had romantic intentions toward her."

"Ah." He nodded. "I confess I did as well for a brief time. But his interest in Miss Keene was of the most paternal, I assure you. However, that is not to say he will not marry another once his mourning has passed."

She cast him an anxious glance.

"You see, Judith, the risk you run? Instead of being content with a home in Brightwell Court and everything you should ever need, you have wagered it all on the chance my father will die without a legitimate son. You are furthermore gambling on Felix's willingness to be as generous as Father, which I doubt, but that is another matter. For if Father marries again, and his wife bears him a son . . . then you lose all. Do you not see, Judith? You turned out to be every bit the gambler your father was, though you say you despised him for it."

Her lips trembled. And though she glared rebelliously, her façade was beginning to crack.

Edward turned and walked slowly back across the room.

"Must I leave, then?" she called after him, her voice deceptively calm.

At the door, he turned and looked back. She stood, facing away from him, the sunlight from the window enshrouding her in an unmerited halo of gold. Perhaps, he thought, that was how God saw all His children. Selfish and fallen, yes. But in the forgiving light of His Son, each wore an unmerited halo.

"My father does not ask it of you. You are his niece. He will always love you."

Her rounded shoulders shook, but he felt no satisfaction, no victory. For whether she stayed or went, in his heart he had bid farewell to this woman he had loved since a boy, as playmate, cousin, confidante, and friend.

❧

Three weeks later, Felix stood stiffly before them in the library, unable to meet Edward's gaze. Instead he trained his eyes on Lord Brightwell's cravat and pronounced as if by rote, ". . . If my uncle will publicly recognize me as his rightful heir and Edward agrees to rescind his claim and not challenge the resulting new will, then we shall take no further action and require no legal recompense for fraud."

Lord Brightwell's eyes blazed. "Recompense? As long as I live, you are entitled to nothing. Nothing."

Felix visibly shrunk at his uncle's outrage.

"Everything I have given you—your tuition and expenses, your annual allowance, all of these came out of generosity of feeling, not obligation."

"I—" Felix chanced to meet the earl's gaze, and any rebuttal quickly faded. Instead, he muttered, "I have always thought so, my lord."

"Then who wrote that little monologue for you? Your mother, I suppose?"

Sheepishly, Felix nodded. "She said that what you have done for me, you have done out of guilt. Not generosity."

"And have I taken in your widowed sister for this same reason? I am to be credited with no Christian charity?"

Felix's chin protruded stubbornly, defensively. "I did not say I concurred with Mamma, my lord. But when I am Lord Brightwell, I shall provide for Judith myself."

"Very proper," the earl drawled. "But are you not putting the mourning coach before the horse? As long as I live, you would only be heir presumptive—no title, no money, no privileges. And know this, nephew—I plan to live for a very long time."

Felix swallowed. "For my part I wish you would," he said earnestly. "I have no great longing to be a peer. Devilish lot of responsibility that."

"I am relieved to hear it. For who knows?" the earl said. "I may even remarry. Have a son of my own, and then *he* shall be my heir and you receive nothing."

"Mamma is afraid of that. She was ever so relieved to hear Miss Keene left."

"Was she indeed?"

"For my part, I had just as soon not be Lord anybody. Except . . . it would help me win the hand of a certain lady."

"Miss Harrington, I presume," Edward said.

The young man's face burned scarlet. "I am afraid so."

Ignoring his admission, Lord Brightwell asked, "Did you not read any law at Oxford, Felix? You must realize, my boy, that there is nothing but scandal to be gained by making this public while I live. There is nothing for Edward to rescind. He is just as much a commoner as you are. Only an eldest son can be heir apparent, and as such has *use* of the courtesy title through my lesser rank of Baron of Bradley, but I still hold the peerage. Do you understand? You can never be Lord Bradley. And would only become Lord Brightwell after my death."

His nephew's face fell.

"You will find, my boy, that not every worthy female requires a title to win her."

Felix's lower lip jutted forth. He was clearly unconvinced.

"Here is what I propose," Lord Brightwell said. "I will write within my will a full confession, disclosing my deception, and accepting full blame, so that any serious consequences befall *me*—I shall be too dead to care—but not Edward, who is innocent of any wrongdoing in this matter. He *will* lose the courtesy title, and many in society will rebuff him when the true nature of his birth is revealed. But as he plans to live quietly, apart from London society, I don't think the repercussions will be overly severe.

"After I am gone, you and the solicitors will take this proof to the Lord Chancellor." Here he put his arm around Felix's shoulder and said in a confidential aside, "You have no real proof at present, my boy. Save one senile old woman who would never betray us to strangers, even were she to live long enough to do so." He removed his arm and continued in his best parliamentary voice, "The Committee for Privileges will review the case and shall, I have every certainty, acknowledge your claim to the peerage." He gave Felix a shrewd look. "Remember, this assumes an absence of a new heir apparent. If I remarry and have a son, then such a will and confession would naturally place him in position to inherit. Do I make myself understood?"

A knowing gleam sparked in Felix's eyes. "Have you some lady in mind, Uncle?"

"Ah. That is my affair, is it not? Now. If you agree—and your mother and sister as well—to handle this quietly and avoid a scandal, then I will continue to provide a generous allowance which will give you the life of a gentleman you desire, and allow you to win the hand of any number of ladies of quality." He stood before his nephew and looked him directly in the eye. "If you do *not* agree and scandal erupts, then you shall not have one shilling from me until after my death and the legal case to follow. Do you agree or not?"

Felix swallowed once more. "I agree."

Lord Brightwell nodded his acknowledgment. "Good. Now. I may very well remarry, but at my age I cannot afford to lay all my eggs, as it were, in that basket. There is every chance you *shall* be the next Lord Brightwell, and if so, I want you to be well prepared to live up to the name. So—" He drew himself up and commanded briskly, "First, there will be no further improprieties with the servants. Second, you *will* finish your coursework and obtain your degree. And third, you shall begin your education in estate management and parliamentary affairs—in the library, Saturday week, nine o'clock. Do I make myself clear?"

"You do, my lord." Felix looked up at Lord Brightwell in wonder. "I must say you astound me, Uncle. I had not thought it of you."

"What had you thought?"

"That you would put me out. So I would not be tempted to . . ."

"Hasten my demise?"

Again Felix's face reddened. "Just so."

"I would never believe it of you, my boy, regardless of the schemers your mother and sister turned out to be. You may not be the most clever boy, nor the most prudent, nor the most gentlemanlike, nor . . ."

Edward cleared his throat.

"Right! But you have a good heart, and I have every hope that with proper education and mentoring you will be a credit to the family yet."

"And my sister?"

"I am sorry to tell you Judith has already left us."

"Left?"

"Yes, she has remarried and is even now on her wedding trip."

Felix gaped. "When was this?"

"Two days ago, I understand. By special license."

"Why was I not told?"

"You shall have to ask Judith that, when she returns from Italy. I did not forbid her to contact you, if that is what you are tempted to think."

"Who on earth did she marry?"

"George Linton."

"Linton? Thunder and turf, you must be joking! That dolt?"

"That dolt, indeed, with his handsome four thousand a year. It seems Judith was not content to wait for you to make good on your promise to provide for her."

Felix shook his head. "I'll be hanged. And not a word to her own brother. And what of the children?"

"They are all still here at present. After the wedding trip, Alexander alone will reside with the happy couple. It seems George Linton is willing to take on the one child, but not three."

Felix frowned. "I don't understand."

"Nor do I," Lord Brightwell said. "But Judith has decided to leave Audrey and Andrew here in my care. If you object, and prefer to engage some qualified person to house and care for them near you at Oxford, to provide for them yourself and see them properly educated, you are welcome to do so."

Felix pulled on the hem of his waistcoat and shifted his weight. "I am fond of them, of course," he faltered. "But I cannot afford . . . and truly, they are no relatives of mine. Not even my sister's, are they? Will not Dominick's mother take them in?"

"It seems the elder Mrs. Howe is stricken with such severe gout and tenuous finances—*her* words, you understand—that she will not be able to do so, much as she might wish it. She will not object to my raising them as my wards, with the stipulation that I bring them to visit her on occasion."

"Your wards?" Felix repeated.

"Yes."

Felix regarded his uncle with something akin to begrudging respect. "Taking in another's children again, are you?" he said drolly.

Lord Brightwell's eyes twinkled. "Yes," he drawled. "I seem to make a habit of it."

Chapter 48

When the Crenshaws' footman handed her Lord Bradley's card, emotions flared like Chinese rockets through her body—panic, fear, hope. She was tempted to refuse to see him but knew she could not do so. Not after his letter of apology. For what if Lord Brightwell was ill? Or something had happened to one of the children?

"Show him up, please."

The ensuing minute seemed an hour, but then she heard footsteps approaching all too soon. She swallowed and took several deep breaths to try to calm herself. To no avail.

When the door opened once more, Olivia rose unsteadily. "Lord Bradley. I . . . I did not expect you."

He bowed. "I am certain you did not." He looked down at his

boots. "And I expected the footman to announce in no uncertain terms that you were not at home, whether you were or not."

"It did cross my mind, I own." Her chuckle sounded forced in her ears. "But I did not wish to cause a stir, when I am but a guest here."

He looked at her through his golden lashes. "An honoured guest, I hope?"

Olivia bit her lip, then smiled. "Rather, yes. My mother as well. They have all gone into Cirencester together or I would introduce you."

He nodded. They stood there awkwardly for a long moment. Finally he cleared his throat and twirled his hat in his hand.

"Oh! Forgive me," Olivia said. "Do be seated, please."

"Actually, I . . . I feel a bit like Andrew in the schoolroom. Too much energy to sit. Would you be so good as to walk with me? I saw a fine garden as I rode in."

"Of course . . . I shall just find my bonnet."

They strolled together through formal gardens enclosed by walls of mottled stone. The sun shone and the air was heavy with the fragrances of rose and lavender.

"You received my letter?" he asked.

"Yes. Though I saw your father added the direction."

He nodded. "I beseeched him to tell me where you were since the day you left, and he finally gave way."

Edward had been so nervous that he had not looked at her squarely, fully, until this moment. He stopped walking and stared. Her rose pink gown had a low square neckline which displayed delicate collarbone as well as a beguiling swell of femininity. A matching pink ribbon drew his attention upward to her long graceful neck. Beneath her bonnet, earrings dangled from small white earlobes, and gleaming coils of dark hair framed her face. Her lips shone and her cheeks blushed most becomingly. "What have they done to you?"

Her lips parted; her blush deepened.

"Forgive me, that came out very wrongly. I meant, well, you look beautiful. Always did, of course, but—I like your hair and . . . well . . . everything."

She dipped her head. "Thank you. My aunt insists on having her abigail arrange my hair and dress me. Takes far too long, I fear."

"Worth it, I assure you."

Her hint of a grin bloomed into a smile.

As they walked on, hands behind their respective backs, he told her about all that had recently happened at Brightwell Court. And all that he had learned.

Olivia stopped, eyes and mouth wide. "Avery Croome is your grandfather!" She shook her head. "I am astounded and yet . . . I should have guessed." She studied his countenance, her blue eyes sparkling. "Indeed I do see a resemblance."

He said dryly, "I don't know whether that is a compliment or not."

"It would not have been a few months ago, but since I have come to know him, it is."

As they walked on, he glanced at her, noticed from her furrowed brow that she was pondering still.

"That means Alice Croome was your mother," she said. "And Mrs. Moore . . . has she known about you all along?"

Edward shook his head.

"No, I did not think so. Did you tell her?"

"Yes."

"How did she react?"

Edward drew in a deep breath. "I am afraid I caused quite a stir belowstairs."

"Oh?"

"Two maids spied me kissing her cheek."

"No!" Olivia said, mock-scandalized, then laughed. "Pray tell me all."

He complied, and they walked and talked for the better part of an hour.

When he finished his tale, she asked, "What will you do now?"

"An excellent question. What will you do?"

She took a deep breath. "Spend the rest of the summer here. Then go to Kent and teach in a girls' school, as I have always longed to do."

"But that wasn't *precisely* what you longed for, was it?"

She shrugged. "Not precisely, no. I had dreamed of Mother and me opening our own school one day. But that must remain a dream for now." She sighed. "I will content myself to assist another experienced schoolmistress and learn all I can in the meanwhile."

"I cannot convince you to return to Brightwell Court?"

"No. As much as I adore Audrey and Andrew, I . . . cannot. I own I am not fit for it after all."

"Nonsense. You are the cleverest, kindest—"

"The solitary life, I mean. Ever only in the company of children. Long hours alone. Not really fitting anywhere. Never to have a true friend. . . . Forgive me! I am prattling on worse than Doris ever did."

He looked at her blankly. "Doris . . . ?"

She pressed her eyes closed. "Exactly."

They walked on, Edward aware that he had made a gaff but not knowing how to remedy it. Instead he said, "Surely you might teach somewhere closer than Kent."

"Perhaps. But there is something appealing about a fresh start far away, now that I know my mother is safe. I have written to the constable in Withington and am still awaiting word on my father's situation."

He cleared his throat. "You have not heard, then? Seeing you, I thought not. There is news, I am afraid—news I wished to deliver in person."

She looked up. "What is it?"

From his coat pocket, he withdrew a segment of newspaper and unfolded it. "Word of your father's trial, the specific charges and likely sentence."

He held it toward her, but she did not reach for it, only regarded it blankly. "Tell me what it says," she whispered.

He breathed deeply, hating to be the bearer of such tidings, guessing how conflicted she must feel. "Your father is being tried for embezzlement, as rumored, and as is the case with servant betraying master, and the staggering amount taken, they expect him to be hung, or at the very least transported for life."

"Dear Lord, no . . ."

"I am sorry, Olivia. Even with your father's failings, this must come as a terrible blow."

Her wide, panicked eyes beseeched his. "But he did not do it! I know he did not. He has been a lot of things, but never a cheat. Never a thief."

His heart clenched to see her so distressed. "I do not mean to cast aspersions, when I have encouraged you to see your father in a more charitable light, but could not a quest for revenge have tempted him to it, if greed would not?"

She nodded. That notion had crossed her mind.

They walked on for several minutes in silence, and then he turned to her once more. "Our solicitor is at your disposal, and whatever funds you need for—"

She gripped his arm. "Take me to him. Will you please? I must see him. Ask him."

He placed his hand over hers, unable to resist the chance to touch her. "I have another idea. You recall I am some acquainted with Sir Fulke and his son, Herbert. Perhaps I might appeal to them, ask for leniency, at least a lesser punishment."

"Do you think them capable of mercy?"

"Sir Fulke? Not likely. If Herbert were there, I might be able to sway him, but as far as I know he is still away. Yet, I would try."

"You would?"

"For you, yes. And I am certain Father would approve."

"Why should you?"

They looked at one another, blue gazes melding.

"Olivia . . ." he said, sounding almost offended. "I think you know the answer to that."

Of my Arithmetic I was very fond, and advanced rapidly.
Mensuration was quite delightful, Fractions, Decimals
and Book keeping.

—MISS WEETON, *JOURNAL OF A GOVERNESS* 1811–25

Chapter 49

$\mathcal{O}$livia waited nervously in the entry hall of the former Meacham estate, now in the possession of Sir Fulke Fitzpatrick.

A quarter of an hour after he had been shown into a room down the corridor, Lord Bradley reemerged, in the company of two men. After a few low words were exchanged, the two men crossed the corridor with the merest glance in her direction and then disappeared into another room. Lord Bradley turned to face her, and she hurried across the marble floor to meet him.

He cleared his throat. "I have good news and rather trying news both, I am afraid. Herbert is in town for the trial. He and his solicitor have agreed to allow you to see the books in question."

"And the trying news?" Olivia whispered.

His blue eyes were somber. "You have one hour, Olivia. It is all I could manage."

She swallowed, then nodded. "Pray for me."

"I shall. I am." He squeezed her hand, then opened the door for her.

Olivia entered an ornate library, where alabaster busts stared blindly from atop tall bookcases of mahogany and brass. A claw-footed table sat at the middle of the room, while fringed chairs of velvet huddled closer to the marble chimneypiece. Above it reigned a gilt-framed portrait of a lace-bosomed dowager, who looked down at Olivia in marked disapproval. Ignoring her, Olivia stepped to the table and sat down. Three books lay before her, illuminated by four tall sash windows. She prayed that old glass slate in her mind, murky from lack of regular use, would come back to her once more. She opened the books in order and slowly ran her finger down the columns, figuring and checking as she went. Everything seemed in order. *Almighty God, please help me. . . .*

An hour later, the door opened. Olivia closed the last book and rose. Into the library walked not two men but seven. Lord Bradley; a black-haired young man she guessed must be Herbert Fitzpatrick; his father, Sir Fulke; the solicitor she had glimpsed earlier; Mr. Smith, the constable; the local magistrate; and another man she did not recognize.

Lord Bradley stepped in the breach between Olivia and the cluster of men. "Sir Fulke, this is Miss Keene, Simon Keene's daughter."

Standing before her was the proud gentleman from the Crown and Crow, now a dozen years older. The years had not been kind to him.

His thin lip curled. "Ah . . . the little trained monkey, all grown."

She felt Lord Bradley stiffen beside her. "Sir Fulke . . ."

Olivia doubted the man even heard Edward's steely warning.

"How fate played into his hands," Sir Fulke continued. "That I should purchase his master's estate and that my own steward would keep him on. How Keene bided his time, earning my steward's trust, learning his way about my business and about my books, then when he was confident in his position, he struck, thinking I would never be the wiser. Well, now fate delivers her cruel twist, and he is caught in his own trap."

Olivia met the man's gaze. "I might say the same of you, sir."

He smirked. "What is that supposed to mean?"

"I am very glad your solicitor and our constable are here today, as well as the local magistrate," Olivia said. "Fate, I believe, is still at work."

"You talk nonsense, ghel. If you think to confuse me with riddles, you are quite mistaken."

Olivia forced a smile and changed tack. "I am glad to see you looking so well, Sir Fulke," she began. "Mr. Smith told me you suffered a hard blow to your head. He thought you might have taken a fall. Down a pair of stairs, perhaps." The second smile came more easily. "It was kind of you not to inform the constable *where* you were injured. For that might have looked very bad for my father."

His eyes narrowed, but he said nothing.

"For the highly esteemed Mrs. Atkins says she found you in our home, unconscious."

As she'd hoped, he did not challenge Mrs. Atkins's word. Everyone in the village respected the midwife. Most had been delivered by her, or entered the world into her hands. Sir Fulke could not have lived in Withington long and not known how highly she was regarded.

Olivia said, "Is it not possible that you very naturally blame Simon Keene for that injury, and that is why you seek such a stern penalty? The very revenge you accuse my father of taking?"

"What are you talking about?"

"I suppose you might have fallen down our stairs, but why you would be abovestairs in our house, where the only rooms are my bedchamber and the old schoolroom, I cannot guess. Is there some reason?"

He stared at her coldly. "No reason I can think of."

"Then is not another explanation more plausible? Were you not, in fact, struck from behind? By some scoundrel too cowardly to fight you face-to-face?"

He made no answer, but there was a wary gleam in his eye.

"It would explain a great deal," Olivia continued. "It would explain why Simon Keene left the village so soon after, as though a guilty man. A fire iron can do a lot of damage. More than any fall down stairs."

"Perhaps, Davies," Sir Fulke said to his solicitor, though his eyes remained on Olivia, "we ought to add assault to our list of charges."

"He admits it, then?" Mr. Smith, the constable, asked.

"Actually, no," Olivia said. "Though I have blamed him these many months for a violent act. As you have blamed him."

"Ah!" Sir Fulke's muddy eyes lit. "Perhaps you seek a bit of revenge yourself. A cruel father, was he?"

She smiled sweetly. "Nothing to you, I am sure."

He studied her, uncertain of her meaning.

"I suppose you had just come to our house to bring my mother more needlework for your dear wife," Olivia continued. "And perhaps Simon Keene burst in and hit you from behind, driven by jealous rage. And you never knew what hit you. You awoke later to find yourself in Mrs. Atkins's office, where she had taken you to recover."

"She saw nothing?" he asked, selecting a cigar from a wooden box on the table and idly rolling it between his fingers.

"Do you mean, did she see my father strike you? Sadly, no."

"Miss Keene," Edward interrupted. "I do not see what . . . this cannot help your father."

"I only want the truth to be revealed," Olivia said. "Does not the truth set one free?"

"Yes, but—"

Sir Fulke interrupted, "My own memory of those events—head injuries being what they are—is vague, Miss Keene," he said dismissively. "When I awoke, I found myself rather in a fog. I thought Mrs. Atkins told me I had fallen down stairs, but I may have mistaken the matter. I later learnt I had been unconscious for more than a day."

With the help of copious amounts of laudanum, Olivia thought.

"It must have been as you said," Sir Fulke said, warming to the notion. "Your father found me in his home, assumed the worst, and struck me down like the coward he is."

Olivia grimaced. "But do not forget, sir, you gave your attacker just cause."

Again those muddy eyes narrowed. "What do you mean?"

"You see, the reason someone struck you from behind—I do not deny that part—was because when this person entered our home, he or she found you violently strangling my mother."

"Preposterous!"

"I agree it sounds so," Olivia said calmly. "And in fact, for the longest time, I believed this fiend, bent on destroying my dear mamma, was my own father, to my shame. But it was not. He was in Cheltenham, in the company of your own steward."

The seventh man, the one she had not recognized, nodded his agreement. "That's right, miss."

Sir Fulke's lip curved in a feline smile. "Miss Keene, your tale-bearing astounds me! You ought to be a writer of novels. You have missed your calling with all that arithmetic nonsense."

Olivia sighed. "If only it were a fiction. But for me it became a nightmare that has haunted me for months."

"If not your father, who?" Sir Fulke asked. "Do you claim some passing tramp or thief struck me?"

She stole a glance at Edward. "I have been mistaken for both in the past. But, no."

"Who, then?" Mr. Smith asked, while the magistrate leaned forward in his chair, watching her closely.

"I stayed late at Miss Cresswell's that evening, tutoring two pupils who had fallen behind. I came home to find chairs overturned and glass smashed against the grate. I heard my mother call out in panic and ran to her bedchamber. It was quite dark, but light enough to see a man with his hands around my mother's throat, squeezing hard. I know what that feels like now. Sharp pain, lungs burning, the surety of death any moment . . ."

"Rubbish, the lot of it!" Sir Fulke exclaimed.

"I did not think. I only knew I must stop the man and save my mother. Before I knew it, I had grasped the fire iron and struck for all I was worth. I thought I might have killed the man. But I did not. He breathed still."

"I was not that man," Sir Fulke said, with a pointed look at the magistrate. "You said yourself the room was dark and you suspected your own father. He must have heard your mother was entertaining gentleman callers. I had certainly heard the rumor myself, though I, of course, did not credit it."

Olivia said coldly, "You lie."

"And *you* would do anything, say anything, to try and spare that vile father of yours. Spin all the tales you like, my dear. But you have no *witness* save yourself."

"I am afraid I do." She nodded to Edward, who opened the door. Dorothea Keene walked in, regal in striped gown and hat, head held high.

Every head turned. The constable gaped like a beached fish.

Sir Fulke instantly paled. "Dorothea!"

Mr. Smith stammered, "Mrs. Keene, we thought . . . after you disappeared, well, everyone thought the worst. I told 'em Keene would never harm you, but few believed me."

"You were right, Mr. Smith," her mother began. "But Sir Fulke would and did. He tried to strangle me. And I was terrified that when he came to, he would try again—and take revenge on whoever struck him. I felt I had no choice but to send my daughter away that very night and to flee the village myself the next morning, though injured."

Sir Fulke's face was beetroot red. "What lies! Preposterous, the lot of it! The whole family is in on it. I know our magistrate and constable are wise enough to see the truth."

Mr. Smith looked like a confused boy. "Why would Sir Fulke mean you any harm, Mrs. Keene?"

Dorothea Keene took a deep breath and faced the constable and magistrate. "Because I refused his advances. Not once but over and over again for several months. He became . . . obsessed . . . with me, though I never gave him any encouragement."

"You did!" Sir Fulke exclaimed, ignoring his solicitor's staying hand and whispered warning.

Her mother continued, "He began coming to our house for his wife's needlework in her stead. I was quite uncomfortable with his calls, but he would not stop. He tried to push himself on me that night, and when I fought back, he . . . he . . . nearly killed me."

"Nonsense! Smith, it is all nonsense!"

Mr. Smith looked flabbergasted and uncertain how to proceed. Sir Fulke's steward sat silent, as did the magistrate, who watched the proceedings in calculated detachment.

Herbert Fitzpatrick rose. "I believe her," he said.

"Shut up, boy!" his father snapped. "Turn against your father, will you? Always were a weak, useless lad."

Herbert flinched, but when he spoke, his voice was calm and cool. "I did not witness the events of that evening, but I was aware of my father's increasingly frequent calls on Mrs. Keene, and my mother's distress because of it. It would not be the first time my father has pursued another woman, though I had never known him to pursue anyone so doggedly before."

"Shut your trap, boy. You are hereby disinherited. Davies! I want a new will." Sir Fulke turned toward the door.

"We are not finished here, Sir Fulke," Olivia said.

"Yes, we are," he said, jaw clenched.

"There is the matter of the embezzlement charge. I have reviewed the books, and my father did not embezzle from you."

"Right," Sir Fulke sneered. "Who did, then?"

Olivia looked at the young man beside the solicitor, his pale face framed by the blackest hair. And in his wary green eyes, she saw once more the dread of disappointing one's father that she recognized in herself, that she recognized from a boy in the Crown and Crow all those years ago. Would, could, this boy, grown now, dare disappoint his father? Own up to the truth which would surely earn his father's wrath and rejection a hundred times over what a lost contest would have done?

The young man looked at her then. Really looked. And whether he recognized her or something in himself, Olivia could not know, but he stood up the straighter for it, and his eyes lit with a strange determination, like a soldier marching into certain, but resigned-to, death.

"No one *embezzled* from you, Father," he began. "But I took it, to keep you from wasting the family's last shilling on gaming and women. You have not given Mother and me enough to live on these last years, so I felt within my rights to take what was needed to pay the bills and keep my mother in the comfort she deserves. Disinherit me if you like—here stands your solicitor at the ready. I have invested wisely. From the interest earned, I can now support Mother and myself—if not in grand fashion, respectable at least. Which is more than I can say for you. Your affairs are in a sorry state indeed, and it does not take an accomplished clerk to figure that out." He turned to Olivia. "Though it did take an accomplished young woman to discover I did it—and to give me the courage to own up to it."

"But . . . ! How dare you," the older gentleman blustered. "I shall disinherit you indeed. Cut you off!"

Herbert said dryly, "Disinherited twice in a single day. How extraordinary."

The steward cleared his throat. "Sir, if I may. The sum your son invested is all that is keeping the family from debtors' prison. Perhaps leniency is in order?"

"He shall never lay his thieving hands on my money."

"What money, Father?" Herbert said. "We have already established your debts outweigh your assets and the investors are dropping like scales off a rotting fish."

Sir Fulke glowered. "And whose fault is that?"

"Yours, sir."

"These rumors and now charges of embezzlement have done it. It is on your head. Yours!"

Herbert looked at his father coldly. "So be it. But Mr. Keene goes free."

"Why should he?"

"Because he is innocent," Olivia's mother said. "And because if you drop all charges, the rest of this sordid business will remain our secret."

The constable objected. "Mrs. Keene, are you sure you want to let him off? I could have him—"

"Quite sure, Mr. Smith." She turned cold eyes on Sir Fulke. "That is, unless he ever comes near me again."

Herbert Fitzpatrick offered Olivia his arm and escorted her from the room while the magistrate, Mrs. Keene, and Sir Fulke sealed the bargain, with Edward, the steward, and the solicitor acting as witnesses.

In the hall, Herbert withdrew a single gold guinea from his waistcoat pocket and pressed it into Olivia's gloved hand. "This is yours, I believe, Miss Keene. You won that long-ago contest and you won today."

"I think we both won," she said. "Thank you for speaking out."

Pulling his gaze from her hand, he looked up ruefully. "Would you have let me keep silent, had I not?"

She smiled gently but shook her head. "I have been silent long enough."

It was all the romance of the nursery and
the poetry of the schoolroom.

—HENRY JAMES, *THE TURN OF THE SCREW*

Chapter 50

The carriage made its way to the far end of Northleach, to the mottled grey-stone prison and magistrate building known as the House of Correction. The arched doorway was flanked on either side by imposing two-story walls.

Edward waited in the carriage with her mother, while Mr. Smith offered Olivia a hand down. The constable led Olivia through the magistrate's building and into a small visitors' room near the keeper's house. Then he disappeared, taking the magistrate's order with him.

Several minutes later, a keeper opened the door and Simon Keene shuffled into the room, head bowed and hands clasped together in front of him as though manacled, though no physical restraint bound him.

Her father looked up and started. Clearly no one had told him who had come to see him. Nor why.

"Livie! I did not think to ever lay eyes on you again."

Her heart was so full to see him that for a moment she could not speak. When she did not, his hopeful expression faded.

"Come to say good-bye?" he asked dully. "Or to rail at me once more?"

"Neither." She sat at the table and gestured her father toward the second chair across from her.

He slumped down. "Surely you've heard I'm done for. It's the noose for me. Or transportation. Fatal the both of them."

"No. You are being released. Did they not tell you?"

He frowned. "Are you dreamin', girl? Out to raise my hopes and dash them as I have disappointed you time and time again?"

"You are innocent."

"Ha! I did not embezzle a farthing, but I am guilty of far worse. It is why I don't care what they do to me now—I have made peace with my maker. I wish I might have told your mother how sorry I am. Begged her pardon—yours as well. If you might forgive me, I could die content enough."

"I do forgive you," Olivia said. "And I hope you will forgive me."

"Forgive you? For what?"

"For thinking the worst of you."

He looked away. "I have given you prodigious cause."

"Perhaps," she allowed. Later, she would confess all that she had thought him guilty of. But not now, not here. He looked low indeed, yet there was an odd new light in his eyes, a peace in his countenance she had not before seen. "Never mind that now. I have had a look at Sir Fulke's books and—"

"Did you indeed?" he interrupted, brows high. "And how did you accomplish that?"

"Lord Brightwell and his son are acquainted with Sir Fulke, and—"

"Brightwell again. I might have known. Has he claimed you as his own?"

"No. The point is they convinced Sir Fulke's son and solicitor to give me an hour with the account books, and do you know what I discovered?"

He shook his head absently, his eyes flitting about her face, as though taking an inventory and committing it to memory.

"The money had been taken over a period of only a few months, more than a year ago. It had been categorized as petty cash, yet withdrawn in large amounts which, when summed, rounded to the pound. Not the work of an accomplished clerk like you, even had you been working for Sir Fulke at the time, which you were not. You are far too clever for such a hack job."

"Who was it, then? Not his steward, I hope? Seemed a decent man to me."

She shook her head. "It was Herbert Fitzpatrick, Sir Fulke's own son. And with good cause, I gather. Do you remember him? The Harrow lad who won that contest in the Crown and Crow?"

"Won?" He humphed. "You let him win—that's what."

She leaned across the table and looked him in the eye. "You are right, I did. Will you never forgive me for it?" Tears blurred her vision, and she was twelve years old all over again.

Tears filled his drooping brown eyes, and her heart ached to see it. "Me forgive you? When it's I who was worse than the devil to you? You who never did me a wrong—well, if you don't count that one contest. . . ." He attempted a grin, which only served to push the tears from his eyes and down his cheeks, thinner than she had ever seen them.

He sighed and slumped back. "I have not had one drop to drink since that night I came the fool to Brightwell Court. I have been praying too, for the first time in my life. That parson, Tugwell, he helped me see—not the error of my ways, for I knew them all too well already—but what was wanting in me. I am far from perfect, I know, but I am changed and changing still. I know it is too late for

Dorothea and me. When news of my hanging reaches her, wherever she is, she will no doubt wed her Oliver after all. I hope she will finally be happy."

Olivia shook her head. "She did not leave you for him. She felt she had to flee because someone was threatening her. Nearly killed her."

His face darkened, thunderstruck. "What? I shall kill the fiend! Who is he? Who?"

"This is exactly why she did not tell you. She knew you would murder the man and end up hanging for it, and she did not want that."

He shook his head regretfully. "Well, it is what I get in the end, at any rate, and I would have rather given my life to protect her." His voice grew thick with emotion. "I would, you know. I would give my life for her."

"I know you would," whispered Dorothea Keene.

Olivia looked over her shoulder. Her mother stood timidly in the threshold. When Olivia looked back at her father, his mouth was slack, expression stunned. He stared at Dorothea as though not believing his eyes. As though for the last time.

"You gave your life for me long ago," she said quietly. "When you married me, even knowing I carried another man's child."

He slowly nodded. "I loved you then, and I love you now. Livie too, though she don't belong to me."

Dorothea shook her head. "But she does. I did visit Brightwell Court once after I lost the first child, but I was never unfaithful to you. I have told you before, and I will tell you until you believe me. She is your daughter. *Yours.*"

Still he stared at his wife, disbelief evident in his expression, but whether disbelief of her words or of her very presence, Olivia was not certain.

"Why are you here?" he asked breathlessly, "Why are you telling me this, when you had already made your escape? When you were already well and free of me?"

Tears brightened Dorothea's eyes. Her whisper grew hoarse. "Perhaps I do not wish to be free."

Hope flared and faded in his dark eyes. "Well, free you'll be, and soon now. I'm to be hung or transported, and men don't come back spry and whole, if they come back at all. Still, I am glad you've come. I asked God to let me see the both of you once more, and He has answered."

"Did you not hear a word I said, Papa?" Olivia exclaimed. "You have been exonerated."

He shook his head in wonder, a rare twinkle in his eyes. "Figured it out when neither the steward nor I could, did you? Caught that Harrow boy out at the last."

She nodded.

"That's my girl. My clever girl."

Olivia's throat tightened, and her heart squeezed to hear him say those long-missed words. She reached across the table and pressed the guinea into his hand, much as Herbert had done. "He returned this."

Simon Keene held the coin in his fingers, turning it this way and that. "Of all the things I have lost in my life, this is the very least I'd want returned to me."

He placed the coin back in her hand, pressing her fingers for a lingering moment.

"You are free to go, Father," she whispered. "We are all of us free."

Olivia finally understood what Mr. Tugwell had tried to tell her. This was how it was for every fallen creature. *Christ bore the penalty we each deserve, to purchase our freedom.*

He shook his head. "I cannot take it in. Free to go . . . where?"

Olivia glanced at her mother. It was not her place to invite him home.

"You will be going back to your Lord Brightwell with his riches and title, no doubt," he went on. "And I would not blame you. Not a bit of it."

"Listen to me," Olivia said. "Lord Brightwell is a very kind and generous man, but he is not my father. That is *your* title, whether you accept it or not."

He studied her, wanting to believe, she could tell, but afraid to do so.

"The man may be an earl," Olivia continued, attempting a grin, "but he is no scholar in arithmetic, I assure you. In fact, he makes rather a muddle of it." She slowly shook her head, looking him directly in the eye. "I long ago inherited your dark hair and mind for numbers. There is no disinheriting me now."

He lifted thin lips in a wobbly smile. "Never."

Edward was pacing outside the prison when Olivia emerged at last. Alone. He searched her face, relieved to see only a trace of the anxiety that had been there before. He exhaled deeply.

"They will be out soon," she said with a tremulous smile. "They wished to speak privately first, as you might imagine."

He nodded and pressed her hand, wondering what the outcome of that discussion would be.

Simon and Dorothea Keene emerged a few minutes later, not arm in arm, but side by side.

Edward stepped forward and shook Mr. Keene's hand. Olivia formally introduced the two men, though they had met under awkward circumstances once before.

Simon Keene thanked Edward for his part, then cleared his throat. "Thing is," he began awkwardly, "it would not be wise for either of us to return to Withington. Too near Fitzpatrick, you understand. And of course, I no longer have a post there. Dorothea here would like to return to the school—"

"Just for a time," Mrs. Keene hastened to clarify. "I feel I should finish out the term."

"And I feel I ought to return to the almshouse," Mr. Keene said, "to speak with that parson again. And then later . . ." He glanced at Dorothea, then away again. "Well, we shall see."

Edward looked at Olivia, who bravely nodded her understanding. He hoped she was not too disappointed there would be no instant reconciliation for her parents. But surely with wise counsel from Mr. Tugwell—and much prayer and patience—they might be reunited soon.

Edward directed the coachman first to St. Aldwyns, where Mrs. Keene bestowed a tentative smile on her husband and embraced Olivia with a promise to see her soon.

They then delivered Mr. Keene to the almshouse as he'd requested. But when they arrived, Charles Tugwell bustled out and insisted Mr. Keene stay in the vicarage guest room. A village shopkeeper, a Miss Ludlow, he believed, followed in the vicar's wake, smiling and waving to Olivia.

When Olivia stepped away to speak with her and Charles, Edward pulled Simon Keene aside.

"I wonder, Mr. Keene, if the position of clerk at Brightwell Court might interest you?"

The man frowned. "You don't want the likes of me in your house, not after everything."

"On the contrary," Edward said. "Father has promoted our man Walters to steward, leaving us without a clerk. And I understand you are very clever with accounts, as is your daughter."

"Are you offering for her sake?"

"And if I am?"

"Your father cannot want me."

"My father has more pressing things on his mind at present—a new will to draft, a new heir to groom, and new wards to oversee."

"And what does Liv—Olivia say to the notion?"

"Why not ask her yourself?" Edward looked over at Olivia, and his chest warmed to see her smiling at him, smiling at them both.

Simon Keene looked over as well, and a slow smile transformed his down-turned features. "Perhaps I shall at that."

❧

Late that evening, after lingering over tea and sandwiches with Lord Brightwell and the children, Edward and Olivia took Audrey and Andrew up to the nursery, bestowing many hugs and kisses before Becky swept them away for bed.

Together they descended the stairs once more, but instead of returning to the library, Edward stopped in the hall.

"Will you join me for a walk through the garden, Olivia?"

She felt a thrill of anticipation. "I will."

They walked along the church wall, through the arbor, and around the side of the house. Seeing the tree from which she had first overheard Edward's secret, she paused beside it, running her fingers over the rough bark and remembering.

As if reading her thoughts, Edward said, "Now this brings back memories. But this time, I shall hide behind the tree with you. Do you mind?"

Olivia shook her head, heart beating fast and her throat suddenly tight.

He stepped forward, and nervous, she stepped back. He stepped closer yet, and her back against the tree, she could retreat no farther, could not move. Did not want to move.

"You do know why I objected to Father claiming you as his daughter, do you not?"

She shrugged, guessing the answer but wanting to hear him say it.

"Because my feelings for you are . . . not at all brotherly."

He ran a finger along her cheek, and she shivered. Then he traced her lips with that same finger, and she could barely breathe. He whispered, "Do you know how long I have wanted to kiss you?"

She shook her head again, not trusting her voice.

"Not when I first saw you behind this tree, I admit. Then I wanted to strangle you." He grimaced. "Forgive me. Poor choice of words, that."

She managed a tremulous grin.

He placed his hands on her shoulders and slowly dragged his warm fingers down her bare arms and then up again. Shivers of pleasure fluttered up her spine.

"I believe it was when I saw you swinging Andrew about on the lawn. Or was it when I found you and Andrew asleep together, your hair down around you and wearing only the thinnest of night-dresses?" He gave her a roguish wink.

She whispered shakily, "Seems I have a great deal to thank Andrew for."

He smiled down at her. Ran his hands up her arms once more, then lifted them to her flushed cheeks. "You are burning."

"I know."

He framed her face with his hands and bent toward her, eyes fixed upon her eyes, then lowering to her mouth. At the last instant, as his lips touched hers, she closed her eyes, focusing her senses on him. The spicy, masculine scent of him, the cool fingers on her cheeks, his warm lips on hers, kissing her in whisper-soft caresses that deepened and intensified with passion.

When he finally broke the kiss, his breathing was haggard and his voice husky. "I love you, Olivia. Have you any idea how much?"

"No," she breathed. "But I hope the number is very, very high."

He kissed her once more, then lifted his head, his gaze caressing her bare neck, her face, her hair, her eyes. "Have I told you how beautiful you look tonight?"

"Several times, yes," she answered, her voice rather breathless.

"You look like a duchess . . . or a countess. I wish I might have made you one."

"I never wanted to be a countess."

"No?"

"All I have wanted, for the longest time now, was simply to be . . ."

When she hesitated, he guessed, "Free? A teacher? Reunited with your mother?"

Olivia shook her head. " . . . yours."

He bestowed upon her a smile so tender that her heart ached to see it.

Suddenly serious, he led her to the veranda, and there, under the light of several torches, looked intently down at her, eyes warm. "I have something for you."

He withdrew an object from his coat pocket. Not a ring, not a jewel box, but a folded piece of paper. He unfolded it with great care and held it out to her.

It took her eyes and mind several seconds to figure out what she was looking at. It was one of Edward's drawn plans for a building project, this one with a garden indicated behind and walking paths around. The scale drawing depicted a kitchen and laundry belowstairs, dining parlor, sitting room, and schoolrooms on the ground floor, and many bedchambers above.

He pointed to where he had labeled the plan in his bold, block printing.

MISS KEENE'S BOARDING AND DAY SCHOOL FOR GIRLS
All accepted, regardless of ability to pay.

Joy swelling within her, she smiled up at him.

He turned the paper over, revealing a second, similar plan. "This one has a few improvements over the original, which I hope you will approve."

The drawings themselves were identical, Olivia realized. Only the title had changed:

THE KEENE AND BRADLEY SCHOOL FOR GIRLS

"You wish to teach school?" she asked, brows high in feigned misunderstanding.

He stroked her chin. "Goose. The Keene refers to your mother. The Bradley refers to you. At least, I hope it will, very soon."

"Ah . . ." She slid her arms around his neck and lifted her face to receive his kiss. "A great improvement indeed."

Epilogue

*F*inally, I can think about that long-ago day in the Crown and Crow without the remorse that plagued me for so many years. Now I grin and sometimes laugh to think how God wove even that into something good. A sum far greater than its parts.

As I sit on a lawn rug on a warm summer's day and look at the dear ones gathered around me, my heart is light and joyful. And amazed.

I watch as Edward, my Edward, tries unsuccessfully to untangle line on a fishing pole, as though his hands are covered in school-room paste.

Shaking his head and wearing one of his famous scowls, Avery Croome limps over and takes the pole from Edward, muttering about the uselessness of modern youth. But beneath his gruff façade, there is a twinkle in his silvery blue eyes (so like Edward's, though I am determined his eyebrows shall never grow as wild), and I know Mr. Croome is thoroughly enjoying himself. I sometimes wish he and Mrs. Moore might wed, but they seem content to simply spend more time in one another's company, now that the hurt and misunderstandings of the past no longer stand between them.

Andrew's birch-bark float sinks into the river, and he calls out with glee. Mr. Croome hurries over, hand to the lad's shoulder, encouraging him and instructing him on how to land the fish. Drawn by Andrew's shout, Lord Brightwell saunters over from the garden in time to admire the brown trout. Edward ruffles Andrew's hair and grumbles good-naturedly about the boy catching three fish while Edward has yet to catch one.

Beside me on the lawn rug, Audrey cheers on her brother, adjusting her bonnet when it threatens to fall back. What a lovely young woman she is becoming. At thirteen, she is nearly my height, and her face has lost its childish roundness. Something tells me that when Amos Tugwell returns from school next term, he shall finally take notice of her.

Audrey bends low and tickles the infant lying on a soft hare rug before us, enjoying the warm breeze on his skin and cooing happily. Our son—Edward's and mine. We named him Avery S. Bradley. The S standing for Simon or Stanton, depending on which grandfather asks the question.

From behind, I hear a tap on the window glass and turn toward Brightwell Court. There at the library window stands my father. How handsome he looks in his clerk's coat and neckcloth. Sober as a Quaker. A flash of Titian red hair appears behind the wavy glass, and there is Felix, holed up with my father and Walters, learning all he can about the running of an estate.

My father lifts a hand in greeting, and I wave back. It does my heart good to have him here, to see him doing so well.

My mother is not numbered among us this afternoon, for she

is busy at the school Edward built for us on the outskirts of Arlington, where she is proprietress and headmistress. How she loves the work and her pupils. I taught beside her the first year, until my Avery was born. Then, as unbelievable as it sounds, we hired Miss Ripley to assist her. The former governess is so pleased to have a place and be spared the workhouse that she follows my mother's edicts and manner of teaching, never once reverting to the harsh discipline she once described to me.

I still call-in at the school at least once a week, to teach arithmetic and to hear how the pupils are getting on. Becky attends there now, as does Dory's younger sister. How satisfying to see them learn and gain confidence as young women of worth.

To reach the school, I must pass by the village lockup. Whenever I do, I cannot help but look at that little place and remember. How long ago it seems. Thankfully so!

Shaking off thoughts of the past, I look at the riverbank once more and watch them—these men of my son's family. Mr. Croome, Lord Brightwell, Edward, Andrew. Great-grandfather, grandfather, father, and adopted brother. And a second grandfather inside. How blessed our Avery is. How blessed we all are.

As if sensing the direction of my thoughts, Edward, line in the water, looks over his shoulder, and our gazes catch. His knowing smile gladdens my heart.

Suddenly his line pulls taut and is nearly jerked from his hand. "I think I have one!" he calls, his voice as excited as a little boy's. Instantly, Mr. Croome is there beside him—hand on Edward's shoulder, leaning near, encouraging, and instructing him on how to land the prize. My heart aches and my eyes burn to see it.

And then the fish, a very tiny fish, is brought to shore to the cheers of Audrey and Andrew. Mr. Croome, his scowl noticeably absent, claps Edward on the back, and says in a hoarse voice, "Well done, lad. Well done."

When Edward looks across at me once more, there are

tears in his dear blue eyes, and answering tears fill my own. I breathe another prayer of thanksgiving for all God has done in our lives.

Well done indeed.

Author's Note

The idea for this novel was inspired by Mahler's Third Symphony, which I heard many years ago on a road trip to Davenport, Iowa. I admit I rarely listen to classical music, but that day, as I did, whole scenes spun forth like a movie in my mind. Today, very little of that original story remains, which—hopefully—means that I have become a better researcher and writer since then. Still, Mahler's Third remains the "soundtrack" of the first two chapters.

Brightwell Court is not a real place, but it was loosely inspired by the very real, very picturesque Bibury Court in the Cotswold village of Bibury, which the artist William Morris called "the most beautiful village in England." Many thanks to author Davis Bunn for recommending that my husband and I take tea there during our first England trip. We happily did so. Not only did we enjoy the ivy-covered Tudor manor, the lovely grounds bordered by the curvy River Coln, and the greedy ducks that nipped at our scones, but I also realized it would make an ideal setting for *The Silent Governess*. I am not the first, nor will I be the last, to set a novel in that idyllic place. If you ever have the opportunity, I hope you will visit Bibury yourself.

I have been fascinated by governesses ever since my sixth-grade teacher read aloud *Jane Eyre* to us, in short increments over several weeks, with real emotion and even mascara-tears. My thanks to Ms. Rebecca Hayes, now Morgan, for sparking my lifelong love of British literature.

As always, heartfelt appreciation to my family, church-family, friends, and Bethany House colleagues for all their encouragement and support. Special thanks to my diligent and thoughtful editor Karen Schurrer and to author Laurie Alice Eakes for her gracious help with historical details.

And with deepest gratitude to God, the giver and fulfiller of dreams, and for His glory.

Soli Deo Gloria.

Reading Group
Discussion Questions

1. Which character in the novel did you most like or relate to? What drew you to that character?

2. The book's opening quote says, "The best proof of wisdom is to talk little, but to hear much. . . ." Do you agree? Have you ever wished too late you had followed this advice?

3. Has a childhood regret remained with you into adulthood? What have you learned about getting past such regrets?

4. What did you learn about the life of governesses that surprised you? Do you think you would have enjoyed being a governess in the early nineteenth century? Why or why not?

5. Governesses were expected to teach literature, poetry, French, Italian, geography, the sciences, religion, arithmetic, needlework, dancing, drawing, and to play a musical instrument. How does this compare with your own (or your children's) education? Anything on the list you wish you'd had the chance to learn?

6. How might discovering that your origins are different from what you've always believed affect you? Would you have reacted differently than Edward?

7. Legal adoption as we know it was not practiced in Regency England. Unless a child was a peer's natural son born in wedlock, he might be left some money but could not inherit his father's title or estate. Women could not usually inherit either. Did this surprise you? Strike you as unfair?

8. Where do you get your identity? From your parents, your profession, your kids, your church, your relationship with God? How has the source of your identity changed over the years?

9. Has your view of God been influenced by your earthly father or another person? Positively or negatively? If negatively, what ways have you found to overcome that influence?

10. Did any character or happening in the novel surprise you? How so? And did you enjoy the twist?

For additional book club resources, please visit
www.bethanyhouse.com/anopenbook.

About the Author

JULIE KLASSEN is a fiction editor with a background in advertising. She has worked in Christian publishing for more than fourteen years, in both marketing and editorial capacities. This is her third novel.

Julie is a graduate of the University of Illinois. She enjoys travel, research, books, BBC period dramas, long hikes, short naps, and coffee with friends.

She and her husband have two sons and live near St. Paul, Minnesota.

For more information about Julie and her books, visit
www.julieklassen.com.

More Regency Fiction From Julie Klassen!

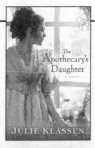

In a world run by men, have her actions ruined the family legacy—and stolen her chance for true love?

The Apothecary's Daughter by Julie Klassen

Both Charlotte and Daniel are determined to protect their secrets—but neither can imagine the sacrifice that will be required.

Lady of Milkweed Manor by Julie Klassen

Jane Austen's Beloved Classics—Go Beyond the Story!

These editions of *Pride and Prejudice* and *Sense and Sensibility* are sprinkled with trivia, notes, facts, and inspiration drawn from Austen's own prayers and writings on faith.

Pride and Prejudice by Jane Austen
Sense and Sensibility by Jane Austen

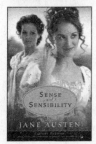